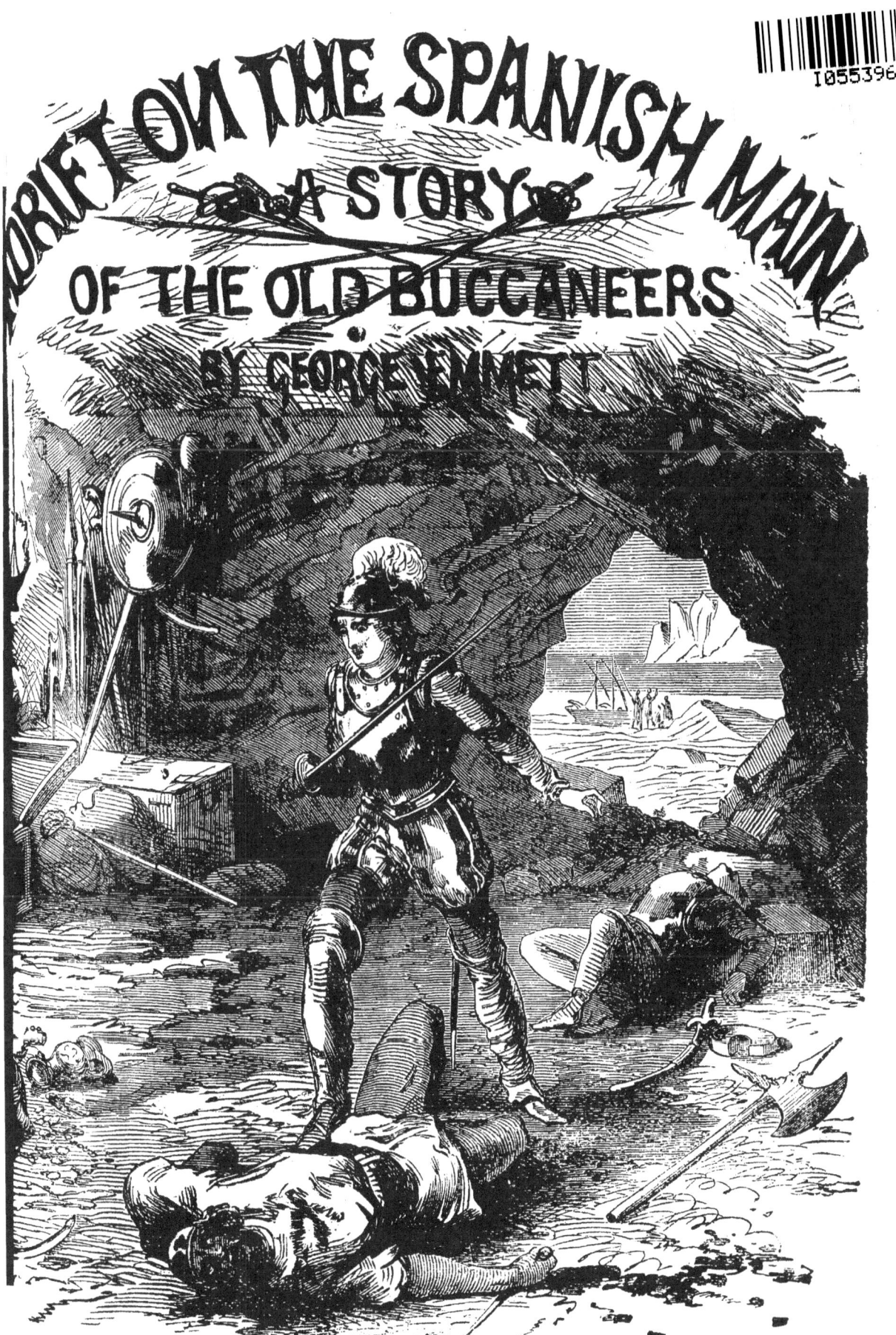

ADRIFT ON THE SPANISH MAIN
A STORY
OF THE OLD BUCCANEERS
BY GEORGE EMMETT

THE TREASURE CAVE.

ADRIFT

ON THE

SPANISH MAIN.

BY

GEORGE EMMETT.

CHAPTER I.

THE SPANISH GALLEON.

"A sail! a sail!" a promised prize to hope,
Her nation—flag—how speaks the telescope?
BYRON.

THE pearl-like light of the dawn was succeeded by the sun rising, as it were, out of the depths of the great ocean, and soon the golden glow lit up the gently undulating waters, and the sails, spars, and rigging of the war ship Bonaventura.

The silken banner of England floated lazily from its staff, and on the high quarter-deck, terminating almost in a point, stood the watchful sentries, the sun's glow flashing and sparkling upon their spear points, steel caps, and corselets.

The Bonaventura, although in size but a fishing smack compared to the mighty war vessels of modern times, was a large vessel when the navy of Great Britain was only in its infancy.

Her tonnage was six hundred tons, and she was manned by one hundred and thirty seamen, thirty gunners, and seventy soldiers.

Insignificant as these items may seem, and the size of Queen Bess's war vessels, our hardy forefathers performed prodigies of valour in much smaller craft, and many of the greatest discoverers sailed round the world, when sailing round the world was a perilous venture, in ships of not one-third the size of the Bonaventura.

With the first flash of the sun upon the decks an officer, garbed in the rich costume of the period, and wearing a long Toledo blade at his hip, came from the gorgeously-appointed state-room, and turning to one of the sentinels, asked—

"Has anything been seen of the chase?"

"The sun has but just risen, Master Rupert," replied the man, and when the blue line disappears there is hope for us."

"How so, knave?"

"The galleon, master Rupert; she cannot be far away."

The officer stood upon a gun, and, shading his eyes with his hand, made a close survey of the glittering waters.

"The Spaniard," he muttered, "has edged away during the night; and I thought it would be so when the dice-box and wine take the reason from older heads than mine."

He stepped from the gun and went below, and upon entering the cabin, was accosted by three officers, who were seated at a table, playing with dice.

"What of the yellow banner, Rupert?" said one. "Has the Don courage enough to flaunt his flag in the sun when the lions of England cast their sheen upon it?"

"Neither his flag nor his vessel is visible," Rupert replied; "and, I fear me, will never be seen by those who tread the deck of the Bonaventura again."

A supercilious sneer played upon the lips of the officer to whose queries Rupert had replied, as he said—

"By all the shaven crowns in Christendom, the boy would make us forget the older hands that rule here! Know you not we have chased the Don from the Canaries to Spanish America, before giving up thought of the dollars? Mark me, lad, we shall stow the yellow metal yet on board this stout ship."

"I hope so, Master Hatton."

"On deck again, boy," said another officer, "and bid the knaves see to the arquebuses, which we have had but little need to use, and tell our trusty armourer to see the sheaves of arrows well filled, the pikes pointed, and the bills sharpened."

Rupert Felton, fourth officer of the Bonaventura, went on deck as desired by his superior, and gave the necessary directions to the armourer.

This done, he ascended the quarter-deck, and unfastening the jewelled snake that held his sword-belt, crossed his hands over the top of the hilt, and stood for some time in deep thought; and, by the working of his handsome

face, it was evident his mind was a prey to strangely disquieting thoughts.

The young officer's musings were broken in upon by Nicholas Hatton, who approached Rupert, and, placing his hand upon his shoulder, said—

"How now, Rupert! what ails thee, lad? Is it the memory of the blue-eyed maidens of fair Albion that takes the ruddy tinge from thy cheek, and gives in its place the hue of a prayer-pattering monk?"

"Albion's maidens are many and fair," answered the handsome officer; "but there's but one face dwells in my memory. God wots I have but one mistress, and that is our royal lady—if another, it is our stout bark."

"Yet," said Hatton, smiling at Rupert's mirth, "men do say Rupert Felton's plume has often been seen under the windows of the black-eyed Rachel, daughter of the rascally Jew who lives upon his fellow-men by the devil's invention—that of usury."

"The tongues of fools must wag, Master Hatton," answered Rupert, "and were I to say that all men are fools, and women shallow and deceitful, I should be but speaking the truth. No, no, Rupert Felton's thoughts were not of these."

"That they are of moment needs no sorcerer to tell," said Nicholas Hatton; and had I not seen thee in the thickest of the fight, I should think it was the fear of meeting the Don whose prowess is so well-known in these seas."

Rupert's eyes kindled at his companion's words, and he drew his shining blade a few inches from the leathern scabbard, but thrust it back as a smile succeeded the look of anger, and said—

"You would know what it is that falls like a pall upon my spirits? I will tell it. It is a dream, Nicholas Hatton. I pray God I may never behold such another!"

"A dream's false shadow clouds thy brow. I fear me, Rupert, the monkish teaching of thy early days has left a mark upon a mind that would have been free from these superstitions, had thine hand been only versed to use the sword and not the pen."

"My hand can do both."

"Ay, Rupert, and well; but to the dream, lad. What was its import?"

"Listen, and you shall hear."

"I listen, friend."

"Last night," said Rupert, "when relieved from the middle watch, I retired and slept, for my eyeballs ached with following the dim lines of the Spanish galleon, and I slept exceedingly sound."

"And"——

"Peace—the tale is soon told. I was taken below the sea—down where the sea-monsters dwell—and the battered timbers of a stout ship lay wedged between the coral rocks; and in my sleep I saw the whitened bones of many men, the flesh from which had been eaten by the shell-fish; and as I gazed upon whitened bones, rusted helms, and corselets, there arose from the timbers of the wreck the figure of one of the golden-haired women of the sea"——

"Proceed, lad; the story is stranger than the dream."

"The woman," continued Rupert, "pointed to where the boxes of gold lay in the wreck, and in a voice weird yet musical bade me gaze upon it, for it was," she said, "to gain that the brave hearts who sailed in the Bonaventura were lost, and as she spoke a horrible monster darted amongst the rotting timbers; and then came floating upward a plank on which shone the name of our stout vessel."

Hatton, though a brave man, was filled with the superstition so prevalent at the period of which we write, and, with cheeks paler than their wont, he hastily asked—

"Then, Rupert, what said the woman?"

"I have told all," cried the young officer, "for, as the plank passed my very feet, I was aroused to take the morning watch."

"The saints preserve us!" said Hatton; "but this is an evil augury, and I will——"

"Look yonder," exclaimed the young man, "and tell me, is that more than a dark cloud ahead?"

"The Santa Fé," said Hatton, his cheeks flushing with joy; "it is her four decks and cumbrous frame driving under that cloud."

The excitement of this discovery caused both officers to forget the incidents of the dream, and Rupert stamped the deck with impatience, as he called out—

"Up, knaves, and cover the masts with canvas. Rouse the loiterers from below, and show the Don what our Royal lady's ship can do to lighten him of his gold and repay the scurvy trick he has played us."

This speech was followed by the appearance of the men from below, and, the watch thus strengthened, the spars of the Bonaventura were soon covered with canvas.

The hull yielded to the influence of the sails, and as the heavy fabric went faster through the water, the seas curled and hissed under her bows, and a white line marked the Bonaventura's track over the pathless deep.

The whole of the officers were on the high deck, and the men who duty it was to attend to the sails were at their stations, ready to obey the slightest wish of Nicholas Hatton.

In the waist the soldiers were grouped, and the gunners, to be out of the way of the sailors, were recumbent between the pieces of artillery, and the small spiral columns of blue smoke that curled about them, told the matches were lighted.

The Bonaventura gained rapidly upon the galleon, for when Rupert first descried the dark object it seemed but a dark speck on the distant line, where the water and clouds apparently mingled; but now—and it was not more than an hour since the chase was sighted—the speck had grown into the well-known magnitude of the Spanish galleon, in the hold of which twenty thousand pounds in bright gold pieces were stored.

There was no movement perceptible on board the galleon until the Bonaventura was within cannon shot; then the large hull that had been rolling lazily upon the billows, and with only a few sails set, began to move forward under the combined powers of canvas and sweeps.

The Spaniard's purpose was soon apparent —he was making an attempt to gain the wind of his foe—then, as though to tantalize those on board the Queen's ship, he wore and went on the opposite tack, as though to put his sailing power against the Bonaventura.

CHAPTER II.

THE ATTACK.

THE manœuvres of the Spaniard were watched with breathless interest by the pursuers, and when the galleon's helm was put a-weather, and the heavy fabric glided majestically forward, the wind over the taffrail, an exclamation of rage came from the lips of Nicholas Hatton.

The exclamation was not alone caused by the galleon's movement; for, in addition to this, the Don hoisted the yellow banner of his imperial master, and saluted the fluttering silk by a salvo from his starboard guns.

"The curse of a true man upon you, insolent Don!" said the master of the Bonaventura. "By our Royal lady and the blessings of our Church, I will never doff arms or armour until the vaunting flag that streams yonder be trampled under foot!"

"A rash vow!" muttered Rupert Felton, as he watched the galleon, "and an impious one to boot."

The chase had now begun to assume the appearance of that which, in former as well as in modern times, is but little liked by a seaman—a stern chase.

Several hours passed without the slightest difference being perceptible in the position of the two vessels.

Both were skilfully commanded, and each commander knew to an inch the extent of canvas his bending masts and extra booms would bear.

"Come this way, Rupert-of-the-Ready-Tongue," said the angry master of the English ship. "Come, boy, and tell me. What is to be done now?"

"Nothing," answered Rupert, "unless the cannoneers have spoilt the wings of yonder vessel."

"See to it, Rupert, see to it; surely there is a piece of brass artillery on deck that will carry the distance?"

Rupert was about to leave the deck, when Nicholas Hatton called him back, and said—

"Tell the knaves whose matches I see burning that I will give to him who shall disable the Spaniard, a string of the finest oriental pearls, to wear around his neck when he goes ashore. Haste, Rupert; and, good youth, should the cannoneers fail, try the skill of your own hand and eye."

While Rupert was busy among the gunners the captain of the Bonaventura turned to Berton and growled—

"Shade of the great Harry!—a king, Berton, who loved wedlock as well as I love the sea—but I would give half the gold below to force yonder Spaniard into a narrow sea, or, for the matter of that, into rough water. What think you, Berton, of the chase?"

"But little; yet, at times, I could swear the tawdry gilding on the stern of yonder vessel becomes plainer when his hull rises on the billows."

"'Tis but the sun playing upon the rascal's patron saint. You have seen the figure, Berton; it is placed below the flag-staff. Ha! the boy has the cannon ready, let us watch the result, and pray it may lame the Don."

Rupert had ordered a piece of ordnance to be run forward, and the gunners, now as fully excited as their superiors, clustered round the gun.

"Steady, knave," said the young officer to the cannoneer, "apply your match when the Spaniard rises upon the waves."

The roar of the piece and the recoil shook the vessel; then followed the usual moments of silent suspense, and every eye was fixed upon the galleon.

"Bravely done!" shouted the captain— "bravely done, my good knave. Send him to me, Rupert, that the reward I have promised may be given."

Captain Hatton took from his neck a string of pearls, and from his hand a valuable ring, set with a single emerald.

These he gave to the gunner; then the men took their stations, ready to leap on board the Spaniard when the vessels touched.

The shot had cut in two the flagstaff, and the proud banner fell into the sea. The next mishap caused by the missile was the splintering of the aftermast, which, held only by the stays after the shot had passed, swayed to and fro for a few moments, then fell over the side.

The confusion on board the Santa Fé was visible from the deck of her pursuer; and the glitter of bills and axes was perceptible as a crowd of the Spaniards worked with a will to rid themselves of the broken mast.

This was soon effected, and the galleon, in obedience to the helm and the shifting of the running sails, swung round and presented her broadside to the foe.

"The Don," said Nicholas Hatton, as he took from his page a heavy sword, "means to show his teeth. Does the insolent, think you, gentlemen, know the quality of this good ship?"

"The Spaniard," said Rupert, "has a rare freight; besides his gold and silver, and valuable stuffs"——

"What are the valuables beyond these things, Rupert?"

"A bevy of fair women," answered the youth, "the wives and daughters of the opulent inhabitants of Panama, the last place, as you may remember, to which the freebooters from Tortugas have applied the sword and fire."

"Marry, cousin, but this is strange; for the freebooters are as eager to make captives of the women and girls as they are to carry off the plunder of a conquered town."

"It is so; but the Panamese had heard of the freebooters' coming, and put their wives and daughters and their jewels on board the Santa Fé."

"By our lady," said Hatton; "you have a discreet tongue. Rupert, to have kept this good news so many days. Why is this, boy? Did you fear to——"

"I wished not to excite the minds of the knaves by the knowledge of these things; for had the galleon escaped, there would have been more disappointment and anger had they known these things."

"The boy is right," said Hatton; "the knaves are at best but an unruly set; so—— Ah! the Spaniard dares to try his powder!"

Three puffs of smoke came from the galleon's top deck, and the missiles passed through the rigging, cutting away two of the lighter sails, and damaging several spars.

Nicholas Hatton's brow became knitted at the prospect of being disabled before he could reach the coveted prize, and he muttered an angry oath that boded ill for the Spanish commander, should he be taken.

Those were rough seamen, the commanders of the navy in the days of Queen Bess, and but little sentiments of mercy had a place in their hearts.

"Send the mariners aloft," said Hatton, "and let them be quick, or their skins shall suffer for the tardiness of their legs."

This was no idle threat the men knew by experience; and nimbly were the damaged sails and rigging repaired and replaced, in spite of the hissing of the iron balls that came from the Spaniards.

"Reply to the Don in the same language, Berton," said the captain; "and you, Rupert, take a score of arquebusiers, and tell them to do their work with effect; and you, Simon Vergrave, line the side with bowmen. Now, gentlemen, away to your stations and be vigilant, for the decks of the Santa Fé are full of men."

The vessels were now within pistol-shot of each other, the galleon motionless on the water; and the English ship, steered in obedience to a gesture from her commander's hand, was moving to the larboard quarter of her foe.

Nicholas Hatton took no more notice of the crowd of steel caps and glittering spear points visible on the Spaniard's deck; neither did he seem sensible of the storm of missiles that poured into his ship, or the return volleys of cannon-balls, bullets, and arrows.

His eyes were fixed upon the canvas of his vessel, save when he looked down at the mariners who were awaiting the orders that would brace the head-yards back.

"Now, my men," he shouted, as the Bonaventura came abeam of the galleon, "be nimble, and the prize is ours. Now, cannoneers, pour in your shot; and, gentlemen, to your posts, and carry the Don by storm."

The whole of the Bonaventura's broadside was poured into the galleon; then the vessels' yards interlocked; and, in defiance of the fire from the Spaniard's deck, the men on the mizen-top ran swiftly to the end of the yard, and lashed the vessels together.

"So—bravely done," said the master of the Bonaventura. "Now, to sweep the deck of England's foe."

He left the high deck, drawing his ponderous sword as he went down the ladder, and passed to where Rupert Felton stood directing the arquebusiers' fire.

"The galleon must be carried, Rupert," he said; "it is but a waste of firing and powder to stand here."

"Twice have I essayed to pass to their deck," answered Rupert, "and each time to meet these points."

He pointed to a triple line of spears held by the Spanish soldiers; and the master of the English ship saw the difficulty of effecting a footing upon the galleon, whose upper decks towered high above the Bonaventura.

"Berton," said Nicholas Hatton, "fill the tops with your bowmen, and you, Rupert, tell the mariners to arm with bills and pikes."

The bowmen swarmed to the tops, and their arrows created a momentary confusion on the Spaniard's deck, for they aimed only at the spearmen whose bristling line had repulsed Rupert's attack.

Nicholas Hatton's attentive eye saw the confusion caused by the bowmen, and in a voice which rose high above the roar of the combat, shouted—

"St. George and Merry England, at them, Rupert Felton, and strike home!"

The young officer brandished his sword, and called out—

"Bills and pikes!—A Rupert! A Rupert!"

The mariners streamed up the galleon's sides, and their bills shivered the spear-shafts of the Spanish soldiery as though the tough wood had been but osier reeds.

Then followed the pikemen—broad-shouldered, brawny fellows, stripped to the waist; and before their muscular arms the Spaniards were swept from the galleon's side like dust before the gale.

CHAPTER III.

THE LAST THROW.

THE galleon was not won, for the soldiers formed but a small portion of the crowd so closely packed upon the deck.

There were the mariners, the mulattoes, and a swarm of slaves, whose liberty would be the reward should the English be driven from the deck.

The cannonade had ceased, and the archers, from the tops of each vessel, had descended, and throwing aside their bows, rushed to the mêlée, armed with pike and sword.

The obstruction removed from the Spaniard's bulwarks, the remainer of the English swarmed up, leaving only the arquebusiers to defend the vessel in case of an attack, or to cover the retreat of their companions should the fight go against them.

Conspicuous by their steel corslets and glittering helms, the English officers led the attack, their Toledo blades clearing a passage through the ranks of the half-nude slaves who were foremost to oppose them.

Rupert Felton's battle-cry was loudest as he forced his way to the waist, and until he came to where the mighty commander of the galleon stood, with the flower of his crew at his back, none opposed the swift strokes of his blade, except to fall gashed and bleeding to the slippery planks.

"An accursed stripling!" said the commander of the galleon. "Have at thee for an island dog!"

Rupert met the downward stroke of his adversary's sword; then, throwing himself into an easy posture of defence, crossed blades with one of Spain's best swordsmen.

"Bide the blow and beware," said Nicholas Hatton, as he carved his way to the young officer's side, "or leave the Don to me, and it may be better."

"The blade so oft used against the Queen's enemies," replied Rupert, "will not fail me now."

He had no time for further speech, for the Don, angry, and lost to all caution, rushed madly upon his youthful adversary, and their blades twisted and curled as they emitted sparks of fire.

A fierce lunge made by the Spaniard caused his death, for the blade struck Rupert's steel collar, and bent nearly double at the moment. The young officer stepped back to prepare for the fatal stroke, and the Spaniard's foot, slipping on the blood-stained deck, he stumbled forward.

Ere he could fall, Rupert's sword passed through his neck, until stopped by the cross hilt. Then it was withdrawn, and sheathed in the body of a plumed and be-jewelled cavalier, who had attempted to plunge his dagger in Rupert's side.

The death of their leader, so far from dispiriting the Spaniards roused them to a pitch of ungovernable fury, and, rejecting the quarter offered by the English, they fought until cut down to a man.

The deck of the richly freighted galleon presented a terrible spectacle when Hatton's standard-bearer for the time drove the iron-shod point of his flag-staff into the high deck, and the rampant Lion of Albion floated proudly over the stern of the captured galleon.

Rupert had gone below at the moment the mariners began to toss the bodies of the slain into the sea.

His rich dress was bespattered with blood, and the blade he held was reeking from point to hilt, and with the light of battle still burning fiercely in his eye, he burst into the gorgeous state-room.

A piercing scream greeted his appearance, and a bevy of Spain's dark-eyed daughters, clustered together in a far-off corner, and uttered prayers to the Virgin and to their particular saints, to save them from the blood-bedabbled form, who they felt assured was about to murder them.

Rupert lowered his sword, and bowing low, said—

"Ladies, be not alarmed. I am no ogre to harm any who have the semblance of what my mother's form was; come, be not alarmed."

His voice and gestures, and, possibly, his handsome face, did much to reassure the frightened women, and they were about to leave their place of refuge, when the shouts of men, and hasty footsteps were heard on the steps that led from the deck to the luxurious state-room.

Rupert would have closed the door, but the half-maddened mariners and soldiers burst it open, and rushed into the cabin, shouting—

"Divide the spoil—let the women be given up to us, and the gold to our masters!"

"Back!" said Rupert, "back, ye black-hearted knaves! Such loveliness is not for such as you. Back, I say! or by the great heaven, I will cut down the first who crosses this mark!"

He pointed to a little pool of blood that had dripped from his sword-point as the blade rested upon the floor, and the men, checked for a moment, drew back.

Their hesitation was but of a few moments, for one of the mariners, a very Hercules in stature, advanced to the front of his companions, and flourishing an ensanguined bill, said—

"The prize is ours, Master Rupert, and the women as much our fair portion as the portion of our masters; so stand aside, ere it is too late."

"That for you, insolent knave!"

Rupert's blade swept the man's head from his body, and as the trunk fell with a thud to the deck, the crowd of mariners rushed forward to avenge their companion's fate.

Rupert went back step by step, until he felt the mast. Against this he stood, and like a tiger at bay, awaited the onslaught of the men, many of whom he had but a short time before led to victory.

They were close upon him, gradually making a circle around him, and more than once his sword had beaten down pike and bill.

Another moment and he would have been slain; but ere this brief space of time could pass, Nicholas Hatton bounded into the state-room, followed by a score of arquebusiers.

The sight that met his eyes was not an uncommon one in those lawless times, for discipline had but little weight with men half maddened by the excitement of battle.

"Open pans!" shouted Hatton to the arquebusiers; "prepare slow matches, and fire upon the first knave who dares raise his hand against his officer."

The soldiers prepared their unwieldy weapons, and Nicholas Hatton turned angrily to the mariners, and said—

"What now, my masters? Have you not had sufficient blood to-day but you must present your weapons at your officer?"

"He has slain our companion," was the sullen answer, "and the law is, blood for blood."

"Is this so, Rupert?"

"It is," was the reply. "The knave was insolent, and I took off both tongue and head, to teach his companions better behaviour."

"It was just," said Nicholas Hatton. "The seaman's law says he shall be punished who knoweth not how to respect his master; so away with you, knaves, and aid those who are taking the gold and rare stuffs to the Bonaventura."

The men sullenly obeyed, and Nicholas Hatton, who lost no opportunity to keep his men in subjection, said to the arquebusiers—

"Send a dozen balls through that plank, there may be a foe there. Ready——"

The balls in their passage from the fire-arms to the plank pointed out would have to pass through the state-room doorway, also through such of the turbulent mariners who were in the way.

The hint was sufficient, even for the most stubborn of them, for there was a hasty rush to reach the ladder, and before the balls splintered the planking the mariners had reached the deck.

"Come, Rupert," said Hatton, "we will attend to the storage of the spoil. And harkye, knaves," he added, turning to the arquebusiers, "throw that carcase into the sea, and remain here to guard the women from molestation."

"I will take charge of——"

"No, Rupert; you are but a sorry figure for a damsel's eyes. Wait until the marks of battle are removed, and the pouncet-box has scented thee with an aroma more delicate than the smell of blood."

The officers went on deck, and, by the hour of sunset, the wealth of the galleon was transferred to the Bonaventura, and the Spanish ladies taken on board and placed in a cabin, under the charge of a sentry, whose piece was loaded, and the smouldering match hung from his waist.

This done, the vessels parted—the galleon with a slow match laid near the powder-room, and the Bonaventura to continue her cruise.

When the watch was set, the officers gathered around the table in the state-room, and the dice-box was resorted to, not only to decide the possession of vast sums by a single throw, but to settle a dispute that had occurred as to the appropriation of the trembling captives, who were praying and sobbing in the next cabin.

"So far," said Nicholas, "the portion is equal. We take each our share of the dark-eyed damsels, and the equal portion leaves one unclaimed."

"And that one," said Berton, "the most lovely of the flock."

"'Sdeath, yes!" said Simon Vergrave, "and I who purpose holding my captives to ransom would give them all for the one who is not yet claimed."

"To hold to ransom!" asked Berton, "by our Lady, I would not ransom her for the wealth of Peru."

"Nor I," said Simon, "but to work, gentlemen. Here are the dice; let us decide who is to possess this paragon of loveliness, whether for ransom or as he lists."

"How are we to throw?" asked Rupert, as his eyes glistened fiercely. "One throw each and the highest to be the winner."

"It is the best way," said Hatton, "so to it. I will begin."

There was an eagerness in the eyes of the men greater than there would have been had the stakes been the immense wealth in the Bonaventura hold.

"Five!" exclaimed Berton, "your chance has gone."

"A curse upon the dice!"

The master of the Bonaventura flung the box upon the table as he spoke, and Berton eagerly dropped the dotted cubes in, and shook them.

"Nine!"

The number was told by every lip; then Simon, as next in rank, threw his chance.

"Fourteen!" he exclaimed; "'tis a good throw. Now, Rupert, try thy luck."

Rupert shook the dice, and his face paled as he tossed them upon the table.

"Fourteen!" he said. "We are equal, Simon Vergrave; try again."

Simon muttered a fierce oath, and again rattled the ivories.

"Twelve!" he exclaimed, passionately, "I will give myself to the Evil One if he spoils my throw, Rupert."

The young officer's hand and lip trembled as he made the final throw, and springing to his feet, he exclaimed—

"Fourteen! she is mine."

Simon Vergrave's face reddened with fury as he brought his clenched fist upon the table, and fiercely exclaimed—

"The foul fiend take thee and the ship, and the girl! I would as soon see her at the bottom of the sea as another's. May thy success be the last——"

Crash—a roar; and the straining of the ship's timbers, a confused rushing to and fro above—then a splintering of wood, and through a hole in the vessel's side the water rushed madly in.

"My dream!" exclaimed Rupert, and his face paled as he clung to the mast—the rushing waters rising rapidly around him.

CHAPTER IV.
THE BUCCANEERS.

MODERN novelists, as a rule, when using the words which head this chapter, have been in the habit of leading their readers to the belief that the terms buccaneers, pirates, and free-booters are synonymous — a mistake the writer will, if the reader has patience to peruse this short chapter, venture to correct.

The earliest account we have of the buccaneers states that a number of hardy, fearless adventurers fixed their abode on the island of Hispaniola, better known now by its more modern name of St. Domingo.

These men used to spend entire months in the forests, hunting the wild bulls, bears, and boars; and when they returned from the chase, they placed the produce on board canoes and sailed to the Isle of Tortugas, which is situate on the western side of St. Domingo.

Tortugas was their market, and to the colonists they gave their salted and smoked meat in exchange for arms, powder, lead, and other articles essential to their profession.

In the language of the country, the places where the hunters salted and dried their meat, and prepared the hides of the animals they had killed, were termed boucans, hence the name buccaneers received by the hunters.

The principal boucans were situate in the peninsula of Savanna, on the north coast of St. Domingo, and on an island in the Bay of Bayaba. They also had a few huts at Port Margot, Mirlabois, Tortugas, and L'Avaché.

St. Domingo, at the time the buccaneers were following their peaceful calling, was under the Spanish rule. This power, at the time, was the most formidable European power —formidable not only in her military and naval resources, but in the vast possessions that had been added by conquest, and one amongst these was the island of St. Domingo.

Spain, although in addition to her overgrown territories she had the command of the treasures of the new world, would not allow the peaceful buccaneers to remain longer in the island; so the idea was conceived of driving them away, or, if possible, to exterminate them.

The execution of this barbarous plan was not a difficult matter, although, as will be seen, it ultimately proved disastrous to the power that caused it.

The buccaneers, unsuspicious of evil, were at their usual avocations—some hunting, others tilling the ground, when the Spanish soldiers fell upon them and massacred all they could find in arms, and those they captured were dragged into slavery.

From this time, the buccaneers, or hunters, were always on the defensive; they no longer went out singly or in pairs to hunt, but in strong parties, and, when attacked by their foes, defended themselves so bravely that the Spaniards, though much superior in numbers, were often defeated.

The tactics of the war now changed; the Spaniards, worsted in nearly every encounter, crept upon the buccaneers at night, and slew all who fell into their hands.

This enraged the buccaneers, and they no longer acted on the defensive alone, but began a war of reprisals, and so bitterly was the fighting continued that the island of St. Domingo became known by the name of Massacre.

For five years this state of things continued; then the Spaniards, finding they could not exterminate the buccaneers, hit upon the plan of depriving them of their means of subsistence.

A general destruction of horned cattle and other animals was ordered and carried out; and the buccaneers, thus deprived of their occupations and resources, were driven to embrace another mode of living, and many of them went to the island of Tortugas, then under the protection of the French flag, and settled as peaceful colonists.

The greater portion, accustomed to the dangers of the forest, scorned a peaceful life, and animated only by one passion—that to be revenged upon the Spaniards—the only way to gain their revenge was to join the freebooters, who were only too glad to obtain such willing recruits.

The freebooters were bands of daring adventurers from all parts of Europe, whose vessels scoured the American seas, their only object being to plunder the richly-freighted Spanish treasure ships, and, if many, they would disembark and attack towns and fortresses.

In this they were secretly aided by France and England, for both countries were jealous of Spain, and nearly always at war with the great power whose riches were increased by the possession of the inexhaustible treasures of Mexico and Peru.

The freebooters, being principally English and French, and owning no authority except the leaders they had chosen, yet used the English or French flags (according to which country was at war with Spain), had not become very formidable until the buccaneers joined them.

Then they became strong in numbers and indifferent to every danger as long as there was a chance of a good booty, and many of them, giving up their wild lives when they had become rich, returned to their native countries; and the news spread so rapidly, that all who loved an adventurous life, made their way across the seas to join the floating republic.

The freebooters became so powerful that both France and England condescended to employ them against the Spaniards—their only pay being the plunder they obtained, their reward, the Letters of Marque the leaders received to legalise their acts.

The pirates, with whose deeds we are all more or less familiar, were of a totally different stamp to the buccaneers or freebooters, for, unlike the two latter, they had no aid given them by any power, neither had they, as in the case of the buccaneers, any wrongs to redress by taking up arms.

The sole object that drew the pirates together was plunder; and so merciless were they in their mode of obtaining it, that friend and foe were alike robbed and murdered; and even amongst themselves there was no principle of honour—no desire to perform gallant deeds or anything else that could bring them within the pale of civilisation.

As will be seen in the course of this story, the buccaneers or freebooters—whichever they may be termed—had some redeeming traits in their mode of warfare and in their treatment of the captives who fell into their hands—traits we seek for in vain in the records of the bloodthirsty pirates, and who, as an old author * justly observes—"Never did make bold descents, attacked no forts, carried not their arms among land forces or into squadrons, but did only cut throats and plunder upon the seas."

CHAPTER V.

ADRIFT ON THE OCEAN.

ONE terrible shriek arose from the doomed ship; the waters, roaring like an avalanche, filled every nook and cranny between her decks.

With the frenzied shriek the stout vessel's timbers grated, as the hull, moved by the influence of a sudden blast of wind, was torn off the rock.

There was then a gurgling noise, as the air was forced upwards; and the Bonaventura, her hold filled with ingots of gold, bars of silver, and boxes of gems and precious stones, went rapidly to the bed of the ocean.

Torn from his grasp on the mast, Rupert Felton was dashed against the top of the cabin, and as a spiral pillar of water shot upward through the hatch, he was carried with it, and tossed by the bubbling waters.

Like a whirlpool, the sea eddied around and above the sunken ship; and among the floating articles that were buffeted about by the white-topped waves, was the form of the young officer.

Scarcely conscious of the act, Rupert clutched a spar that was whirling around him, and until the disturbed surface of the ocean became calm, he clasped the wood with both arms, and so tightly, that death alone could have released his grasp.

It seemed as though the grim destroyer was but mocking the young officer with the prospect of escape; for, during the short time that the waters foamed and bubbled above the lost ship, Rupert was hurled against the many bulky articles that were tossing about.

The collision bruised his limbs and wounded his body, and the blood trickled from more than one cut about his hands and face.

Senseless, save for the instinct of self-preservation that caused him to cling to the spar, Rupert lay for some hours upon the bosom of the deep.

The balmy southern breeze wafted the spar and its burden many miles from where the ship had gone down, and when the solitary youth recovered sufficient of his faculties to be fully aware of his position, he raised his head and looked around for some trace of the lost vessel.

No object greeted his anxious look save the boundless expanse of sunlit sea and the equally interminable sky.

"I am indeed lost," murmured the castaway, as he sank back upon the spar. "Lost—lost!"

He lay until the night set in, in a stupor produced by the terrible fate that had befallen his gallant and gay companions, and his

* Charlevoix.

despair at being thus left alone upon the ocean.

The night passed; and to the solitary mariner the hours seemed days, and when the sun arose in its grandeur and the fiery beams played upon his upturned head, he wished it was night again, for the heat caused him the most intense thirst, and, coupled with the bruised and weakened state of his body, compelled him to forget the effect the salt water would have upon the salivatory glands.

The pangs caused by intense thirst are at all times terrible to endure, but in the midst of the ocean, where water is so near that the outstretched hand may touch it, the sufferings are trebled.

Thrice the castaway immersed his fingers in the salt water, and by this means sought to allay his thirst.

For a few seconds this cooled his mouth and moistened his tongue—then his thirst returned with tenfold intensity.

Rupert cried aloud in his agony, and for some moments there was a determination within him to end his torments by rolling off the spar into the briny flood.

"I would do it," he said; but those who commit the sin of self-destruction are trebly cursed. No; I will endeavour to bear with my misery until the end. That can't be long—another day at most."

An hour after this he was aroused from his despair by a sudden shadow falling across the ocean.

The young officer raised his head, and to his joy beheld the blazing sun darkened by a cloud.

He gazed long and steadily at the dark vapour as roll after roll swept across the sun. Then watching the direction taken by them murmured——

"If the wind but keeps up, they will come this way. Then, please heaven, I shall be saved from a portion of such torments as must be felt only by the accursed."

Rupert had been long enough at sea to distinguish the rising of a rain-cloud, but never before had he watched the dark masses rising with such feverish anxiety as in the present instance.

It was not until near sunset that the dark clouds drifted above the lone voyager; then the rain fell in large drops, and so heavily that Rupert was wet through to the skin in a few moments.

This was a pleasure instead of an inconvenience; for his skin, dried by the torrid rays of the sun, felt delightfully cool; and to assuage his thirst he sucked the sleeve of his jacket, and when satisfied felt stronger and more hopeful than ever.

The rain still fell in torrents, and the castaway, knowing that rainstorms were rare in these latitudes, tried to devise some mode of saving a little of the precious fluid.

Until now he had not thought of examining the spar that had proved his salvation; so he lost no time in doing so before the approaching brief twilight should come upon him.

It proved to be the foretopmast of the Bonaventura (a heavy piece of timber), which he remembered, when he saw the thickest end torn and jagged, had been shot in two by the fire from the Santa Fé.

He remembered also seeing another spar rigged in its place, and a curious sensation passed over the young officer when he thought of the useless portion of the mast having been the means of so far saving his life, while the new one he had been at so much trouble to see rigged in its place was many fathoms below the surface of the ocean.

Sitting astride his "ship," he joyfully beheld a piece of the torn canvass still attached. This was nearly two yards square, and Rupert, having his sword yet hanging at his hip, drew the blade and cut away the cordage that held the moiety of the sail.

This done, the canvass was spread out, the four corners were fastened with string, and a vessel nearly square was made to hold the water.

Long the ocean wanderer sat with the canvas bag; and, as the rain still fell heavily, he hoped to see it fill.

The sun set, and the evening shadows came over the waters, but still not a drop of the priceless fluid remained in the canvas, and to Rupert's mind there came a fact that he had long been unwilling to believe.

The sail-cloth was not waterproof; thus the rain, as fast as it fell, filtered through.

With a despairing cry, he let the bag fall from his aching arms; and, losing his spirits, gave way to the despondency natural to one so circumstanced.

The night was passed as the previous night had been—in praying for the dawn; and long before the gray tints appeared the rain ceased, and the warm winds fanned the officer's cheeks.

This, he knew, was a sure forerunner of a hot day; and his heart fell, for there was no probability of the rain again descending for several days.

Should he not be picked up before then, he shuddered as the terrible prospect, in all its horrors, came before his mind.

Again, should he be found by one of the Spanish ships, what would be his fate when those on board discovered from whence he came?—for the Bonaventura had been a fearful scourge to the richly-laden vessels when on their way to Spain with treasure taken from the mines of the New World.

These and similar thoughts racked his brain until another day shed its beams upon the ocean; and that day was passed in suffering, for the pangs of hunger now beset him.

Another night came, and by this time his face had become pale, his cheeks hollow, and his eyes seemed ready to burst from their sockets for the want of that sleep he dared not take, fearing the frail thing that supported him would roll over should he lose his balance.

The next day came, and the sun seemed fiercer than ever; and, like the preceding days, nothing met his eyes save the boundless view of sky and water.

"My last day of life," said the sufferer; "for I have scarcely strength to keep my grasp upon this spar. To-night will, should I not be discovered, end alike my life and torture of body and mind."

All through that day he gnawed a silver button torn off his dress, and to cool his parched and cracking lips, sucked the pommel of his cross-hilted sword.

He kissed the cross and prayed for a deliverance from his wretchedness; prayed, as a Catholic, to the saints; and prayed as one of the new faith, that was at that time making its way with all classes of Englishmen; but no welcome sail followed these prayers, so he closed his eyes and waited for the fate that seemed imminent, and impossible to escape.

The bosom of the great ocean was as peaceful as an inland lake; and the wind, balmy and gentle, occasionally came from the west, but with such slight force that the solitary voyager's frail craft scarcely moved.

Such being the state of the ocean, Rupert scarcely clasped the spar until startled by a sudden jerk that nearly overset him.

So strong is the instinct of self-preservation that the castaway, although firmly convinced his end was near, clung with both hands to his support; and when the spar vibrated under him, his soul was filled with alarm.

He knew the deep contained many strange monsters; and at the period of which we write, superstition and fable were rife amongst the mariners, and their minds pictured the inhabitants of the sea as monsters whose mission was to devour all of the human species who came within reach of their jaws.

The motion of the spar soon ceased, and the English officer, whose cheek had never paled in furious fight, now became bloodless, and his frame quivered like one who had been suddenly attacked with rigours.

He had gazed down into the clear water, and there beheld what appeared to be a supernatural denizen of the deep.

Its body was black and perfectly smooth; its head of a terrible form; the mouth tremendously large for the body; and the lower jaw protruded far beyond the upper.

Both jaws were full of teeth, and on the top of the creature's head was a hideous conformation formed of thin plates not unlike talc in colour.

These plates were likewise armed with teeth; and the large eyes, that were set far up the head, seemed to the startled mariner to gaze vacantly upward.

Rupert prayed again, for he felt assured that the strange and terrible thing was an enemy sent by the Prince of Darkness to drag him to the infernal regions, which, for all he knew, might be under the bed of the ocean.

To confirm Rupert's opinion, he saw the black visitor's tail and body move; and when it did so, the spar went hither and thither as the short broad fins paddled the water.

He felt as though his brain would split, for the horrible brute's mouth opened and shut occasionally, and yet the creature was firmly attached to the spar.

Nearly an hour passed, yet the visitor from below did not shift his position, and Rupert, whose supernatural fears began to subside, began to look upon it with less fear, and suddenly clasping his hands he almost shrieked—

"Removed."

The mystery was now explained. He had recognised his visitor as the "sucking fish," and the hideous scaly protuberance on the top of its head as the sucker furnished by nature for the creature, when tired, to attach itself to anything that floated.

The sucking fish, being but an indifferent swimmer, attaches itself to floating timbers, to the keels of vessels, and by this means is conveyed from place to place without the trouble of swimming.

His mind now quieted, the castaway saw, in the appearance of the sucking fish, the answer to his prayer that he might not die of starvation.

The sucker would supply him with food for a couple of days at least—but how was he to catch it?

He was weak, and in such a position that he could only grasp the fish by the tail, and he knew a strong man could not pull the echeneis from its hole by a backward pull. The curious apparatus on its head required pushing forward, and that way alone would tax his muscular power.

He was not long in making up his mind what to do. The front of his silken doublet was ornamented with gold cord. To tear off sufficient of this to form a running noose was the work of a few moments, and to pass the noose round the thickest part of the sucker occupied a very long space of time.

This done, and the knot pulled tight, he held the end of the cord in his left hand, and with the right drew his sword.

A swift and sure downward blow and the fish was decapitated, then the black body was drawn up, and there was no time lost by the starving officer in cutting off a portion and eating it.

This incident made Rupert hopeful, and when night came on he clung tighter to the spar, and prayed that the morrow would reveal the land or the masts of a vessel.

Scarcely had these lowly muttered words left his lips than the spar came in contact with a hard substance, and Rupert, putting up his hands, felt the hull of a vessel, and gave a scream of joy and thankfulness.

CHAPTER VI.

THE BRETHREN OF THE COAST.

THE buccaneers, and their allies, the freebooters, attacked and took the Island of Tortugas from the Spaniards, and having fortified their rendezvous, they set about forming that formidable organisation known as the Brethren of the Coast.

This powerful league was composed of three bands. The hunters, who passed the greater portion of their time in chase of the beasts of the forests, to supply the settlement and the fleet with dried meat.

The second band were termed "inhabitants." Their duty was to cultivate the ground, and, in conjunction with the hunters, defend the island in the absence of the fleet.

The third portion of the brethren were the buccaneers, whose sole occupation was to capture the Spanish treasure-ships.

The combined bands, when their numbers were increased by the daily arrival of adventurers from all parts of Europe, met at a great council, and, after some discussion, framed a code of laws for their government, which we will briefly explain, as many of the events to be chronicled cannot well be understood unless the reader is acquainted with the laws of the brethren.

Perfect equality was one article of the code; thus every man was entitled to an equal share of everything that fell into the hands of the band.

Every man also had a vote in the selection of a leader, and to prevent any quarrels about the Spanish girls who should be captured, no man was permitted, under penalty of death, to take one on board a ship; those who deserted the band were likewise punished.

Any man pilfering from a "brother" was to have his nose and ears slit, and then the offender was to be taken and left upon a desert island.

When on board the vessels any fighting between the brethren was prohibited, under the penalty of having the right hand chopped off. All quarrels were to stand over until the ship returned to the island, then the antagonists were allowed to meet in presence of their comrades and decide the matter by pistol or rapier.

Every man, under the same penalty, was compelled to keep his arms always ready for service. These arms consisted of a sabre, a brace of pistols, and a fusee (a weapon answering to the modern rifle).

The arms and armour of the band were of the richest and most costly make, for a species of rivalry soon sprang up among them, and, to use a well-known phrase, they tried to "cut each other out" by the splendour of their weapons.

There were certain rewards for gallant action. For instance, the man who hauled down the enemy's flag and ran up the buccaneers' in its place received a large sum of money.

There was also a reward for the first man who scaled the wall of a fort or mounted the side of a ship.

When the vessels were at anchor, and their crews ashore, any man who did not repair on board at the first signal was severely punished.

Every man upon becoming a member of the strange brethren had to take an oath that he would faithfully abide the laws or forfeit his life.

The swearing-in of a new brother was a strange proceeding. The men knelt upon one knee, and held their swords aloft, while a monk, with a crucifix before him, swore the new comer as a faithful member of the league.

Then, while the bright blades and the symbol of the cross were above him, the neophyte was suddenly told he had no mercy to expect should he infringe but one article of their code.

There was no mercy ever shown to any member of the band who offended. A short trial, the ring of firearms, and all was over.

It cannot be wondered at that a band of men, the bravest and most reckless to be found, should soon become the terror of the seas.

About two days before the opening of this story, a stately vessel lay off the Buccaneers' Isle; the crew were ashore, save half-a-dozen hands who kept a strict watch seaward.

Suddenly a canoe shot under the bows, and a solitary rower, in reply to the sentinel's stern hail, answered—

"St. Domingo."

"Come on board, St. Domingo," was the reply, as the sentry extinguished under his foot the slow match he had ignited on the first approach of the canoe.

The rower rapidly ascended, and was met by the buccaneer officer in charge, with the words—

"What news?"

"Good news," said the man. "The Santa Fé, loaded with specie, has put to sea, and the wind comes from the west, so there is no time to lose."

"None," said the officer; "so we will give the signal."

Three blows upon the ship's bell smartly given, and almost as the sound reached the land crowds of men were seen running to where a number of canoes lay.

They were on board in less than fifteen minutes; the anchor weighed, and the vessel standing out to sea.

The officers stood together on the poop busily discussing the amount of plunder on board the Santa Fé, when the officer, who had been in charge of the ship, caused some commotion among his companions by saying—

"We have only a chance of the galleon being on this side of the bay, if she has passed the English ship. The Bonaventura is in these seas."

"The Bonaventura!"

Here followed a volley of strong language from the bearded buccaneers, for the Queen's ship was known to be as swift a sailer as any vessel afloat, and her captain one of the keenest upon the scent of a pirate vessel.

"What says Captain Levausseur to this news?" asked one of the officers, turning to a tall, soldierly-looking man who stood a little apart. "Does he believe the Bonaventura will take the galleon from under our very guns?"

Levausseur turned and faced the group, and, stroking his grizzled beard, replied—

"It is the misfortune of war if we lose the Santa Fé. If we gain her decks so much the better, but you have all prayed well, comrades, before coming on board?"

"We have," was the half-laughing reply, "Stannard here sang the 'Magnificat,' and I he 'Miserere,' while our English and Pro-

testant comrades used their Bibles, and one and all sang and prayed for a grand prize."

"And your songs and prayers," said Levausseur, "will be heard; for the Santa Fé is richly laden, not only with gold in ingots, and silver in bars, but in young women and girls, who escaped the sacking of the town our brethren lately captured."

"Our men need wives," said Stannard, "and the day may yet come when the need will be supplied, for the custom of bringing women from France and the Low Countries is but a sorry way to stock the island with women."

"Yet it answers," said the captain, "so far, at least; but I should prefer the dark-eyed beauties of Spain to the refuse of the northern countries."

The officers kept up their conversation until the sun set, then they dispersed—some to sleep, others to throw the dice and play away their shares in the prospective prize.

Day after day passed and no sign of the galleon, and the hope of meeting her became but slight.

They went about and tacked over the distance they had passed, still the same unbroken surface of the ocean.

The buccaneers chafed under this disappointment, and several times were on the point of returning to the island, but the hope that the galleon had been delayed in consequence of a calm that set in the third day of the buccaneers' cruise caused them to still remain out.

After passing so many days in suspense, the cry of "A sail to leeward!" acted like a charm upon the buccaneers. Every man rushed on deck.

The vessel's course was changed, and there was joy on every face when the distant speck grew into the bulky outlines of the galleon.

"Gentlemen," said Levausseur, "your prayers and paters are rewarded; for yonder is the Santa Fé, and before an hour our cannon will be playing upon her hull."

The men gave a shout of joy, and the cannoneers ignited their matches ready to cripple the richly freighted ship.

CHAPTER VII.

THE DEATH SHIP.

A LOOSE rope blown about by the wind struck Rupert across the face, and as he eagerly clutched it with both hands, the hull of the vessel swayed towards him, and the spar, so long his home upon the waters, was tossed about by the wash of the waves against the vessel.

Rupert put forth all his strength to retain possession of the rope, and the spar slid from beneath him.

He was left now with his body up to the waist in water, and despairing of being able to retain the rope, he called aloud for assistance.

There was no response, so he repeated the cry, but the large, dark hull only moved slowly through the water—all on her decks was as silent as the tomb.

THE WATER RUSHED IN.

"There is but a sorry watch kept on board," thought the young officer. "Yet this is a large vessel, and in these seas there are those who would take advantage of a sleeping crew."

There seemed no prospect of receiving any assistance until the sun should arouse the mariners, and it was with an aching heart the castaway looked forward to passing the night in his forlorn condition.

He did not despair while life remained, but in his exhausted state he knew there was but slight hope of his being able to cling to the rope until the morning came.

Nerved by the dread prospect of dying when succour was so near, he made another attempt to ascend the side of the ship.

He succeeded in rising clear of the water; then the rope slipped through his hands, and but for the knot at the end, the young officer would have been drawn beneath the hull.

It required but little support to keep his body floating on the surface of the ocean, so, panting and breathless, Rupert lay flat on the sea, one hand alone keeping him in this position.

Again he raised his voice—not loud, yet sufficiently high to be heard had there been any watchers on the deck.

There was no response, so Rupert, praying for sufficient strength to enable him to pass the few hours that yet remained before the dawn, resigned himself to await with fortitude the appearance of the first streak of the new day.

The fear of sharks was not absent from Rupert's mind as he lay upon the water; but to dispel this terrible idea from his mind, he began to form conjectures as to the size and nationality of the vessel.

Speculating upon this, and endeavouring to judge by the motion of the hull whether there was a heavy cargo or not on board, the manner in which the vessel rode the waves struck the young sailor as being very singular.

He knew there was breeze enough to keep the sails steady, and had they been properly set, when the vessel rolled, the canvas must necessarily fall against the mast.

The flapping of the sail was wanting; and this, with the peculiar roll of the hull, caused Rupert to think that not only were the watch asleep, but the helmsman also, for the tiller-ropes, instead of making that peculiar cheeping rattle when the wheel is moved, were silent.

The hypothesis formed by Rupert was, that the rudder, in consequence of the neglect of those on board, had become jammed; thus the ropes were held slantingly.

This was confirmed by the way in which the vessel lurched from side to side, her bows parting first one way then another, the points as variable as the breeze.

Trying to solve the cause of this strange mode of traversing the deep occupied the castaway's thoughts for some time; and, as he was thus engaged, the moon, which had hitherto been veiled by drifting banks of black clouds, suddenly appeared.

The white gleaming disc of night's queen shed its pale light upon the waves in a radiant line, which slowly widened until it reached the hull of the vessel.

Rupert turned his eyes upwards and beheld the towering side of a very large vessel.

The examination of the vessel's size was only a secondary thought; for within half a handspike's distance of the loose rope, there hung a rope ladder.

The castaway gave a joyful cry when he saw this; and, bringing his body erect, he took a firm grasp of the rope with his right hand; he then turned towards the hull of the vessel, and extending his left hand tried to grasp the ladder.

The eager fingers were within a few inches only of the coveted prize, and the thought came to Rupert's mind that he was fated to be made the victim of disappointment.

A wave curling against the hull threw Rupert's body in the required direction, and caused his fingers to close upon the ladder.

A momemt more, and the right hand was taken from the rope, and placed beside the left; then Rupert, with a joyful heart, placed his feet upon the bottom rung of the ladder.

As he slowly ascended the towering side, he saw the vessel had many decks—he passed one, then another, and another, and yet the bulwark was not reached; then the moon became obscured, and he boarded the vessel in the darkness.

When the castaway's foot touched the deck, he fell into an attitude of prayer, and thanked the Great Power that had watched over his fate.

The prayer over, Rupert arose and went towards the poop, and the moonbeams falling upon the deck just as he reached the main-mast, revealed the deck covered with men.

They were lying about in all positions—groups were between the guns, others clustered around the masts, and all apparently in a deep slumber.

It was a deep sleep—the sleep of death—and Rupert, not at first realising the true condition of the mariners, struck one of the recumbent forms with the toe of his heavy boot, and said—

"Wake, my masters! this is but a scurvy watch to keep."

There came no reply, no sign of life, and Rupert stooping for a moment, saw a ghastly face, and a pair of fixed, glassy eyes.

He reeled backwards, and, clasping his brow, exclaimed—

"Great heaven! 'Tis a death ship, and I have but left one death to meet another yet more fearful."

There was not light enough to reveal the blood-stains upon the deck, and the stiffened wounds that were visible upon more than one ace.

Supported by the mainmast, Rupert stood for some time, his eyes covered by one hand, in the vain attempt to shut out the horrible scene.

The castaway could not pause to try and discover the cause of the terrible appearance of the ship's decks. He saw not the pools of blood, nor the gaping wounds. His mind was filled with but one terrible idea, and the few words he said, while leaning against the mast, explained the fearful sensation that filled his breast.

"It is a plague-ship."

The face he had gazed upon, under the pale moonbeams, looked grim and ghastly; and now the fancy had become rooted in his mind—he fancied the air was tainted with the horrible disease.

Nay, more—he felt his limbs and senses succumbing to the fell atmosphere, and, giving a moan of hopeless anguish, he fell to the deck senseless.

He knew not that the cause of his weakness was the effect of the singular voyage, when adrift upon the spar, and the faint odour that he breathed was but the exhalations of the pools of blood.

CHAPTER VIII.

PURSUED BY CANNIBALS.

THE strange sight revealed by the tropical sun when its fierce rays fell upon the form of the young sailor as he sat astride the spar that was between him and eternity was not the only singular object upon the Spanish Main.

Some twenty miles to leeward of Rupert's now abandoned spar, and shortly after the young officer reached the deck of the plague-ship, was a peculiar craft, tenanted by two persons.

One was a man—a very giant in stature and muscular development—the other was of the opposite sex, and a being of wondrous beauty.

The man was in the very prime of his years—his companion but just budding into womanhood, and by her long raven tresses, olive-tinted complexion, large dark eyes, and roundness of form, a daughter of sunny Spain.

The man's complexion and face bespoke a more northern latitude, and his speech, when he turned from time to time to address his fellow-voyager, told he came from Britain's sea-girt isle.

The craft that held this pair of voyagers was of the smallest kind capable of carrying their weight, being nothing more than an empty shot-box, with a portion of a vessel's spanker boom fastened transversely across the open top.

The box was square, and seemed between six and seven feet across, and in depth was not more than three feet.

There was only about twelve inches of the strange craft visible above the surface, the remainder being submerged by the weight of its living burden, and the heavy spar.

The singular vessel made but little way through the water, for there was nothing to supply either the place of oars or a sail. Even had there been, the man could not have used either one or the other, for at the last moment the ill-balanced craft threatened to turn over and capsize.

This would have happened long ago, but for the boom which extended many feet over the sides of the box. Consequently, when there was a disposition for the latter to heel over, the edge of the boom struck the water before the edge of the frail barque could be submerged and fill, and the spar, by its buoyancy enabled the man to right the vessel again.

Seemingly regardless of the danger that menaced both vessel and crew, the man was standing erect, a foot on each side of the boom, while the young girl crouched at his feet, her dark eyes turned appealingly heavenward, and her hands clasped and lying listlessly in her lap.

With one hand the man shaded his eyes, and after a long survey of the glittering ocean, he slowly settled down to a sitting posture, and began to paddle with the palms of his hands, and the strangely-shaped craft went slowly through the water.

"The worst of the danger," said the man, "is now over, lady. God grant we may never know such a night again."

The girl turned her eyes upon the speaker, and in a low voice, replied—

"The saints forbid! Should we escape, oh! how well shall you be rewarded for your bravery in saving me from those dreadful men!"

She spoke English very plainly, this Spanish maiden; for, when a child, she had been reared in a Spanish prison, used exclusively for the detention of the English sailors and soldiers captured during the great wars, and her father was governor of the place.

"I want no reward, lady," said the man, in as gentle a tone as could come from his great chest. "I have little sisters at home, and I am doing as I would others would do by them should they be brought to so sore a strait as you have been brought to."

"My father is rich, and "—

"I want not his riches. It is the cursed greed of my countrymen for Spanish gold that has brought this evil upon us all. Hush! is that a voice, or the cry of a sea-bird?"

The girl listened intently. Then, as her face became paler than before, she whispered in terrified accents—

"It is a voice—the voice of one of those dreadful men!"

The man made no reply, but unsheathing the long knife that hung in a leathern case at his hip, he placed the weapon at his feet, and continued to paddle with increased force, and the effect of this was to move the slight structure faster over the bosom of the interminable deep.

"It is the raft," he muttered, "and if once we are overtaken, this poor child will be sure to suffer. I have no fear for myself. I am strong, and can do battle with any among them who will try the issue. What, after all, if it should have been but our imagination about the voice? I hope it is!"

The hopeful words belied the man's actions, for he continued with might and main to urge the craft quicker in a direction contrary to that in which he had fancied the tones of a man's voice had proceeded.

Had it been daylight, or had the moon but continued to shed her light upon the sea after the English mariner had reseated himself on the frail embarkation, he would have seen an object that in a moment would have cleared up all doubts about the cause of the voice he had heard.

Close to his craft the moonlight would have revealed another structure—a raft of some size, fashioned from many of the articles that had been about the deck of a large ship.

And on this structure he would have seen nearly a dozen men, most of them busily urging the raft through the water with every article they could possibly use for an oar.

So close did the strange craft pass the shot-box and the broken boom, that the back-wash of the latter caused the smaller embarkation to rock to and fro, until there seemed a possibility that she would not right again.

The English mariner had good cause to know the raft and its occupants, for it was not many hours since he had, with his companion, escaped from it, and only in time to save the young and beautiful girl from a most fearful fate.

The occupants of both rafts, if the shot-box may be so termed, had all belonged to one vessel—the ill-fated Bonaventura.

When the vessel foundered, and the waters had subsided a little, the fragments that had floated upwards were strangely mingled with a number of the crew and many of her helpless captives.

All who were on deck were left struggling in the eddying waters, as the ship went down; and those who had presence of mind sufficient to enable them to make an effort to save their lives, clung to such of the floating objects that passed near enough to be grasped.

Those who missed their grasp were whirled far away, and many who clung to such things as afforded a chance of keeping them afloat were unable to retain their hold, and perished.

One of the captives—the beautiful Spanish girl, for whose possession the officers were throwing the dice—was on the deck at the time the ship went down.

She clung to a spar; but her hold was not sufficient to retain it, when the sea leaped and roared over the grave of the good ship.

She would have perished but for the friendly arm of the gigantic English seaman, who was near enough to save her before she went below the troubled surface.

Those who were left, drawn together and under the guidance of the English giant, brought the planks and barrels together and formed a raft.

It was a task of some difficulty, but life was at stake, so the strongest swimmers swam to and fro and collected the "drift."

The bad and indifferent swimmers were enabled to sustain themselves in the water without much fatigue, and at the same time make themselves of great service in fastening the various articles together, as they were brought to one spot.

The raft grew rapidly, and the tired men were glad when the last fragment was collected and fastened to the embarkation, as then they were to be in part rewarded for their toil.

Not only rewarded by being in possession of a structure that kept them afloat, but in receiving a share of the contents of a huge butt of canary.

The half-emptied vessel that held the wine had shot up from the ship some time after the Bonaventura went down.

Possibly the buoyancy of the cask had been so great that it had broken its way through the shattered timbers of the ship.

The swimmers lost no time in speculations of this description; the vessel and its contents were there—that was all they cared for.

The gigantic English mariner had taken the lead in the construction of the raft; now he took charge of the butt of wine, and no voice was raised against his self-election as leader of the band of castaways.

He was known to be a man of dogged resolution and unimpeachable valour, a matchless swordsman, and one not unacquainted with the art of war, as it was then understood, and a skilful mariner.

His position on board the lost ship had been a little above that of a seaman, an under officer, answering to the post held by a boatswain at times.

Coupled with these qualifications, the gigantic mariner's muscular strength had its weight with the men, who quickly submitted to his commands.

Mark Luton, or, as he was more generally named, Stronghand, stood over the wine cask, and turning his bearded face from one to the other of the survivors, said—

"Hark ye, my comrades, the raft is small, but that portion formed by the shot-case must be kept sacred for the use of the Spanish girl. My words are understood—let none approach the shot-case under penalty of death."

"She is but a prisoner," said a soldier, brutally. "Why should she have more space allowed than——"

"Keep your prating tongue between your teeth, comrade," said Stronghand; "or it may be slit."

The soldier quailed before the giant's fierce eyes; and, trying to force a laugh, said—

"I did but jest. Stronghand is right. Come, let us taste the sack those fishes have sent up from below."

The soldier's steel cap was the only drinking vessel they had, and from it they all drank. Then Stronghand went to where the beautiful Spaniard cowered, and proffered her a draught.

She smiled her gratitude to her preserver, and, to his surprise, said, in good English—

"The saints be praised for their mercy in sending me so kind a friend. Isand Veletezzy's heart cannot express all she would say."

"There is no need, lady. I will protect you as though you were my sister; so be under no alarm from these men. They shall not harm you."

Isand drank a small quantity of the wine, and Stronghand returned the steel cap to the soldier.

With such pieces of the wreck as were suitable one portion of the men propelled the raft while the others slept.

They relieved each other in turn, and so the night and day passed. Then another night, then a hot scorching day, and the last of the precious wine was consumed.

The consequence of subsisting alone upon the canary was foretold by Stronghand. The want of it made the survivors more ravenous for food and water than if they had been totally without the stimulant.

Days passed, and the crew of the raft began to lose all hope of being picked up by a passing vessel, or reaching the land. Then, as hunger began to gnaw their vitals, and thirst to render them furious, the one idea took possession of their minds—

They must have food or die!

Food! Where was it to be obtained? There was nothing to be seen on the surface of the tranquil sea that could assuage their thirst or moderate their hunger.

Where was it to come from, then?

The question was asked and answered by the groups of wolfish-looking men, who were huddled together on the raft—asked by their husky whispers, and answered by the longing, famished gaze that from time to time turned towards the beautiful girl, who crouched in that part of the raft assigned by the herculean seaman to her use.

Stronghand kept apart from his companions. He lay between them and the shot-box, his long knife hilt brought close to his hand.

He knew what was passing in their minds, and determined the sacrifice should not be while he had strength to prevent it.

"We must eat or die!"

Time after time were these words used by the famished wretches, and their hungry eyes were fixed upon Isand.

Who can tell the horrid thoughts of these men as they looked upon the beautiful girl?

Did they long for the cannibal repast because her flesh was whiter and more delicate than that of their companions, one of whom could have been sacrificed by lot to keep the remainder alive.

Perhaps these were the thoughts that occupied their minds, for no mention was made of drawing lots; but at the word food, every haggard face was turned towards the Spanish girl and her protector.

At last the crisis came. The terrible pangs could no longer be checked, and the famished crew drew close to the shot-box, and one spoke to the gigantic mariner.

"Comrade," he said, "we are dying. Food we must have, and while the captive lives it is not meet that we should draw lots."

Stronghand had expected this, and was prepared. He rose from the recumbent position he had so long assumed, and, facing the speaker, said—

"It must be so. The girl must die, but not now."

"We are famished."

"It is hard; but that which has so long been borne can be borne a few hours longer."

There was a murmur of dissent from the hungry group, and Stronghand, placing his had upon the hilt of his knife, said—

"I repeat it must be borne until sunrise to-morrow; if we do not sight a vessel by that time, or the land is not in sight, this knife shall cut the girl's throat. Such is my determination; and any amongst you who attempts to thwart my will shall die, and become food for us all."

It was not long to wait, for the sun was slowly sinking; and, after all, a vessel would possibly come near the raft.

They had no animosity against the girl, but food was necessary, and this food must be supplied by the captive, or one of their own number.

The latter course was the most natural under the circumstances.

Looking forward with horrible eagerness for the dawn of another day, the cannibal crew huddled together again, and betook themselves to the occupation of chewing buttons or the hilts of their knives, or anything that would promote the flow of saliva to their parched tongues.

The sun set, and night came upon the ocean; and Stronghand drew his knife, and stepping lightly into the shot-box, placed his hand upon the Spanish girl's shoulder.

She shrank from his touch, and tried to move away, for she expected her last hour had come.

"Be not afraid," whispered Stronghand, "in a few minutes we shall be free from the raft, and if fate so wills it you will be preserved from these men."

She took the mariner's rough hand between her wasted palms, and pressed it to her lips. Then Stronghand quickly cut the lashings that held the shot-box to the raft, and using his hands as paddles, noiselessly glided away.

With the first streak of the new day, the hungry wretches looked eagerly around, and a howl of rage came from their parched lips.

The captive had escaped, and their leader had robbed them of the expected banquet, for he had escaped; so had the shot-box and a broken spar that had been lashed across it.

They gnashed their teeth with impotent rage, howled like so many famishing hyenas; then one, with a fearful oath, called upon his companions to use the oars and pursue the traitor and their expected victim.

Despair and anger gave them strength, and they plied the oars until they were exhausted.

A short interval of rest; then the labour was resumed; and until the sun again sank as it were in the depth of the great ocean, they toiled, but still no sign of the runaways.

Then they desisted, and the raft was allowed to drift about at the mercy of the wind; and the pangs of hunger, heightened by the disappointment they had suffered, seemed to increase tenfold.

"Comrades," said the soldier, "we must eat or perish; there is nothing left now but to draw lots."

They looked from one to the other. The fate they had doomed the beautiful girl to was very fearful when it came to the terrible climax, that one of their own number must die.

"It need not be done now," continued the soldier; "the morning must decide whether we all die, or one give up his life that the rest may live."

Little did the famished wretches know that at the very moment the soldier was speaking, his voice was heard by the Spanish girl and her companion.

The light of another day broke upon the ocean, and one of the castaways stood in the centre of the raft, eagerly scanning the surrounding expanse of water.

Suddenly his eyes became fixed upon something; and after a brief gaze, his haggard face flushed with hope.

"The oars, the oars!" he cried, frantically. "The woman is but a short distance from us!"

The castaways sprang from their listless attitude, and not an oar was touched until all had satisfied themselves that the hope was not a false one.

A dark object to windward was the cause

of this commotion; an object not larger than the wing of a bird; but the men who were adrift knew it could be no other than the shot-box, and the smallness of its appearance was caused by the larger raft being so low in the water.

The strength of limb that, under no excitement to call it forth, seemed gone, now returned, and the raft was propelled with tolerable quickness, and one of the castaways stationed in the centre directed the course of the strange craft.

It was not long before their coming was seen by Stronghand; then he used all his power to escape.

The attempt was hopeless. What could he do with only the palms of his hands to impel the shot-box through the water, while his pursuers had several pieces of timber that admirably served for oars?

The hopelessness of the struggle soon became apparent; and Stronghand gave in and prepared to defend his charge.

He knew the battle would be a desperate one; and as he bared his brawny arm and clutched the hilt of his knife, he muttered—

"The fight will be not only for the captive, but against me for aiding her escape. Let it be so. Perhaps one of the pursuers may serve the purpose she is wanted for."

The raft came on with increased velocity; and the shot-box, lying almost in its course, was struck, and immediately capsized, throwing its occupants into the sea.

This was an accident totally unexpected by the herculean seaman, and he went beneath the surface, as one of the men on the raft clutched the beautiful girl by her raven tresses.

Other hands were thrust forth, and Isand was dragged on board the raft, and the soldier, with a billet of wood raised, stood awaiting the appearance of Stronghand's head, to deal a blow that would strike him senseless.

With horrible cries the famished wretches gathered around the girl, all eager to glue their lips upon her white throat, and drink ——

But it is too horrible for description. The girl was senseless, and knew not of the close proximity of the ghoul-like faces—knew not that her head was drawn back by one of the castaways, who made a grasp of her long hair—knew not that her neck was rudely bared, and the knife-edge was being tested to make an incision across her throat.

With a cry like a wounded tiger, Stronghand came to the surface, and placing his knife between his teeth, tried to scramble on board the raft.

One downward stroke from the billet of wood and his grip relaxed, and he disappeared beneath the ocean.

CHAPTER IX.
THE WARSPITE AND THE GALLEON.

THE buccaneers watched the movements of the huge galleon, calculating the time that would elapse before they were alongside and in possession of her deck.

Once there, the prize would be theirs; for, by the buccaneers' law, no man dared retreat from an enemy's ship.

They must conquer or die, and this terrible spirit governing their actions no doubt gave them the victory, in defiance of the general inferiority of their numbers.

There was a strangeness in the movements of the galleon that excited the surpise of the officers of the Warspite.

Judging by the distance that intervened between the vessels, there was every reason to believe the look-out on board the galleon had seen the approach of the Warspite, yet no notice was taken, for the treasure ship kept her bows in a direct line with the hull of the buccaneer.

"The Spaniard is bold," remarked Levausseur, "or she mistakes us for a friend."

"A mistake it will be as well not to rectify," said an officer, "for the Sant Fé has a large force on board, and there will be a saving of life on both sides if we get alongside in peace."

"By the rood!" exclaimed Levausseur," the Spaniard there does not know this vessel has changed master. Is that it, Tallot?"

"I would wager so," answered Tallot. "It is not three months since we took this vessel from the Dons, and the news has not reached the Santa Fé, or her commander would not bear down upon us."

"It must be so," said the leader of the buccaneers, "and we will hoist the yellow flag, until it is time to run up our colours. By the way, which flag do we sail under now?"

"The English."

"Have the silk ready to run up when the Spanish colours are lowered."

The vessels were within half cannon shot of each other, when the yellow banner was hoisted.

All eyes were turned towards the galleon, and the men laughed as they speculated upon the astonishment that would come upon the Spaniards when they knew the trick that was being played upon them

"He does not answer the flag," said Tallot; "what does it mean?"

Captain Levausseur had been narrowly scrutinizing the appearance of the galleon, and when his lieutenant asked this question he turned and answered—

"It means more than I can understand, unless it is the fact of his flag-staff having been shot away that causes"——

A puff of smoke from the galleon's bow, then the boom of a gun was followed by the whistle of a shot amongst the rigging.

There was a confused and angry shout from the buccaneers as the crushing of wood was heard overhead, and the stentorian voice of their leader shouted—

"The spar is crippled; up men and repair the mischief. Cannoneers, do your duty."

The Warspite's foremast was cut in two, and before the men could reach the top the upper portion of the spar toppled over, and its weight snapped the cordage. With this disaster, another shot came from the galleon and smashed in the Warspite's bows.

"Ten thoushand devils!" roared Levausseur; "the Spaniards have been taking lessons in gunnery, and we are their first target, for never before has such practice"——

Another shot, equally as well aimed as its predecessors, crashed through the port bow, and dismounted a gun.

The fire of the buccanneers began to rage furiously, and many of their shots struck the huge hull close to the water-line.

Levausseur and his officers stormed and raved at the cannoneers, but they failed to silence the single gun that played with such murderous effect upon their vessel.

"The wind is in league with the Spaniards," said Levausseur, "for there is scarcely enough to spread the folds of"——

Crash! Another shot tore through the bows and raked the Warspite from stem to stern, knocking over guns and gunners in its passage, and finally tearing its way out through the woodwork over the state-room windows.

"Gentlemen," said Levausseur, "the wind has gone down, and we are becalmed. The saints give the Spaniards courage to use their sweeps and come down upon us."

Both vessels were now lying still upon the ocean, the tropical breeze having died away to a zephyr. So sudden had been the change that Levausseur had failed to bring the Warspite's broadside to bear upon the galleon.

He had but three tiers of artillery that were able to reply to the Santa Fé's terrible single gun, and for some time the contest continued the buccaneers' ship suffering every time the puff of smoke rolled out from the galleon's port.

The brethren of the coast worked their guns in silence, and the officers paced to and fro, eagerly watching for the appearance of the galleon's sweeps.

They waited in vain, for there was no sign of life on or about the large vessel, save the solitary cloud of smoke that came at short intervals from the bows.

"The foul fiend must be in league with yon vessel," said Levausseur, stamping the deck angrily, "for no Spaniard could work such mischief unaided."

"What is to be done?" Tallot asked. "Every time we fire, it is returned by that infernal gun."

"Ah! What is that crash?"

"The whole of the steering gear," answered Tallot; "and until something is rigged to supply its place let us hope the wind will keep down."

The leader of the buccaneers chafed like a caged lion, and turning fiercely to his officers said—

"Stop that useless cannonade, and set every man to work repairing damages."

The order was obeyed, and soon after the Warspite's guns ceased firing the Spaniard was silent; then Levausseur saw the sudden splash of the anchor as it was released.

"Sound the depth of water, Tallot," he said to the lieutenant; "or, by the rood, we shall be overreached by the Don."

The lead was cast, and, to the surprise of the buccaneers, they found there was not more than twenty feet of water beneath their vessel.

"Let go the anchor," said Levausseur, when received Tallot's report, "and place a couple of men with axes ready to cut the cable should it be necessary."

When this command was carried into effect, the buccaneer chief, addressing his companion, said—

"The Don, mayhap, thinks the current, if there is one in these seas, will swing the galleon's broadside towards us; but he has forgotten ours is the smallest vessel, and will yield sooner to the grip of the anchor than the galleon."

"If it does," said Tallot, "we shall have the advantage."

"We shall. Then I will sink the accursed craft, were there ten times the quantity of treasure on board."

"The water not being very deep," said Tallot, "it would be possible to lift the treasure, after the galleon is sunk."

"True, true," said Levausseur. "When the galleon is sent to the bottom, not before."

The buccaneers watched with anxious faces for the vessels to yield to the cables, but the day began to close in, and neither hull had moved.

"The sea is like a mill-pond," said Levausseur; "but, after all, it may be better for us that it is so."

A slight change had taken place in the appearance of the galleon's sails, since the anchor had been dropped, but not a shot had been fired from the gun.

There was no change in the position of the vessels when the sun set, and the tropical twilight soon deepened into darkness.

With the first appearance of the gloom Levausseur's face kindled with joy, and, calling his officers together, he said in a tone far different to that he had used since the galleon's fire had damaged his vessel, and ruffled his temper—

"Gentlemen, the prize is ours, if we can use the hour of darkness that precedes the rising of the moon. The boats, comrades, must do the work; they can creep like silent shadows over the waters, and the Spaniard can be boarded and won. See to it. Let every boat be ready, and every man on board will go with us. The ship will not break from her anchor, even should the wind rise before we return."

This plan, so in accordance with the freebooters' mode of fighting, was hailed with satisfaction, and soon the boats were noiselessly lowered.

There were not sufficient boats to hold the whole of the crew; but there being a number of canoes on board, sufficient of these were added to the flotilla to convey the entire force.

A few words will suffice to describe these canoes, and the uses the buccaneers made of them.

They were nothing more than logs of wood hollowed out, so as to contain from two to twenty men. Their capabilities, of course, the result of the size of the log from which the canoe was fashion d.

The buccaneers, in their plundering excursions upon the Spanish possessions, were able to send spies up the small creeks and shallow rivers in these vessels; and a rower, who was expert with the paddles, could travel quicker and with less fear of discovery than in a ship's boat.

The flotilla moved silently from the ship, and pulled for the galleon.

They did not row direct for the Spanish vessel; but following Levausseur, who was in the largest boat, described a half-circle, and when past the Santa Fê the buccaneers' flotilla approached the stern of the Spanish ship, their boats and canoes forming a crescent.

Like shadows they reached the large vessel; then the leading boats shot past the Santa Fé's sides, and the centre of the crescent crowded under the high stern.

The click of a flint upon the pan of a pistol was the signal to board, and with their bright blades clenched in their teeth the buccaneers swarmed up the galleon's sides and reached the deck.

CHAPTER X.
A SHIP—A SHIP.

THE famished wretches crowded yet closer to the man who held the Spanish girl, and called loudly upon him to draw the knife across her white throat.

"It is a sin, comrades," he said; "but it must be done."

"Stay your hand," shouted the soldier, who had struck Stronghand. "We are saved. Look! A ship—a ship!"

The seaman who held Isand's raven tresses allowed the senseless girl's head to fall, and, starting to his feet, shaded his eyes with his open hand, and cried, joyfully—

"A ship—a ship!"

The remainder of the castaways took up the welcome sound, and while their attention was absorbed by the distant dark spot upon the horizon, Stronghand appeared on the other side of the raft.

He was bleeding from a wound in the forehead, and the man who had given him the blow was the first to go to the herculean mariner's assistance.

"Comrade," said the soldier, as he helped Stronghand on board, "I am sorry for giving you that blow; but you would have done the same had"——

"Say not a word," answered the giant. "I played you false, broke my plighted word by leaving the raft, and deserved ill at the hands of yourself and companions."

"Then you forgive me?"

"Here's my hand on't, and Mark Luton never broke faith when it was pledged by a grip of his hand."

It was a grip, and the soldier's fingers were compressed as though in a vice, and while it lasted he suffered martyrdom.

"I was not a false prophet," remarked Stronghand, "when I said a ship would cross our way. By the rood, I was right, for ever since I came on board the raft her lower yards were visible."

The soldiers gave a joyful assent to Stronghand's words, then went to the group of castaways, whose every faculty was absorbed by the sight of the distant ship.

Stronghand, without one word at the cause of the sudden change that had come over the feelings of the ocean wanderers, knelt beside the senseless Spanish girl.

He raised her head, and gently parting the closed eyelids, watched the edges come together again, and knew by this she yet lived.

"A moment later," thought the giant, "and that knife would have ended the life of as fair a creature as ever breathed the sunny air of Spain."

Supporting her head with such articles as he could find to serve the purpose of a pillow, he threw a piece of sail cloth over the recumbent form.

"Nature will restore her," he muttered, "better than rough usage of mine. Until she recovers, I will watch yon ship."

The whole of the masts and sails were now visible, and a portion of the hull greeted the herculean mariner's eyes as he arose and joined the anxious group of starving men.

"What think you, Stronghand?" the soldier asked. "Will yon vessel come within reach of our voices?"

Stronghand took a long and steady look at the vessel before he answered.

"I would the fellow did not yaw so much, and it were better for our hopes if there were a few men on the yards.'

The castaways listened with breathless interest to the words of a man whose nautical skill was so far above his position.

"You hold out but little hope, comrade."

"I said not so," answered Mark Luton; "but I would we had the means of hoisting a signal, or making ourselves heard."

The hope that had been so feverishly burning in the hearts of the stowaways was a little damped; and with less of joy in their voices the men kept asking Stronghand to describe the position of the vessel.

"She is coming directly upon us," said the mariner; "but whether she will keep her course is more than I can foretell. That, comrades, is in the hands of One who has saved us from a grave in the hold of the Bonaventura; and, methinks, an offering of prayers would perhaps assist in our deliverance."

The rough occupants of the raft were but little accustomed to pray; but when the deep voice of the giant fell upon their ears and the fear of a horrible death strong upon them, they bent their knees by one impulse, and prayed the ship would save them.

It seemed as though the appeal had been heard and answered, for the light breeze freshened a little, and the sunlit canvas filled and impelled the huge vessel faster towards them.

The hope that had begun to leave their breasts now returned with tenfold force, and many war-worn veterans actually shed tears of joy at the prospect of their speedy deliverance from a terrible doom.

The hope seemed well founded, for the vessel did not swerve a point from her course; and when her bows were within half a mile of the raft, Stronghand, in a voice less calm than usual, cried—

"Now, together, let us hail our deliverer from death."

The men did as they were desired, and, weak as they were, the joint cry was raised to a shout, and it seemed impossible to the castaways that it should be unheard on board the vessel.

"The swinging of the tiller," muttered Stronghand, "and the wash of the sea against the ship's sides would prevent a cry like this being heard. But I must keep that to myself; it will be cruel to damp their hope of deliverance."

If they were heard, no notice was taken by those on board the vessel, for not a seaman was visible on the bows or rigging.

"To the oars," said Stronghand. "We must lessen the distance, and run the danger of being struck by yon vessel's bows "——

"Our cry has been heard," came from several throats. "See—see; she ships her yards, and "——

Here followed a scream of anguish from the distracted men, for the dark fabric that had been speeding so swiftly towards them, suddenly fell off before the men, and the breeze catching the canvas caused the huge hull to reel slightly, and the sun flashed upon her broadside as she started in the new direction.

Several of the poor wretches had fallen senseless when this terrible calamity occurred, others stood, with clasped hands and starting eyeballs, watching the rapidly receding vessel.

"Courage, courage," said the giant seaman, "there is yet hope. See, the sails flap against the mast—a sure omen of a coming calm. Ah! said I not so? See, the vessel is motionless; now let all who value life work at the oars."

Stronghand drew the shot-box on board as he spoke, and by a slight effort of his mighty strength, tore the planks into strips, and gave them to the men who were without any means of aiding the progress of the raft towards the becalmed ship.

The men who had swooned were aroused by the indefatigable Stronghand, by a plentiful shower of salt water.

The castaways worked as though such suffering as theirs, entailed by exposure and want of food, had never been known by them, and the Spanish girl, recovering from her stupor, uttered a gladsome cry, for the raft, when her eyes unclosed, was overshadowed by the towering hull of a large ship.

The castaways yelled with delight as they neared the vessel, yet there was no sign of their cries being heard by the mariners who were on the deck.

Stronghand had cast the plank he had been using for an oar into the sea, and rising upon one knee, he gripped the hilt of his long knife, and issued commands to the excited rowers.

"Be prepared," he said, "for a blow. Drive the raft close to the hull, and join her there, and give me time to drive my blade into the timber. Before a man moves, remember the knife will be our only hold."

They did as they were directed, and the knife-blade struck the hull just above the water-line, and but for the giant's grip upon the hilt, the raft would have recoiled from the force of the concussion, and been driven away.

Ten minutes later the raft formed from the property of the engulphed Bonaventura was floating away untenanted.

CHAPTER XI.

RUPERT-THE-READY.

WHEN Rupert recovered from the stupor that fell upon him after he had reached the galleon's deck, the sun was high in the heavens.

The young officer raised himself upon one hand, and placing the other upon his throbbing brow, gazed around.

His breath came short and quick as his eyes took in the ghastly scene, and from between his white and parched lips came the words—

"It is the Santa Fé!"

The first object upon which his eyes fastened told him the name of the vessel—this object was the dead body of the Spanish noble who had commanded the galleon.

He lay near the mainmast, where he fell when Rupert's sword passed through his body.

Near him were several of the crew, and the whole extent of the deck was likewise covered with blood-bedabbled bodies, broken weapons, and dark streams that were penetrating their way into the hitherto spotless planks.

Rupert knew a slow match had been placed near the powder room, and his first thought when the feelings of horror had a little subsided, was about the fuzee.

"It may not have burned to the end," he thought, "and while I lie here, the powder may ignite, and blow the ship into fragments."

The possibility of this doom overtaking him after all the dangers he had passed, gave the young officer sufficient strength to struggle to his feet.

He leant against the mast for a few seconds, and the raging thirst that consumed him caused the recollection of the slow match to pass from his mind.

He looked eagerly, madly around for water, and in response to his frenzied gaze there stood near the foremast a barrel of water.

The vessel was uncovered, and the sun was playing upon the clear liquid, causing it to flash and sparkle with a brilliancy that was more welcome to the sufferer than had the sheen come from the most priceless stones and jewels.

Rupert's brain swam with delirious joy as he reeled towards the barrel, and, when his hands clutched the iron-bound rim, he gave a cry of joy.

Greedily he placed his cracked lips to the water and drank what was to him the most delicious draught that had ever passed his lips.

He laved his face and hands; held the precious fluid in his palms, and suffered it to drop through his fingers; the poor fellow was delirious with joy, and could scarcely realize the actual possession of the cask and its contents.

No elixir concocted by the sages of old to heal wounds, bruises, and all ills that the flesh can suffer, ever worked such a wondrous cure as the draught of water did upon Rupert Felton.

The dizziness left his brain, his limbs became stronger and better able to support his body; and the gloom that had fallen upon his mind was dispelled, and, despite the fact that he was the only living thing upon the large ship, he felt a buoyancy of spirits that seemed impossible under the circumstances.

Suddenly the remembrance of the slow match came to him.

"I had forgotten that," said Rupert, " and in the midst of my rejoicings there has been every possibility of my body taking an upward direction with the timbers of this vessel and the remnants of mortality that lie around."

He went towards the main hatch as he spoke, and, descending to the powder-room, discovered the cause of the slow match not doing its duty.

A Spanish mariner's body lay near the match, and the red stream that had flowed from a sword-thrust in his side had extinguished the smouldering light.

"This knave," thought Rupert, "must have, in a measure, recovered after we left the vessel, and found his way here; and Death, which had but sported with him for a brief space, overtook him when he came near the match. I have cause to be thankful; for this man's death has not only saved my life, but given me a stout vessel, well provisioned, well armed, and strong in artillery and stores."

A sudden light illumined the young officer's eyes as he spoke, and it faded as quickly as it had come.

The cause of this the young officer's muttered words soon explained.

"Foolish thought!" he said. "Yet had I but a few men from my native island I would take the fortune the gods have provided me, and my dream of command and boundless wealth would be realised."

He passed slowly to the state-room, and a pang shot through his heart as he stepped over the stain that marked the spot where he had swept off the head of the man whose mutinous conduct had entailed such a fearful punishment.

"Even with that man," he soliloquised, "whom I sacrificed in my anger, I would attempt the management of this ship, and"——

He gazed at the place where the beautiful Spanish girl had crouched when he entered the state-room, and a sigh came from his lips.

"The monsters of the deep," he muttered, "had no need of so dainty a morsel for their ruthless maws, yet perhaps it is as well as it is so, for, were she alive and left to my company, there is but little to gainsay that the strange feeling at my heart would not have ripened into love, and that would have marred my dream of conquest."

There was abundance of the choicest food in the state-room, so Rupert began to assuage the growing pangs of hunger.

"It is ever thus with me," so ran his thoughts. "Here have I been saved from a terrible doom, yet I am not content. I have water, food, wine, and a mighty vessel, yet I would, if it were possible, conjure up men to serve under me, and in time I would rove the seas, my ship my kingdom, my crew my subjects, and——but the dream is too wild—too wild. I shall have to await the coming of a ship, or a storm may arise, and—and as I cannot work the—the sails, the "——

His head fell forward, and exhausted nature sought relief in a sleep that was as powerful as though the young officer had passed to his last slumber.

The hours passed swiftly, and he showed no signs of awaking, until a noise on the deck above caused him to start.

"A plague upon my dream!" he muttered. "I thought the dead were alive and peopling the deck, and "——

He became as pale as a corpse, and grasped the table, for there was the unmistakeable sound of footsteps on the deck.

"Can the dead return?—no! Yet it cannot be aught else, for there was no ship in sight when I sank into that sleep."

Again the hasty shuffling of feet; and, borne on the wind down to the state-room came a man's voice.

Rupert took off the superstitious dread that came upon him, and snatching a rapier and pistol from the floor, he waited the result of the mysterious sounds.

His heart beat faster than usual when he saw, by the slight movement of the ladder that led to the state-room, some person descending.

The idea of a spirit, or spirits, having possession of the vessel was abandoned when Rupert saw the ladder move.

"Beings of no substance," he thought, "do not tread as heavily as that. My visitor, let him be friend or foe, is not proof against steel or lead."

He raised the pistol, and took a firmer grip of the cross-hilted sword, as the man descended; then both weapons were lowered, and the young officer sprang forward, a glad cry coming from his lips; then the words—

"Mark Luton, of the Bonaventura!"

"Aye, Master Rupert-the-Ready; or is it

your shadow that has come here from the bottom of the sea?"

"Rupert Felton in the flesh, Mark," answered the young officer. "But tell me how camest thou here?"

"Most strangely, Master Rupert; that I will tell you when I have been on deck, and make known to my comrades that there is something on board besides the carcases of the Dons.

"Your comrades, Master Stronghand?"

"Ay, Master Rupert, we count twelve in all, and a Spanish girl, thirteen; an unlucky number, the old wives say, but this time a lucky one."

"A girl—one of the captives?"

"Ay, Master Rupert—the girl the gentlemen shook the dice for. She has come on board with us."

Rupert's eyes sparkled, and his face was radiant with joy, but he controlled his feelings sufficiently to say to the mariner—

"Go on deck, Mark. Go on deck, good Stronghand, and I will provide food for those who have come on board."

Stronghand hastened up the ladder; and his haste was not only to impart the welcome news that food was to be obtained on board the galleon, but to check the famishing men from drinking too much water, for he had left them around the cask, from which Rupert had drunk his delicious draught.

When the mariners had quitted the stateroom, the young officer stood with his head raised, his nostrils dilated, and a flush of pride upon his handsome face.

"By the Gods!" he exclaimed, "this is more than I could have desired, had my power been equal to the necromancer's who could conjure spirits from the ocean depths; for here I have enough men to manage this ship and the beautiful Spaniard for my bride."

His lips trembled with excitement as there arose before his mind visions of conquest and deeds of daring, in which he was the master spirit, and with flushed cheeks and proud mien he went on deck, where a shout greeted him, for he had been loved by the hardy mariners of the Bonaventura.

"Rupert-the-Ready," they cried, "for a leader, and a stout vessel our home is a mercy we little expected when adrift on the Spanish Main."

Rupert heard the words that so well accorded with his own views, and, gracefully saluting the men, he said—

"It shall be so. Men of every clime seek adventure, fame, and profit in these seas. We will but follow their example; and, owing no allegiance but to ourselves, the bond that unites us will be stronger than ever sailed under the silken banner of England's Queen."

A feeble shout greeted these words, and Rupert continued—

"A few words will seal the bargain; then, comrades, food and wine await you below. Here, Mark Luton, you shall be our lieutenant, and you, Firebrand, our master of artillery; that is all we can appoint until our fortune sends us more hands. Away, knaves,

and remember while you eat that long fasting requires but little eating."

There was a rush below by all save Stronghand. He waited to hear how Rupert came on board; and when the young officer told the story, Mark Luton, in as few words as possible, told all that had taken place since the raft had been formed and deserted.

"Firebrand," he said, in conclusion, "is made by you our master of artillery. He is worthy of the service, for a better skilled artilleryman never blew match; but for this, I fear, the blow he struck me would have to be atoned for."

"Forget it, Mark," said Rupert, taking the giant's hand; "and receive my thanks for the service you have rendered the lady. A murrain upon me, there she lies in a stupor for want of food, while our tongues are wagging. Hasten, Mark, and bring such dainties as may suit her palate; and, at the same time, tell the knaves to be quick, for the deck needs clearing of the dead and the sails attending to."

Stronghand went below, and the young officer bathed the beautiful girl's lips and face with cold water, and the grateful look that came from her dark eyes confirmed the passion that he felt.

Like a mother tending a child, the officer fed the young girl, and while thus engaged, he happened to look over the bows of the ship.

Something he saw startled him, for he with a hasty apology, placed Isand's head upon a coil of rope, and starting to his feet, stamped the deck, and called out—

"Mark Luton! Firebrand! Up—up—all of ye! There is a ship bearing down upon us."

He was answered by Stronghand and the soldier; and the former, when he saw the vessel, beheld, with the acuteness of a seaman when upon his watch, the outlines of a Spanish man-of-war."

"This is a bad beginning, Master Rupert," he said. "A ship of war, and the knaves who are below have tasted the wine till their senses have departed."

"Curses upon them!" said Rupert. "Bear the maiden to a place of safety—then we must fight the Don. We are but three in number, but the stake at issue will make us a host."

CHAPTER XII.

BOARDING THE ENEMY.

THE Spanish maiden was taken below by Stronghand, and, when he returned, he lent his powerful aid to cast loose one of the bow guns.

The piece was of the largest make, and the barrel of great length, and Firebrand, after sponging the tube, said—

"The bore is true to a hair's-breadth; and if she carries a ball well, we may yet do the Don some mischief before he can reach us."

"By the rood," said Rupert, "we must spoil his sailing, or our voyage will come to a premature end."

"I would wager," said Stronghand, "a duke's ransom against an old doublet that yon Spaniard has seen the smoke from an English cannon before to-day."

"Know you the vessel, Stronghand?" Rupert asked. "I had fancies her trim was familiar."

"Do you remember the long cruise we had in the Bayaha, Master Rupert?"

"Of a surety I do, Mark; it was a wearisome time, for we were so long becalmed."

"That is the cruise, Master Rupert; and we were waiting for the appearance of the Spanish galleon"——

"Not so; for"——

"I crave your patience; the galleon we were on the look-out for was the Holy Trinity."

"Ah! most true; yes, it was the Holy Trinity."

"She came, Master Rupert, with the land breeze, and you may remember we could not carry her because she sailed in concert with a vessel of war."

"Yes, it was so; and the vessel of war you think is this one?"

"Ay, Master Rupert, it is the same, although there has been some alteration in her spars and rigging. The Dons most likely have done this to make their ship look more like ours, for the set of those sails is after the fashion of our nation."

Rupert's attention was taken from the gun to the spars and canvas of the strange ship, and, after a few moments' survey, he said—

"It is as you say, yet I cannot well understand why the Dons should do this."

"It is easy, Master Rupert,; for with that rig and the English colours, they can creep upon the small vessels of the adventurers who infest these seas in quest of plunder, and carry them by the board."

During the few moments occupied by this conversation, the gun had been loaded, and Firebrand, the artilleryman, was upon one knee taking aim at the strange ship.

The prow of the galleon was much higher than the bows of the enemy's ship, and Firebrand rapped out an oath because he could not depress the muzzle of his piece sufficiently low to bring it to bear upon the foeman's hull.

"There goes the Don's flag," exclaimed Stronghand, as the Spanish colours were displayed over the enemy's stern. "I knew I had not been deceived."

"We have no staff left to display our silk," said Rupert, "thanks to Firebrand, who knocked away the Santa Fé's flagstaff before we closed with her."

"We can fight as well without colours as with them," said the artilleryman. "Now, Master Rupert, the gun is ready, and only waits your orders to fire."

"Fire," said Rupert, "and the saints speed your shot; for with this wind the Don will soon be upon us, and then our"——

Rupert's concluding words were lost in the roar of the piece, and the three simultaneously exclaimed—

"Bravely sped! the Don's rigging has suffered."

Firebrand had aimed at the foremast, and his shot was successful. The gun was quickly reloaded, and Firebrand, before applying the match, said——

"I would we could raise the muzzle a few inches, then I could do some damage to the Spaniard's timbers."

"That is easy," said Stronghand, snatching up a billet of wood. "Now, Master Rupert, and you, Firebrand, put forth your strength, and we will place this beneath the wheels."

Stronghand put his shoulder under the breech of the gun, and, aided by his companions, raised it sufficiently high to admit the thick piece of wood being placed under the carriage.

Firebrand glanced down the piece, and with much satisfaction said—

"The elevation is as perfect as though the master of the Queen's artillery had devised it. "Shall I apply the match, Master Rupert?"

"Aye, there is no time to be lost, and not a shot must be wasted."

"Not one, fair sir."

The artillerist applied the match, and, to the joy of the three adventurers, the ball lodged in the bows of the Spaniard.

"St. George and Old England!" exclaimed Rupert joyfully, "thou art a pearl beyond price, Firebrand; let us try another such shot."

They did so, and the result was more successful, for a gun was overturned.

The enemy, foiled in their attempt to bear down upon the galleon, began a furious fire.

Stripped to the waist, and black with smoke, the three Englishmen worked at their ponderous piece of ordnance, until the wind fell, and a calm reigned above the ocean.

Then they took a few moments' respite, and Stronghand ran below, and brought up a couple of bottles of wine.

"I kicked the brutes," he said, "but beyond a grunt there was but little sign of life. A murrain upon the wine! But for that we should have been able to pound yonder ship into fragments, for these guns —— Ah!"

"What is the matter, Stronghand?"

The gigantic seaman had his eyes fixed upon a dark speck on the distant line of sky, that seemed to touch the water.

"There," he said, "is a sign which never yet spoke falsely. We shall have a storm ere long, Master Rupert."

"Let it come," said the young officer. "But not before we have beaten our foe. To the gun again, comrade!"

The destructive piece was soon blazing away again, every shot taking effect upon the supposed Spanish man-of-war.

"Master Rupert," said Stronghand, "I have an idea by which I think we can compel the banner of Philip of Spain to strike."

"Name it, good Mark."

THE BUCCANEERS' OATH.

"The calm," said Stronghand, "will last for many hours; at the least until the drunkards below have recovered their senses."

"It will do that without doubt."

"Such being the case Master Rupert, it will be easy enough for us to lift the anchor again."

"The anchor! that is safe enough on the"——

"At present it is safe, but I would suggest we let it go, and trust to the chance of a fluke gripping the bottom."

"Even so. What then?"

"The current will swing the galleon broadside to bear upon the Don, then we can work

the guns that are better placed than this one."

"By our Lady, a wondrous thought! It shall be done, Mark; and, if we cannot raise it again, a few blows from a bill will cut the strands of the rope."

"You agree, Master Rupert?"

"I do and gladly."

"The Don," remarked Firebrand, "is of such gentle manner that his guns cease their roar while we drop the anchor.

The guns on the enemy's ship were, as Firebrand said, suddenly silenced; and the next sound that broke the silence was the

3

splash of the galleon's anchor, when the three adventurers released the hawser.

They watched the effect this would have upon the foe, and Stronghand smiled graciously when he saw the movement repeated by the enemy.

"A good example," said Rupert, "is not lost upon our foe."

"No, Master Rupert," answered the giant; "but his politeness in following our way has overcome the more solid virtue, yclept discretion."

"How do you make that apparent, Goliath?"

"Our decks are higher, Master Rupert, and a broadside from the cannon, if those muddle-skulled knaves recover from their stupor in time for us to use a tier, will knock King Philip's spars and sails about the heads of his men."

"A good fall for us," said Rupert, "if yonder sticks were down; for, truth to tell, we should have fared but scurvily had the Don come to close quarters."

"Our throats would have been slit," answered the giant; "for no Spaniard would have kept us for ransom—at least I speak for myself," he added, "for I know not one who would ransom my carcase, except the serving wench at the wine shop near St. Clement Danes, and she would never possess the number of gold pieces."

"Bah!" replied Firebrand, "it were better a man's throat were slit than he should linger out his days in the dungeons of Philip of Spain."

Rupert made no remark, but a shade of sadness passed over his handsome face when he thought that not one of his noble house would ransom him, even to the extent of a single piece of gold.

"They would sooner," was the bitter thought, "I were in the Bonaventura's hold, or my life taken by a Spaniard, than give one groat towards my deliverance."

There was too much truth in this, or Rupert Felton, the presumptive heir to a noble house, would not gladly have seized the opportunity to become an adventurer upon the Spanish main.

However bitter the recollections of his private wrongs were, and the reflections called up by the remarks of his companions, he soon forgot them, for a pleasant smile wreathed his lips as he said—

"Ransom or throat-slitting matters but little to us now; we are safe until the wind rises, for the Spaniard has no sweeps, or he would have used them, instead of letting his anchor fall."

"When the wind rises," said Stronghand, "it will benefit him but little, for there will be enough to do on yonder ship, with her damaged rigging, to keep the hull before the gale."

"Mayhap," said Rupert, "it will be but prudent for us to attend to the sails, for should a strong breeze come we are but ill prepared."

Stronghand growled assent, and set an example to remedy the evil, by bracing the yards, and taking in the lighter canvas.

The three adventurers, finding their antagonist kept his guns silent, were glad enough to follow the same plan, for they had worked very hard, and were glad of a little rest to recruit their strength.

"But for our voyage since the Bonaventura went down," said the giant, as he lay at full length beside a gun, "we could have kept up the fire; but as it is, I am even fain to seek a respite from labour."

"My body," said Rupert, "is as painful as though I had been well cudgelled, and my eyes feel as though a little slumber would be grateful."

"Have it, Master Rupert," said the giant. "I will keep watch."

"No," said the young officer; "the current may swing us round, and I would fain be ready to help in the work we shall have to do."

"It is time," growled Mark, "these knaves were brought to their senses. What say you, Master Rupert, if we go below and rouse them? Firebrand, here, can keep watch."

"It is a good thought. Come."

Stronghand smiled grimly as he filled a couple of vessels with water, and, following his young leader, went below.

The mariners were under the table, not one showing any sign of life; and as the officer and his companion stood for a moment regarding them, the latter said—

"It has always puzzled my brains, Master Rupert, to know why a man, and a Christian, should drink so freely of that which produces such a result as this. By the rood, one would think there must be a joy in this filthy condition."

"There is," said Rupert, "but the pain that follows scarcely repays it."

The herculean mariner and his leader carried the table a short distance from the senseless seamen; then the former raised one of the vessels of water above his head, dryly remarking—

"Some prefer to mix their wine with water before drinking. These knaves prefer it mixed afterwards."

He dashed the cold water over the men, drenching their garments, and producing such a shock, that several sprang to their feet with cries of alarm.

"How, now, you knaves!" said Stronghand; "is it meet we should do battle to save your swilling throats from the Spanish knives? Up with you, quick, or I will dry your damp carcases with this."

He picked up a broken spear shaft, as he spoke, and this, coupled with the cold water, soon restored the seamen to a sense of what had taken place since they succumbed to the Spaniard's wine.

"By the saints," said one, "there must have been poison in the bottles, or"—

"Find your way on deck, and keep your tongue until it is wanted. Away, quick!"

The men sullenly obeyed, and as Rupert and Stronghand followed, the giant said—

"Beshrew me, Master Rupert, but I have a good thought."

"Its import, Mark!"

"To take the Spaniard, Master Rupert—take him while he sleeps; for King Philip's men keep, as you know, but a scurvy watch."

"Your plan?"

"Take the barge boat—it is quite sound—and board the Don as soon as night sets in."

"The project is good, but we have not sufficient men."

"Plenty, Master Rupert; the Spaniards will not see our numbers in the dark; an English shot, a volley from our pistols and arquebusses, and the Don is won."

"But the Santa.Fé? she may drift."

"If we do not return, Master Rupert before the storm rises, we shall not require the Santa Fé, or any fabric that floats upon the ocean."

Two hours later the adventurers stepped into their boat. They were armed to the teeth, and every man carried either pistol or arquebuss to increase the noise when they should board the Spaniard.

Eight men worked the oars, and Firebrand steered the boat; the remainder were in the bows, ready to spring on board the enemy's vessel.

The muffled oars gave no sound, and the Englishmen, unchallenged, reached the Spanish vessel. Then Rupert gave the signal, and ran up the ladder, followed by his companions.

CHAPTER XIII.

A FIGHT IN THE DARK.

WHEN the buccaneers reached the galleon's deck, they gave a shout of triumph, and Levausseur, in a voice of thunder, said—

"Spare none! spare none! Strike home, hearts of oak!"

The clash of swords and the detonation of firearms followed the buccaneer leader's words.

Levausseur and that portion of the men who had landed on the starboard quarter, reached the galleon's mainmast before a foe came near enough to cross blades with them. Here they were assailed by a group of silent determined men, who gave back blow for blow and held the buccaneers at bay.

The night was so dark that the combatants were invisible to each other, save when the flash of a pistol or arquebuss reflected transiently a gleam of polished corselet or helm.

The buccaneers, enraged at the sturdy resistance of their foes, sought by sheer strength to clear a passage to the poop.

But every time they sought by that manner to break through the compact body of men who were drawn across the deck, they were met by pike, bill, and spear, and compelled to fight desperately to keep the slight advantage they had gained by their sudden boarding of the galleon.

When the remainder of the men from the starboard division of boats joined Levausseur he hoped to be able to carry the deck.

He stepped back from the front rank of the combatants, and went to the galleon's bulwark, and there met the last man as he scrambled over the side.

"Return," he said to the buccaneer, "and cut adrift every boat. There must be no means of retreat. We must capture the galleon, or die on her decks."

The buccaneer descended, and Lavausseur waited until he returned, and asked—

"Have you done my bidding?"

"I have, sir. Every boat is cut loose, and will be adrift in a few moments."

"'Tis well."

The buccaneer leader grit his teeth angrily as he spoke; then, springing upon a gun, shouted, in a voice heard high above the rattle of steel blades, as they fell upon helm and corslet.

"The boats are cut loose! The brethren of the coast must either conquer or die!"

This was a usual practice of the desperate men when their foes were more than usually stubborn, and the result was, the buccaneers, incited to frenzy by the knowledge that all means of retreat was cut off, fought like demons, and were victorious against the most fearful odds.

The effect in this instance was as usual; the brethren of the coast fought desperately, but without their usual success.

It seemed as though the Spaniards understood Lavausseur's words, for they emulated the buccaneer's bravery and lusty blows.

Lavausseur alternately prayed and cursed for the light. He knew full well that unless it was possible to bear down a foe by sheer impetuosity, when fighting in the dark, there was nothing to be done save hold the ground he had already gained.

He was also aware that combats of this description were seldom of much importance in their result.

"A malison upon the night!" he muttered; but for this we should be masters of the galleon and her treasures."

The fury of the combat began to subside, as the opposing parties became sensible that there was no advantage to be gained by a continuation of the fight until the moon should shed light sufficient to reveal each other's positions on the deck.

Although the fight had continued for some time, but little mischief had been done, save to the sword blades, many of which were jagged by coming against the edge of an opponent's weapon, or the curved rim of an iron head-piece.

The men's bodies and heads being protected by defensive armour, there was no loss of life, for the light was necessary to aid the sword-point against a vulnerable part.

Several were bleeding from cuts across the face and arms, and a few had been trodden under foot, overthrown by the savage rush that was made from time to time and as savagely repelled.

The occasional clash of a sword against sword; then the sound of strife ended, and the combatants, separated by the mainmast, stood leaning upon their weapons grimly, and silently awaiting the moment to renew the struggle, the end of which would be the possession of the galleon, or an utter extermination of the vanquished.

It wanted a brief time for the moon to rise, for the pale light that precedes the appearance of the glorious disc of silver was slowly being visible in the distant horizon.

The rival mariners' faces were eagerly turned in the direction of the pale gleam, when a bank of heavy clouds swept across the heavens, and all became as dark as ever.

The sudden change in the appearance of the heavens was followed by the whistling of the wind through the rigging; and by the swiftness with which the yards swung round, and the violent manner in which the canvas flapped against the masts, it was evident a gale was fast sweeping across the ocean.

Levausseur's men were in possession of the fore part of the galleon, and the buccaneer chief, knowing the danger of riding upon a single anchor during such weather as was expected, at once sent a man to break the hawser in two.

He determined at the same time to make a desperate effort to obtain possession of the galleon. Thinking his adversaries were not on the alert, he shouted—

"At them, hearts of oak, and the prize is ours!"

The men sprang forward, and were met by their active opponents, and the combat was resumed. The uproar was aided by the moaning of the wind, and the "sough" of the water, as the hitherto quiet surface became disturbed.

Levausseur placed himself in front of his men, and strove to cut a passage through his opponents.

He succeeded in penetrating the first rank when the dark clouds that had obscured the moon were parted, and the light shining upon the deck revealed a sight that caused every weapon to be lowered, and a mingled cry of rage and astonishment to come from the buccaneers and their leader.

CHAPTER XIV.

THE AMBUSCADE.

LIKE the galleon's deck, the Warspite was in total darkness, when the survivors of the Bonaventura scrambled on board.

They were cat-like and cautious in their movements, their object being to surprise and capture the Spaniards, not to fight, and run the risk of defeat.

They stood in a group near the gangway, and Rupert whispered—

"This is but a scurvy way of taking care of a ship, but it is to our advantage. What think you, Stronghand, of our chance of success?"

"It opens fairly enough," answered the giant, in a subdued whisper, "although the absence from deck of the watch is not more than I anticipated."

"How so?"

"I was a prisoner on board once, Master Rupert, and saw how they kept watch and ward. No sooner was the middle-watch set than the officers went below, and soon the men followed, one by one, until the deck was left to take care of itself."

"This was in an open sea, Mark?"

"Not so, Master Rupert; I saw it only when we were at anchor, as in this case."

"The knaves deserve punishment, but we have profited by their idleness. Now, Mark, let us hear what is best to be done to secure the prize."

"The watch will come upon deck, Master Rupert, when it is time. The task will be easy to capture and bind them as they leave the ladder."

"The noise will arouse their followers."

"Not so," said the giant. "Six of our men can lie close to the hatch, and be ready to gag the knaves as they ascend; the remainder can lie under the guns to aid if necessary."

"Then, Mark?"

"Then, Master Rupert, when we have gagged all we can, will be the time for our battle-cry to be raised, and, speeding below, we shall capture the whole of the foemen before they can arm and resist."

"By my ancestors, but the plan is good. Let us adopt it; and, should we succeed, I shall take it as a good omen of our future fortune."

"Success is certain, Master Rupert."

The men were placed as the giant had suggested; and, thanks to the absence of any lighted lanterns on the masts or booms, Rupert and Stronghand sat at the foot of the foremast, listening intently for the least sound; but the time passed, and all remained as silent as the tomb.

"It must be past the middle-watch," said Rupert, who became tired of the silence and the cramped position he had assumed. "Would it not be better we made an attempt to carry the ship without waiting to gag the watch?"

"It would be imprudent, Master Rupert; for the chances are, we should be descending at the very moment the sleepy knaves are coming on deck."

"True, Mark, true; yet——Ah! what is that sound?—it is not unlike the ring of steel, and the voices of men in combat."

Stronghand listened intently for a few moments, then answered—

"We are not far from land, and the air is so still, that the least sound can be heard many miles."

"What think you it is?"

"A wine-shop brawl, perhaps, or a combat between a party of roystering gallants and the watch. It can be nothing else."

"I would not stake my head upon the truth of your surmise, Mark."

"Why, Master Rupert?"

"Because I saw no sign of land when on board the Santa Fé."

"Even so, Master Rupert. I am not mistaken, for the land lies very low; and the quietude that reigns over the water enables us to hear even the peal of a bell though no view of the belfry is to be attained. It is a common occurence in these seas."

"You may be right, Mark; but I repeat, I would not stake my life upon the truth of your words."

"You have staked your life for less, Master Rupert."

"What mean you?"

"The plot concocted by Antony Babington, Master Rupert."

"Speak, Mark, or by the foul fiend "——

"I crave your patience, Master Rupert; I have not yet spoken "——

"In the fiend's name, do so, then."

"I will; the plot of one Antony Babington* to murder his lawful queen, the virgin Elizabeth."

"Well, Mark Luton, of what concern is this to me?"

"None at this time; but it might have gone hard with you, Master Rupert, had it not been for the smith who lamed your horse the day you were on the road to Derbyshire."

"You were the smith, Mark Luton; I thought we had met before the day I went on board the Bonaventura."

"I am that smith, Master Rupert, who had turned mariner, and came to England to become a smith; then, when I knew you were to serve on the Bonaventura I took service again as a mariner."

"Because I —— But what mean you, Mark?"

"I will tell that anon. Now, I will speak of the day I lamed your charger. Do you know why I lamed your beast?"

"I am not a necromancer, Mark."

"Shall I tell you?"

"I listen."

"It was this," said the *ci-devant* smith. "You were on your way to join those mad-brained fools who had a picture drawn of themselves in a group, and a motto painted beneath, stating how they were pledged to take away the life of Queen Bess."

"I do not deny this," gasped Rupert; but why should you take "——

"That will be told anon, Master Rupert. I do but mention it now that you may have confidence in me."

"I have, Mark," said Rupert, grasping the giant's hand; "but a true man's curse upon the plot of which you speak. But for that, Mary of Scotland would not have suffered the block."

"Mary of Scotland," was the stern reply, "should have been more the queen and less a woman, whose vanity was pleased by every handsome face, and "——

"By the great "——

"Hush, Master Rupert, I crave your pardon. She has gone—let her follies and frivolities go with her. And now to cast up our chances of being masters of this vessel."

"It will be a matter of pleasanter gossip," said Rupert; "and as the night wears on

apace, I would advise we make a descent upon those sluggards."

"Such was the thought that came to my mind, Master Rupert. I will go below. Be on the alert, for I may need assistance."

Stronghand glided from his place of concealment and went below; and Rupert, who was eagerly listening for his follower's return, was astonished at the hasty manner in which Stronghand ran up the ladder.

"The ship is deserted, Master Rupert," he said. "I have been below, and the lamps are still burning. There are arms and apparel cast about the cabin as though the wearers had doffed silken doublets and daggers for buff and iron."

"'Tis plain, Mark Luton," exclaimed Rupert, "the Spaniards have passed us in the dark and boarded the Santa Fé."

"I fear so, Master Rupert; but it is not too late to rescue the galleon. To the boat—to the boat!"

"Too late," said Rupert. "Hear you not the storm sweeping across the waters? Cut the cable adrift, and every man stand by the sails."

The order came too late. The crippled vessel, having no steering gear, was unmanageable when the storm arose; for, as soon as the cable was cut, she began to move swiftly through the water, her speed increasing every moment.

"We are lost, Master Rupert," said the giant, moodily. "Our prow is towards the shore, and the waters are leaping after us; and, thanks to the Firebrand's cannon practice, there is neither sail nor wheel. Ah!"

The moon shone out brightly at this moment, and a cry of horror came from the men.

The ship was driving in amongst the line of breakers, that seethed and hissed a few fathoms ahead.

There was no hope now. The vessel, impelled forward, was hurled upon a rock. There was a crash—a mighty wave swept the decks from stem to stern, and the survivors of the Bonaventura were washed into the roaring waters.

One moment they were engulphed, the next they were thrown high and dry upon the rocks; and there, bruised and senseless, they remained until the sun rose the next morning.

Stronghand was the first to explore the coast, and when he returned it was with a joyful heart.

"Master Rupert and comrades," he said, "we have still our swords. Below, in a roadway cut through the heart of the rocks, a procession of Spanish ecclesiastics approaches. Come, let us to an ambuscade, and capture them."

"For what purpose, Mark?"

"For ransom, Master Rupert—for the vessels of silver and gold they carry with them; for money that will purchase a ship that we may cruise in quest of the galleon, and the beautiful maiden left on board."

Rupert needed no further incentive. He called upon the men to follow, and, leaping

---

* Those familar with the history of England will need no explanation of this historical fact.

lightly from rock to rock, reached a hollow that seemed fashioned by nature for the purpose of an ambuscade.

Here the adventurers stood, with drawn blades, ready to sally out upon the procession of Spanish churchmen, whose rich vestments and jewelled ornaments were worth a king's ransom.

CHAPTER XV

THE GALLEON AGROUND.

THERE was ample cause for the anger and astonishment of the buccaneers when the moonlight streamed upon the decks of the Santa Fé.

In the darkness and their eagerness to fall upon the Spaniards, the men led by Levausseur had mistaken their companions, who had ascended the opposite side of the vessel, for the Spanish crew, and the same cause had led the assaulting party to mistake Levausseur's men for the foe.

Hence the stubborn fight that had occurred in the dark; and now there was light sufficient to see the extent of the mischief done, the buccaneers gnashed their teeth with fury at the sight of many a score of their companions lying dead upon the deck.

There were nearly as many dangerously wounded; and Levausseur, in a voice of concentrated bitterness, said—

"We have made a profitable night's work, my masters, and the"—

One of the buccaneers who had gone below rushed on deck at this moment, and going to Levausseur, said—

"There is a Spanish girl in the state-room, sir, but not a mariner or soldier is to be found between decks."

"Bring her here."

The man went upon his errand, and soon returned with the unfortunate girl.

She looked wildly around, and her eyes at last singling out the leader of the fierce band, she dropped upon her knees before him, and, clasping her hands, pleaded—

"Save me, sir! Save me from the brutal men who are searching the decks!"

Levausseur was past the age when female loveliness could soften his heart, or it would have been melted at the sight of so much beauty and distress.

"Rise!" he said, grimly. "I am not a priest or a king that you should kneel to me."

The girl did so, and stood, with her hands meekly crossed, wondering inwardly why fate had selected her to pass through such strange and varied fortune.

"Where is the crew of this vessel?" the buccaneer leader asked. "Quick, girl! I have not time to waste in idleness."

"The crew of the Santa Fé," she answered, "have long since passed away."

"What mean you?"

"The foemen's steel," she said, "has slain the many gallant men who sailed in this vessel."

"Is the girl mad?" The buccaneer stamped the deck impatiently as he spoke. "Speak—and in the way that I can understand you."

"I have but replied to your question," she said. "The men of the Santa Fé were killed by their enemies!"

"By the rood, woman, you speak in parables. Was it the dead who engaged my ship, and battered both masts and hull with their guns?"

"The guns were worked by three men," she answered, "and these men were the enemies of Spain, and masters of this ship."

"Three men to hold their own against my ship and fourscore good mariners?"

"I am speaking the truth."

"An incomprehensible truth to me. Quick, tell me what has become of these men?"

"They left in a boat not long before you came on board."

"Malediction!" exclaimed Levausseur, "the villains have by this time attained possession of the Warspite. What ho, there! to the boats, let us—— But no, I have had every boat cut adrift, and all chance of being revenged upon the knaves who have worked us such evil has passed away."

He paced angrily to and fro the deck for a few moments, then, turning suddenly upon the Spanish maiden, said fiercely—

"This galleon is called the Santa Fé?"

"It is."

"And her freight of gold and silver, where is it, girl?"

"At the bottom of the sea, with the bodies of those who caused the decks of this ship to run with blood."

"Is the girl mad?" Levausseur asked, turning to Tallot, "or but trying to laugh in our faces?"

"Neither," said the second officer. "Since you ask my opinion, I should say she is but answering your questions as you put them, instead of telling the strange story of this night's work, and the stranger tale of the galleon's buried treasure."

"There is much that is true in your words, Tallot. I will question the girl; meanwhile, do you cut the hawser and attend to the sails, for the wind is rising, and upon our quickness alone depend the chances of regaining the Warspite."

The officer went to execute the chief's commands, and the latter, seating himself upon a gun, said to the Spanish girl—

"We are unused to solving riddles, girl; so, as you hope for my protection against my unruly followers, tell me the truthful story of the disappearance of the galleon's crew, and the loss of her treasures."

The Spanish maiden obeyed, by relating all that had occurred since the Bonaventura's men first boarded the galleon—the fight—the shipwreck—her sufferings upon the raft—and the strange escape of Rupert Felton from a watery grave."

Levausseur listened intently, and, when she had concluded, he said—

"A marvellous story, girl, and that portion which relates to the attack upon my vessel not the least marvellous. Are you sure there were but three men giving me battle?"

"I am sure; for the others were overcome by the wine they drank, and were not able to ascend the ladder until a short time before the boat left to surprise the vessel from which you came."

Levausseur's first thought, after he had sent the girl below, and placed a sentry over the cabin, was to bear down upon the War-spite and wrest her from the English mariners.

"I bear Queen Elizabeth's men but little goodwill," thought the buccaneer; "and this night's work does not lessen the feeling, and should I be fortunate enough to have them in my power, they shall have but a short shrift before gracing the yard-arm."

The large sails were spread, and everything seemed likely to favour the execution of his wishes, for the breeze was rapidly rising and the huge vessel, manned by such a strong crew, was easily handled.

Already her prow was turned towards the Warspite, and the mighty fabric began to move through the water; but ere it had gained much way, the breeze fell off, and the sails flapped and fluttered against the masts.

Then, as suddenly as it had fallen, the wind swept across the water, the sails bellied out, and before the yards could be braced, the galleon swung round and tore through the waves as unmanageable as a runaway steed.

"A storm," said the buccaneer, "and one that will test our seamanship to ride through with damaged sails and rigging."

He sprang upon the poop with intention of giving orders to the men who stood by the ropes; but before a command left his lips, the gale burst upon them with terrible fury.

All attempts to arrest the vessel's progress were futile, and when the roar of the sea became mingled with the shriek of the winds, there came a sudden crash, and the galleon shivered from keel to truck. She had struck upon a sunken rock, and the buccaneers gave a cry of horror when the waves began to break over the deck.

CHAPTER XVI.

THE BUCCANEERS' FLEET.

UNTIL the first gleam of the coming day began to appear in the leaden-coloured sky, the galleon swayed to and fro upon the reef, her stout timbers shivering and groaning as the storm shrieked and howled around and above.

The sea ran mountains high, dashing against the vessel's sides, and descending in mighty volumes over the deck, and such of the buccaneers as were incautious enough not to cling to the ropes or ring-bolts, were hurled into the surf, and their bodies beaten into a shapeless mass against the sides of the doomed ship.

The men, rough and brutal as they were, were awed by the terrible conflict of the elements, and giving themselves up for lost, prayed, wept, and cursed in turns at the misfortune that had befallen them.

Many—and these were the most reckless—attempted to quit the deck, and find a momentary respite from the horrible scene by descending to the spirit-room.

They would have succeeded, but for the grim and resolute leader and his lieutenant, who stood at the hatchway, their swords drawn ready to cut down the man who dared attempt to break the orders of the brotherhood.

"Back, my masters!" said Levausseur, sternly. "There is no way down here, except over our bodies. Remember your oath, "No man to quit the deck of his vessel either in storm or battle under the penalty of death.'"

The men paused—not irresolute. They looked at each other, and as plainly as words could speak, asked—

"What are these men to us now? We must die! Let us overpower them and obtain our wishes."

It was an apt illustration of "belling the cat." None liked to be first to encounter their ready weapons, and the scene around was too appalling for any concerted measures to be adopted.

"Harkee, my men," said the grim leader, when the storm lulled sufficiently for his voice to be heard, "there is yet a chance for our lives. Wait until the day dawns, that we may see the coast—it will be better than attempting to pass here, for he who does so will as surely die as those who remain faithful to their oaths will live, should the galleon hold together until the light dispels the darkness."

The men sullenly retired until the morning came. The two resolute officers, whose courage had not for one moment failed them during the long and terrible night, saw there was but little hope, for the sea, for several fathoms around the vessel, was covered with a white foam—a sure sign that all who attempted to go towards the land would be buffeted to death by the breakers that hissed and seethed above the hidden rocks.

"There is no hope for us, Tallot," said Levausseur, "we have kept a dangerous vigil for no good purpose."

"No hope!" said the lieutenant, "for the timbers are beginning to part, and through every crevice the angry water finds its way into the hold."

"The hull rides easier now," responded Levausseur, "than it has done since we struck—the cause may be the weight of water in the hold."

"Without a doubt, that is the cause."

"By my manhood, Tallot," exclaimed Levausseur, changing the subject, "the events of this fearful night have driven the memory of that dark-eyed girl from my mind. Go below, and see what has become of her, for in her terror she may fall into the flood I now hear surging in the hold beneath us."

Tallot sheathed his sword; and when he had descended half-way down the ladder, he paused and said—

"There will be prudence in not telling the knaves the vessel is filling. They are already difficult to "—

"Away! There is no need for this advice, for while there is a hope of life, I will not do anything to lessen it; and telling the men of this new danger will have but one result—that, the loss of all power over them."

Tallot went below, and Levausseur eagerly watched the slowly rising light, and as the inky darkness began to roll away, the hope of life became stronger in his breast.

The lieutenant returned after a few minutes' absence, and taking up his former position as sentry, said—

"The water has risen beyond the lower deck, and the Spanish girl is in the state-room beneath us, clinging to a crucifix. I spoke to her, but her senses are too much occupied in prayer to note my words."

"Let her remain where she is. How long, think you, will it be before the sea reaches the state-room?"

"Not while the hull remains on the reef, for the water will not rise above the level of the sea; and if I mistake not, the surf beats less roughly, and the wind howls less fiercely than before the dawn."

"I am of a like opinion. Its truth we shall soon ascertain, for see, there is the first glow of the sun."

Slowly, and it seemed to the anxious watchers an age, the sun rose, and as the rosy beams spread, getting brighter every moment, the wind went down, and the white-topped waves reared their crests less high.

Soon came the full blaze of the glorious orb of day upon the troubled waters, and before the golden light had driven the last lowering clouds from the sky, the sea became as calm as a mill-pond, and the wind died away to a gentle murmur.

"Our great danger is past," said the buccaneer leader. "We are safe from the elements, and but for the loss of our boats could reach the land."

"But a sorry change," said Tallot, "to leave this vessel, disabled as she is, to seek a shore where captivity is certain, to be followed by a speedy death."

"Bah!" said Levausseur. "We are strong enough to capture a Spanish town and make conditions with the inhabitants."

"Not on this coast," said Tallot, "for there are numerous companies of soldiers scattered along the seaboard, and the governor of New Spain has his camp not many miles inland."

"Are we to remain here like caged rats?" Levausseur asked, "and when we have eaten all the provisions that are not yet spoilt by the water, to make a raft of the spars and endeavour to reach our isle? Is this your plan, because a few hundred Spanish soldiers are near?"

"No," said Tallot. "I would advise, if my advice is worth following, that we endeavour to bring the first vessel that passes to our side, and if it is a Spaniard, the sight of this galleon will deceive him, and"—

"Once on board, the ship is ours, a goodly plan and one worth following; but should a vessel not pass until we have consumed all that is eatable?"

"We must form a large raft and take the first vessel we sight. Should we not meet one—By heaven! fortune is good to us.'

Tallot pointed to a distant speck, and a joyful shout came from the buccaneers, for the news spread like wildfire that a vessel was in sight.

Soon all was bustle and anxiety on board the water-logged galleon, and the sunlight flashed upon sword blade, helm, and corselet as the buccaneers set about cleaning their arms, ready to do battle with the very men whom they expected to save them.

The distant outlines of a vessel was followed by another; and, finally, four vessels, with their sails all spread, to catch the slight breeze, stood in towards the reefs.

"A fleet of Spanish merchants," said Levausseur. "See, the leading ship keeps off. The others have rounded to, and are taking in their sails."

The vessel designated by the buccaneer leader as the leading ship stood steadily in towards the galleon, until within half a mile; then, as though aware of the reefs, she likewise hove to, and the sails were taken in as a boat left the side.

"Ready, men. Keep your arms out of sight," said Levausseur. "Do not move until you have my command."

The buccaneers crouched like tigers at the spring, and the boat shot forward, and was soon within hail of the galleon; and when Levausseur saw the rowers, he said, half angrily—

"There is no need of further combat. It is a boat well known to us, and yonder is our fleet."

He spoke truly, for when the officer in charge of the boat reached the deck, he, much to the mortification of Levausseur and the unlucky crew, related, in a joyful voice, the capture of Vera Cruz, and the immense amount of treasure on board the fleet; and, in conclusion, said—

"I am now going to meet the bishop and his brother preachers, to extract from them a million of piastres in money and vessels of gold and silver."

He descended the galleon's side, and entered the boat, bidding Levausseur fire a signal for assistance from the fleet.

CHAPTER XVII.
A DESPERATE FEAT OF THE OLD BUCCANEERS.

THE officer had spoken the truth when he told Levausseur that Vera Cruz had been taken by the small force that lay off the sunken reefs.

The desperate courage that could execute such an undertaking proves the stuff of which the "Brotherhood" were composed; for neither the history of ancient nor modern times can show such a feat of arms as this.

It is no idle fiction, for the account is yet extant in the annals of the New World and general history, and, although it terms the hardy buccanners a horde of pirates, does not deny their brilliant courage, dogged resolution, and quickness of stratagem in effecting their object.

Some idea may be formed of the temerity of such an enterprise when it is considered that Vera Cruz was garrisoned by three thousand men of that very nation which was held in high repute for its military character.

Besides these there were eight hundred men and sixty cannons in a neighbouring fort called St. Jean-de-Luz, which was covered on one side by the sea, and on the other by the city; and in twenty-four hours six thousand armed men could be assembled in the environs for the defence of Vera Cruz.

The leader of the buccanners, who was intimately acquainted with the spot, as well as with the surrounding country, informed his companions in arms that the Spaniards in this district had been accustomed to stand a first attack very well, but that, as soon as success appeared doubtful, they never failed to carry away or to deposit their riches in the ground, and to save themselves in the woods; and, consequently, that they must act with prudence, and endeavour at once to astonish the enemy by an irresistible onslaught.

To the assailants this was a secret highly valuable to be known, and equally important to be kept.

There was, indeed, no fear that the freebooters would themselves disclose it; their own interests recommended to them the most rigid discretion on this occasion.

And they knew, as experience had taught them, the lesson that wherever they appeared the Spaniards and their partisans would employ every possible manœuvre against them, and that the plan of their enterprise would be frustrated the moment it should become known.

Notice of the intended attack was communicated to the buccaneers, though only in a general manner, and notwithstanding the majority of the freebooters opposed a plan the execution of which was apparently beset with insurmountable difficulties.

Their commander, who knew that the bright prospect of a rich booty would triumph over their repugnance, ordered some Spanish prisoners to be brought before the assembly, who informed them that in a few days two ships laden with treasures would arrive at Vera Cruz from Goado.

This news made them decisive, and it was determined to set sail without delay. The freebooters who were about to embark in the expedition were reviewed, their number amounting to twelve hundred.

It was agreed that as soon as they should approach Vera Cruz all the buccaneers should go on board two ships with the exception of some seamen, who were to continue at sea, in order to manage and guard the rest of the fleet, and who were not to appear until after the complete success of the enterprise.

The design of this manœuvre was to conceal the real strength of the freebooters, and to induce the enemy to think that the two ships they had seen arrive were those expected from Goado.

In fact, on the appearance of the two ships, the Spaniards flocked down to the shore impatient to receive the cargo with which they supposed these vessels were laden, and of which they stood greatly in need.

The sight of the Spanish flag, which the buccaneers hoisted, occasioned universal joy. As the ships continued at some distance, and seemed rather to stand out than to avail themselves of the wind that favoured them, the Spaniards began to entertain some doubts.

These were communicated to the governor, Don Louis de Cordova, who, giving no credit to them, maintained that the two ships in question were really those which had been expected, and that he recognised them by their signals.

He returned a similar answer to the commander of Fort St. John, who warned him to be on his guard. The night at length came on, and every one retired quietly to rest, on the assurance of a man who had so much interest in being well informed.

The freebooters availed themselves fully of these circumstances. The two ships in the rear, which had not been discovered, advanced under protection of the darkness and of the serenity that universally prevailed.

The disembarking was effected at midnight, near old Vera Cruz, which was deserted, and was situated at the distance of five miles from the new town of that name.

The guards, who were stationed on the shore, were surprised and killed. They next met with some slaves, whom they engaged to serve them as guides by promising to give them liberty.

Before day they were at the gates of Vera Cruz; and as soon as they were opened the freebooters suddenly rushed in and put to death every one that opposed their passage.

A select body marched to the fort, which served, on the land side, to defend the city, and carried it by assault. They found twelve pieces of cannon of a large bore, and commenced their first sweep by firing several shots against the place.

The soldiers awoke in amazement, and for some time continued motionless, as the very day on which this success was gained was the anniversary of some great festival. They thought some of the principal inhabitants had commenced its solemnities at an earlier hour than usual. They mistook for cries of joy the shouts of the assailants with which the streets re-echoed, and by a chance of which, perhaps, a second instance does not occur in military annals, they were the last to learn that the enemy was the master of the place whose defence had been committed to them.

It was not till that moment that they ran to arms, vociferating what everyone already knew, that the robbers were in the city.

Hitherto the freebooters had used their easy victory with some degree of moderation, but they became furious so soon as they experienced any opposition, and they cut to pieces everyone they met.

In a very little time all the soldiers were either killed, wounded, disarmed, or put to flight, and the principal inhabitants were made prisoners without having had leisure to place themselves and their wealth in safety, as was always their practice on similar occasions.

At length the massacre terminated, and the tumult was appeased.

All the prisoners, whose numbers greatly exceeded that of the victors, were shut up in the principal church, at the gates of which were placed heaps of gunpowder, and sentinels were stationed with matches in their hands in order to set them on fire and blow up the building on the first mutinous cry that should be heard.

Thus, in the compass of a very few hours, and with the loss of only a few of their comrades, the buccaneers were masters of one of the richest and most beautiful cities in America.

Pillaging was their next consideration, and they spent twenty-four hours in embarking on board their ships whatever was valuable or convenient for their use.

Their plunder, which consisted of gold and silver, in cash, jewels, cochineal, and other costly commodities, amounted in value to upwards of one million sterling.

These treasures, however, were nothing in comparison to what they might have been able to carry away from so wealthy a city if they had not been pressed for time, for they were apprehensive lest the very numerous soldiery, who were dispersed among the surrounding districts should assemble together and march against Vera Cruz.

They were, therefore, obliged to shorten their harvest for the present, with the intention, however, of speedily returning to reap more abundantly—an expectation which certainly could not appear illusory.

The freebooters were accustomed to consider everything belonging to the Spaniards as their own property, and when they reappeared in any places which they had only half pillaged, they never failed to obtain ample interest for the capitals which they had, as it were, lent them only for a limited time.

At Vera Cruz they did not neglect the subsidiary and rapid means of increasing their plunder, by exacting a ransom for the confined prisoners.

For this purpose they sent into the church a Spanish priest, who from the pulpit announced, in a few words, the imperious will of the conquerors to his affrighted audience, and conjured them instantly to comply, if they wished to purchase their lives and their liberty.

This forcible address produced the desired effect. As most of the prisoners in their flight from their houses had carried with them their money and jewels, a collection was made immediately, and the amount of nearly forty thousand pounds obtained.

This sum the freebooters thought too moderate, but it was necessary to reconcile their safety with their cupidity.

Already it was rumoured that the Viceroy of New Spain was marching against them with considerable forces, when a fortunate and unsuspected circumstance occurred to favour them.

The Bishop of Vera Cruz was actually visiting his diocese at the time he heard of the fatal event which had just taken place in his see.

Apprehensive that still greater misfortunes would be inflicted on his flock if they did not speedily appease the freebooters, he exerted all his zeal to collect above a hundred and fifty thousand pounds (English money).

CHAPTER XVIII.

RUPERT OBTAINS THE FREEBOOTERS' BOOTY.

THE churchman, headed by an important personage, whose vestments proclaimed him a bishop, came slowly past the place where Rupert and his followers lurked.

Bringing up the rear of the procession was a roughly-fashioned cart, drawn by a mule, and as it jolted over the uneven ground, there came upon the mariners' ears the pleasant jingle of money, and the clatter of silver plate.

"What think you of that, Master Rupert?" said Stronghand. "It is a pleasant sound."

"To men who have not a coin in their possession, it is; but, truth to tell, Mark, I like not this robbing like a cut-purse, or highway thief."

"Qualms, Master Rupert, befitting men who have the wherewithal to purchase a vessel, arms, and stores, but not for us who need the necessary sum."

"But the Church, Mark—is it not sacrilege think you?"

"Sacrilege!" laughed the giant. "I'll warrant me these same sleek priests have but lately pillaged the pious of these goodly vessels and moneys, by the threat of excommunication of —— But, hist, now is our opportunity."

Stronghand did not give Rupert time to take the lead, but calling upon his men to follow, he rapidly descended the rocks, and came face to face with the mitred bishop.

Great was the giant's surprise when the prelate and his companions, instead of showing any symptoms of fear or surprise, gravely drew up their mules, and beckoned to the driver to bring the cart to the front.

"Here is the ransom," said the bishop, addressing Rupert. "It is of the full value of a million of piastres, though not all in coin. The vessels of silver and gold are of the weight that make up the sum."

Rupert was staggered by this address, but Stronghand prevented him from replying, by coming forward and saying—

"Right reverend father, we doubt not your word, and your punctuality in bringing the ransom is a proof of your honesty of purpose."

"Reward the poor priest," said the bishop. "He has brought the ransom many miles, and will take it to the boat if you will but deal justly with him."

"Reward, sir," said Stronghand. "We will gladly purchase his mule and cart if he will sell it for a fair price. Come, priest, what sum do you fix?"

The man, who had evidently expected his throat to be cut rather than to meet with this civility from the fierce buccaneers, bowed with great humility, as he said, in Spanish—

"To you, fair sir, I leave the price of my mule and the belongings."

"Be it so," said Stronghand. "Go to the cart and fill that pouch which hangs at your girdle with piastres."

"I pray you, sir, do not make sport of a——"

Stronghand, who had a tolerably good idea for whom the ransom was intended, knew there was no time to be lost; so he snatched the pouch from the priest's side, and striding to the cart, crammed it to the mouth with piastres.

"See the priests do not rob you," he whispered, as he thrust the bag into the extended mule-driver's hands. "Now, away, before they get sight of the money."

The man needed no second bidding. He stayed only to kiss the large brown hand of his benefactor, and sped rapidly out of sight, hugging to his breast sufficient money to make him wealthy for life.

"Now, reverend sir," said Stronghand, "we will wish you, one and all, a prosperous journey and hearty welcome from your flock."

"The hostages for whom this ransom is intended," said the bishop, "I do not see them in your company."

"They will be at the city before your mules can amble the distance," said Stronghand. "Do you doubt me, holy sir?"

"Alas!" replied the bishop, "I have no choice but to believe you. So farewell, and may the Allwise Ruler soften your hearts, and turn you from the path you have so long followed to the disturbance of our coasts. Farewell."

The clerical procession rode away, and Stronghand, taking the mule by the bridle, laughed outright, and said—

"By the rood, Master Rupert, fortune has played into our hands; but now our riches are likely to be burdensome, for I know not what to do with them."

"Next to your boldness," said Rupert, "the amount of wealth so easily surrendered to your keeping by those wretches astonishes me."

"There is no need, Master Rupert, for astonishment. A few words will explain the matter. This goodly store of wealth is a ransom for prisoners held by one of the buccaneer bands, and this is the place where it was to be paid over. Our arrival was fortunate, for we have been mistaken for the freebooters, and the ransom was readily handed over to our keeping."

"But the prisoners, Mark, for whom this was intended? Will it be just to deprive them of their liberty, and perhaps draw down upon them the wrath of their captors."

"I am afraid, Master Rupert, we shall have——Surround the cart, comrades; hither come the rightful receivers of the ransom."

The men drew their swords, and drew up before the cart, and Rupert stepped to the front of his companions, ready to parley with the leader of a dozen brawny buccaneers, who came from the direction of the sea.

"There will be some hot work soon," muttered Stronghand; "for Master Rupert's temper will not brook the insolence he is sure to receive from yon barn-door cock in eagle's plumes."

Stronghand was right; there was hot work soon, and the result was unlooked for by either party.

CHAPTER XIX.

AN UNEXPECTED INTERRUPTION TO THE COMBAT.

THE buccaneers halted when they came within a dozen yards of Rupert's men, and looked inquiringly into each other's faces.

"By the God of war!" exclaimed the buccaneer leader, "these knaves are as much unlike the shaven crowns we expected to meet as we are unlike veiled nuns."

He came forward as he said these words, and Rupert, without moving from the position he had taken when the freebooters first appeared, said—

"What ho, my masters! a fair day to you all."

"An English tongue!" muttered the buccaneer. Then aloud—"A fair day to ye all, and a safe journey from hence."

"The wish is mutual," said Rupert, "for we would that you were safely hence."

"If a stout ship," said the buccaneer, "can take us, we shall have a safe journey. But tell me, young sir, does that cart contain the equipage of your party?"

"It contains our property, sir."

"Possession gives you the claim to its ownership," said the buccaneer; "but if every man had his own, I would say yon cart holds that for which I came ashore."

"Possibly," said Rupert; "and as it has fallen into the hands of men who are well able to hold their own, you can return to your boat I see yonder"——

"Ho! ho! young Springhold, know you to whom you speak?"

"Sufficient to repeat my words if necessary."

"The fire is rising," muttered Stronghand, "and their blades will cross ere yonder gull's white wings reach seaward."

"Bah! you are short of your reason, boy. Know you that I am third in command of the buccaneers of the coast, and these men I have with me are capable of carrying a town without any help from their trusty leaders. Think of all this before you cause the steel to be drawn."

Rupert's eyes glittered, and his breast rose and fell under the steel corselet that covered his body; his fiery nature could ill brook the freebooter's boastful words.

"Harkee," he exclaimed, fiercely; "I care not if you are chief of the lower regions, and your men devils in men's shape—you shall not touch a piastre of this ransom while my arm can wield a sword."

"Well done, bully boy," grinned Stronghand. "Bring on the fight, lad, and the prize will the sooner be ours."

"Is this your final answer?" the buccaneer asked, tightening his buff sword-belt. "I give you time to answer."

"You have had my answer."

"So be it. Have at you, then!"

"A Rupert! a Rupert!" shouted the remnant of the Bonaventura's crew. "Down with the pirates!"

The buccaneer officer's and Rupert's blades crossed, and the followers of each rushed to the fight.

Stronghand alone stood quietly, leaning on a heavy battle-axe. The giant knew there would be plenty of time for him to begin when his companions needed assistance.

Rupert's opponent was a dexterous swordsman, but he lacked the suppleness of wrist and the quick eye of his young antagonist.

They had not exchanged a dozen passes before the freebooter found it would require all his skill to keep Rupert's sword-point from finding its way between his chin and the top of his steel collar.

"The boy," he thought, "has some knowledge of fence; and if I value my life, it will be better if I stand on the defensive alone."

The combat between Rupert's followers and the buccaneers raged furiously, and with little advantage on either side, until the latter, closing shoulder to shoulder, forced the Bonaventuras backwards, and for a moment the treasure-cart was in the buccaneers' possession.

One of the latter had the mule by the bridle, and was in the act of leading him away, when Stronghand strode forward, and, seizing the buccaneer by the throat and waist, lifted him from the ground.

For a few seconds the grim giant held the man above his head, then, as though he had been but a feather's weight, hurled him against the rocks.

The hapless wretch gave a wild shriek, then fell to the ground dead, his back being broken by the force with which he came upon the stones.

Stronghand backed the mule and the treasure-cart to a cleft by the roadside; then, seizing his heavy axe, ran to the aid of his companions, who were falling back before the hardy freebooters.

His presence was a host.

"What ho, my masters!" he roared, sweeping the first line of buccaneers back with his battle-axe, "are ye so tired of life that ye care not for my arm?"

The buccaneers hesitated a moment before again advancing, and Stronghand, whose quick eyes noticed every movement, called out to his companions—

"St. George and merry England! Strike home!"

He led the way, and the freebooters were scattered like autumn leaves before the gale. Their leader had been beaten on one knee

by Rupert, and the young officer, with his sword-point at his opponent's throat, said—

"Yield, or die!"

"I yield," said the buccaneer, lowering his sword, "ransom or no ransom."

"It is well. Now call upon your fellows to do the same, or "——

There came the clatter of horses' hoofs upon the rocky road, and a body of Spanish cavalry swept down, and cut off the retreat of the buccaneers, who were flying towards their tent.

At the same moment the rocks were lined with King Philip's arquebusiers. Both buccaneers and Rupert's men were surrounded by a foe who hated the English seamen as much as they hated the freebooters.

"Trapped!" exclaimed Rupert. "Draw together, my men."

"We must surrender," said Stronghand; "there is not the slightest chance to escape these men."

The leader of the soldiery was the Viceroy of New Spain—a man famed at the time for his military prowess.

He had marched upon Vera Cruz, but too late to save the town from the freebooters; and while chafing at the disappoinment, the churchmen returned to the city, and related to the governor the giving up of the ransom.

The Spaniard saw there was yet a chance for a blow to be struck against the foe; also time to recover the treasure, should the buccaneers not have reached their boats and carried it off.

Hastily ordering a regiment of cavalry to be mustered, he sent them on in advance, to cut off the freebooters' retreat by the sea.

The road to the beach was a long way farther than that taken by the infantry, and thus it was both parties arrived together, and at the very moment when victory had fallen to the men led by Rupert and his herculean lieutenant, Stronghand.

Don Juan Alvarez rode in front of the troopers, and waving his sword, exclaimed—

"Caught at last, miscreants! Surrender, or you will be shot down where you stand!"

"Try and gain time, Master Rupert," whispered the giant; "the buccaneers may have aid from their vessel—if so, we can hold our ground against a legion of the Spaniards."

Rupert acted up to this suggestion, and approaching the governor, lowered his sword as a token of parley, and said—

"Circumstanced as we are, there seems no other course than to surrender; yet I would fain make honourable conditions "——

"Conditions, pirate! A short shrift and a shorter rope, is the only condition I can offer."

Rupert's face flushed with indignation as he answered—

"I am no pirate, although an enemy of Spain. I have fought honourably under the banner of my country, and claim the conditions of a soldier taken in fair combat."

The Spaniard was about to speak, when the leader of the buccaneers came forward and said—

A GHASTLY VISION MET HIS VIEW.

"The officer speaks truly. He belongs not to the brethren of the coast, and by mistake the ransom was paid over to him by the churchman, and it was for its possession we were contending when your men came up."

"So—so! You are a pirate?"

"I am a freebooter," the officer proudly answered, "and an enemy to Spain!"

"Yet beard me to my teeth."

The buccaneer motioned for his men to collect in a body, and answered—

"I do. Look yonder—see you the masts of those ships? These are the men who stormed Panama, captured Rancherio, won Vera Cruz, and upon more than one occasion the vessels singly have fought and captured sixty-gun ships, bearing your country's flag."

The Spaniard bit his lips with anger. He knew the truth of the buccaneer's words.

"Of what avail," he asked, "is this to our parley?"

"Nothing, only to tell you if we surrender honourably, and you dare to break your word, the men who have done the deeds I have brought to your mind, will take such a vengeance upon you that you had better never been born."

4

The Spaniard, although enraged at the buccaneer's words, was perfectly well aware that the brethren of the coast were capable of any atrocity to avenge their comrades.

But for this, and the knowledge that he would fall by the assassin's knife, or any foul turn would be revenged with fire and sword, Don Juan Alvarez would have had the daring speaker slain where he stood.

"You have a glib tongue," he said, "one that wags well, even when the raising of my hand would be followed by a dozen balls in your body."

"That hand," was the reply, "had better be chopped off than be raised for such a purpose."

"A bold assertion of yours," said the Don, "and I would falsify it, but for the lives of my countrymen who are on board your ship."

"Come," said the buccaneer, "we but lose time. Name your conditions of surrender."

"They are soon made," said Don Alvarez. "You and your men are prisoners until the hostages you have on board ship are given up."

"And the treasure," said the buccaneer, "what of that?"

The Spaniard reflected for a moment; then a smile played over his lips, as he pointed to Rupert, and said—

"This officer and his men, you say, are not of your band?"

"They are not."

"How came they here?"

"That," said Rupert, "I will answer. We were shipwrecked and cast ashore near this place."

"The storm of last night wrecked your vessel?"

"Yes."

"I understand now how you became possessed of the ransom—the holy fathers mistook you for the freebooters?"

"Yes," said Rupert. "They surrendered it to our keeping without asking a question."

"And when the pirates came, you fought to retain it?"

"We did."

"The result was, you were the conquerors?"

"We were."

"Under these circumstances," said the Spaniard, addressing the buccaneer, "the treasure cannot affect you; so that part of the conditions of surrender can be set aside."

The buccaneer looked savagely at Rupert as he muttered—

"The fool had better have kept his counsel."

Then aloud to the governor—

"Be it so. We surrender as prisoners of war—the officers to wear their swords."

"That condition," said the Spaniard, "can only extend to the shipwrecked mariners. You will have to deliver your arms to my keeping until the exchange of prisoners takes place."

"Be it so," said the buccaneer, reluctantly giving up his sword. "Now, Sir Spaniard, as the wind is fair, and my companions in arms do not wish to be delayed, it will be as well that you, send a message to them at once."

"I will do so, when I have arranged with these men;" he referred to Rupert and his followers. "You will surrender as prisoners taken in fair combat, and await your exchange as prisoners of war."

Rupert bowed and sheathed his sword; then the Spanish soldiers, at a signal from their leader, closed around their captives, and the Don said—

"Handle arms, and shoot down the first man who attempts to escape."

The whole of the prisoners, except Rupert, Stronghand, and Firebrand, were deprived of their arms; then the trumpets blew a march, and the party began their march to Vera Cruz.

CHAPTER XX.

RUPERT'S STRATAGEM.

THE signal from the water-logged galleon was answered by the buccaneers sending a boat from the nearest ship; and when the officers in charge discovered the occupants of the Santa Fé were a portion of the brotherhood, another signal was made for more boats to be sent to convey the men to the fleet.

Tallot took charge of the beautiful Spanish girl, and when they went on board the buccaneer ship, the grim leader said to Lavausseur—

"Is that all the booty in exchange for your vessel?"

"That is all," said Levausseur, "and had the storm not abated, we should have gone to the bottom of the sea."

"Better to have escaped that fate," said the freebooter, "than to have died in possession of a shipload of treasure."

"Far better," said Levausseur; "but I regret the loss of my vessel, for never a better bark rode the billows."

"She went down, then, after you had rescued the treasure from the galleon?"

"No," said Levausseur; it is a strange story, and the telling will be better over a bottle of Canary."

"Come below, then," said the leader, "and we shall be able to talk in peace."

The officers went below, and Levausseur told the other the strange manner in which he had lost his vessel.

"So," said the buccaneer, "it was the Bonaventura's men who fought your vessel, and afterwards carried her off. This is strange! For the English ships have no orders to act in a hostile manner towards us."

"That is true."

"Therefore," continued the buccaneer, "unless the fellows bear any animosity towards you, there must have been a mistake."

"Now I remember," said Levausseur, "I hoisted the Spanish flag, and kept it flying during the fight."

"That explains matters, Levausseur. The

Englishmen took you for a Spaniard, and you made a similar mistake. Did I understand these men fought your vessel, and with a single gun?"

"So the Spanish girl states, and there is no reason for me to think she has lied."

"What think you they have done with the Warspite?"

"Either run out to sea, or the ship has gone to pieces on the reefs."

"The latter, I think; for when we rounded the point this morning, the water was strewed with fragments of a wreck."

"It must have been the Warspite," said Levausseur, sadly. "She has gone, and her captors with her."

"I am sorry for that," said the buccaneer, "for the men would have been welcome additions to our band."

An attendant came to the cabin door, and receiving permission to enter, said—

"There is a boat coming from the shore, sir."

"Well, it is our men returning with the ransom, is it not?"

"No, sir; there is only one man in the boat."

"Surely," said the buccaneer, rising, "the Spaniards have not fallen upon our men instead of delivering the ransom?"

He went on deck, followed by Levausseur, and the boat soon came close enough for them to distinguish the solitary rower.

"It is not one of our men," said the buccaneer, "and not a Spaniard, by the fashion of his steel cap and white plume."

"The cap is of English make," said Levausseur, "so is the corselet."

The boat was soon alongside, and the rower, by the swift manner in which he ascended the ladder, was evidently well used to the sea.

"Do I address the commander of this vessel?" he asked Levausseur, and the latter pointed to the buccaneer chief, who said—

"I command this vessel and the fleet that lies within cannon shot."

The stranger bowed, and said—

"I bring news for you. The boat's crew you sent to receive the ransom have been captured by the Governor of New Spain."

"Malediction! and has he dared to make them prisoners?"

"He has; and I am the bearer of the conditions of ransom."

"And who, in the fiend's name, are you that have an English tongue for the service of Spain?"

"My name is Rupert Felton," was the reply. "At present a prisoner of war on parole to bring you the governor's conditions."

The buccaneer looked less angrily at Rupert, as he said—

"I crave your pardon, sir. I had thought you were a renegade, and in the pay of Philip of Spain. I am glad it is otherwise. Now I await your commands."

Rupert had been advised by Stronghand before he left the Spanish prison not to mention the loss of the Warspite.

"For," said the giant, "those freebooters, Master Rupert, are not particular when a man is in their power."

"I am desired by Don Alvarez," said Rupert, "to inform you that the fortune of war has placed your men in his hands, and he holds them to ransom against the citizens of distinction you have taken from Vera Cruz."

"And the ransom, what of that, your sir?"

"The governor made no mention of the money collected by the churchmen."

"Was that delivered by the praying hypocrites, or was there an ambuscade formed for my men?"

"The money was gathered and delivered, and not until after the churchmen were on their way to the city did the Spanish troops arrive. They came, I believe, from the viceroy's camp, which is situate some four or five miles from the beach."

The buccaneer chief motioned to Levausseur to follow him to the stern of the vessel, and out of earshot of the mariners who were moving about near the mizenmast.

"Think you," said the buccaneer, "there is any reason to doubt this youth's statement about the coming of the Spaniards upon our men?"

"I should think not. He seems open and honest," said Levausseur, "and worthy of belief."

"If so," said the buccaneer, "the loss of our men is but the fortune of war, and I must treat honourably with the Spaniards."

"It will be as well," said Levausseur, "to redeem the men by surrendering the hostages you hold."

"But the ransom?"

"Let that pass. The way to Vera Cruz or any town on the coast is always open, and the loss can be made up and interest taken."

The buccaneer laughed and said—

"Let us be thankful that Spain's possessions are always open to replenish our coffers."

"And her sunken reefs," added Levausseur, "to sink or wreck our ships."

They turned and walked towards the spot where Rupert had stood, and discovered the young officer with his sword drawn and facing Tallot, who at this moment unsheathed his weapon.

The buccaneer chief strode angrily forward, and placing his hand upon Rupert's shoulder, said—

"How now, young sir? You forget where you stand."

Like an angry lion, Rupert turned, and inserting his fingers in the rim of the chief's corselet, hurled him back, saying—

"Keep your hand from me, pirate!"

The buccaneer turned white with passion, and drew his blade; but before he could use it, Levausseur came forward, and said—

"A game cock, by the rood! Patience, comrade, let us hear the cause of the quarrel between him and Tallot."

Rupert saw the second blade drawn upon

him, and placing his back against the mast, said, mockingly—

"So much for the brave brotherhood of the sea! Bah! Let me settle with one before a second draws upon me."

The buccaneer chief sheathed his weapon, and said—

"The younker is unworthy of my arm. I was wrong to place a hand upon him."

"You were!" said Levausseur. "Now let us hear the cause of Tallot drawing upon him."

Tallot, keeping upon the defensive, answered Levausseur by saying—

"The Spanish maiden we brought from the galleon came on deck during the time you were speaking, and essayed to have speech with this gallant. I bade her return from whence she came, and this stranger drew upon me."

"What know you of the maiden?"

Rupert turned to Levausseur, and answered—

"More than is my purpose to tell. But we waste time and words. This knave "——

"Knave!" roared Tallot. "Knave!"

"Knave and pirate!" said Rupert—"thrust me back, and but for your interference"—to the buccaneer chief—"my blade would have, ere this, wiped out the contamination of his touch."

"Methinks," said Levausseur, "you are early tired of life to challenge Tallot, the best swordsman of the brethren of the coast. Have a care, young sir! And remember, if you fall, it will be said by our foe that we slew their messenger, and thus disgraced our name."

"I will risk my life upon the issue," said Rupert, "if you, sir, will permit of the trial."

Levausseur turned to the buccaneer chief, who went over to Tallot, and whispered—

"Wound, but do not slay this crowing cock."

Tallot smiled assent. He was confident he could do as he wished with the young officer.

"Have at you," he said, "and your blood be upon your own head."

Rupert laughed as the blades crossed, and after a few passes Tallot's blade spun upward, and caught in the rigging.

"Crave my pardon, or you die."

He placed the point of his weapon against the buccaneer's throat, and would have spitted him, had not the required apology been given.

"By the Virgin," said the buccaneer chief, to Levausseur, "this youth fences like a demon. He has disarmed our best swordsman in less time than a monk could have counted a bead!"

"His skill is in advance of his years," said Levausseur. "Do you propose crossing blades with him?"

"By the Mass, no," laughed the buccaneer, "I have too much at stake to risk being spitted by that master of fence."

Rupert came forward, and with his sword saluted the buccaneer officer, and said—

"I await your commands, but ere I leave your vessel I would apologise for so roughly shaking your hand from my shoulder, and at the same time thank you for allowing me to cross blades with your officer."

"Honest as well as brave," thought Levausseur. "My faith, how he would rise were he to join the brethren of the coast."

The buccaneer chief admired Rupert's frank and manly speech and bearing.

"Well spoken," he said; "let the matter be forgotten. Now to answer the Spaniard's message. Tell him we are willing to make the exchange when and where he wishes."

"Upon that head," said Rupert, "I am instructed to say that the hostages can return with me, and your men can bring the boat back to the ship."

"A good plan; but think you the Don means fair?"

"He is a soldier," said Rupert, "and will keep his word. If you doubt it, I will pledge my untarnished honour."

"That I am willing to accept as a pledge; but should the Don deceive you?"

Rupert's answer struck the buccaneer's fancy, and increased his admiration for the speaker.

"Should he do so," said Rupert, "I will slay him before his guards."

"Enough," said the buccaneer; "the hostages shall accompany you."

He called to an attendant, and bade him bring the citizens of Vera Cruz to the gangway, and place them in the boat that was fastened alongside.

The man went upon his errand, and the buccaneer said to Rupert—

"Waiting an exchange of prisoners is a wearisome time for you. What think you of your being ransomed, and joining our band?"

Rupert reflected for a few moments. The offer was not to be despised, but his mind was filled with a desire to become a rover on the Spanish Main, and rule absolute monarch over his band.

Though a prisoner on parole, he did not give up all hope of having his wish accomplished. He did not tell the buccaneer these views, but in a courteous manner declined the offer.

"Now, sir," he said in conclusion, "there is yet another matter I would speak with you upon; that is, the ransom of the Spanish maiden you have on board."

"She is held by Levausseur," said the buccaneer; "to him you must appeal."

"To what ransom do you hold the maiden?" said Rupert; "do not name it too high, for she is but the daughter of a prison governor."

"Five thousand piastres."

Rupert was startled by the sum named, and shaking his head, said—

"I fear me the father will not be able to collect that sum; will you allow me private speech with her?"

The buccaneer bowed acquiescence. Rupert went to the after-hatch, and passed close to Tallot, who was leaning against the bulwark, looking savage and moody at the defeat he had sustained.

The hostages were coming up the steps,

and Rupert was hailed by them as their deliverer from the power of the buccaneers.

One of them caught the young officer's hand, and raising it to his lips, said—

"Thanks, young sir; to you I owe my life. May the Virgin give me the opportunity of proving my thanks."

Like the lightning's flash there came to Rupert's brain a stratagem by which the beautiful maiden could escape.

CHAPTER XXI.

THE TREASURE CAVE.

"THE Virgin," said Rupert, "has heard your prayers. You can serve me, and without risk to your life."

"To the risk of my life, young sir, you may command me."

"This way, under the shadow of the deck. Now, strip off your outer garments, and quickly, for every moment is precious."

The Spaniard obeyed, silent with amazement, until Rupert snatched the attire from the ground, then he said—

"A strange request, young sir, and my appearance in but my under clothes will "—

"A long cloak hangs on yonder peg. It has been left by one of your countrymen. Take it, and away, for the boat is being brought under the ladder."

Leaving the young Spaniard to possess himself of the cloak, Rupert entered the cabin, and before the lovely girl could speak, he hastily said—

"Maiden, these is a chance of your deliverance, and, on your speed in doing as I bid you, rests the result. Don this apparel, and range your clothes upon yonder couch in the semblance of a human form. This done, open your window, and step into the boat that is beneath."

He left the cabin before the girl could reply, and when he reached the deck, Levausseur met him, and asked—

"What says the girl ?"

"She is fearful of the result," was the dubious reply, "but prays that I may be successful."

"It matters but little," said Levausseur, "for a maiden is worth more than the ransom, for we are short of wives on the island."

Rupert's face flushed at the buccaneer's words, but in as calm a tone as though he felt not the least interest in the result, he said—

"I will appeal to the father, and if the ransom does not come within an hour from this, you can sail, and portion the girl to whom you like."

"A good arrangement."

"And until then," said Rupert, "it will be as well to leave the maiden in peace and in ignorance of her fate."

"She will be alone until the time for sailing arrives."

Rupert saluted the buccaneer, and pointing to the hostages who were standing at the gangway, said—

"It will be as well that I descend, for the boat is but light, and the weight of so many men will have to be adjusted."

"Farewell," said the buccaneer chief, as Rupert began to descend the ladder. "Remember my offer, and at the Isle of Tortugas you will always find a welcome."

"Thanks, a prosperous return ; I shall not forget. Did you know," Rupert thought, "all I could tell, and that which will be told by your men when they return, your welcome would have a different savour."

He assisted two of the hostages into the boat; then, as though by accident, unfastened the rope and pushed the boat astern, at the same time holding the line that hung from the vessel's side.

"Silence, my masters," he said to those on the ladder ; "we shall return in a moment."

The stern of the boat swung round under the cabin window, and Rupert assisted the girl into it, and softly drew the window close.

So quickly did he manage this, that the buccaneers did not notice the boat having left the gangway until Rupert was bringing it to its former position by pulling upon the "guess warp."

"A plague upon my clumsy knot," he said. "Had there been a heavy sea on, the boat would have been adrift."

The few buccaneers who were leaning over the side smiled grimly at the Spaniards who were clinging to the ladder and shaking with fear.

The whole of the citizens were soon seated in the boat, and Rupert placed four of the strongest at the oars, and taking charge of the rudder, gave the word to push off.

The Spaniards worked manfully, for their escape from the ship, they felt, was not a certainty until they were safely ashore again.

Rupert's lips wore rather a contemptuous appearance when he saw the frantic efforts the rowers made to keep time ; but his attention was soon drawn from the men by the young Spanish girl who sat near him.

She said but little until the boat was near the shore, for up to that time her eyes were fixed upon the buccaneers' vessel, in expectation every moment to behold the boats lowered and the buccaneers in chase.

"Heaven, young sir," she said, "will reward you for the good deed you have this day done. I cannot but give you thanks, and that is but a slight reward."

"It is all I need, lady—all I shall require when I place you in your father's hands."

"My father," she said, "is far from here, and it is as well, for he hates your nation, and would, despite the good service you have done him, thrust you into a dungeon in the castle of which he is keeper."

"I would brave him," said Rupert, "were he near, for then you would be in safety."

"I shall be in safety, young sir," she replied, "for I have an aged relative, superioress of a convent that stands a league below Vera Cruz."

The boat touched the beach as she finished speaking; and when Rupert told the rowers to pull stronger in order to ground the light craft the Spanish governor and several soldiers came forward to receive the liberated captives.

Isand remained with Rupert, and the governor came forward to speak to the stranger, but her protector prevented him by relating how he had saved the beautiful girl, and asking permission to see her safely to the convent.

"You have my permission," said the governor; "and it will be as well you start at once, for the buccaneers may discover her escape."

"I will depart, sir, when the exchange of prisoners is made."

"They are here."

As the governor spoke, the buccaneers came down the roadway, escorted by a detachment of Spanish soldiers.

Their arms were placed in the boat, and, until the men were seated and pulling towards the ship, Rupert stood on the beach.

"Remember your parole," said the governor, as Rupert turned away. "I shall expect you at evensong at the fort of Santa Luz."

"I shall be with you," said Rupert. "Meanwhile, bid my comrades be at rest regarding my safety. Come, maiden," he added, "we have a league to travel, and the road is rough."

A league, and in the society of the girl he had already begun to love, was to Rupert too short a distance.

He burned to tell the maiden the sentiment he felt, but at every attempt the words died away, and he substituted others relating to her strange escape or the beautiful scenery by which they were surrounded.

In the midst of one of these speeches the girl gave a slight exclamation of fear, and drew closer to her companion.

Rupert's hand went to his sword-hilt, but there was no cause to draw the blade, for the girl pointed to a small orifice in the rock, and whispered—

"The demon's cave."

Rupert's less superstitious nature caused him to smile at Isand's exclamation, and she saw it and said—

"You smile, young sir, but you know not the legend of that fearful place."

"I am willing to hear it, lady; more willing when it is told by your lips."

"It is said," she answered, "that the people who ruled in this land before Spain conquered this vast country, placed their treasure in that cave. Many have gone through the opening, lured by the prospect of wealth, but none ever returned save one, and he lived only to fall at the entrance."

"Did he speak?"

"No; but there was evidence in his clenched hands of the wealth inside, for they were filled with precious stones."

"Has no one entered since?"

"None; for the place is accursed, and not the boldest warrior would pass into the jaws of that fearful cavern, not for the wealth of New Spain."

Rupert made no reply, but his adventurous spirit was aroused, and he determined, when he should have placed the girl in the convent, he would return and explore the mysteries of the cavern or perish in the attempt.

CHAPTER XXII.
RUPERT IN THE TREASURE CAVE.

THEY ascended a path cut in the rocks, and Rupert, looking inland, saw the turrets of a stone structure rising above the foliage of a romantic forest.

The building was not more than half a mile from where the young officer stood, and he knew, unless he could bring his mind to the state necessary for him to make the declaration of love to his beautiful companion, the opportunity would be lost.

"The distance is but short," he said, "yet I must say the words, or be for ever lost. By the rood, I would sooner face a row of Spain's pikemen than make this avowal."

"There stands the convent," the Spanish girl said; "and now, young sir, we must part, for it would be ill for my name were you to be seen with me by any of the sisterhood."

"Part, maiden, and so soon? Can you not bear with me until the gates of yonder building are reached?"

"Young sir," replied the beautiful girl, "my deep gratitude would forbid me to be discourteous to you; but powerful reasons tell me it will be better we part at once, and for "——

"Ever," she was about to add, but her voice trembled with emotion, and the word was left unsaid.

Rupert noted her agitation, but ascribed it to a far different cause to the real one.

The young soldier was but little versed in the ways of love; his training had been the camp, the battle-field, and on shipboard.

"Your wish," he said, "must be law to me, lovely maiden. Yet I would know that it is not my presence that is so distasteful that it cannot be borne for the distance that lies between this and the convent."

Rupert stuttered so over his speech, that he felt a blush of shame tinge his cheeks as he thought how deficient he was in the courtly phrases of the gallants of the time.

"Beshrew my rough schooling," he thought, "it has taught me to handle a Toledo blade, to fill a breach, and navigate a ship; but when in beauty's presence I am but as a country lout."

The absence of these unmeaning set phrases was a surer way to the Spanish girl's heart than Rupert imagined.

Like the sensible portion of her modern sisters she admired the manliness of the young soldier, who could speak to her in common-place, sensible language, instead of using those absurd metaphors that must in the end disgust every woman of sense.

"Your presence," she answered, and her eyes sought the ground as she spoke, "is far from distasteful, young sir; and my deepest regret is, that I cannot obtain for you the welcome and thanks of my relatives."

"Enough maiden," said Rupert, "I accept your explanation; we must part. I am not of your country or faith, and my presence near the convent would be sufficient to bring the wrath of the fanatical sisterhood upon you. Farewell!"

He held out his hand as he spoke, and a thrill went through his frame when he felt the small fingers he clasped tremble.

"Farewell!" said Isand, "may the Virgin be your protector through life. My prayers at matins and evening song will be for your welfare, and so long as I live the memory of your goodness will remain in my memory."

Rupert unconsciously drew the girl closer to him, as he said—

"Through life, maiden, the remembrance of you will live in my heart; and if I have a regret, it is that we have ever met."

She raised her eyes to his face, and Rupert saw they were filled with tears.

"I too am sorry we have met," she said; "but in the cells of yonder convent prayer and fasting will take from my heart the—the"——

"Speak! speak! Do you then feel as I feel? Do you"——

"Hush! Dreams—wild dreams, that can never be realised," she answered. "Yet they were blissful; and this"——

"You love me then, beautiful girl. Say, is it so?"

"No—no! gratitude. I dare not love. Yonder convent is my home. My father has dedicated me to the Church. I must obey his wishes; but for that, I could reply to you in words that would"——

Rupert waited not to hear the conclusion of her speech, but impatiently drew her to his breast.

She remained passive for a moment, then with a wild cry broke away, and said—

"This must not be. Farewell, and Heaven speed you!"

"One moment," said Rupert. "I would have a token of our parting—that ring upon your finger, and in return take this."

They exchanged rings. Then the girl, as though fearful that her resolution would fail her, raised his hand to her lips, and fled towards the convent.

Rupert watched her for a few moments, then striking the hilt of his sword angrily, he said—

"She shall be mine! Once free from my parole, and at the head of a gallant band, I will level the walls of yonder building to the ground if they refuse to give her egress from the gates."

He stood upon the rock until the trees shut out the girl's form from his sight; then he turned and went slowly towards the cave.

He stood for a few seconds at the entrance, then drawing his sword, stepped inside.

The place was in total darkness; and when Rupert had passed a few feet inside, a dizziness came over him, and he would have fallen, had he not rushed to the entrance again, and refilled his lungs with fresh air.

"Foul vapour," he said, "this is the cause of the treasure-seekers being compelled to remain in the cave."

He felt dizzy and confused for a few moments; then the thought came to his mind of a mode by which he could destroy sufficient of the foul air to enable him to explore the cave with safety.

"Fire," muttered Rupert, "will absorb the noisome vapour. I have my flint and tinder, the gods be praised!"

A small flat box held the useful article, and Rupert stood at the entrance of the cave until the tinder ignited.

To this he applied the end of a piece of slow match, such as was used by the arquebusiers, and blowing the smouldering end into a flame, he again advanced.

Near the centre of the roof was a large keg, and upon examination there was sufficient oil to burn for at least an hour.

The cotton preserved by the oil was yet useful, and after some difficulty the adventurer succeeded in igniting the lamp.

He was compelled again to retire, and breathe the pure air, and by the time he returned the lamp threw out sufficient light to enable him to see the contents of the cave.

The Spanish girl's words were true, several men had entered the cave, and never returned.

There was the body of a man lying in the centre of the cavern, his flesh blackened by the noisome vapour, and near the entrance was another, who had fallen before he could reach the outer air.

Turning from these sickening sights, Rupert beheld the vast treasures that were scattered about, as though placed there in haste.

There were diamonds from the mines of Mexico, amethysts, cat's-eyes, turquoises, camelias, and emeralds, some of the latter of a prodigious size.

There were vessels of jasper from very remote mountains, statues and pedestals from the quarries of Zecalso.

In addition to these precious products of the country, there were vessels of gold and silver, leathern bags of money, and arms of a curious make, the blades of the finest steel, and the shafts and hilts a-gleam with precious stones.

Rupert's brain swam at the sight of these vast treasures, and he reeled like a drunken man.

The foul air, but slightly consumed by the lamp, had taken possession of his faculties, and he had but strength to stagger to the entrance, when the lamp went out, and the devil's cave was buried in darkness.

He fell face downward but a few yards from the entrance, and his face, so recently full of hope and joy, assumed the pallor of death.

CHAPTER XXIII.

SPANISH GRATITUDE.

WHEN the maiden reached the gates of the convent she saw a group of armed men lounging about, and to her surprise she recognised the guards of the prison of which her father was governor.

"My father," she said to one of the men, "is he here?"

"Yes, lady," was the reply. "Thanks to the Virgin, we have found you at last!"

"Have you been in search of me?"

"We have. There came a report that the galleon was wrecked upon the coast, and we have been searching along the whole seaboard for you."

Isand passed through the gate, and the men, freed from her presence, passed jokes about the singularity of her attire.

In the chamber where the abbess received the people belonging to the outer world the maiden found her father.

He uttered an exclamation of delight when Isand ran towards him, and was loud in his praises of the saints who had restored her to his arms.

"Said I not so?" he said to the abbess. "Were not my words true when I said the Church would not lose so good a daughter?"

The abbess assented, and to the young girl said—

"Those garments are a strange covering for limbs so delicate. Come, my daughter, I will provide thee with a more fitting raiment."

"Not the robes of the Church, mother," the poor girl replied. "I am not worthy yet to wear them; for my poor mind is torn and distracted with matters of the outer world."

"A sister," said the abbess, "who has this day taken the vows and the robes of our order will supply you with the raiment she has cast aside. Come, child."

The girl followed, and when in the cell exchanging her garb for one more fitting to her sex, she fell upon her knees and prayed to forget that handsome youth whose remembrance came more vividly to her mind, when she stood in the cold, dreary cell that would soon be her home.

The abbess's quick ears overheard the prayer, and, catching the name she used, smiled grimly.

"The strength you pray for," she said, coming to the kneeling girl, "will be granted; but first your heart must be cleansed by a full and open confession."

Isand's religious fears were easily excited, and she bowed her head and poured forth her story of love to the immoveable, icy woman, whose feelings had long been deadened to human passion or feeling.

"'Tis a serious matter," said the abbess; "you have sinned, and sinned deeply, in thus turning your heart to a stranger, and one not of "——

"I know it," moaned Isand, "but I am but young, and, for a time, the remembrance that I was destined for the Church left my mind."

"So much greater the sin," was the stern answer. "Your faith is but little to be thus easily weaned from the glorious life your pious father has destined you for. But come, let us return to the parent you have so deeply wronged."

The Spaniard saw his daughter's agitation and the vain effort she made to keep the tears from falling down her pale cheeks, and with as much affection as his haughty spirit could show, he took her hand and said—

"What now, child?—why do you grieve?"

"There is deep cause for her contrition," said the stony-hearted abbess, "for she has erred—nay, deeply sinned against you and the holy Church."

The Spaniard looked strangely at the speaker, and as his fingers closed over the ivory hilt of a dagger that hung from his belt, he fiercely exclaimed—

"A daughter of mine bring disgrace upon our house! Speak, girl! What is the meaning of these words?"

"No violence beneath this roof," said the abbess sternly. "Let the girl speak. Down upon your knees, daughter, and repeat the story you told me in the novice's cell."

Terrified by the abbess's words and her father's angry expression of fury, Isand knelt before her parent and told him the story of the shipwreck—how Stronghand had saved her life, and the manner in which Rupert had taken her from the buccaneers' vessel.

"He risked his life for me," she said, "and I could not but be grateful to one who had done so much for me. That feeling soon changed. Do not frown, father—I could not help it. I loved him, and love him yet."

"Daughter! minion! by the "——

"The secret would have remained buried in my heart until I had taken the vows," she went on, "but for the lady abbess overhearing my prayer for strength to drive his image from my heart."

"Who is this man?"

"He is English by birth "——

"English! an enemy to our country and faith, a sea robber, a "——

"No," said the girl. "He's an officer of the royal forces—a noble and gallant "——

"Silence, girl! Tell me when you last saw this viper who has filled your young heart with sentiments so hostile to the life which, in accordance with my vow, I devoted you to."

"I left him in sight of the convent walls, father."

The Spaniard jumped to his feet as he furiously exclaimed—

"A heretic, and dwelling with a daughter of the Church within sight of these holy walls. To you, lady abbess, I leave the care of this girl. I will hunt down the wolf who would have stolen a lamb from your fold."

"Stay, father!" said the girl, imploringly. "Heed him not—he is hot-tongued, and unused to brook the slightest speech "——

"Silence, girl "——

"Nay, father, I will be heard. Your life is dear to me, and I would not have you meet this Englishman, who is more skilful of fence than the sword-master of King Philip's army."

The Spaniard's lip curled with contempt as he said—

"By the saints, should the island dog draw upon me, I will spit him as readily as Lopez the cook spits a bird."

"Father, hear me"——
He tore himself from the girl's feeble grasp, and rushed from the convent; and bidding his men follow, went towards the seashore.

"There is an accursed Englishman," he said, "an enemy to our country, hidden hereabouts. Keep a sharp eye, my men, and the first who sights him shall receive a rich reward."

They reached the rocks, and explored every hollow capable of hiding a man, and when one of the single-masted boats ran ashore, the Spaniard hastened towards it, and eagerly questioned the fisherman.

"No, master," was the reply; "the saints be praised, we have seen no English robber except a fleet of them which is now putting out to sea."

"Has any boat left the shore within this last hour?"

"No; the boat that left conveyed the sea robbers to their ship—that was more than an hour since."

"He cannot have escaped," said the angry Spaniard. "Come, men, let us search further down the"——

An exclamation from one of the soldiers stayed the prison-governor's further speech.

"See yonder," the man said; "there is an armed man near the mouth of the Devil's Cave. I can see the sun flash upon his corslet and sword-hilt."

The Spaniards hastened to the spot, and when they reached the stranger found him, as they thought, dead.

CHAPTER XXIV.
AN UNEXPECTED DELIVERANCE.

THE governor unbuckled Rupert's corslet, and placing his hand inside the young officer's doublet, said—

"He lives! Make a litter by crossing your spears. Quick! about it, men."

They promptly obeyed, and followed the governor, who turned towards the convent.

"There seems but little life in the heretic's body," muttered the governor, "and while that little remains, I would be sure this is the man I seek."

To assure himself upon this point the Spaniard had ordered Rupert to be taken to the convent, feeling assured if his daughter saw the Englishman—and he was the one she had confessed to loving—her demeanour, when his senseless form was laid at her feet, would explain the matter.

The porteress at the convent refused to admit the—as she thought—dead man, and the Spanish governor, with an angry oath, strode past the woman, and went to the chamber where he had left his daughter.

He found her cowering at the abbess's feet, and when he entered, Isand's face brightened, but it changed when her father's stern voice said—

"Come this way, girl."

He took her by the wrist, and led her to the gate, and when she saw the pallid face of the senseless officer she ran forward, and kneeling by the prostrate body, moaned—

"They have killed him! O Father in Heaven! let me die too!"

"Enough," said her grim parent. "This is the man, now what to do with him is the next question."

The abbess, who stood at his elbow, whispered an answer to the half-muttered query.

"We have dungeons beneath the cloisters," she said. "One is at your service until the heretic has recovered sufficiently to be taken to your castle."

"Thanks," said Don Veletzy. "The way, lady abbess, to these dungeons?"

"Under the third window, on the north side of the convent is a door; take the heretic there. I will descend by the cloister, and meet you."

She placed her hand upon the beautiful girl's shoulder, and said, imperiously—

"Follow me, novice, this is no place for you, exposed to the gaze of the soldiers."

Isand slowly rose, and her love mastering the fear she felt, she suddenly stooped over Rupert and kissed his pale forehead.

A howl of rage from her father, and a stifled shriek from the abbess followed this act, and the poor girl to escape their reviling, went swiftly towards the convent door.

Don Veletzy had Rupert raised from the ground and taken to the place indicated by the abbess, and they were not there but a few moments, when the iron door swung silently inwards and disclosed a flight of stone steps.

The abbess motioned for the men to follow her, and selecting a key as she passed down the gloomy corridor, stopped before a dungeon.

The lock was well in order, for the bolt shot silently back when the woman applied the key.

She went inside and lit a taper, and the light revealed the interior of the murky chamber.

The place was empty, save for a rough table and stool. In one corner was a heap of mildewed straw, and near this was a huge iron ring set in the stone flooring.

The damp had congregated on the walls, and in some places, formed by the fungi, were patches of green, dank vegetation, of strange and uncouth shape.

The soldiers placed Rupert upon the straw, then withdrew, leaving the abbess and the Don bending over the captive.

"There seems but little need to have brought him here," the abbess said, "for the angel of death has set his seal upon him."

"Not so," replied the Don. "His heart beats strongly, and his pulse speaks of health. He has but been stunned."

"If so," said the abbess, "he will recover without the leech's skill. Time will do all that is necessary."

"Such was my thought," replied the Don, "so, with your permission, I will leave the heretic here until I return from Vera Cruz."

"You are welcome to the use of the dungeon," replied the abbess, "and the heretic will not die of starvation, for a lay sister will place bread and water within his reach."

They left the cell, and as the door closed, Rupert raised himself upon one arm, and listened to the key being withdrawn from the lock.

"By the rood!" he muttered, "I had much to do to keep still when that beautiful girl kissed my forehead. But it is as well I did so, for had I showed signs of life, there were many spears and sword-blades ready to do the Don's bidding, and if I mistake not, that would have been to exterminate the heretic who had taught his daughter to love him."

Rupert's consciousness had returned when the soldiers brought him to the convent door.

Trained from his early boyhood to exercise the greatest self-control over his feelings, he had still feigned insensibility, and did not even unclose his eyes to ascertain by whom he was surrounded.

He heard the voice of the abbess and Isand's father, and his quick perception told him all that had occurred.

"I have been picked up by this fanatical Don," he thought, "and brought here by his men, for my body rests upon a litter made by crossed pike staves. I must still feign insensibility, and wait for the opportunity to see how many men surround me."

The opportunity came when they halted for a moment at the door in the north wall.

One hasty glance showed the group of soldiers, and Rupert, depending upon the suddenness of his attack, would have started to his feet, and cut his way through; but, to his dismay, his sword had been detached from his belt.

His corselet and helm were also gone, and in this defenceless condition he knew it would be impossible to escape from the many spears that were around him.

"If the Don meditates my death," Rupert justly thought, "he could execute his wish by ordering one of his men to drive a weapon through my body. He dares not order this, therefore he intends but to keep me to ransom."

Reasoning thus, he was placed in the dungeon, and the conversation he heard between the Don and the abbess enlightened him a little upon the former's intentions.

"It is cowardly to make war upon women," he soliloquised, "but I have no other resource; so when the lay sister brings my meagre diet, I must take advantage of her weakness, and make my escape; there is nothing else to be done."

He waited long for the coming of the nun, but the day waned, and night took the place of the glorious southern sun.

"By my manhood!" exclaimed the young soldier, as he paused in his walk to and fro in the dungeon, "but it seems the sisterhood mean to leave me here to die without even the bread and water promised by the abbess. My curse be upon——"

He paused, for the key was placed in the lock, and when the massive door swung slowly back, he gave an exclamation of joy and surprise.

CHAPTER XXV.
THE LAST.

IT was the unexpected sight of the beautiful Spanish girl that caused Rupert's exclamation for she entered his prison pale and trembling.

In her hand was a huge lantern, the ghostly light gleaming through the talc sides added to the marble paleness of her features.

Rupert would have rushed forward, and enfolded her in his arms, for the remembrance of that kiss she had given him told there was no longer any necessity for his passion to be concealed.

He was in the act of advancing for this purpose, when she whispered—

"Follow me, young sir, and pray the Virgin the danger I have placed myself in may be the means of your freedom."

"Maiden," said Rupert, "sooner would I rot in this cell than aught of harm should happen to you——"

"Come," she said, impatiently interrupting him, "there is no danger to me, unless we are discovered. For you there is great danger in staying here, for they will take your life."

She moved through the doorway as she spoke, and Rupert followed.

"Tell me," he whispered, taking her hand as they passed down the gloomy passage, "in what shape is the danger of which you speak?"

"For freeing you," she answered. "If I am discovered, I shall be immured in one of the dungeons, and left to perish. But, quick! and all will be well."

"Where is the abbess?" Rupert asked. "Tell me, maiden, how it is that you have been able to open my dungeon door?"

"It is soon told," she answered. "I was placed in the novices' cell, and thinking of your danger I could not sleep. The door was locked, but I forced it back with a silver bodkin, and went to the abbess's chamber. She was asleep, and I took the keys that lay on a table near her bed. Then I came to your dungeon."

"Then," said Rupert, "you will be discovered by the bolt of your cell being withdrawn."

"It is a spring bolt, and if I can replace the keys on the abbess's table, I can close the door of my cell. But here we are at the gate. Now, adieu for ever!"

Rupert caught her in his arms as he said—

"Farewell! Should the fortune of war enable me to return before you have taken the vow, will you fly with me?"

"No—no. I dare not. I am——"

"I will come, Isand, and tear you from the steps of the altar——"

"No; I must submit to my fate. Do not strive to turn my heart from the life my father has doomed me."

"Is you heart in that life? Would you not sooner be with me, the mistress of a proud ship, and a hundred gallant men ready to do your bidding? Answer me this."

"I should; but it can never be. No—no. Farewell! In a month's time, I shall take the vows—then——"

"Before then, if I live," said Rupert, "you shall be mine. I swear it."

She broke away from the young soldier, and gently pushed him through the open portal; then the door closed, and Rupert, scarcely comprehending the change that had taken place, staggered forward.

The cool night air playing upon his hot brow soon revived him, and he went in the direction of the fort, where he had to surrender his parole.

The night was dark, and the absence of roadways soon led him far from the place he wished to reach.

He stumbled on, until the gray light of the morning enabled him to see the surrounding objects.

To his surprise, he was within a dozen yards of the entrance to the Demon's Cave.

"Fate," muttered Rupert, "has brought me here. I am unarmed. Inside this cave there are arms and armour, and"——

The falling of loose stones and sand from the rocks now caused Rupert to seek a cover in the thick brushwood that grew at the very entrance of the cave.

His first thought was that he had been seen by some of the outlying Spanish sentries, who were watching the coast, apprehensive of another attack from the buccaneers.

Great was his surprise when he heard a well-known voice say—

"I could have sworn to it, Mark; there was a figure standing direct in our path."

"It must have been fancy," replied Stronghand, "yet I thought something came down the rocks. Mayhap it was an animal of some kind; but whatever it is we have no time to lose in the search. Master Rupert, the governor tells me, is in danger, and we must to the rescue."

"That is so," answered Firebrand, "but where this convent stands is a mystery, for we have been all night tumbling and"——

"I am here, my friends," said Rupert, as he came out of the brushwood, "and right glad I am to meet you."

"Master Rupert's voice!" said the giant, "the governor spoke falsely then?"

He gripped the young officer's hand as they met, and Rupert said—

"There was some truth in the viceroy's words, Mark, for I have but just escaped from the dungeons of a convent, and, as you see, am unarmed—not even a dagger to hold my life."

Half a dozen weapons were put forth for Rupert to take his choice from; but he waved them back, saying—

"Near to us we have arms and treasure, enough to equip a fleet; but first, before we speak of these matters, tell me how it is you have been liberated."

"The good citizens you saved from the buccaneers," said Stronghand, "interceded for us, and the Don gave us our liberty, at the same time making known that you had been captured by one of his countrymen, over whom he had no command."

"No command?" Rupert repeated. "The Viceroy of New Spain is all-powerful here."

"Not so, Master Rupert," said Stronghand, "or he would have ordered your release. He gave us our liberty, and had we not found you the convent walls would not have kept us from your cell."

"Thanks, my brave companions, but it is better a less powerful arm has saved me."

"The story, Master Rupert, will be welcome."

"You shall have it, Mark; but first I would learn if you have any of the grape's generous juice, for I am chilled to the very bone."

"A plague upon my forgetfulness!" said the giant, holding a leather bottle of wine towards his chief; "I had not thought of this."

A draught of the rich liquor warmed Rupert's frame. Then he told his companions of his visit to the cave and subsequent adventures.

"By my manhood!" said the giant, "but the maiden deserves a better fate than she will meet in the cloisters. What say you, Master Rupert, to a rescue?"

"It is not yet time. When we have a vessel large enough to remove the treasures in this cave we will take the goods the gods have provided and the girl at the same time."

"My eyes hunger for a sight of these marvels," said Stronghand. "Let us explore the cave; but first it will be as well to give egress to the foul air."

"How?"

"A very simple way, Master Rupert. This is the entrance you say?"

"Yes."

"Then, by boring a hole through the roof the noxious vapour will escape."

"A good thought. Let us begin at once."

They clambered up the rocks, and after a long search the heavy pike Stronghand had used to probe the earth went through between the sand that had collected over the hole, used formerly as a means of egress for the smoke from the cave.

"By the saints," said Stronghand, "the vapour is noisome; it taints the clear morning air like a pestilence; let us enter."

The sun rode high in the heavens when the adventurers emerged from the cave.

Rupert had armed himself from the multitude of weapons that lay around, and every man carried in the leathern pouch that hung from his belt a portion of the gold.

They closed the orifice in the roof, then rolled a number of heavy stones against the entrance to keep the cave secure until they could return.

There was no necessity for this, for not a Spaniard would have ventured beyond the opening for a king's ransom.

"Now," said Rupert, "let us make terms with one of the fishermen yonder, and at the port of Carthagena we can purchase a stout vessel."

The terms were soon made, and the man who sold his boat blessed every saint in the calendar for the lucky day's work.

Stronghand was busy spreading the sail, when a shot whistled past his ears, and before the boat was half its length from the shore Isand's father waded in the water, followed by a dozen of his men.

"The foul fiend has aided your escape," he said to Rupert, " but this time you die."

He clutched the gunwale as he spoke, and Stronghand, extending his brawny arm, grasped the governor by the collar of his doublet and dragged him in.

The sail filled, and the fishing-boat shot out upon the waves, and his excellency was a prisoner, his men staring after him in blank confusion.

"Now, Master Rupert," said the giant, "shall we cut the Don's throat?"

"Not so, Mark. Pitch him overboard, and if he can swim to land so much the better for himself."

In a moment the Spaniard was raised above the giant's head and hurled into the sea, and when he rose to the surface he struck out for the shore, cursing bitterly at his defeat.

When he reached the beach he yelled to his men to fire, but the boat was out of range of their weapons, and before the sun had set the adventurers were prevented from going to the port of Carthagena by the appearance of an English man-of-war. They were taken on board, and, by virtue of this service, compelled to serve with the crew.

This mishap, for a time, prevented Rupert's scheme from being carried into execution, and as the land faded from his view, he paced moodily to and fro the deck, thinking of the inmate of the convent, and wondering whether they had parted for ever.

. . . .

The destruction of the Spanish Armada is an event in English history with which every schoolboy is familiar.

But as the numerous incidents connected with the memorable period, when this "invincible" fleet was—partly by the interposition of Providence in the shape of violent winds and storms, and partly by the skill and valour of our English admirals and sailors—irretrievably crippled and destroyed, are of that interesting nature, which, when heightened by the colouring of romance, cannot fail to be acceptable to our readers, we do not hesitate to use them in the present instance as the groundwork of our story.

With its principal characters the reader has already made acquaintance in the tale entitled "Adrift on the Spanish Main," to which this will form the sequel.

It is not my intention to trouble my readers with any dry historical details, save those which will be comprised in a few lines, and which are absolutely necessary to place them in possession of a few facts connected with our story, at starting.

It was in the reign of Queen Elizabeth of glorious memory, A.D., 1587, when the haughty and intriguing Philip II of Spain, the husband of Mary, Elizabeth's late sister, intent upon invading the English shores, was preparing the formidable fleet which he in his pride termed " the invincible," but which he subsequently found to his cost to be utterly impotent against the combined forces of Heaven and Englishmen.

The news of such mighty preparations reached England, and so great were they that it was rumoured the Spaniards had provisions of bread and wine for 40,000 men for a whole year.

That our favoured island was the point against which this mighty armament was to be directed was discovered by the agents of Sir Francis Walsingham, secretary to Queen Elizabeth, one of whose favourite maxims my young readers will do well to remember:—" Knowledge is never too dear."

The moment the safety of the nation appeared in prospect of being imperilled the most energetic measures were at once taken to meet the invaders.

Then, as now, Englishmen were Englishmen, and with one heart and voice rallied around their Queen, to support her in the impending struggle.

Elizabeth wanted neither a loyal people, brave admirals and sailors, or watchful and indefatigible spies, who used their courage and their wits, and perilled their lives to learn the secrets of the enemy.

In many a strange disguise, and by many a daring expedient, were the plans of the foe discovered, and information forwarded to the proper quarter in England.

Nor were the Spaniards, being accustomed to plotting themselves, ignorant that such measures were in constant operation.

The misfortune—for them—was, that they generally made the discovery too late to neutralise its effects, and when they could only vent their spleen and wrath in unavailing oaths and threats of vengeance.

Sometimes, however, the spies on either side were detected in their perilous game, and, in that case, the masquerade generally had a tragical ending.

Little mercy was shown, and the result of this mutual espionage and severity was to render both sides particularly watchful and cautious in such hair-breadth undertakings.

Without further remarks, then, let us commence our history.

CHAPTER XXVI.

THREE OLD FRIENDS.

THE sun was setting red and fiery over the Atlantic, where it washes the north-west coast of Spain, when a small vessel, manned by a crew of three persons, might have been seen gradually nearing the shore.

Any one used to naval tactics would have observed a kind of caution—if I may use such a term in reference to a lifeless boat—in the manner in which it drew towards the land.

The coast generally was rocky, but not entirely so. Here and there the rocky barrier

RUPERT AT THE HELM.

divided, and left spaces of sand and shingle, which formed small creeks, and offered a landing place to small vessels like that of which we are now speaking.

She bore the Spanish flag, and the bronzed complexions and dress of those on board gave no indication that they did not serve under the yellow ensign, although one could hardly have reconciled the extreme caution of their approach with the fact of their being sons of the soil.

Neither did they seek the shore by one of the sloping sandy creeks; but instead, guided their vessel into an indented position of the rocky coast ridge, that looked like a bay in miniature, and there they lay snug and secure from observation, concealed by the rocks that rose on either side.

Having reached this haven, they seemed to experience the relief men feel when they have accomplished a task of difficulty, or at least the first and most important step towards it.

They looked complacently in each other's faces, and smiled silently, making for the present no remark.

A grappling iron was thrown over the vessel's side, the hooked end of which dug into the craggy edges of the rock, and kept the boat from drifting back to sea.

The three men then leisurely filled their pipes with the newly discovered fragrant weed which Sir Walter Raleigh had lately introduced into England, and striking a light with a flint and steel, lay down placidly on deck and smoked, and waited patiently.

Their gaze was generally bent on a fortress, almost at the water's edge, that loomed forth at no great distance, bold and dark in the half light.

As they lay prone on the deck, leaning carelessly on their elbows, their heads could hardly have been seen above the gunwale at a little distance.

Save from the thin blue smoke of the tobacco, which betrayed the presence of the smokers, the boat might have been empty.

There they lay, smoking thoughtfully, their looks usually fastened on the fortress, that seemed for them a kind of magnetic attraction, but ever and anon directing their glances across the open sea, on which the dying crimson of the setting sun quietly rested.

Slowly it sank beneath the horizon, taking with it the rose-coloured gorgeous clouds that surrounded it, and leaving only the cold blue sky, that looked for a time doubly chilly from the contrast caused by the departure of the great luminary.

But by degrees the stars came rapidly peering and twinkling through the blue expanse over their heads, till at last it looked like a vast spangled robe.

And then the moon appeared, lighting up the ocean with her silver radiance, and, causing the fortress to stand out in bolder relief than ever.

It seemed strange to see those men lying there with apparently no motive.

They might have been fishermen, but the boat was not a fishing smack, and a close observer might have seen they wore the uniform of Spanish officers, and were armed with swords and pistols.

And besides this, there was an expression of intellect in their keen looks that betokened them of a more intellectual class than that of the "toilers of the deep."

One of the three was of herculean build, and possessed that calm repose of manner which implies contempt of danger, and which not unfrequently accompanies superior size and strength.

The second of the party, though very inferior in bulk, was nevertheless remarkable for his youthful appearance, the symmetry of his limbs, and the careless grace of his attitude.

The third had neither the peculiarities of the first nor the second, but still presented a stalwart form, and a power of muscle that promised well for a friend, or bad for an enemy in case of contest.

After remaining silent for some time, they, as if by common consent, fixed their eyes upon each other, and after a second or two's silent inspection broke into a quiet, but genuine laugh—a laugh in which there was nothing at all foreign, but on the contrary genuine English in all its quality.

"By Saint George," exclaimed the burly captain, "I can but laugh, when I think of all the vicissitudes we have gone through, that we should be here all together again, engaged in perhaps one of the most perilous enterprises we have ever yet attempted. But I like it well for all that," he added. "The greater the danger, the greater the skill required to work safely through it."

This was spoken in pure English—so pure that it at once gave the lie to their dress, complexion, and the flag under which they steered.

The youngest of the party rejoined: "True, good Mark; we have our work to do, and if we can only succeed in hoodwinking the governor of yonder fortress as successfully as we have the Spanish outlookers, we may carry away all information we require, and a flask of ripe canary into the bargain."

"Ha, ha!" laughed the third, "I can't help marvelling that we, with our stained faces, our foreign uniforms, and the yellow rag that flutters aloft, should have been able so completely to throw salt water into the eyes of our Spanish friends. It makes me laugh to think of it."

"Our enterprise is undoubtedly worthy of the days of chivalry," returned Rupert. "It was not for nought we braved the dangers of the Spanish Main, since we learnt the language that now stands us in such good stead."

"Yes," remarked Mark Luton, in a tone of great satisfaction, "we may look upon our knowledge of that as the principal cause of our being here; but for that we should never have been honoured with the task of watching the enemy's movements on their own ground."

"Never! of what use should we be, not understanding what was spoken to us? By all the saints in the calendar, I love this work! it keeps the heart and brain in healthy exercise. I love it! I love it!"

It was Rupert who spoke these words, and as they came spontaneously from his heart to his lips, he stretched forth his hands as though he would have embraced the very thought with esctacy if he could have done so.

"I love it also," echoed Mark warmly, "it suits my nature. I always loved danger—I always shall!"

"And I!" exclaimed Firebrand.

My readers are doubtless curious to know the precise business in which our three old acquaintances are engaged in at this particular spot at such an eventful time.

A few words will suffice to explain.

Circumstances had brought Rupert the Ready into the notice of Sir Francis Walsingham.

Brave, skilful, and acute himself, he could detect the same qualities in others; and no sooner did he learn that Rupert was acquainted with the Spanish language than he at once marked him as one of his agents abroad—in other words, as a spy upon the enemy's actions.

Rupert naturally introduced his friends, Mark Luton and Firebrand, to the Secretary, who took them into his service at once; and it was now in the capacity of spies that they were lying quietly amongst the rocks on the Spanish coast until the evening should have closed in, and they could approach the fortress, where, by passing themselves off as Spanish captains, they would be able to extract the information from the governor without exciting his suspicions.

The moonbeams now lay broadly upon the waters, but the vessel in which they were was wrapped in shadow, so that detection was almost impossible.

The time had arrived when they were to proceed to the fortress.

They were eager to accomplish their mission, and, if not fearful, at least naturally anxious for its successful issue.

"It is time!" exclaimed Rupert, knocking the ash from his pipe.

"I am with you," cried Mark.

"And I," echoed Firebrand.

The trio sprang to their feet.

But no sooner had they done this, than Rupert made a sudden pause, and laying his hand on Mark Luton's shoulder pointed seaward.

"Look yonder!" he exclaimed eagerly.

Stronghand looked eagerly, shaded his eyes with his hand, and so did his companion Firebrand.

"What do you take it to be?" inquired Rupert.

"A vessel undoubtedly of about the same size as our own," replied Mark.

"She seems to be making for the shore."

"Yes—I think so."

"Is she English, or Spanish, or Dutch? can you make out?"

"No, by the Rood! she may be all the colours of the rainbow upon close inspection, but she looks dark enough at present."

"We'll take the liberty of watching our interesting friend yonder," observed Rupert, placing his glass to his eye.

"Can you discern any one on board?"

"Not yet."

As Rupert spoke, he handed the glass to his companions, each of whom looked through it in turn.

"She is evidently coming towards the shore," said Mark; "there is no doubt of that."

"We will wait and see," said Rupert.

They filled their pipes, and sat down quietly to watch the approach of the small craft.

The breeze had freshened as the day declined, and there was a stiffish breeze that sent the vessel rapidly through the waves, with the white foam splashing over her bows.

Nearer and nearer it came on.

"By all that's strange! would it not be wonderful if they ran into our creek here?" said Firebrand.

"They will not do that," replied Rupert; "their course is a little more south. If you observe, they are between us and the fortress."

"Ay, true, so they are," assented Firebrand.

They were now so near that Mark Luton proposed they should make their way to the beach, over the rocks, while the distance was yet great enough to render recognition by the new comers—who were evidently approaching the shore—impossible.

In a few moments our comrades were, as quickly as possible, picking their way over the craggy, slippery, jagged rocks, and in a short time they were safely on the shore, snugly ensconced behind a projecting rock awaiting the arrival of the vessel.

Nor had they long to wait.

Singular enough, as the boat drew near it was seen to be manned by three men only—their own number.

"That's easy work, Ru," said Mark, in a low tone, "only one to one. I'd rather there had been six."

"Are they Spaniards?" inquired Rupert. "Yes!" he exclaimed immediately, asking and answering his own question in a breath. "There is no doubt of that."

"What do they want here?" remarked Stronghand.

"Perhaps they are bound for the same destination as ourselves," replied Rupert, laughing softly.

"Ah, ah," chuckled his companions.

"Sh!" whispered Rupert, cautiously as the next moment the boat's keel grated on the sand.

The men leaped ashore instantly, one carrying in his hand a kind of triple iron hook attached to a rope.

This he wedged firmly against a fragment of rock, quite unconscious how near he was to three of his foes, who were quietly watching him, and having done so returned to the boat and made the end of the rope fast to the prow.

He then rejoined his companions.

CHAPTER XXVII

THE SPANISH SPIES.

THE men were thorough Spaniards, dark and swarthy, with large moustaches and pointed beards; though for the matter of that so were the Englishmen, only the complexions of the latter were counterfeit, being dyed with a particular juice, for obvious reasons.

"Praise to the saints," said one, "we are safe thus far."

"You're not to the end of your journey yet though, my friend," thought the Englishmen.

"We have some fair intelligence to communicate to old Don Xavier touching the preparations of these English heretics," the first speaker went on.

"Ha! ha!" laughed his companions, "spice your information well, Diego, and we shall make the old commandant jump in his shoes for joy."

"Depend on me, Ortez," replied the other. "The old rogue knows well enough there'll be some English gold rolling into his coffers before long. He's hospitable, and will feast us royally for our good news."

"By St. Geronimo, I am in a mood to sup to-night," cried the third, who had not yet spoken. "I trust the Santa Maria will show herself before long, for I am famished."

"Patience, Juan," advised his friend, "and you shall not only sup, but perhaps be permitted to see the pretty English senora, whom the crew of the Esperanza left there, so I was informed two days since, under the gallant keeping of the Don."

"Then, by the mass, I wish the Santa Maria would show herself. Must we wait for this despatch from Don Pedro de Valdis, the captain? Is it positively necessary?"

"Undoubtedly. It is our introduction, and if we wish for supper and the smiles of beauty it will be as well not to go without it."

Don Juan looked out wistfully across the sea, the appearance of which had changed.

The wind had increased, and blew in sharp fitful gusts, driving the clouds heavily from the south-west.

Ever and anon the moon was obscured.

The sea also began to foam, and there was every prospect of a heavy gale.

"Madre de Dios!" exclaimed Juan, "this is unkind! We are going to have a storm, and shall most probably miss the despatch."

He shuddered as a gust of wind went rushing past.

It was growing extremely and unaccountably cold.

"I think," said Don Diego, "we are going to be frozen by a sudden winter."

The three Spaniards shuddered simultaneously.

The cold penetrated to their very marrow.

"Come! come! Come, Santa Maria!" exclaimed Don Juan, whose teeth chattered, and who was longing for his supper.

"Ah, see!" cried Captain Ortez, as he pointed to a dark mass in the distance. "There's the Santa Maria!"

"The good saints be blessed for it!" fervently ejaculated Juan. "Shall I loose the grappling iron?" he asked, eagerly.

"Not yet, amigo!" answered Ortez.

"I should think not!" echoed Rupert, in a low tone, from behind the rock, as he planted his foot upon the shaft of the hooks.

The conversation that had taken place between the Spaniards had been distinctly overheard by our English friends, who were close at hand, concealed behind a rock.

They had secured valuable information, and they saw at once the course to be pursued.

They must have the letter of introduction

that was at that moment on board the Santa Maria.

The Spaniards renewed their conversation at this moment, and the dark hull of the lofty many-decked Spaniard appeared in the now somewhat misty distance.

"I will go out and meet the vessel!" said Captain Ortez; "I can run the boat along in a wind like this, like an arrow from a bow."

A fierce gust rushed past him as he spoke, and almost swept him off his feet.

"You can let loose the grappling iron now, my friend," said he to Juan.

"This instant!" exclaimed the eager young man, who was something of a glutton.

He rushed towards the spot, and, to his great surprise, discovered what appeared to be a brother captain, seated on the rope, and his back coolly leaning against the shaft of the grappling iron, with two other Spaniards—apparently his friends—close by.

"Ha!" he cried, starting back, "I did not know any one was here."

"Oh, yes!" answered Rupert, in very good Spanish, smiling at the same time, "we're all here—I mean myself and my two little brothers!"

"Little!" murmured Juan, glancing at Stronghand, whose head reached his shoulder, seated as he was.

The other two Spaniards, hearing voices, advanced, and their surprise was equal to that of their companion at the sight of the Englishmen.

"So, senors," said Stronghand, before they had recovered their breath, "you are going to the fortress, eh?"

"Yes, undoubtedly!" they replied, "but we must first get the letter from the vessel now passing. Have the goodness to rise, you are sitting on the grappling hooks."

Rupert smiled, but did not move.

"It's a very rough night," he remarked.

"That's nothing," replied Captain Ortez, rather irritably; "I am used to such weather."

"Are you not afraid of it?"

"Not at all?"

"It might capsize your boat."

"No matter!"

"Think of your wife and children."

"I have none!"

"Indeed?"

"Yes, indeed! get up!"

Still Rupert did not move.

The Spaniard swore a very impatient oath.

"Rise, senor, or——"

"Go on, my friend," quietly observed Rupert, whilst his companions enjoyed the joke immensely, "or what?"

"I shall be compelled to remove you by force," answered the captain, sternly.

"You had better not do that, my friend," replied Rupert; "the fact is, I don't think it safe for you to go on such a night as this—I don't indeed!"

"Not safe, but I must go."

"I beg you will not; I had much rather you did not."

"Confound you, I tell you I will go."

He extended his arm as he spoke and grasped the collar of Rupert's coat.

But the young Englishman quietly laid his grip upon Captain Ortez's wrist with an intensity that very much astonished the Spaniard.

"Excuse me, you will do nothing of the kind."

"Not go !" spluttered the captain, extremely wrath and indignant, "who says I shall not ?"

"I do," quietly answered Rupert.

"You ?"

"Yes, I."

"Well, but why—in the name of Sathanas and all his legions—why ?"

"Because I object," returned Rupert grimly.

The Spaniard made a fierce lunge, just as a hooked fish might have made ; but it was no use—Rupert still grasped his wrist.

The two Spaniards advanced indignantly.

"This is insulting," they cried.

"Oh nonsense, senors," answered Mark.

"Why does this gentleman persist in retaining our friend ?" they asked.

"Didn't you hear ?" returned Mark, definitely, "because he does not intend him to go !"

"But why ?" they all shouted in concert, violently.

"Because I've made up my mind to go myself," answered Rupert, decidedly.

"You !" they exclaimed, glaring at him.

"Yes, I. The fact is, my friends—I don't mind telling you in confidence—but I require the letter you wish to fetch from the captain of the Santa Maria myself. It's essential to my peace of mind that I should have it, and have it I will !"

The Spaniards were completely staggered by this cool language, spoken in their native tongue, and drew themselves up as stiff as ramrods.

"This is language, senors, we are not accustomed to," exclaimed Don Diego, "you must apologise."

"Pooh !" coolly replied Rupert.

"Pooh !" echoed Mark Luton.

"Pooh !" finished Frebrand.

The Spaniards foamed with passion. Their very moustaches curled at the ends with wrath.

They stamped and swore wicked oaths, and looked vindictive and bloodthirsty.

"You will not apologise ?" they cried.

"On no account !" returned the Englishmen, very coolly.

"Then you must fight us !" shouted the Spaniards, drawing their swords.

"Do you particularly wish to be killed ?" inquired Rupert kindly.

"We wish particularly to kill you—that is what we wish !" they cried.

"Amiable individuals !" thought Rupert.

"And we will kill you !" they cried, "come on !"

"If you can !" answered the Englishmen.

"Ha, ha," yelled the exasperated Dons, as they crossed blades ; but as they were about to commence, a brilliant flash of lightning darted so vividly across the sky, now black with clouds, that they recoiled.

Before they had time to recover themselves a peal of thunder, loud enough to wake the dead, rolled over their heads.

They paused.

The flash of lightning had shown them the Santa Maria bearing down under full sail, and within a mile distance.

"We must put an end to this," whispered Rupert to his friends ; "it is time to start."

The Spaniards having recovered themselves came at once to guard.

But they had sadly misjudged their powers, for within three minutes from the moment of attack they were disarmed and lying on their backs, with a strong hand pressing somewhat unpleasantly upon their windpipes.

They began to struggle, but a slight intimation with the sword's point warned them that they were in hands that would not be trifled with.

"Lie still, senors ! pray lie still !" growled Firebrand, "or there's no knowing what may happen."

He spoke with a kind of gruff entreaty, but the Senor Juan, who had fallen to his share, plunged violently, so that he was obliged to tap him rather sharply with the hilt of his sword on the head.

At length they were induced to realise their position, and lay still, uttering curses not loud, but particularly deep.

"'Tis a rough night," exclaimed the mellow voice of Mark Luton.

"It is," assented Rupert, in a tone of suppressed mirth ; and were we to leave these poor fellows here in this unprotected state, they might possibly be blown away. We must tie them down in the boat."

The Spaniards groaned. But there was no escape.

Rope was produced, and their hands were tightly bound together at the wrists behind them.

Their ankles were also wound up with strong cord, and fastened off with knots such as English sailors know how to tie.

The Spaniards were completely helpless, and lay groaning and lamenting on the ground.

And a new phase in the character of the elements appeared.

The wind increased in fury, and a violent storm of hail and snow came bursting like a torrent from the burdened clouds.

The massive Spanish galleon was seen approaching through the dense shower that shrouded her like a gauze veil.

"There's not a moment to be lost !" cried Rupert. "Look you to the formidable Don."

"By heaven !" 'tis a rough night. Is it safe to venture ?" exclaimed Stronghand.

"Safe, Mark ?" returned Rupert, "we have braved too many dangers to fear now. Besides, I must have that letter, if only for the fun of the thing. You'll see I shall return with it."

He got into the boat as he spoke, and lighted the lantern that hung suspended to the mast.

"Now then, loose away, and push her off!" cried Rupert.

Stronghand and Firebrand planted their shoulders against the bows, and pushed with all their strength.

But the keel was too firmly wedged into the sand, and it would not move.

"We must have more weight," cried Mark.

Suddenly he thought of the captives.

"You must help, senors," he exclaimed to them.

An unanimous refusal was the reply.

"If you refuse I'll throw you three into the sea to feed the fishes. Come Firebrand!" cried Mark, "dead weights are better than nothing. Bring our prisoners here."

The hapless Dons were hoisted up, dripping and half frozen from their recumbent position, and placed in a leaning posture against the prow of the stranded boat, as utterly helpless as three sacks of grain, or three logs of wood.

Then Stronghand and Firebrand added their strength.

"Now then! altogether! Yeo hoy! hoy! hoy!"

The wind came with a sudden blast, whirling past like a fierce hurricane.

The sail filled, and with a sudden grating sound, as though her keel had been suddenly rasped from stem to stern, the vessel reeled, swung round, and dashed like lightning through the foaming billows.

A tremendous splash was heard, and the three unhappy tied-up Spaniards fell backwards into the sea, from which they were presently hauled out by the legs by Mark and Firebrand.

In the meantime, Rupert grasped the tiller, the hail and snow dashing in his face, sped onwards, to meet the Santa Maria, and obtain the letter.

CHAPTER XXVIII.
AN ADVENTURE IN THE CAVERN.

His companions, Stronghand and Firebrand, stood watching the small vessel as it tore almost wildly through the waters.

In fact they would have liked to have gone with him, and shared the danger, whatever it might be ; but Rupert deemed it more prudent to go alone on board the Santa Maria, feeling he could account for himself better than for three strangers, to the captain, and without exciting any suspicion.

Had any less experienced sailor been alone in that boat in such a furious wind, and in such a sea, they might have trembled for his safety. As it was, they knew that Rupert was thoroughly equal to the perils of the moment.

His was an eye quick to perceive, and a hand prompt to execute, any piece of nautical strategy that was necessary to the safety of his vessel, and they therefore had less fear of his safe return than the furious weather seemed to justify.

However, as the craft gradually became more and more indistinct, and as the snow still continued to fall heavily, they began to think about seeking a temporary shelter in their own boat, which still lay snugly moored in the rocky creek where they had left her.

Their thoughts had been diverted for the moment, and all remembrance of their prisoners banished from their minds, by the departure of their adventurous comrade, and the necessity for getting under cover was probably suggested by a pitiful groan from the half-frozen Spaniards, who still lay drenched, and utterly unable to help themselves, on the beach.

Mark and his companion considered a moment. They had no particular affection for the dark-complexioned individuals at their feet; but they were Englishmen, and having put their foes hors de combat, they did not wish to leave them to utter destruction.

"It will be next to impossible to carry them across those slippery rocks," remarked Stronghand, "where we could hardly keep our own footing; we must look and see whether there be any natural shelter or hollow where we can leave them for the present."

They moved from the spot to reconnoitre. The Spaniards moaned piteously, and turned their heads wistfully as the Englishmen receded from their view.

The latter, however, did not trouble themselves about their prisoners, being perfectly convinced of their perfect inability to escape, or in fact, do anything but roll, but proceeded towards the rocks.

At brief intervals the moon gleamed forth from behind masses of dark clouds, and it was during one of these temporary illuminations they descried a cavity in the rocks that seemed to promise shelter.

They approached and entered cautiously. That is to say they were about to enter, when a peculiar sound caused them to pause.

It was that of some one—a man they thought—who, in a very lugubrious and mournful tone, seemed to be pouring out his complaints through the medium of his vocal organ.

Voice he had none, it being extremely hoarse, and grating and the poetry was a little worse than the voice.

The doggrel ran thus—

"From Injy I sail'd, O dear! O dear!
For England bound, O dear! O dear!
I never shall get there now I fear;
For the Spaniards caught me and drop'd me here,
And I feel altogether uncommonly queer.
Diddle dum, di, doodle day."

The serious tone of the invisible vocalist, and the peculiarity of his song, struck our Englishmen as decidedly ludicrous.

They accordingly did what most Englishmen would have done in acknowledgment—laughed. Not loudly, but to themselves.

"That's English, isn't it?" said Mark, in a low tone, to Firebrand.

"It sounds very much like it," answered his companion, "the refrain especially—

'diddle dum, di, doodle day,' is particularly English."

"The sounds seemed to come from the inside of this cave," remarked Stronghand. "Let us enter."

They went in.

All was profoundly dark, and the substance they trod on appeared to be very much like a thick layer of dried leaves.

So soft was it that their footfalls were not heard.

With hands outstretched, and keeping close to the sides of the cave, they made a circuit of the interior, until they stood once more at the entrance.

They, however, encountered nothing living —nothing but the rugged inequalities of the cavern walls.

"'Tis strange what voice that could have been," said Stronghand. "If we had not both heard it I should have looked upon it as fancy. Any one there?" he asked directing his voice into the darkness.

"Diddle dum, di, doodle day," was the faint scarcely audible reply.

"It's some sea monster having a game with us, I think," suggested Firebrand; "I've heard there are such things."

"So have I," returned his comrade, "but I never saw any yet."

"I wish we had a light," Firebrand exclaimed, as he ran his nose against a projecting piece of rock.

"I think we may accomplish that," said Mark, as he took from his pocket a flint and steel, and a small packet of tinder. "I thought these might be useful, so I brought them with me."

A few strokes of the metal against the stone sufficed to kindle the tinder.

Firebrand gathered up, with his hands, a heap of the soft material that formed the carpet, as it were, of the cavern, and Mark placed the tinder beneath it.

He then fanned it gently with his hat until, being dry, it burst into a flame.

It then became perceptible that it was sea-weeds that had been collected and placed there, perhaps by shipwrecked mariners, to add to the warmth and comfort of the interior.

There being plenty of it they heaped it on the burning mass unsparingly, and as the flames increased they revealed some broken spars and planks that greatly assisted in increasing the bonfire and enabling our adventurers to look about them.

It was a cavern, but not of any great extent, being no more than about forty feet in length and fifteen in breadth, near the opening, but it grew gradually narrower, until at the extreme end it came almost to a point.

But here there was a peculiarity.

A natural cavity presented itself in the rock, exactly resembling that of an old-fashioned fireplace; and still further to carry out the similarity, the upper part of the cavity was hollow, as a chimney would be, and extended upwards to an apparently indefinite extent.

"See," exclaimed Stronghand, who was exploring the recesses, "here is a regular old-fashioned hearth and fire-place carved by dame nature, in a cave."

"Our fire would burn better here, I think," observed Firebrand, "than where it is, and give more light and heat."

"I think so, too," said Mark. "It will not be difficulty to move it."

Accordingly, using two flat pieces of plank for the purpose, they contrived to transfer the smouldering ashes from their central position to the end of the cavern.

This operation had to a great extent extinguished the fire, they, therefore heaped on more of the dry sea-weed and some pieces of wood, and left it to burn up, while they went to bring in their Spanish friends from the outside. Taking them one by one by the head and heels, they carried them into the cavern, and placed them near the fire.

The visages of the three Spaniards gradually lost their expression of despair as they caught sight of the welcome blaze.

They were all but frozen, and the mere idea of being first thawed and afterwards dried was pleasant so contemplate.

The fire, too, began to recover itself, and Mark threw on some more pieces of wood that crackled and blazed, and added greatly to the heat.

In a very short time the Spaniards under its influence began to steam like three baked potatoes.

"Ah!" they exclaimed, "this is pleasant! —this is delightful!"

"I want my supper," murmured the hungry Juan.

"I wish they would untie our hands," remarked Don Diegos.

"Senors Inglese!" exclaimed Captain Ortez, boldly, "in the name of my friends allow me to request you to untie our hands."

"Impossible!"

"But, senor, remember we are Spaniards."

"That is the very reason why we tie you."

"But we are also gentlemen!" urged the captain, with great dignity, "Spanish gentlemen!"

"Possibly you may be," replied Stronghand, in a tone that left considerable room for a doubt whether he quite believed the assertion.

Captain Ortez noted the tone, and it excited his strong indignation.

He was steaming on the outside, and boiling within.

"You speak, sir, as though you doubted my words," he said, fiercely; "you evidently do not believe me."

"I believe in nothing Spanish but one thing," replied Stronghand, with frigid coolness.

"What is that?"

"Spanish onions!"

The faces of the three Dons turned yellow with rage, at which the Englishmen laughed.

"You shall pay for this one day, rascals!" cried Captain Ortez, grinning spitefully, "depend on that."

"Ha! ha! ha!" laughed the Englishmen again.

"Ha! ha! ha!" echoed a voice that seemed

to come from nowhere, and sounded very hollow. Every one heard it.

The Spaniards paused and looked at one another mysteriously.

"What was that?" they whispered.

"It is the same voice we heard before," said Mark, in a low tone to his comrade, "whence does it come?"

This seemed a very difficult point to discover, so Stronghand threw on some more wood, and resolved to think no more about it.

The Spaniards, however, were not able to dismiss the incident from their minds so easily.

"Was it the voice of our patron saint?" asked Don Diego.

"If it was," returned Juan, in a melancholy tone; "he was laughing at us, and he would not do that."

"Certainly not!" acquiesced Captain Ortez, with moody, knitted brows; "this cave is the resort of evil spirits; the voice we heard was not a human voice—the laugh was hollow and unearthly; I fancy I can hear it now, and ——"

"Diddle dum di, doodle day," sang the mysterious, unseen being.

"There! did you hear?" exclaimed Ortez, the perspiration bedewing his brow, "it is the voice of the spirit."

"What did it say?" inquired Juan, with much trepidation.

"Deedledum day didle doo," answered the captain, with much solemnity.

"What does it mean?"

"Who can translate the language of another world?" returned Captain Ortez; "I know not what it means; it is evidently some powerful incantation."

"Do these English know what it means?" asked Juan.

"It means the fire wants stirring," answered Stronghand, with a laugh that appeared terribly reckless to the superstitious Spaniards, at the same time raising the burning mass that blazed and crackled fiercely, and sent a shower of sparks flying up the rocky chimney.

And now came a new surprise, as the voice again fell on the ears of all present.

It spoke now in ejaculations, and seemed to suggest very strongly that some one was up the chimney who seemed to be divided between the necessity of yielding to the momentarily increasing heat of the flame and a desire to be jolly under difficulties. It was something to this effect—

"Diddledum-di-doodle—oh! how warm it's getting all of a sudden—I think some one's been lighting a fire underneath—oh, yes! that must be it—and I got up here to get out of the way. Out of the frying-pan into the—oh! oh! it's getting hotter than ever—oh, dear! oh, diddledum-di-doodle—oh, murder! oh, scissors! fire! I'm scorching! Old Nick himself could'nt stand this! oh! oh! o——h!"

At this juncture the speaker, whoever he was, came down the chimney with a sudden crash, that startled the three Dons terrifically.

They began mumbling their prayers, and almost rolled over one another in their efforts to get out of the way.

The new comer, who had pitched head first into the midst of the fire, rolled also.

In fact he turned a summersault, as the shortest way of getting out of the burning mass, and fell on his back, from which position he scrambled up, and went on his knees in a penitental attitude, his hands clasped, his hair (all that had not been singed off) standing on end, and his eyes and mouth full of grey ashes.

"I beg your pardon, gentlemen," he gasped excitedly, "I—I didn't know I was intruding. I-a-diddle-dum-di. no! I don't mean that —strike me but hear me; no, I mean hear me but don't strike me. I've jest come from the Injies! I've been taken prisoner by the Spaniards; my name's Peter Flight! I've got a father and mother, and sisters and brothers in London all, expecting me; spare my life; I feel very queer, and in short, diddle-dum-di-doodle-day!"

And with this eccentric termination to his rambling account the youth, for he was but young, and particularly tall for his age, collapsed, and did a quiet faint, using the back of Captain Ortez for his pillow, who howled out in Spanish that the evil spirit had got him.

Stronghand looked at Firebrand, and then at the luckless Peter.

"This is a fellow-countryman, not a Spaniard," he said, "we must help him."

They accordingly raised him, and Stronghand gave him a draught of brandy from his flask, which revived him so rapidly that he was soon able to sit up and relate his history in a more collected and definite manner.

This, however, we must leave for another chapter, whilst we follow our hero, Rupert the Ready.

CHAPTER XXIX.

NEARLY LOST.

HE, in the meantime, utterly regardless of the fury of the elements, the angry sea that roared around him, the frozen sleet that the wind dashed fiercely in his face, till he was almost blinded; intent only upon one object, that of obtaining the despatches for the governor of the fortress, was rapidly nearing the Santa Maria.

The wind was so boisterous that it may easily be imagined his strength and skill were taxed to the utmost to keep the little craft he was in from being suddenly capsized.

But Rupert, besides possessing great physical strength and energy, was a skilful seaman; and never were these qualities in greater requisition than on this night.

Clinging to the tiller with one hand, sometimes standing, but oftener forced on his knees by the fury of the blast, and grasping the bowline that restrained the sail, he guided the frail vessel as a skilful rider might have done a wild horse, and in a short time drew near the massive Spanish galleon.

In spite of the strain on his own energies at that time, he had full power to observe that the giant vessel, though her sails were reefed, was rolling heavily.

The Santa Maria was one of the largest of the Spanish fleet, and as he approached the colossal monster, with her four decks towering upwards like a floating castle, the thought crossed him that he would rather be even in the small boat he was then guiding than in the unwieldly galleon on which he gazed.

"These Spaniards boast of their ships," he soliloquized, "but let them look to them well in such a storm as this. At any moment I should not be surprised to see that floating citadel devoured by the raging waves. She is not fairly balanced. Let them look to her."

There was no time for speculation or soliloquy, for at that moment the fore-topmast of the galleon, yielding to a sudden squall, snapped like a dry twig, only with a much louder crash, and hung suspended by its tackle.

"That's the beginning," he thought, "what will the end be?"

He heard the captain's voice shouting to the crew to cut away the fragment of the mast, and the next moment he was under the lofty stern of the Spaniard.

He had been sighted by someone on board, and when he raised his voice for a rope one was immediately thrown to him.

To this he made his own vessel fast, and then came the questions bawled through a speaking-trumpet; "Who are you? From whence?"

"From Captain Ortez, for the governor's despatches," Rupert called in return, also through a speaking-trumpet.

This was instantly communicated to the captain, who desired him to come on board.

Another rope was thrown him, and by the aid of this, he rapidly clambered up the sides of the galleon, and stood upon deck.

Here everything was in confusion.

The sailors swarmed like bees up the shrouds, cutting the broken topmast away.

Angry exclamations and vehement oaths burst from the lips of those engaged continually, and jarred upon Rupert's ears, especially at such a critical time. They seemed to rival in fierceness and outrival in malignity, the elemental discord then prevailing.

He had, however, not long to wait, being almost instantly conducted to the captain's cabin.

The captain was not there at the moment he entered, but instead a fierce-looking man of some fifty years of age, who regarded him with eager looks of surprise if not suspicion.

Rupert, aware of his critical position if the deception he was practising were discovered, had prepared himself for any circumstances that might await him.

He, therefore, heeded little the keen glance of the only occupant of the cabin besides himself, whose name was Don Alonzo di Aguilar, nor was he surprised to hear him mutter in a low tone of suspicion—

"Captain Diego! Umph!"

At this moment the captain, Don Pedro de Valdis, came into the cabin.

He too started, and looked intently at Rupert, who returned his gaze boldly but courteously.

Don Alonzo rose as the captain entered, and whispering a few words in his ear, with a farewell glance at Rupert went out by another door.

The captain fixed his eyes upon the counterfeit Spaniard for an instant, and then said with stern abruptness,

"You are not Captain Ortez. Why do you take his name?"

"Pardon me, senor, I have not done so," replied Rupert firmly, but respectfully.

"You were announced to me by that name," cried Don Pedro, irritably.

"It must have been some mistake then, captain. I said that I had come from, not that I was Captain Ortez," Rupert explained.

"What is your name?"

Rupert paused for a moment; he had never thought of a fictitious name until that moment, and he felt painfully alive to his neglect.

"Do you not understand me?" cried the captain, irritably; "I ask your name?"

Luckily he remembered that of one of his prisoners, and answered immediately with the utmost frankness,

"Juan de Vasquez."

Still more luckily for him, the captain was not personally acquainted with the young man whose name he had assumed.

"Juan de Vasquez!" repeated the commander, thoughtfully. "You are one of Captain Ortez's officers, are you not?"

"Yes, senor."

"And you come for the governor's despatches?"

"I do, senor."

"Why did he not come himself?"

"He is indisposed, senor, from a violent blow received during the gale to-night, and was unequal to the task of guiding the boat in such stormy weather. Seeing his anxiety, I volunteered my services, which he accepted."

The captain seemed satisfied.

"Where is Captain Ortez now?"

"He his waiting on the beach with Captain Diego for my return with the despatches."

The account given by Rupert so definitely appeared sufficient guarantee to the commander for its truth.

He smiled as he said, "You shall have the despatch;" and going to a small cabinet affixed to the side of the cabin he took from it a sealed letter, which he gave to Rupert, who felt a thrill of joy as his fingers closed upon the packet.

He took from his pouch a small oil-skin case, in which he placed it carefully, and having done so, thrust it into his under vest, next his body.

He had hardly taken this precaution when the vessel lurched so heavily that it was with the utmost difficulty he kept his legs.

Captain Pedro clung to the table, which was a fixture, for support till the vessel righted herself.

"By the mass!" exclaimed he, "this is a night to be remembered. Even the Santa Maria feels it."

"You will excuse me, captain," said Rupert, whose generous nature recoiled from the thought of even his enemies being hurried into eternity at a moment's notice; "but unless you cut away your masts, I fear the Santa Maria will feel more yet than she has ever done."

The captain looked up with sudden indignation at this ominous suggestion.

"Cut away her masts?" he echoed, frowning upon the daring suggester of such demolition. "Do you imagine, sir, I have been all my life at sea without knowing how to manage my ship? What causes you to suggest such a piece of madness?"

"The vessel is overbalanced, senor, replied Rupert, "I am sure of it. It is that which makes her roll so heavily."

"Psha!" exclaimed Don Pedro, scornfully. "You must be mad. What could a vessel like the Santa Maria do without her masts?"

"Better on a night like this than with them. Without them she might float; with them, I think, she is in great peril."

"Psha, you are young and foolish!" cried Don Pedro, passionately; "you will know better what——"

A sudden and terrific crash on deck, and another fearful lurch of the ship, prevented the captain finishing the sentence.

"Good heavens! what is that?" he exclaimed, turning pale.

Before Rupert could give his opinion a piercing shriek, clear and distinct above all the confusion, and trampling of feet overhead reached their ears. Rupert started, and answered the captain's question by asking another.

"Was not that a woman's voice?" he said.

"Likely enough," replied Don Pedro, coolly; "we have women on board. 'Tis nothing. It is not of women I am thinking."

The cabin door opened at this juncture, and one of the lieutenants entered.

"The foremast has gone by the board, senor," he said; "but I think it is a relief rather than a detriment, the vessel seems to ride easier."

The captain glanced at Rupert, whose thoughts were picturing a woman in distress, and who had scarcely noticed the lieutenant's words.

"I shall be on deck in a moment myself," said Pedro, in a tone of subdued irritation, to his officer, who instantly departed.

Hardly had the door closed when again a wild scream penetrated the apartment in which they stood, followed by the appealing cry—

"Help! help me, for the love of heaven!"

Rupert's blood rushed like lightning through his veins.

It was not only a woman's cry for help, but it was an English woman's and that had doubly enlisted his sympathies.

He advanced a step.

"Do you hear that, captain?" he exclaimed indignantly. "You do not surely permit women to be insulted on board this vessel?"

"She is a prisoner, and she is English," replied the captain, indifferently; "do not trouble yourself about her. You have your despatches, you had better depart."

"Not till I am assured of the woman's safety whose cry I have twice heard," returned Rupert, his eyes flashing with indignation. "Who but a base coward would think of countenancing violence to one of the weaker sex, simply because she is a woman and a prisoner? who but a Spaniard?"

Rupert almost hissed these words in the captain's ear, but before he could reply the female voice was again distinctly heard.

"You have cruelly severed me from my family," it cried, "and I am in your power a helpless captive, but rather than yield myself to the vile dishonour you propose, I would die a thousand deaths! Release me, villain! help, help!"

"By heaven! this is too much," exclaimed Rupert, glaring around him like a chained tiger; longing to fly to the rescue, yet ignorant where to direct his course.

At that moment there was a violent scuffling heard at the small door by which Don Alonzo had made his exit, and the screams within were renewed.

"Help, help! Mercy! If you are a gentleman! if you are a man!"

Rupert hesitated no longer.

He drew his sword, and flew towards the door.

The captain placed himself before it, and drew a long bright-barrelled pistol from his belt, which having cocked he presented at our hero, as he said—

"Now if you wish to deliver your despatch, depart while you have the power. Another moment and it will be too late."

"I would not depart though your whole crew stood with their weapons pointed at my breast, until I had tried at least to rescue that poor girl from your clutches, whoever or whatever she may be."

Rupert made a bound like the spring of a panther, and at the same moment the door was burst open inwardly with such sudden force, that Don Pedro was thrown forward on his face, and his pistol exploding, the bullet which he had intended for Rupert's brains was firmly imbedded in the floor of the cabin.

Simultaneously with this a young girl of not more than seventeen years of age, clad only in a loose night dress, her dark hair falling in wild disorder over her fair shoulders, and her eyes gleaming like fire sparks with terror and despair, rushed desperately into the room, followed by Don Alonzo di Aquilar, pale and fierce with excitement and thwarted passion.

The young girl glanced for an instant at Rupert, who stood with his drawn sword ready for an attack, and without hesitation, staggered forward, and sinking at his feet threw her arms round his waist, with desperate intensity, and cried—

"Oh, save me! Save me, senor, from that man!"

"That will I to the last drop of my blood," exclaimed Rupert in his own language.

Never in his life had he seen anything in the shape of woman half so lovely as the fair pleader that knelt before him.

With a cry of joy she recognised her native tongue.

"You are not a Spaniard?" she asked eagerly.

"No, lady, heaven be praised!" answered Rupert, "I am an Englishman, your own countryman; and I'll die before any here shall lay a finger upon you for harm."

The beautiful girl rose from her knees, and glanced at him with trustful gratitude.

The captain had risen to his feet, and now stood by the side of his friend Alonzo.

Both had their swords drawn.

"Release that girl, vile heretic!" shouted the latter, in a voice hoarse with rage.

"I will, when you can take her from me, and not before," returned Rupert with a scornful laugh.

Don Alonzo, without another word, attacked the young sailor like a savage wolf, but at the third blow, Rupert sent his sword flying to the other end of the cabin.

The next moment the captain's weapon followed that of his friend.

Both were disarmed.

"There is not a moment to be lost!" whispered Rupert to the young girl.

At this moment the captain struck a gong violently, and the trampling of feet was heard approaching the cabin.

"If I am taken now all is lost," thought Rupert.

In a moment his mind was made up.

With one blow he dashed out the light and rushed out of the cabin, accompanied by the young girl.

The two baffled Dons followed, but the door was closed.

They tugged at the handle; it refused to open.

Rupert had locked it on the outside.

Foiled in this, the captain hammered at the gong furiously.

Don Alonzo joined in with a volley of fierce oaths.

Rupert waited not but hurried on.

He met several of the crew who asked in a bewildered manner what was the matter.

"The captain wants you," answered Rupert in Spanish, and forward they pressed, leaving him and his fair charge to reach the deck.

The storm was still raging, but Rupert thought not of that.

His chief anxiety was to find himself on board his tiny craft, and with his lovely countrywoman safely at his side.

He hurried along the quarter-deck to the spot where his boat had been tethered.

To his horror the rope had snapped—the boat was gone.

He heard, too, the cries of pursuit.

He felt desperate; to be taken now was death to one, if not both.

The voices of the captain and Don Alonzo, who had been released by the crew, were heard urging on the men to follow.

They would soon be upon them, and what could his single arm avail against so many.

He glanced despairingly out across the stormy waters.

His beautiful companion saw and read that glance rightly.

"There is no hope," she cried.

"None, lady," said Rupert, sadly. "At least, only one; but death is preferable to dishonour?"

"Yes, yes!" she cried firmly; "death a thousand times sooner!"

"Dare you meet the fate that awaits us there?" Rupert asked, pointing to the raging waters.

"Yes, I dare!" she replied; "where you go I will follow."

"Come then," he cried.

As he spoke he hastily divested himself of all superfluous clothing, so that nothing might impede his actions, and then passing his arm round the waist of the young girl he steadied her as she mounted a gun carriage.

In an instant he was at her side.

Clinging to the shrouds with one hand, and still supporting her with his encircling arm, they reached the edge of the bulwarks.

It was enough to appal the stoutest heart to gaze down into the dark pitiless waters, but the thought that it was their only chance of escape from foes still more pitiless decided them.

They remained silent an instant, and each uttered a brief prayer to heaven for mercy —their last, they thought.

"Close your eyes, lady," said Rupert gently, "and when I give the signal leap off with me."

The captain and crew at this moment came crowding up the hatchway, and a loud shout told him they were seen.

A report of fire-arms was heard, and the bullets whistled past and over their heads without effect.

CHAPTER XXX.

PETER FLIGHT'S VICISSITUDES.

"Now!" whispered Rupert.

At once they sprang forward, and the next moment were engulphed in the raging billows.

At first Rupert who was an excellent swimmer, struck out desperately, but it was a vain struggle.

It was only prolonging misery.

The fierce waves dashed over their heads, a deadly agonising despair seized them, and one bitter, desperate cry burst from their throats.

With a last frantic effort their outstretched hands sought to grasp something, if only a straw or a weed, to stand between them and death, but there was nothing.

The fierce blast mocked their wail of anguish; their eyes grew dim and their ears rang with strange music.

Surely all would soon be over.

No! Suddenly Rupert's hand came in contact with a rope.

He grasped it with the strong instinct of self-preservation.

It was firmly fastened to some solid object, and this recalled his failing senses back to life.

He glanced upwards faintly, and as the pale moon peered from a tier of clouds, he recognised the foremast of the Spaniard floating upright in the water, and knew that he was clinging to it.

A sense of safety rushed across his mind; hope sprang up once more in his breast, and clasping the now insensible but lovely burden he could hardly support to his breast, he prayed fervently for her sake that he might live.

* * * * * *

Peter Flight, however, before he was in a condition to give any account of himself, found it necessary to remove the ashes from his eyes and mouth.

This having been accomplished, he rose from his seat on the ground, and went through a slight series of gymnastic evolutions with his arms and legs, in order to ascertain, for his own private satisfaction, that all his joints and muscles were in proper working order.

While he was thus engaged, Mark and Firebrand had an opportunity of contemplating the individual who had been thrown in their way in such a sudden and remarkable manner.

He appeared to be a youth of about nineteen years of age, who had not yet done growing.

Being inclined to be tall, rather than strong and robust in limb, he presented—as boys often do, between the neutral ages of boyhood and manhood—a somewhat lanky and half-starved appearance.

Nevertheless, there was an evidence of spirit in him, from the manner in which he had previously chaunted his misfortunes in verse, to the chorus "diddledum di doodle day," and the energy with which he now, as it were, pulled himself together, without the least regard to the presence of lookers on.

His actions were thoroughly English, and both Stronghand and Firebrand watched him with much satisfaction and amusement.

Peter's face was naturally pale; and as he had had nothing to eat for a couple of days, it was now pinched and drawn in at the cheeks

His features were small, and his nose slightly inclined to turn up; but his round eyes, that twinkled with an unmistakeable spark of fun, and his black hair, set off a countenance that might have been called a comic edition of honesty and good humour, combined with pluck and spirit.

It was quite a treat to our English adventurers, as they waited in the cavern, to watch their countryman's evolutions.

He commenced with a succession of sneezes. rendered imperative by the ash that had intruded itself up his nostrils; then he cleared his throat by a decided and energetic cough, that made the trembling Spaniards shudder again; after this he stalked several times to and fro, throughout the entire length of the cave; then he swung his arms round successively, till he looked like a human Catherine wheel; and finally kicked out in a most fierce and determined manner, first with one leg and then with the other; winding up his performance with a royal salute from his right toe on the hind quarters of the doughty Captain Ortez, whose curled up position certainly offered a very excellent mark for a chance shot.

The Spaniard yelled and rolled over his companions with great precipitation, and Peter, perfectly satisfied, at the state of his limbs, joints, &c., and altogether very much refreshed by his performance, turned towards his fellow-countrymen, with a face genial and smiling, and which his recent exertions had set all a-glow.

"Now, gentlemen, I'm all right," he exclaimed.

"Take another pull at the flask," said Stronghand, handing him the liquor, "and then let us hear your adventures—it will serve to pass away the time."

Peter took the proffered pull with great readiness, and became eloquent immediately.

"My name's Peter, gentlemen— Peter Flight, eldest son of Toby Flight, tailor, of Cripplegate Ward, in the City of London— long live the Queen!"

Mark and Firebrand laughed at this introductory flourish, and Peter continued:

"I've got a lot of young brothers and sisters, at home; I forget at this moment whether it's eleven or twelve—no matter I am the eldest. Dad wanted to make me a tailor, but no! I was of an adventurous disposition, and my soul—I've a great soul, gentlemen—revolted at the idea of stitching doublets and jerkins, besides, I couldn't abear the sitting crossed-legged, my legs wouldn't stand it. I had, moreover, heard of foreign countries, and I longed to cross the sea, and penetrate those distant regions, where fierce tigers and other interesting animals run wild about the streets, and look in at the window upon people as they sit at the social meal, and where deadly snakes are found in your bedroom early in the morning coiled up in your boots !

"I expressed my opinion to my worthy father, who didn't believe in anything but tailoring, and he——"

"Objected ?" put in Mark.

"Yes, by the gods !" exclaimed Peter, he said decidedly I shouldn't go! He was positive; so was I—the dispute waxed warm and the end of it was my paternal relative assaulted me—me his first-born—with the sleeve-board !"

"Is it possible ?" exclaimed Firebrand with affected surprise.

"It is a positive fact !" replied Peter, "I don't mind telling you in confidence, but dad laid me across his knee, and—and administered corporal punishment—in other words, thrashed me soundly. I won't say where he hit me—the honour of a young Briton for-

RUPERT BEFORE THE GOVERNOR OF THE CASTLE.

bids; but you might have heard the whacks on London-bridge, and I couldn't sit down for a fortnight!"

"Poor fellow!" ejaculated Stronghand, sympathetically.

"Poor fellow!" echoed the heroic Peter, in a tone of intense scorn, and an expression on his face to match, "No nothing of the sort; that thrashing was the making of me!"

"Oh, indeed!" said Mark.

"Yes," continued Peter, waving his hand majestically, "I didn't say much at the time, but I thought a great deal, and at the end of a fortnight I quietly packed up my traps, which consisted of a pair of boots, a rapier, and a magnificent pistol without a lock, and left my father's house before breakfast."

"Brave boy!" exclaimed Stronghand.

"I was no longer a boy!" returned Peter, grandly, "the whacking I received, had made me a man! I went down to the docks—fortune favoured me. An English merchant about to sail for the West Injies wanted a boy—I mean a man of all work. As I undertook to do everything that the human frame could possibly be expected to do, Master Stephen Mountjoy received me with favour, and accordingly I embarked with him. He had with him two uncommonly handsome girls—his daughters Adela and Helen.

"Of course you fell in love with one of them?" remarked Firebrand, smiling.

"I did more than that," returned Peter, consequentialy; "I fell in love with both!"

"You are a bold youth," Stronghand exclaimed.

"Yes I am," acquiesced Peter, "ever since that severe castigation with the sleeve-board, my courage has developed in a wonderful manner!"

"And did you confess your passion?"

"Of course I did—I was candid. I told them they were two ducks, and that I adored them both."

"And what did they reply?"

"They burst into a fit of laughter, and called me a great goose!"

"That was insulting—wasn't it?"

"Rather! the blood of the Flights was up, but I reflected that making love to my master's daughters wasn't in the list of my duties; and as I thought I'd been a little over hasty myself, I forgave the 'laughter' and the 'goose' and thought no more about it.

"We arrived at Madras safely, and though I didn't meet any tigers or elephants in the streets, or find a boa constrictor in my pocket or boots all the time I was there, I liked the place very well. My employer, Stephen Mountjoy, was quite a merchant prince, and I had plenty to do trotting about with him. He began to take quite a fancy to me. I was his valet, head clerk, secretary, and in short, general factotum.

"Many a time have I found my knowledge of tailoring stand me in good stead—many a button have I stitched on to the doubtlet of my worthy master, but now, alas!——"

Peter sighed. Sad reflections seemed to crowd across his mind.

"The mention of your master seems to have made you melancholy," said Stronghand.

"It has—it has!" whispered Peter. "We were such a happy family—master, me, and the young ladies. They, too, were just beginning to appreciate me when—oh dear! oh, dear!"

Peter broke down again, but recovering himself, went on.

"We staid at Madras two years, and then, it being rumoured that there was likely to be an invasion of England by the Spaniards, the master thought it would be as well to get back to London before it began.

"I too, was all a-fire to be there—weapon in hand ready to receive them! So we set sail.

"All went very well till we came in sight of the Spanish coast, and then one day we found ourselves surrounded by a lot of ugly-looking floating castles. In fact, I thought they must have been a party of fortresses come out for a stroll, and got to sea by mistake. However they turned out to be ships—Spanish ships. Well, of course, though ours was a merchantman, not a fighting ship, we did our best to keep off the Dons, but they were too strong for us. They hemmed us in, boarded us, and made prisoners of the ship and all in her.

"There was a general sharing of the spoil. Everyone took something or somebody. An ugly-looking, long-moustached captain that commanded the Santa Maria claimed poor Miss Adela; another equally unpleasant individual from the Esperanza took possession of Miss Helen, while the master himself was seized upon by a third party."

"And what was their ultimate fate?" inquired Mark Luton.

"That's more than I can say, replied Peter, shaking his head dolefully. "I only remember hearing the captain of the Esperanza say with a grin as he received Miss Adela, something about 'St. Nicholas,' pointing at the same time towards the shore."

"St. Nicholas," echoed Stronghand, looking expressively at his comrade, "that is the name of the fort yonder, whither we are bound. If she should be be there——"

He broke off suddenly and turned again to Peter.

"And what became of the other young lady and the rest?" he asked.

"Goodness only knows; I don't," answered Peter. "They seemed to me to be all carried off in different directions."

"And into whose hands did you fall?" asked Firebrand.

"Into nobody's. No one seemed to care anything at all about me," answered Peter, "and from what I could guess from their pointings and ugly gestures, there appeared to be a benevolent intention on the part of the Spaniards to blow up the captured English vessel, and me with it. But as I didn't quite coincide in this arrangement, I quietly dropped myself overboard and swam ashore."

"You must be a good swimmer," remarked Stronghand, rather doubtfully.

"No, I can't say I am," confessed the candid Peter, "but I took care to provide myself with a couple of oars. One of these under each arm kept me afloat, and all I had to do was to kick out with my legs."

"Ah, I see, you didn't swim—you kicked yourself ashore," said Firebrand, laughing.

"Yes, I think that was more like it," admitted Peter rather moodily, "and here I've been for the last two days with nothing to eat but a leathern belt and the stuffings of half a dozen buttons. If you happen to have anything in the shape of food, for goodness sake let's have it. If not—much as I dislike foreign meat, I shall certainly be compelled to cut a slice off one of those Dons there."

Peter drew his hanger as he spoke, and with a very ravenous and hungry expression in his features, pointed very expressively with the weapon towards the huddled up Spaniards, who having been long since dried, began to emit an odour not very unlike burnt feathers.

They had contrived so to place themselves that they could peep with one eye at the Englishmen.

The terribly significant action of the famished Peter was distinctly seen and thoroughly appreciated by each one of them, and they quaked inwardly with profound terror.

"Oh, Madre de Dios," groaned Juan de Vasquez, "instead of having supper, we shall be eaten alive."

This miserable anticipation elicited a groan from his companions in distress.

Of this the Englishmen took no notice, but Stronghand said to Peter.

"We have a store of dried meat and bread, together with other necessaries in the boat, so you'll require no Spanish cutlets to-night, at least."

Mark Luton glanced laughingly towards the prisoners, and at once went out of the cave to fetch some provisions.

CHAPTER XXXI.

PETER AND THE SPANIARDS.

IN a few moments he returned with food and a small keg of water, upon which Peter pounced with the avidity resulting from his two days' fast.

The hungry Spaniards watched him with sensations that may be better imagined than described, and looked wistfully towards Stronghand, who, divining their thoughts, said—

"You, senors, who have fared sumptuously to-day, can well afford to wait for twenty-four hours or so without eating. It will do you good."

A deep growl was the only reply.

Mark Luton and Firebrand began now to feel anxious respecting their comrade Rupert.

He had been some time absent, and they would fain have seen him back again.

"I would Rupert were on shore again," exclaimed Mark; "'tis an awful night to be out at sea and in that Spanish soup-plate."

This remark was a contemptuous allusion to the galley in which Rupert the Ready had embarked upon his daring venture.

"Let us go down to the beach and see if he be in sight," suggested Firebrand; "with our glasses we may descry something of him."

"I was going to propose the same thing," answered Stronghand. "Our prisoners are so well bound they cannot possibly escape, and besides our gallant friend Peter will look after them."

"That will I, noble—"he paused. "Excuse me, what are your names?"

"Stronghand and Firebrand," was the answer.

"Very good! Then noble Stronghand and Firebrand," continued Peter, with his mouth full, "I will answer for the safe keeping of these enemies of our country with my life."

"If you need weapons there are some," said Mark, pointing to several he had brought from the boat.

"Thanks!" exclaimed Peter.

Stronghand and his companion stood for an instant at the entrance of the cave, looking out upon the night.

The gale still roared and rushed fiercely past as though it would have swept them away, together with the rocks on which they stood.

"Let us go forth," cried Mark.

"I am with you," said Firebrand.

At this moment a sound, startling from its peculiarity, was borne upon the rushing wind to their ears, and then as suddenly ceased.

It was not the crash of thunder, nor the deafening roar of an explosion, nor yet the wild shriek of a hundred drowning souls, and yet it seemed more awful than any of these.

It rather resembled one mighty gasp for life, as though in that convulsive effort some mighty giant had breathed out his soul, and then came a more awful stillness, as though the very elements stood still, appalled at some tremendous devastation they had accomplished.

Stronghand and Firebrand looked in each other's faces, and read in the mutual glance of their eyes the thought that some dire peril had fallen on one they almost feared to name.

There was an instant's pause, and then with one voice they exclaimed—

"To the beach!" and hurried forward.

Peter in the meantime had concluded his meal, and felt much revived in consequence.

He sat pondering upon past, present, and future events, wondering whether he should ever meet his master and his two fair daughters again, and if so, which it would be his fate to marry.

He became so absorbed that the three Spaniards came to the conclusion that he had fallen asleep.

They were naturally anxious, if possible, to burst their bonds and escape.

Now, if ever, was the time, whilst the two powerful Englishmen were absent, and there was only one long-legged stripling left to guard them.

If they could once get free from the ropes that bound them, they could easily overpower him they thought.

Once out of the cave, aided by the obscurity of night, they could soon reach the fort, where they could detail their wrongs to the governor, and perhaps return with numbers to turn the tables on their captors by capturing them in their turn.

It was worth an effort at least.

Peter still kept motionless—wide awake, but lost in thought.

He had prepared himself, however, like a

skilful general, for a sudden attack, and therefore felt no anxiety about his prisoners.

The Spaniards, being bound hand and feet —the former of these members being tied behind them—it was difficult to arrive at an upright position without a risk of falling.

However, with much effort, and a considerable deal of struggle to keep their balance, they contrived at length to gain their feet, and then they were not much better off, but stood leaning against each other like three unhappy, helpless Guy Fawkeses.

If they could by some means bring the ropes that bound them into immediate proximity with the red-hot ashes, that might possibly sever them.

They could not walk to the fire.

There was only one way to reach it, and that was to jump.

It was a brilliant idea, suggested by the hungry Juan, and carried unanimously.

"Yes, we will jump!" they whispered very softly.

Accordingly, all being ready, they jumped, and did not fall.

Then there was a slight pause, and an eager glance towards their custodian.

No notice, however, being taken by that chivalrous but absorbed individual, they jumped again.

This time, however, not so successfully, as there seemed a general inclination to overbalance, and they had to lean against each other with the utmost perseverance to keep themselves from falling.

Unconsciously Don Juan had set his foot on some hot embers, and as he dug his lower extremities as firmly as possible into the ground to maintain his balance, he very speedily began to feel the full benefit of the burning ash.

At first he determined with Spartan resolution to "grin and bear it;" but under the intense anguish of the burn, while he did the first, he forgot the second, and yelled lustily.

The watchful Peter, startled from his reverie, seized upon all his weapons at once, and confronted the enemy fiercely.

His appearance was certainly startling.

Two large rapiers in his belt, a knife in his mouth, and a long barrelled pistol in each hand, together with a huge sombrero stuck on the back of his head, made up a combination of terrors, which, in addition to the fierce expression of his features was irresistible.

There was also an originality about the manner in which he held his firearms; since, while he presented the left-hand pistol with the muzzle towards the head of Señor Juan, he caused Captain Lorenzo Ortez horrors unutterable by aiming straight in his eye with the butt-end of the right.

This, however, was not perceived by Peter in his haste.

Neither was it observed by the rest, so the mistake did not matter in the least; the result was all the same.

It produced a panic, and that was sufficient.

The terrified Spaniards, who expected nothing less than a bullet at least, perhaps two, in their bodies at the shortest possible notice, stood hobbling about nervously, their knees knocking together, with blanched, yellow physiognomies, and chattering teeth.

"So, senor yellow boys, you thought you were going to escape—did you?" exclaimed Peter, in a stern and awful voice.

The Spaniards, who only understood the threatening tone, but not the words, addressed to them, gasped out something in Spanish, which Peter in his turn did not comprehend; but it seemed something in the way of appeal.

At least, so Mr. Flight, junior, translated it.

But he shook his head fiercely in reply.

"Mercy! no, no — no mercy! bullets! death! gore! decapitation! perforation! and destruction!" he said.

The Spaniards groaned piteously, and swayed to and fro like agitated poplars.

Peter coolly proceeded to cock the pistols, and place the rapiers on the ground on each side of him.

He then screwed up one eye, and contemplated the Dons ferociously with the other.

"Now," he said, in a firm voice and decided manner, "business is business! and when I've anything to do I like to do it at once!"

He then coolly picked up a sword and pistol, and stood upright on his feet.

"Prisoners!" he exclaimed, "I find you attempting to escape; I therefore sentence you to instant execution!"

As he spoke he presented the pistol at the head of Captain Lorenzo Ortez, who made frantic efforts to thrust himself between his two friends, who, however, backed him up so manfully that retreat was impossible.

"Now, now, now, I will give gold! I am rich!" he yelled out in Spanish. "Do not shoot me! shoot my friends instead! spare me, and I will make your fortune!"

But this generous appeal was quite thrown away upon Peter, who frowned more sternly than ever from beneath the wide sombrero, and said—

"I shall shoot you first, and then decapitate you all!"

He elevated the point of his pistol, and fired.

There was a terrific bang that echoed through the cave like thunder.

The bullet, as Peter intended, flew over their heads, and flattened itself against the rock behind them, fragments of which flew out upon their heads rather sharply.

They were all confident they were mortally wounded, and in this belief their legs gave way under them, and they once more lay curled up on the ground like three periwinkles without their shells.

Peter, perfectly satisfied with the result of his performance, made up the fire, accommodated the Spaniards with a kick all round, and walked to the entrance of the cavern, where he stood looking out and listening to the shrill blast.

CHAPTER XXXII.

A NIGHT OF AWFUL PERIL.

RUPERT'S prayer was answered.

Hardly had it passed his lips when he felt his heart, which a few moments before had been ready to sink with despair, buoyed up with a new and sudden hope.

The giant mast, from the superior length of the part submerged, and which was bound with iron bands, floated in an upright position.

A considerable portion of tackle and rope still remained attached to the upper portion, and in this Rupert entwined himself as firmly as possible.

It was a matter of great difficulty to do this, since his left arm was entirely occupied in supporting the senseless form of the young English girl, who still lay senseless on his breast.

It taxed his powers to the very utmost in that raging sea to keep her head above water, especially weakened as he was with his previous exertion.

Without the greatest care his precious charge might have been quietly and easily drowned in his arms.

But in the new impulse of hope that a merciful heaven had given him, he felt that her life must be preserved.

It was this feeling that prompted him to struggle still, and to feel that even in that apparently hopeless position deliverance still might come.

He glanced down at the pale face of the beautiful creature he held clasped to his breast so helpless and unconscious, and he felt he loved her for that very helplessness.

He felt that, though comparatively strangers to each other, it would have almost broken his heart to think those lustrous dark eyes would never open to look on him again.

Once more he sent up a brief, but fervent ejaculation to the ruler of the winds and waves, that she might be spared.

As if in answer to his petition, Adela Mountjoy, for it was she, sighed deeply, and then with a convulsive shudder opened her eyes wildly, and gazed around her.

A terrified shriek burst from her lips, but Rupert gently soothed her, so far as he could.

"Hush, lady! Do not despair," he cried. "Remember, you are no longer on board the Spaniard."

"Oh no, no, no!" she gasped. "Thank heaven for that."

"Our only enemies now are the elements," said Rupert, soothingly.

"And they are less fierce than men," she replied, as though she appreciated the consolation.

"Do not speak or cry out," Rupert continued; "husband your strength. The mast to which we are clinging will float, and with the returning light of day a vessel may come in sight, or some deliverance may arise to proved that heaven never forgets those who trust its mercy."

Rupert said this to inspire hope in the breast of the timid, shivering maiden who clung to him, though he was obliged to confess even to himself that their position was imminently critical.

It might chance that with the morning light the boats of the Santa Maria would put off, and they again fall into the captain's hands. If so their doom was certain.

There was, however, still one strong hope, and that was that his staunch comrades, finding that he did not return would start in search.

It was this thought that cheered him more than any other.

Still, under any circumstances, his position and that of his companions would be perilous, even if they discovered him.

The task they had undertaken was in itself hazardous in the extreme, and burdened with the additional responsibility of providing for and preserving a young and beautiful girl on a hostile shore, where every one they encountered was a foe, it would be almost more than mortal power could perform.

Still, however, he tried to hope the best, and to a great extent succeeded.

But now a new and unexpected danger awaited them.

The captain of the Santa Maria, and his friend Don Alonzo di Aguilar, utterly foiled by the desperate leap of Rupert and Adela into the waves, were still consoled by the thought that they had escaped one danger to perish miserably by another.

Their surprise and chagrin may therefore be imagined when after a few moments, and just as Don Alonzo was biting his lip moodily and execrating the fate that had robbed him of so rich and beautiful a prize as Adela Mountjoy, one of the crew pointed eagerly to the spot where in the dark waters the faint moonbeams fell with their chill light upon the white forms of those whom they imagined to be buried in the ocean's depths.

At first superstition caused a shudder of horror, from the idea that they gazed upon the spirits of the departed, rising in judgment against them from the yawning waves.

But as they strained their eyes upon the strange sight, and perceived the floating mast to which Rupert clung with Adela in his fostering arms, they saw and understood that it was the living and not the dead they gazed upon, and that those whom they would have made their victims had escaped from their hands at last.

For a moment the sight seemed to paralyze their faculties, and then came the thought that they might yet be captured.

The sea was raging violently, and the monster galleon rolled like some unwieldy denizen of the deep that seemed ill at rest.

The captain, however, believed profoundly in the Santa Maria, and laughed to scorn the ominous but true forebodings of Rupert the Ready.

As for Don Alonzo, his passion rekindled at the sight of Adela, and without troubling himself about any thing but the repossession of his beautiful prize, he cordially acquiesced in the command—

"Let two boats be manned instantly!"

It was almost an insane order on such a night, but then Don Alonzo was not going in either, and that made all the difference.

Had he been compelled to join the dangerous expedition, he would not have been so eager.

The orders were, however, promptly obeyed.

The boats were, with much difficulty, got over the vessel's side, and twenty-four seamen were floating in a few minutes between life and death.

The Captain bawled his last orders through his speaking trumpet, and they fell hoarse and grating on the ears of those who heard them.

"Bring them on board alive, if possible; if not dead!"

Then, as if in rebuke at the cruel mandate, a hollow peal of thunder moaned across the heavens, followed by a fierce squall that dashed the frail boats madly upwards, and sent a heavy sea like a broadside clean over the bows of the galleon.

The vessel reeled with the mighty shock, but recovered herself, and the captain laughed in impious confidence.

"Did you see that?" he observed to his friend, Don Alonzo, boastfully, "and that English gaillard, had the impertinence to hint that the Santa Maria was in danger—psha!"

Don Alonzo, whatever he might have thought, did not say much. His eyes were fixed upon the boat.

Don Alonzo, however, remarked in a dry abstracted manner, shrugging his shoulders as he spoke—

"You have lost your foremast, Pedro."

"We may lose them all," was the reply, "and still the Santa Maria will float."

The captain was right there.

Had she lost her masts, he would have been comparatively safe. Her peril lay in her not having lost them.

Both Don Pedro and Don Alonzo watched the boats.

The night was somewhat misty, and the spray dashed at frequent intervals in Rupert's face, prevented him seeing distinctly.

He, however, kept his glances divided between the galleon and the shore.

He observed the shock the vessel had received from the last rush of the angry waters over her deck, and in spite of his own critical position, his natural goodness of heart made him shudder as he saw her roll heavily under it, ere she could right herself again.

"Good Heaven!" he cried, "I thought it was all over then. Though they are my enemies, I would not see so many poor souls hurried into eternity at a moment's notice. Heaven help them!"

While he uttered this petition he little knew the intentions towards himself of those for whom he prayed.

He was soon, however, apprised of them.

Hardly had the words left his lips, when he discerned the two dark objects rising and falling at intervals, between himself and the hull of the Spaniard.

"We are seen," he cried, "and they are coming to take us."

A very few moments convinced him that he was right in his conjecture.

Every moment brought the boats nearer.

Adela Mountjoy, who had now fully recovered consciousness, and whose eyes rested trustfully on the face of him who supported her, as though she would in that earnest gaze have kept her drooping spirits from yielding to the despair that well-nigh overpowered her, saw from the change of expression in his features, and the fixed look of his eye that something unusual had happened, or that some new peril was at hand.

"What is the matter?" she asked, faintly, a sickening sensation creeping over her heart as she did so, yet she hardly knew why. "Why do you look so earnestly?" she added.

She had not even the energy left to turn her head, but trusted to Rupert for the answer to her question.

He gazed down sadly into her pale face, and in a voice of mingled despair and bitterness, though he strove to control it, said—

"They have put out the boats, and are coming to take us."

A spasm of intense dread spread over Adela's lovely features at these words, and he could feel her cling to him more convulsively than ever.

"You will not let them take me," she murmured in a broken voice. "I would rather die than fall into their hands."

It was a terrible alternative, but there was an earnestness in her tone that proved she was prepared to welcome a watery grave rather than be recaptured by the Spaniards.

"Promise me," she continued, pleadingly, "that, if the worst come, and there is no chance of escape, you will let me sink beneath the waves that encircle us, and not fall again into his hands!"

She shuddered as she spoke, more at the idea of such a fate than in the contemplation of the death she voluntarily accepted in preference.

Rupert bent down to her assuringly, and said in a low, earnest tone—

"I promise you they shall never take you—alive at least."

"Oh, thank you. You will let me die rather?"

Rupert could hardly force himself to speak the word, but with effort he answered—

"Yes!" and then in a firmer tone he whispered, as he strained her to his breast, "we will die together!"

"Then I do not fear," was Adela's reply.

The boats were now close at hand, rising and falling on the mountainous waves.

Rupert could distinctly see the fierce swarthy faces of the crew, and they could see him and his fair companion.

At this juncture, too, a blue light ignited on the deck of the galleon, spread a glare over the surface of the ocean, rendering objects as distinct as in the day.

Half of the crew of each boat served the oars, the remaining half carried fire-arms in their hands.

There seemed little hope now unless the violent motion of the boats should prevent the possibility of the men taking aim.

The galleys had now advanced to within twenty yards of the floating mast to which Rupert clung.

The Spanish lieutenant shouted through his speaking-trumpet—

"Our orders are to take you, and convey you on board the Santa Maria."

"We heed not your orders," Rupert shouted in return, with all the reckless defiance of despair, "since we are resolved not to be taken."

"You cannot escape us!" again bawled the officer, "we must capture you, alive or dead; our orders are imperative, therefore yield yourselves!"

"Not though you were backed by your whole fleet!" cried Rupert.

"You defy us!" roared the lieutenant.

"We do! you, your captain, and your country—all!"

There was a slight pause of preparation, and then came the hoarse command—

"Fire!"

There was a report of musketry, and several bullets came crashing into the mast over Rupert's head, but neither he nor his charge was injured. Rupert laughed loudly in desperate defiance, but his laugh suddenly ceased, for as the smoke of the volley cleared away, nothing remained but a vacant space.

Neither boats nor foes were left upon the surface of the waves.

All were gone!

The mighty deep had swallowed them up, and the lurid blue light from the Spaniard's deck had lighted them to their ocean grave.

Once more Rupert's heart glowed with hope at this signal deliverance.

"Heaven has interposed in our behalf!" he cried, "our enemies have perished."

But the retribution was not yet complete. Another and far more awful catastrophe was yet to follow.

A loud cry of rage and dismay had burst from the throats of the Spanish captain and crew as they saw the boats engulphed, and this had hardly died away, when a tremendous and overpowering body of water swept over the quarters of the Santa Maria, carrying with it death and destruction, extinguishing the ghastly light, and shrouding the terrible moment in appalling darkness.

The giant vessel quivered and reeled like a scared thing under the mighty shock, but ere she could recover herself, another sea of equal magnitude swept her decks from stem to stern.

She reeled, lurched, and then a wild, despairing, heart-sickening cry burst from the doomed crew, for they felt their hour was come.

It was this cry that reached the ears of Mark Luton and Firebrand, as they stood in the cavern.

And the hour had come!

For a moment the galleon hung, as it were, oscillating between sea and sky, at a terrific angle, of about 35 degrees, and then rolled over, utterly vanquished.

For a moment only she remained as though stunned and motionless, keel upwards, and then with a sudden plunge disappeared with her living freight and costly treasure into the ocean depths, never to rise again.

And now arose a new and more imminent peril than any our hero and heroine had yet experienced.

The appalling spectacle of the foundering of the Santa Maria had rivetted their eyes and almost stopped the pulses of their hearts.

So absorbed were they for the time that they did not hear friendly voices shouting to them.

It was not till Rupert observed they were being borne onwards with lightning rapidity that he awoke to the consciousness that they were under the influence of some sudden and mighty power.

They were not hurried forward in a straight line, but whirled round and round in a circle till his brain reeled again.

Adela clung to him and gasped for breath.

"Good Heaven! what is this?" she cried.

Rupert glanced downwards, and the sight that met his gaze answered the question.

They were on the edge of a gigantic whirlpool, whose depths from the rapidity of the spiral motion looked like polished glass, and gradually they were being sucked within it.

A cry of horror burst from his agonised soul as he cried in utter despair—

"We are in the vortex of the sinking ship! Heaven help us, for there is no other hope!"

CHAPTER XXXIII.

IN THE DEPTHS OF THE WHIRLPOOL.

A SHUDDER of terror thrilled through the frame of Adela Mountjoy, as Rupert's words fell almost like a death-knell on her ear, but she uttered no cry.

The poor girl, in her helplessness, simply clung to her only earthly protector still more tenaciously, although, as a Christian, woman she felt the full force of the word—"Heaven alone can save us!"

Once, only for an instant, she turned her head and glanced aside, and then her eye looked down into the polished depths of the vortex, on the edge of which they were being whirled round and round with incredible swiftness.

The motion was so rapid and so steady that it was hardly like motion; and yet it was too palpable that they were being hurried on to an appalling, apparently inevitable doom.

Her brain reeled at the sight, and she felt giddy and sick; but the moment was one of that overpowering intensity that she did not faint.

There seemed a stern necessity that compelled every sense to retain its full vitality during that awful crisis.

Round! round! round! round! they whirled, as though some mighty engine was in operation to stir the dark waters into that terrific gyration, on the surface of which they were borne as helplessly as twigs or straws.

But this did not last long.

Gradually they began to descend.

There was no escaping the dreadful fact that the vast eddy was gradually sucking them into its rapacious jaws.

Lower and lower they were sinking with remorseless certainty.

Now, as they looked up, they could see distinctly that they were hemmed in on every side by the smooth wall of revolving waters.

All that could be seen else was the sky, with its stormy clouds over their heads.

Then a strange fascination seemed to seize them, and they found their eyes fastening again, with a species of irresistible attraction, on the whirling element that held them captive in its spiral stream.

Lower and lower they sank.

Down! down! down! till the dark polished sides of the vortex towered above them like walls of steel.

They no longer experienced terror.

Every sense of dread seemed absorbed in a kind of entranced curiosity.

They were enthralled—fascinated—spell-bound.

It was under this strange and terrible fascination both Rupert and Adela found themselves noticing the most trivial circumstances.

Now and then a minute fragment of wood would arrest their attention, as it whirled round; then a tiny cluster of sea sand; presently a piece of paper like an open letter appeared on the surface for an instant.

They began to conjecture as to how long that letter had been written, who had written it, and what might be its contents.

"It might have been a love-letter," thought Adela, "written by some young sailor to his mistress. The poor girl will never get it now!" she repeated.

Then she went on to wonder if the writer of the letter was dead, whether he had gone to the bottom with the doomed ship, or whether he was at that moment struggling for life in the fierce waters; if so, how sincerely she pitied him, though without a thought of pity for her own fate.

Rupert also went through a similar mental commentary on the floating scrap of paper.

"It must be a despatch," he thought; "something important, most probably—some critical intelligence perhaps. It would never reach its destination now at all events. It might rise to the surface in time, and be picked up. How strange if it should fall into the hands of an English vessel! What important news it might contain," &c., &c.

It may seem almost absurd to mention these passing ideas that entered the brains of Rupert and Adela at that moment, as being too trivial to have found a place in their minds in such a momentous crisis.

But what boy or man is there amongst us, who has been in situations of imminent peril, who has not in a second's space found his whole life rushing before him, even to the most minute and insignificant details?

We all know the wonderful rapidity of thought under such circumstances.

Nor is its peculiarity less remarkable than its rapidity.

Many a great hero, when a sudden and violent death has stared him in the face, has in that awful moment forgotten the weightier sins of his past life, and found himself dwelling on the comparatively trivial act of an angry blow given to a dog, when he was a schoolboy fifty years ago.

It is rather in this latter phase we must regard the strange abstraction of our hero and heroine.

Their minds seemed to be diverted from their danger that was still increasing every moment.

They were going quietly to destruction in a kind of dreamy torpor.

Presently, however, voices reached their ears.

Rupert recognised them at once, but they excited no emotion.

Nor did Adela attempt to arouse him to the fact, although she also heard them distinctly.

She too was influenced in the same manner as her companion.

But though they seemed so oblivious to their awful peril (it was perhaps a merciful interposition of Providence that they were so), they were perfectly conscious of passing events, as the following dialogue will prove:—

"That is Mark's voice," said Rupert, dreamily, as Stronghand's powerful halloo came echoing over the stormy ocean.

"Who is Mark?" Adela inquired in a quiet, calm tone, in which there was hardly any curiosity.

"Mark Luton — dear old Mark! — my friend," replied Rupert, "a big, strong giant, and a staunch, true man."

He spoke as placidly as though he had been seated by Adela's side in some quiet country nook in his own island.

"Ha! there's Firebrand's voice, too," he continued, with as little emotion as before.

"Who is Firebrand—another friend?"

"Yes!"

"Why do they call?"

"They have come in search of me in the boat."

It did not seem to strike Rupert to call out in return.

Nor did Adela suggest any such effort. She simply ejaculated "Oh!" and then added, "will they find us?"

Rupert did not reply. The idea had suddenly struck him that the boat which contained his friends would be drawn into the whirlpool in which they themselves were engulphed, and he was now in a curious state of mental cogitation as to the result of such a catastrophe.

Would the vessel float on the edge, or would it sink gradually, as they had done? Would it descend low enough in the vortex for them to reach it? If so, what a strange meeting !—how astonished Stronghand and Firebrand would be to meet him in that watery abyss !

Again the shouts of his friends reached his ears.

This time they burst in suddenly upon his abstraction, and to a certain extent broke the lethargic spell that bound him.

It seemed to have had a similar effect upon Adela, for she uttered a shrill cry.

They were beginning to awake to the horror of their position.

The shriek of the young girl, following upon the shouts of his comrades, brought Rupert back completely to a state of consciousness, and he then discovered to his horror that by some means or other he had lost his hold of the mast that had hitherto supported them.

Whether in his state of temporary forgetfulness he had unconsciously relaxed his hold, or whether the violent eddy had broken the rope to which he clung, he knew not.

All that he did know was that he was severed from the frail refuge, and that the mast was being hurried on before him quite out of arm's reach.

It was with a feeling of agonising despair that he realised this truth, and a wild cry burst from him—

"Mark ! Firebrand ! we are here ! For Heaven's sake help us !" he shouted.

A cheering cry was wafted towards him.

"They hear us !" he cried, and then in a gloomy tone, he added, "but how can they reach us here ?"

Adela looked piteously around her, and her heart sank within her at the utter hopelessness of the prospect.

"Rupert ahoy !" shouted Stronghand again.

It gladdened his heart to hear the friendly voice, but at the same moment the peril his companions would be in, were they caught in the whirlpool, rushed across him.

He had now awakened from his dream, and his soul recoiled from the thought of involving his friends in a snare that would inevitably destroy them without the smallest chance of rescuing him or his companion.

He felt he would have given the world if he could have warned them.

He now shouted wildly—

"Keep away ! do not approach or you will be lost !"

But still he heard the cries of his friends.

His voice, however, had been against the wind, and though it had reached the ears of his staunch comrades, the warning his words conveyed was utterly inaudible.

One circumstance, however, was remarkable, that though they were going gradually down—down—lower and lower, they did not sink beneath the surface of the water.

But this Rupert attributed justly to the rapid whirl of the vortex.

But this would not avail them long.

They were rapidly reaching the bottom, and then they would be overwhelmed.

He glanced down at Adela, and, as if moved by a similar impulse, she looked up.

Their eyes met, and in that mutual gaze they understood each other's thoughts.

"There is no hope !" murmured the young girl, faintly.

"None !" replied Rupert, in a sad voice.

Again came the cry across the waters—

"Rupert the Ready—ahoy !"

It sounded that time almost like a mockery, and he felt too heart-sick to reply.

His head sank moodily forward, and he closed his eyes involuntarily, whilst the whirling motion of the fierce eddy seemed stronger than ever.

Round they went still with giddy rapidity—round—round—round — round — yet still they sank not.

Rupert was a brave man, but his heart sickened at the thought of being entombed with his lovely burden in that pitiless gulf.

Every moment, too, as the shouts of his friends drew nearer, he expected to see the vessel in which they had embarked come rushing and plunging down into the vortex.

With a kind of horror-stricken anticipation he looked suddenly upwards, with a start, as though to meet the realization of the horrid catastrophe.

But, instead, to his great astonishment, the water wall around him had sensibly decreased in height, and even while he was endeavouring to account for this circumstance, he felt that they were gradually ascending, and once more there flashed across his breast the cheering hope that they might yet be rescued from the very jaws of destruction.

He could shout now, and he did so—frantically, wildly—still continuing to ascend like a cork to the surface.

"Mark—Firebrand ! help ! help !"

"We are here, Rupert. What cheer, mate ?" was the answer.

The vast whirlpool had now closed its yawning mouth, and Rupert and Adela once more floated on the crested waves, whilst at a short distance from them the small craft, manned by Mark Luton and Firebrand, was bounding towards them as though conscious her errand was one of life and death.

Rupert was exhausted.

He had scarcely power to make an effort. He could only gasp—

"Quick, Mark, quick ! my strength is gone."

The next moment the boat had reached him.

The strong arms of Mark Luton, grasped his, and he felt himself and his now senseless burden hoisted on board.

Then with a last thought of the dire peril he had escaped on that eventful night, and a thrill of gratitude that he was once more in safety, a dark mist gathered over his fainting senses, and he remembered no more.

CHAPTER XXXIV.

THE PHANTOM BARK.

THE events of the last chapter, although they took some time to describe, occupied in reality but a few moments.

Not more than five minutes elapsed from the foundering of the ill-fated Santa Maria to the moment when Rupert and Adela were safely hauled on board the English galley.

The violence of the gale had now in a great measure abated, and there was every prospect of being able to reach the shore, at the point from which they started, with ease and safety.

A heavy mist, however, hung over the waters that still foamed and swelled from the effects of the recent hurricane.

However, our adventurers were provided with a lantern, the rays of which lighted up the compass, and thus they were enabled to steer their course with sufficient certainty.

They had, moreover, provisions in the vessel, wine, and brandy, and with the latter restoratives Rupert and his fair charge were soon restored to life and consciousness.

Stronghand, as he gazed upon the lifeless pair, had wondered to himself how Rupert came to be thus fettered with a young and beautiful girl, and though he felt quite convinced that his chivalrous comrade would be able to account satisfactorily for his interesting though responsible charge as soon as he was able to speak, still Mark could not in the meanwhile avoid sundry doubts rising in his mind as to what they should possibly do with her.

A woman at such a time, and circumstanced as they were, was the very last encumbrance he would have bargained for.

Let not my readers, however, on this account accuse Stronghand of any lack of chivalrous feeling.

On the contrary, with all his size and strength he had a kind and generous spirit; and when he regretted the presence of Adela, it was quite as much for her own sake as on account of himself and his companions.

It may be remembered also that precisely similar thoughts had occurred to Rupert himself.

The young officer was soon himself again, and able to relate to Stronghand the circumstances under which Adela had claimed his protection, together with the sinking of the galleon, and their subsequent perils in the vortex of the whirlpool.

"I never thought to have seen you again, old comrade," he exclaimed affectionately, extending his hand to Mark Luton, who took it, and returned the grasp with equal sincerity.

"Never mind, captain," he replied, "'all's well that ends well!' Let us rejoice that for once in your life you were mistaken."

"My brave preserver!" Adela exclaimed, addressing Rupert in a voice that trembled with emotion, "how can I thank you for your generous care? But for you I must have perished miserably. May heaven reward you!"

Rupert assured her gallantly that he was already rewarded for his poor services in the pleasure he felt at seeing her in safety, so far restored, and last, not least, so close still to his side.

Adela was snugly wrapped in a warm sea cloak which, though it obscured the beauty of her figure, added greatly to her comfort, chilled as she had been by her immersion in the water.

The vessel bounded over the waves, and seemed to promise a speedy arrival at the land, where they hoped to find a fire awaiting them in the cavern, when suddenly Firebrand exclaimed in a hasty whisper—

"Look to larboard!"

Every one looked with eager gaze at the sight which presented itself.

Englishmen are not, as a rule, inclined to superstition, but there are times when peculiar circumstances may render even them liable to unusual impressions.

This moment was one of these peculiar times; and the sight that so impressed them seemed to invest itself with a mystery, which on another occasion might have been easily accounted for.

And now, what was this strange phenomenon, on which the eyes of all in the little bark were so intently fixed? It was this:

At a short distance—not more than forty yards off—was a vessel, apparently the counterpart of their own, floating upon the waves, and proceeding seemingly in the same direction.

Thus far, perhaps there was nothing particularly strange in such an appearance.

In that boisterous night other vessels besides their own might have been seeking to gain the shore.

But this vessel—at first barely perceptible —was suddenly shrouded in a halo of lurid unearthly light, which seemed to pierce the mist, and reveal the bark and crew in marvellous distinctness.

Although the wind blew boisterously, not a sail or a rope appeared affected by the blast. There was no angry fluttering of the one, or quivering of the other.

The vessel, too, was crowded with men, whose fixed-set features wore the ghastly pallor and rigidity of corpses.

Had vessel and crew been carved out of some solid substance, or petrified suddenly into stone, they could not have been more set and motionless—save that motion only which the waves imparted to the bark itself, as it floated on their bosom.

The Englishmen uttered not a word, but kept their eyes fixed on the mysterious vessel, as though fearing to speak, lest the illusion should be dispelled.

At length—in a whisper that from its intensity was more impressive than the loudest tone, Rupert suddenly exclaimed:

"'Tis they! 'Tis they!"

"Who?" asked his comrades in a subdued voice, but with equal earnestness.

"The drowned crew of the Santa Maria," he answered, "I recognize the face of the captain."

Even as he spoke the phantom bark vanished into a mist and was seen no more.

For a few moments there was a dead silence, and then, as though ashamed of the impression he had felt, Stronghand remarked—

"It must have been fancy—what think you, Rupert?"

"We all saw this strange sight—we could not all have been deceived," replied Rupert.

"It may have been some illusion, caused by the moon shining through the mist," suggested Mark.

Rupert shook his head seriously, and observed—

"I know not whether I am growing superstitious, or whether my narrow escape tonight from destruction has left me liable to spectral impressions, but I feel a conviction—laugh at me if you will—that there was no life in the crew we have just looked upon."

"I never yet heard of a dead crew guiding a vessel on a night like this, or any other night for the matter of that," said Stronghand.

"It seemed strange, though, their disappearing so suddenly," remarked Firebrand.

"It did so certainly," acquiesced Mark.

"It was more than strange," continued Rupert, "and until we stand once more safe and sound on dry land, I shall feel inclined to consider it an evil omen."

"Dismiss your fears, then," cried Stronghand, with an assuring laugh, "for we are close upon the shore."

The mist had almost entirely disappeared, and Rupert with much satisfaction, distinctly saw the rocks along the coast.

In a few moments their bark was once more sheltered in the creek where they had moored her at the opening of this story.

The young Englishman was then more than half inclined to think that the strange spectral appearance had been the result of an overwrought brain, and, dismissing it from his mind, turned his attention to the somewhat difficult task of conveying the beautiful girl he had saved to the cavern.

There was only one way, and that was to carry her, and he frankly told her so.

Adela offered no squeamish objections.

Rupert had saved her life, and she shrank not from trusting herself in his arms.

Accordingly wrapping her carefully in the cloak, he raised her, as he would have done a child, and with equal tenderness.

Firebrand led the way with a lantern, and Mark followed behind, laden with sundry bodily comforts in the shape of food and wine, and ready to stretch forth his powerful arm in case of a slip.

It taxed Rupert's strength to the utmost to keep his footing over the irregular rocks; but at length the passage was accomplished, and they all stood safely on the beach.

A few moments more brought them to the cavern, where Peter having effectually quieted the three dons, and made up a roaring fire, was anxiously awaiting them.

No sooner did he catch a glimpse of Adela's beautiful face, peering like a sunbeam from the dark cloak in which she was enveloped, than he uttered an exultant shout.

"Hurrah! hurrah!" he cried, "she's found, she's found! God bless our gracious Queen! hurrah!"

What particular connection there might have been between this invocation and the restoration of Adela Mountjoy, was not exactly clear. But Peter was in the habit of using this expression when exhilarated, and that he was so now there was no doubt.

He capered about, and snapped his fingers, and gave various symptoms of mental aberration, until a howl from Captain Ortez informed him he had planted his heel on that gentleman's dignified nose.

He then suddenly ceased, and approached his master's daughter.

The young lady was delighted to see the good-hearted fellow, and welcomed him warmly.

"I rejoice to see you, Peter! I was afraid those wicked Spaniards had killed you," she said, offering him a very white hand from beneath her cloak, which he took eagerly and raised to his lips, in a kind of respectful rapture.

"That would have been of no consequence," cried Peter, "but I was afraid they'd killed you; that would have been a catastrophe too horrible to contemplate; but I see they haven't! you still live. We shall see old London again! Cheapside and Cripplegate—old dad, old mother, the old shop, and the eleven little Flights; not to mention the sleeve-board, and the cat. It's too much happiness! hurrah! diddledum di doodle day!"

Having uttered this with the utmost heartiness, he squatted himself down on the ground by the side of Adela, who seemed absorbed in sad recollections.

"I fear I shall never again behold my poor father and sister," she said, mournfully, with the tears in her eyes.

O yes, you will!" exclaimed Peter, in a tone of the utmost confidence. "Now we've found one of the family we shall be sure to find the rest, I feel certain of it!"

At this moment Rupert approached.

"We have made such preparations for a meal as our circumstances will permit, and you need support, Miss Adela," he said.

The young girl thanked him with a sweet smile as he assisted her to the provisions.

They had fasted a considerable time, and the repast strengthened and refreshed them.

The three hungry Spaniards, also, came in for a share, and having, after serious investigation, made the discovery that they had not got six bullets each in their bodies, contrived to eat what was placed before them, their hands being untied during supper.

They looked very blank, however, when Peter informed them that stimulants were decidedly unfit for them in their present state, and that they must be content with the pure element of water, and think themselves lucky to get that.

They groaned, curled their moustaches, and finally drank the invigorating fluid, though with many grimaces and contortions of feature.

The meal being finished, the Spaniards were tied up again, and borne off to an adjacent cave which Peter had discovered, the entrance to which was very small, and against which they rolled a heavy mass of rock—as Peter considerately remarked—to prevent them from rolling out.

This done, Adela was left in the charge of

Peter, who, at his own special request, was pledged to guard her with his life, whilst Rupert and his comrades proceeded along the coast to Fort St. Nicholas.

It was nearly midnight when they approached the fortress.

The sentinel challenged them from the battlements above.

"Who goes there?"

"Friends of Spain, and his Majesty Philip the Second."

"What is your errand?"

"Despatches from the Santa Maria."

"Bueno! Good!"

The sentinel, apparently satisfied with the answers he received, continued his march, and Stronghand grasping an iron ring in the wall, gave it a jerk that caused the bell with which it communicated to send forth an iron clang that echoed again through the courtyard of the old fortress.

In a few moments there were evident signs that the summons had been heard.

Lights flashed, and feet came hurrying along, and very shortly an iron wicket opened, and the face of an ancient seneschal appeared, reconnoitring the applicants.

The same questions were put and answered as before, after which the seneschal retired with his information, and in a short time returned.

There was a prodigious rattling of chains and drawing of bolts, and then the ponderous gate swung open slowly, creaking on its hinges as if in great bodily pain.

"Enter, senors!" cried the seneschal.

A small escort of armed soldiers with torches lined the stone passage, and as our daring adventurers passed through, and the portals closed, they faced round and followed them as they, conducted by the old seneschal, went towards the habitable portion of the building.

CHAPTER XXXV.

IN THE FORTRESS.

AT the porch they were met by Don Xavier himself, a pompous, corpulent, sallow, little man, of apparently about fifty years old, who wore an enormous ruff, and a rapier of such inconvenient length that it seemed surprising he had not long ago broken his neck over it.

His Excellency bowed elaborately as they entered, and bade them welcome with grand hauteur, glancing at the same time with a peculiar expression at Rupert's deshabille.

Before leaping into the sea he had discarded his doubtlet, and whatever clothing he could with propriety get rid of he had thrown aside.

Don Xavier looked somewhat ruefully, if not suspiciously, at the undress that appeared to demand an explanation.

Rupert's mind was at that moment utterly abstracted.

As he crossed the courtyard of the fortress his attention had been attracted to a small window, through the iron bars of which a young and beautiful face, shaded by a mass of golden hair, peered anxiously upon the scene below.

The young lady held a lamp in her hand, and the light shone upon her features, and, though his glance was necessarily only momentary, he distinctly saw her face, and was struck with a resemblance he fancied he recognised between it and that of Adela Mountjoy.

He found himself meditating upon this circumstance, and wondering whether there was any relationship between them.

Had he been in the cavern when Peter related the capture of the English vessel by the Spaniards he would have had little doubt about the matter.

One thing he felt certain of, and that was that the young lady, whoever she might be, was English.

"How strange it would be," he mused, "if Adela and she were sisters!"

His meditations were suddenly put a stop to by Mark Luton laying his hand upon his shoulder, and saying in a peculiar tone, which Rupert understood—

"Captain! his Excellency the Governor wishes to speak to you."

"A thousand pardons!" exclaimed Rupert, starting from his reverie, and apologising; "what does your Excellency wish to remark?"

"That I feel particularly chilly, senor, myself, and that I am profoundly surprised to see you in your present state of undress on such a night."

Rupert, who had given no particular thought to his personal appearance, glanced a little ruefully at his imperfect toilette, so little suitable for an official visit.

But he recovered himself instantly with great self-possession, and replied—

"It was my great anxiety to convey the despatch to your Excellency immediately, that induced me to come just as I am."

"Oh yes, yes!" exclaimed the Governor eagerly; "you have the despatch?"

"Yes, your Excellency; and I have great reason to rejoice at being able to reply in the affirmative, since I well-nigh lost my life in preserving it."

"Is it possible?"

"Yes, your Excellency; the boat in which I went out to meet the Santa Maria capsized, and I had to swim ashore."

"Saints preserve us! and you brought the despatch in safety through all?"

"I did, your Excellency."

"Brave man!—then you have just left the Santa Maria?"

"Not an hour ago, senor."

"And you saw Captain de Valdis?"

"It was from his hand I received the despatch."

Rupert did not mention the loss of the Spanish galleon and her crew, but left the governor in ignorance of that catastrophe.

Don Xavier seemed highly pleased that the document he considered so important was in a state of preservation; his eyes sparkled, and he gave his grey moustaches a self-congratulatory twirl, and wriggled his short neck complacently in his voluminous ruff.

"I am very much pleased with your

A FEARFUL APPARITION.

conduct, young man," he said to Rupert, in a tone of patronising condescension, which the latter did not particularly appreciate. "But come, senors," he added, "let us adjourn to the supper-room; the wind here is enough to chill the marrow in one's bones. But first, whom have I the honour of receiving?—your names?"

"Captain Lorenzo Ortez," said Rupert, boldly.

"Captain Diego, and Juan de Vasquez," added Stronghand and Firebrand respectively.

"Very good, then follow me!" exclaimed Don Xavier.

The governor led the way along a wide

stone corridor, which branched off right and left into smaller passages.

But he kept straight on until he reached the end, where there was a door, which he opened.

"Enter, senors," he cried, as he went into the apartment.

It was a large room into which our adventurers entered; and if somewhat heavy and sombre in its hangings and furniture, was nevertheless warm and comfortable.

A roaring fire blazed in the grate, and a candelabra of wax tapers diffused a pleasant light around, and afforded a delightful contrast to the dark, cheerless scene without.

The table was garnished with a profusion of bottles and the remains of a repast.

The Don rubbed his hands cheerfully; his small eyes twinkled, and his sallow cheek almost glowed, as he surveyed the table first and then his guests.

"I have already taken a slight repast, senors," he said; "but I shall endeavour to sup again out of compliment to you."

The Don was a great gourmand, and the arrival of the Englishmen, whom he fully believed to be his own countrymen, was a good excuse for an additional gorge.

"Come gentlemen," he cried, "pledge me in the red wine of Oporto."

"The wine being poured out, the governor raised his glass.

"Your health, senors," he exclaimed.

Our friends bowed, and the glasses were emptied.

It was delicious wine, and it glowed through the veins of the drinkers with exhilarating effect. The Don then rang the bell energetically. A domestic entered.

"What does your Excellency require?" he asked.

"Supper immediately," said the Don, sharply.

"What will your Excellency please to take?"

"Everything there is in the larder!" shouted Don Xavier. I have company."

The startled servitor disappeared with the utmost alacrity, and the Don turned to his guests.

"Now, senor," said he, addressing Rupert, "while the supper is coming, if you will oblige me with the despatch, I will run through it; though I fear after your immersion in the water it will not be very legible."

Rupert smiled at this remark.

"I am rather methodical in my arrangements," he replied; "though I may get wet myself, I always keep my papers dry."

As he spoke, he drew from his vest the oil-skin pouch, which he unrolled, and displayed to the eyes of the governor the despatch perfectly dry.

"Good! very clever, indeed!" exclaimed the latter admiringly, as he took the paper eagerly. Before he read it, however, his eye rested on Rupert, who was in his shirt sleeves.

"It offends my sight somewhat, senor," he remarked, "to see you so indifferently

clad. If you will step into the ante-chamber yonder" (he pointed as he spoke to a door marked by a dark-coloured arras), "you will find a chest full of wearing apparel, from which you are at liberty to select."

Rupert inclined his head in acknowledgment, and said—

"Your Excellency will perhaps extend a similar favour to my comrades, who have been pretty well drenched in their efforts to save me."

"Oh certainly," replied the governor, "you will find plenty there."

The Englishmen raised the arras and passed through into an adjoining chamber, whilst Don Xavier proceeded to read the despatch.

The apartment was dimly lighted by a couple of wax tapers, and was somewhat gloomy, compared with that they had just quitted.

The wall was panelled with dark wood, and the floor was planked with a substance that had the appearance of mahogany.

A large chest stood against the wall.

"By the mass!" exclaimed Stronghand, as he raised the lid and gazed at the quantity of rich doublets and trunk hose with which it was filled, "his Excellency keeps a good wardrobe for the accommodation of his friends. Now, gentlemen, help yourselves!" he added, as he tossed the garments out on to the floor.

Two of our adventurers were not long in making a selection, and the garments being rich in material and trimming, the exchange was decidedly for the better.

"I think we shall do honour to the governor's feast," said Rupert, as he glanced at his silk velvet doublet of purple and gold, with considerable complacency.

"Pardie! comrades, I foresee you will have all honour to yourselves, for not one of these gewgaws will fit me," remarked Stronghand, after several abortive attempts to insinuate his giant limbs into the garments.

"Never mind, Mark," replied Rupert consolingly; "after all, it is the man and not the dress in which the honour centres."

"Oh I'm perfectly content," answered Mark; "I can sup with as good appetite in my own clothes, as in those of any Spaniard."

"And I," acquiesced Firebrand; "still this change of costume may be useful at a pinch."

"It would be a pinch indeed if I were to squeeze myself into any of them," added Stronghand, laughing.

Rupert's eyes fell upon a pair of pistols on a ledge in a corner.

"They may be useful," he said, as he took them up, "loaded too! better and better!"

He slid one into each of his pockets as he spoke.

"This is a dreary-looking apartment enough," remarked Firebrand, as he gazed around. "Do you remark that narrow door?"

He pointed to a portion of the wall in which the outline of such means of egress revealed itself.

"It is too narrow for a door; it must be a closet," said Stronghand.

"I am not so sure of that," added Rupert; "these old fortresses are usually full of such narrow outlets."

"The shortest way to arrive at the truth, will be to open it if possible," said Firebrand.

It had no handle, and while Rupert was employing his eyes in searching for some knob, or spring, that might answer a similar purpose, his attention was arrested by a plaintive voice in a tone of earnest supplication.

In an instant everything else was forgotten as he and his companions listened intently.

Their eyes being now accustomed to the dim light, they observed another door, which they had not previously noticed.

"The voice comes from thence," Rupert remarked softly, as he listened, "the speaker, too, is a woman—an English woman!" he added, with sudden eagerness, "What says she?"

He strained his ear to catch the speaker's words, and his effort was rewarded.

"Merciful heaven, preserve my father and my dear sister, Adela, and grant that we may be spared to meet again!" were gently wafted to him from the adjoining chamber.

Rupert as the voice ceased, thought once more of the young girl he had seen looking down upon him from the window overlooking the courtyard. Her likeness to Adela Mountjoy had struck him forcibly at the time, and now that name breathed by her lips confirmed him in the impression that she must be indeed her sister.

He tapped gently at the door, but there was no answer.

"Has she fallen asleep?" he murmured to himself.

He tapped again, and a soft voice within inquired—

"Who knocks?"

"A friend," was the answer, "come close to the door; I dare not speak loudly."

"I am here," whispered the voice.

"Is your name Helen Mountjoy?"

"Alas, yes!"

"Friends are near; your sister is in safety; do not despair, but hope," whispered Rupert.

At this moment the Don's voice was heard calling them to supper.

"I dare not stay longer or I shall excite suspicion," Rupert exclaimed in a low tone, "but comfort yourself with the thought that you are not forgotten."

He had hardly ceased, when the arras was raised, and the Don, who was impatient to commence feeding, exclaimed loudly—

"Supper waits, senors!"

They replied instantly to the summons, and entered the adjoining chamber where the repast was served, radiant in the governor's costume, Stronghand alone excepted, who could find nothing that would come within a mile of him, and who consequently wore his own clothes.

CHAPTER XXXVI.
THE TEST OF COURAGE.

THE table groaned under the weight of the viands.

Soup, flesh, and fowl, pasties and fruit were mingled together in tempting but bewildering profusion.

Don Xavier had evidently been pleased with the contents of the despatch, and proceeded to assist his guests with much expedition.

The supper was excellent, and our heroes were not indisposed to enjoy it.

The Governor ate and drank like a true glutton, but his guests were more cautious.

As the rich wine mounted to the brain of the former, he began to grow grandly defiant, and to speak as though there was not his equal in the world.

"Drink, senors, drink!" he cried, "no man is a true Spaniard who shirks his glass!"

He drained another bumper, and then continued—

"Ah these cursed Inglese, what trouble they give us! But we shall teach them a lesson before long! yes, yes, a severe lesson!"

"Or perhaps we shall teach you one," thought his guests, who were watching him with much satisfaction.

"Ha, ha!" he laughed, continuing his subject, "they must be mad, quite mad. See here!" as he spoke he unfolded the despatch and placed it before them on the table.

The wine he had drunk had caused him to forget his usual caution, or it is probable he would not have done this.

"See, see, my friends," he continued, with boisterous elation, "of course it is private, strictly private, but you are my friends, and I trust you. See what a naval force we have. Here I am informed from undoubted authority that our Armada consists of one hundred and fifty giant ships, capable of carrying more than eight thousand mariners, and two thousand eight hundred great brass cannon of all kinds."

The enthusiastic and considerably inebriated Don pointed rapturously to the letters of the despatch which danced about before him so as to be hardly intelligible.

"Besides," he continued in a very hiccuping manner, "twenty caravels for the service of the army, and a host of smaller boats for transporting our soldiers on board the vessels. Well it may be called the Invincible Armada! who could withstand it?"

"There is only one country that would have any chance against such a mighty force," answered Rupert, quietly sipping his wine.

"And what country is that?" inquired Don Xavier, trying to look straight at Rupert.

"England, senor Governor!" Rupert replied bluntly.

"England!" scornfully laughed his Excellency.

"Psha! it's impossible—what can England do with her poor little forty cockleshells of boats? I am informed on this same reliable authority she has not one more! Not one!" He again pointed triumphantly to the despatch, and repeated—

"What can she do with forty against a hundred and fifty such vessels as we have?"

"She can build others, senor," replied Rupert, smiling.

"But even supposing she had only the forty cockleshells you allude to, they would be manned and commanded by hearts of oak! Does your Excellency understand what kind of hearts they are?"

"Hearts of devils! no!" cried the Governor, annoyed at Rupert's peculiar tone; "what have I to do with hearts of oak? They are not Spanish hearts, are they?"

"No!" replied the Englishmen, with a simultaneous burst.

"Of course not!" added the Don, shaking his head knowingly.

"Your Excellency is unquestionably right," said Rupert, drily; "they are composed of an entirely different material altogether."

The Don was pacified at finding some one agreed with him in this particular, and drank off two bumpers of wine in succession.

"We shall annihilate the pestilential heretics! roast them in their own fires!" he hiccupped, folding up the despatch, and attempting to put it in his pouch, but dropping it instead.

Rupert quietly put his foot upon it, and at a convenient opportunity, stooped down, and picking it up put it into his own pocket.

"By St. Nicholas, there'll be the finest collection of instruments of torture ever invented!" the bloodthirsty and drunken Governor went on.

"Little do these English pigs imagine what we have in store for them! the thumbscrews! the iron collars! the racks and pincers! Ho! ho! I'll go to England, and see the bonfires! I hate 'em! I hate 'em!"

Don Xavier struck the table ferociously, and upset his glass, but seizing another he dashed some wine into it, and rose from his seat, swaying to and fro unsteadily.

"The Spaniards are a brave race!" he cried. "I am a brave man—"

"When you're drunk!" thought the Englishmen.

"So was my father, Don Alphonso of blessed memory, before me. We're all brave!"

The Don paused suddenly and looked fiercely at the Englishmen, who regarded him with the most provoking unconcern.

"Are you three gentlemen brave?" he demanded.

"We do not consider ourselves cowards, Sir Governor, though we do not hold it good to make a boast of it," Rupert replied. "Our motto is 'deeds not words!'"

"Ay, by the saints! A very good motto!" assented the Don, sitting down rather abruptly, but still not losing his subject. "Let's put it to the proof. Dare either of you go into that anteroom, open a narrow closet you will see there in the wall, and bring me what you find in it?"

The Englishmen rose instantaneously. They remembered having noticed the closet alluded to.

"We all dare!" they replied, feeling strongly inclined to take the insulting drunkard by the throat and throttle him.

"All dare!" echoed the Governor, scornfully. "Sparrows are brave in a flock. Who will go alone?"

"I will!" said Rupert.

"Go then, senor! Press the round knob on the right side of the closet, and the door will open." Rupert threw a glance of contempt at the pompous commandant, and went at once into the antechamber.

The Governor sat listening attentively, chuckling as he did so.

Mark Luton and Firebrand, not quite certain that Don Xavier might not suspect their assumed character and contemplate treachery, also listened; their hands secretly placed upon the hilts of their swords.

Rupert in the meantime, had discovered the knob in the wall, which looked like a knot in the wood, and was about the size of a shilling.

Pausing only for an instant to wonder what it was that required so much courage to fetch, he pressed his thumb against the knob.

It yielded instantly, and as it did so the door flew open, and from it started, in the dim light, a figure which caused Rupert, not unnaturally, to recoil with involuntary horror.

This figure was a human skeleton, which, nevertheless, appeared to be endowed with motion, since, as it emerged from its hiding place, it stretched forth one of its long bony fleshless arms towards him.

Rupert remained motionless for a moment, gazing upon the ghastly relic of frail mortality, as it stood with its grinning jaws and eyeless sockets, in a kind of hideous mockery before him.

But his self-possession speedily returned.

"This is some trick of that old drunkard," he said to himself, "an interesting plaything truly. But since my bony friend seems disinclined to return to his cupboard again, we'll try the effect of a little gentle persuasion. It will at all events put a stop to the worthy governor's practical joking for a time, in this particular at least.

So saying he drew his cutlass.

"Now, Senor Lantern Jaws!" he exclaimed, as with a swift downward stroke he cleft the skull of the skeleton, and divided the spinal column. Two more smashing blows right and left, and the unsightly mass of bones fell with a crash on the floor.

The governor who had been listening with the most intense eagerness, started up at the noise.

"Aha!" he cried, exultingly, "I knew he could not face that, he has fainted; ha, ha, how brave!"

He staggered to the arras, pulled it aside and entered the antechamber, with a volley of sneers on his tongue, expecting to find Rupert prostrate on the ground.

Instead of this, however, the only prostrate thing he found was the skeleton, Rupert being on his feet, perfectly calm and collected, with his friends Mark and Firebrand on each side of him, and wearing an expression on his features, which, had Don Xavier been less under the influence of his cups, would have warned him not to go too far.

The Governor could scarcely believe his eyes when he saw the anatomical specimen so entirely demolished.

"You have destroyed my skeleton!" he shouted; "it was the remains of some English vagabond cast upon this coast, and I had put it together with springs, at a large price, to amuse myself and excite my friends' terrors, and now you have annihilated it!"

"I have proved that I did not fear it, at all events," replied Rupert, sternly, "and given you an opportunity of proving your skill in anatomy by putting it together again."

So saying, he strode haughtily from the room, followed by his comrades.

"We'll teach this braggart a lesson before we've done with him," whispered Rupert as they seated themselves at the table once more, and coolly replenished their glasses.

The Governor followed almost immediately. He arrived at his chair in a very zig-zag manner, and though he had appeared annoyed at the destruction of his skeleton, he seemed to have recovered his temper perfectly.

"By Saint Antonio!" he exclaimed, addressing himself to Rupert, particularly, "you are indeed a brave man; I could mention to you a score of names who have swooned dead off at the sudden appearance of that skeleton."

"Yes!" replied Rupert, with undisguised contempt, "but they were Spaniards!"

"And are not you?" demanded the Don, with a sudden start that almost seemed to sober him.

"Spaniards without nerve, I was about to say," Rupert added, not wishing at present to excite the Governor's suspicions.

Don Xavier appeared to be satisfied with this explanation, and drank several glasses in succession, with great zest.

"If we were the cowards you seem to imagine us," continued Rupert the Ready, "you would never have received the despatch, for we were attacked by three scoundrels who had dyed their faces, and would have imposed themselves upon us for Spaniards, but who in reality were spies— English spies, who sought to rob us of our prize."

"And you fought with them, and overcame them?" hiccupped the governor, admiringly.

"Certainly!" answered Rupert, "bound them hand and foot."

"Kicked them—ducked them — the impostors!" added Stronghand and Firebrand.

"Good! good! I love you for that; nothing is too bad for these English scarecrows!" cried the Governor fervently; "fill, and let us drink extermination to the detested race, and to their bastard Queen."

The hot blood flushed in the faces of our adventurers at this insulting proposal.

Stronghand made a step forward, and extended his finger and thumb ominously in the direction of the Don's nose, but Rupert quietly restrained him.

"Let us fill, my friends," he cried gaily, "his Excellency is a little excited, and knows not what he says."

"Eh! what's that?" exclaimed Don Xavier. "Not know what I—?"

"Come senor!" interrupted Rupert, who had quietly whispered to his companions, "our glasses are full. We wait for you. Come, the toast!"

The Governor, with a very shaky hand, filled his glass to overflowing.

In his eagerness for the toast he had forgotten Rupert's remark, and now pulled himself up by the arms of the chair to a perpendicular position.

Our English friends were already on their legs.

"Raise your glasses, senors," cried Don Xavier.

The glasses were raised.

"Now," he cried, "let us drink destruction to England, destruction to the English swine, and to their bastard Que—!"

He was not allowed to proceed further, for the three Englishmen, having taken deliberate aim, discharged their bumpers full in the face of the doughty Spaniard, who fell back in his chair half-blinded, entirely astonished, and thoroughly drenched with red wine, where he lay puffing and gasping for breath.

"Oh, Santa Maria! I'm murdered!" he groaned.

"Why, senor, what's the matter?" inquired Rupert, coolly, as though nothing had happened.

"Matter!" spluttered his enraged Excellency, "you villains! You base, unmannerly rapscallions! I'll, I'll!"

The Governor tried to rise, but finding it impossible, he lay back in his chair, foaming with fury, and glaring fiercely at the English trio.

At this moment the clanging bell of the fortress rang furiously.

Rupert and his friends looked inquiringly at one another. The seneschal entered.

The old man was too accustomed to see the commandant in a maudlin state of inebriation to be in any way astonished at his present state, so he merely delivered his message.

"Three gentlemen to see his Excellency on most important business."

"What gentlemen?" demanded the Don hoarsely, struggling to preserve his dignity. "Their names?"

"Senor Juan de Vasquez, Captain Diego, and Captain Lorenzo Ortez," replied the old major domo.

A slight thrill passed through the frames of our adventurers at this announcement.

The very men whose names they had assumed were at the gate.

CHAPTER XXXVII.

AN UNEXPECTED ARRIVAL.

A SIMILAR kind of astonishment rushed through the muddled brain of his intoxicated Excellency, but it seemed to clear his faculties and to banish the recent affront he had received from his memory.

He turned towards Rupert and his comrades, and regarded them with an inquiring, bewildered gaze, as though seeking an explanation.

He was evidently in a fog, and required helping out of it.

"There must be some mistake!" he exclaimed at length.

"A terrible mistake!" echoed the Englishmen. "Your Excellency will never admit them?"

"Certainly not," replied the Don. "Send them away, Sancho!" he cried, to the seneschal.

The old man departed, and the Governor, tired of wine, poured out a bumper of brandy for a change, and swallowed it.

He had hardly done this when the old man returned.

"What now?" roared the Don, irritably.

"The strangers refuse to go before they have seen your Excellency," said the ancient retainer. "They say they have been attacked on the road, and have important matters to reveal. Am I to admit them?"

"Admit them! strangers too; at this time of night? are you mad? no—no!"

Suddenly a thought struck Rupert, that they might, by a little finesse, turn the tables completely upon the new comers.

He whispered a few words to the Governor, who appeared reconciled.

"Perhaps you had better see them," suggested Rupert, "and in the event of any danger, you may remember we are here to protect you."

"Protect me!" echoed his Excellency; "me? Am I not a Spaniard? and does not every Spaniard know how to protect himself?"

"Undoubtedly," returned Rupert, "but these are traitors! ruffians! fierce as tigers! in short, they are English, and your Excellency must know very well that one Englishman is more than a match for any three Spaniards!"

The Governor uttered an angry growl of contradiction, but Rupert checked him by suggesting—

"Who can stand against treachery?"

"Well, certainly, there's truth in what you say," remarked Don Xavier. "As you are here——"

"You may depend upon our looking after your safety with the most rigid carefulness," added Rupert.

"I'll imprison the scoundrels! I'll starve the base heretics!" cried the Governor, excitedly. "You can let them in, Sancho, and let the guard follow them, and remain without, in case of need."

The seneschal departed.

"Suppose we wait in the anteroom," suggested Rupert, "we can then——"

"Too far away to be of any service," interrupted Don Xavier, whom Rupert's words had rendered apprehensive. "Couldn't you conceal yourselves somewhere nearer at hand?"

"Beneath the table," proposed Stronghand; "that would conceal us, and we should be close to your Excellency."

"Ah yes, the table!" cried the Governor, catching eagerly at the idea, in spite of all his courage; "that will do!"

At that moment there was a rattling of arms, and footsteps were heard approaching mingled with a confusion of excited voices.

The Englishmen disappeared beneath the table, and the Don took a copious draught of brandy.

He had hardly swallowed the potent liquor when the door burst open, and the three Dons, who were left in apparent security in the cavern, rushed hastily into the apartment.

As they spoke all at once, and with great volubility, their grievances were very incomprehensible to the Governor, who roared to them to speak one at a time.

"We have been assaulted and betrayed, your Excellency!" cried Captain Ortez.

"Insulted, drenched, and starved!" continued Juan de Vasquez.

"Kicked, scorched, and fired at!" wound up Captain Diego.

"Well!" returned his Excellency, in the most unsympathising of tones, "what did you mean by permitting it?—are you not Spaniards?" he added, scornfully.

"We are, senor! true Spaniards!" they replied eagerly; "but we were set upon by a dozen fierce Englishmen—spies—whilst we were waiting for the despatches for your Excellency, and——"

"You lie, you villains!" suddenly burst forth the Don, fiercely; "there's not a word of truth in what you say. It is you who are English; I can tell it in a moment by your vile accent. You are no Spaniards at all, base impostors! You see I know you, though you have dyed your ugly faces."

The Don had worked himself up to a state of great exasperation and excitement, and, rising to his feet, shook his clenched fist in the faces of his countrymen, who were at once thunderstruck and indignant.

"Dyed our faces!" they exclaimed, "what do you mean, senor?"

"Do not dare ask me questions, vile heretics!" roared the Governor, who waxed more and more furious, and felt for his rapier, which he had quietly drawn beforehand, and placed by the side of his chair, and which Stronghand had as quietly removed.

Not being able to find it he grew more and more irritable.

"You have walked into the lion's den!" he shouted, "I'll imprison you, load you with chains, feed you on mouldy bread and muddy water, you English dogs!"

This was a little more than the Spaniards could bear.

Though they had been influenced by

superstituous terrors in the cavern; still now they were in a well-lighted room, with only an irate commandant to oppose, they could not endure the torrent of invective he poured upon them.

Their eyes glared fiercely upon the Don.

"You must apologise!" they shouted in return.

"Apologise! ha, ha!" laughed the Governor, scornfully; "apologise!—to whom?—to Captain Diego—or Don Juan de Vasquez—or Captain Lorenzo Ortez?" he inquired in a bitterly sneering tone.

"To all!" they cried, drawing their swords, which they had picked up again on the beach. "Diavolos! you have insulted our honour, and blood alone can wash away the stain!"

They made a rush forward as they spoke, and the Governor deprived of his weapon, and seeing no other at hand, snatched up a heavy glass decanter, and hurled it in the faces of the advancing enemy.

Captain Diego was the victim. The bottle struck him on the mouth, and with a yell of pain he fell sprawling backwards.

His companions darted upon the Governor just as his hand grasped a silver flagon, and clutched him fiercely.

Furious at his insults, their rapiers were at his throat, and his life, to all appearance, not worth a moment's purchase.

The Governor seemed to think so too, for he roared lustily for help.

But his assailants were too incensed to heed his cries.

He was powerless in their grasp.

Their weapons were drawn back to deal the fatal stroke, when suddenly their legs were knocked from under them, by some unseen power, and they fell precipitately to the ground.

Before they had time to recover themselves, or even to imagine what had produced this startling effect, Mark Luton and Firebrand were upon them, and had wrested their weapons from their hands.

Rupert at the same time secured the sword of Captain Diego, whom the decanter had brought low.

At the same moment the door opened, and a file of soldiers in breastplates and steel morions, marched in and filled up the entrance.

"Take these dogs!" cried the Governor, "and lock them up in the cell. They have attempted my life, and shall be shot to-morrow!"

In vain the unfortunate Spaniards exclaimed against this sentence, and protested their innocence. They were hurried out unceremoniously.

Although the original idea Rupert and his comrades had in thus turning the tables upon the three Spaniards was that they would be imprisoned and so kept from any interference with their plans, it was by no means the wish of the Englishmen that the extreme sentence contemplated by the Governor should be carried out.

The Don, however, thought differently, and as he was a compound of superstition,

selfishness, and cruelty, and hated England and everything English with true Spanish ferocity, his temper, inflamed with frequent drinking, led him to dwell with delight upon the prospect of seeing three of his country's enemies shot before breakfast the next morning.

The excitement of the events that had recently occurred had had the effect of sobering the Governor, and he began to think of retiring for the night, in order to wake up fresh for the exhilarating exhibition.

But the Don, though fond of the pleasures of the table, was nevertheless as cautious as he was timid and suspicious, and never went to bed before visiting the different departments of the fortress in order to see that all was safe for the night.

"Come, senors!" he said, "another bumper, and then I am going my rounds, previous to retiring to rest. If you choose to accompany me you can do so."

Our Englishmen declined the proffered bumper, but accepted the invitation to attend the Governor on his visit of inspection.

It would give them some opportunity of gaining a knowledge of the interior which might be of service.

The Don, having poured out and drunk his wine in solitary dignity, rang the bell, which reverberated with a tremendous clang through the vaulted passages, until it gradually died away in the distance.

It had hardly ceased when two soldiers entered, bearing links.

They were evidently accustomed to the duty for which they were summoned, and stood grim and mute as statues, waiting till their lord and master should pass out.

They were not kept long, for the Don said abruptly—

"Now, gentlemen!"

The door was opened by one of the torch-bearers, and they passed out, following the Governor, the soldiers leading the way.

The air struck chill as they left the warm supper-room, and the yellow glare of the links shed a ghastly light through the dark stone passage that sent forth echoes at every step.

The cold air seemed quite to revive the commandant, who strode forward with all the pride of conscious authority.

Along the walls of the passage at intervals hung various portions of armour and defensive weapons, comprising old breastplates, gorgets, helmets, and iron gauntlets, mingled with pikes and swords, curtel axes, and formidable maces studded with iron spikes, the silent memorials of many a bloody fray.

From all of these the brightness had long since departed, and now from their posts against the wall they seemed to look down, upon those who went to and fro, like the ghosts of departed warriors.

Don Xavier grew eloquent as he paused before these martial relics, and went into bombastic ecstacies as he boasted of the countries that had yielded to the prowess of Spain.

"I see many trophies here," remarked

Rupert, coolly, " of different kinds, but I see none from one country."

" Which is that?" demanded the Governor.

" England !" returned the Englishmen with one voice, that caused such a tremendous echo that it made the torches flicker as though a stream of cold air had blown suddenly past them.

" England's day has yet to come, and it will not be long," said the commandant, confidently.

" We shall see," replied Rupert quietly.

They went on a little further, when the Don paused.

" What think you of this?" he cried, pointing to the stone floor under their feet.

His companions looked down, but saw nothing.

" Of what ?" they asked.

" Stand back a little and I will show you," he replied, waving his hand importantly.

They drew back a few paces, and the Don placed his foot upon a particular spot in a niche in the wall.

" Now," he cried, turning to them, " observe the effect which a simple stamp of my foot will produce."

He paused an instant, and then raising his heel he brought it down sharply on the stone beneath.

The effect was instantaneous.

A sharp click was heard, and then with a slight crash a portion of the stone floor in front of them suddenly fell in, leaving a dark, yawning chasm, about eight feet in width, and extending from side to side of the passage.

There was something appalling in the suddenness with which this effect was produced, and terribly significant in the use to which it could be applied.

" Well, senors, what think you of this?" he asked.

The Englishmen were silent.

The yawning chasm spoke too much of treachery to claim their admiration.

The Governor observed their silence, and, imputing it to awe, said in a tone of much satisfaction—

" An advancing foe could be easily stopped by such a contrivance as this. Look down," he cried, " there is plenty of room for visitors !"

There was a horrible malignity in the grin which accompanied these words, that betrayed the cruel nature of the speaker.

With a thrill of disgust, not fear, Rupert, Mark, and Firebrand, approached the brink of the aperture.

An earthy and sepulchral odour ascended from its recesses, as they looked down that was almost sickening.

Don Xavier seized a torch from one of the silent soldiers and held it over the abyss.

It revealed a large well of apparently great depth.

" I call this the death-trap !" said the Don, " because whoever descends into its jaws, never comes out alive !"

He returned to the niche in the wall,

and grasped an iron ring that projected slightly.

" I will now close it," he said.

He pulled the ring, as he spoke, and with a steady upward motion, the massive trap ascended and filled up the cavity as before.

As he released the ring which flew back with a spring to the wall, a sound like the clasping of an iron snap was heard, and the Governor pronounced the trap firm and safe, and proved his words by walking over it.

It was not without some involuntary misgiving the Englishmen passed across the fatal spot ; but they did so, boldly.

The last curiosity they came to was an old massive-looking arm-chair with a high back.

" This," said Don Xavier, regarding the antique piece of gloomy furniture affectionately, " was given me by my friend, Cardinal Agapidoz. It came from the torture chamber of the Holy Inquisition."

" And what is its use ?" asked Firebrand.

" Sit down in it and prove its use practically," said the Don, with a sinister smile.

" I admire practical experiments as a rule," answered Firebrand, eyeing the Governor sternly, " but there are some a little too practical, and—"

" Oh, you are afraid—"

" Afraid !" exclaimed Firebrand with a suddenness that made the Don retreat a few paces ; " you shall see, but let me warn you not to play any tricks upon me."

" No, no," returned the Governor, " I had no such intention."

Without another word Firebrand threw himself into the chair.

No sooner had he done so than he found himself firmly clasped at the waist, throat, and ankles, by strong iron bands, that sprang forth as if by magic, and rendered him utterly powerless.

Beyond this, however, he felt no inconvenience.

The position was nevertheless trying, especially as it seemed to afford Don Xavier the most lively satisfaction.

Nay, even Firebrand's comrades could scarcely forbear smiling at his rueful expression.

" Am I to be kept here all night?" he asked, in no very amiable tones, of the Governor.

" Oh no," answered that personage, " I am going to release you."

As the Don spoke he placed his hand behind the back of the chair, and turned a screw.

Instantly the springs unfastened themselves and sprang back into their former places, where they lay crouched and invisible.

Firebrand started up and shook himself impatiently.

But his good humour returned with his freedom.

" By the rood," he said, " your Excellency is well provided with accommodation for all comers."

The Governor, who took this for a compliment, smiled grimly, and proceeded on his round.

Rupert and his companions followed.

Don Xavier crossed the courtyard, and went straight to the guard-room, where a group of soldiers were reclining on the ground before the red ashes of a fire.

The men arose as the Governor appeared.

"Call the sergeant," he cried sharply.

The sergeant soon made his appearance, and the Governor gave him some directions with reference to the execution of the unfortunate Spaniards.

He then returned to the interior, rubbing his hands with much heartiness.

Rupert, as he followed, glanced up at the window, where he had previously seen the light, but it was no longer visible.

"She sleeps," he thought.

The moonbeams, however, fell upon the iron grating, and the massive buttress beneath, and lit them up with a chill brightness.

"I will rescue her from this place if I can," murmured Rupert, to his friends, "but how?"

CHAPTER XXXVIII

THE SENTINEL'S SHOT.

THE room in which the Englishmen were lodged was large, and, if not particularly inviting in appearance, was at least rendered tolerable from the fact of their being together.

The Don had escorted them to the door of their chamber with extreme politeness, and left them there, reminding them of the treat in store for them on the following morning, and promising to arouse them at daybreak to witness the execution of the heretic spies.

They listened as the Governor retired, and almost immediately heard a door bang.

"His Excellency is not far removed from us," said Stronghand.

"I scarcely know whether to consider that to our advantage or the contrary," returned Rupert.

"It will enable us, at all events, to keep our eyes upon him," suggested Firebrand.

"True, it will."

"Well, what think you of our adventure?" asked Rupert.

"So far, so good," answered Mark Luton, "you have the despatch, which is one important point."

"Yes; and if we could transmit it to England, it would be valuable to Sir Francis for the intelligence it contains. But that is an after consideration, the first thing to be done is to consider our position here."

"The Governor suspects nothing."

"No; he is as blind as a bat at present—still there is no knowing how soon his eyes may be opened. These poor devils of Spaniards will be sure to make a strong demonstration when they know they are to be shot."

"What course then do you recommend?"

"As speedy a departure from this treacherous den as possible."

"To-night?"

"Yes. But it is not only ourselves we have to think of—there is the young English girl."

"Ah, true, I had forgotten her."

"There are guards and sentinels on the watch, and in case of an alarm——"

"We could fight our way through a host!" exclaimed Stronghand and Firebrand, grasping the handles of their swords."

"I quite believe that," returned Rupert, smiling at his companions' confidence, "but it would not be a safe position for the fair prisoner we seek to rescue."

"No," continued his comrades thoughtfully, "a woman in the midst of us would fetter us terribly."

"Still," continued Rupert, "the attempt must be made, only the utmost caution will be necessary. I would rather not return at all to Adela Mountjoy than fail to take her sister with me."

"Have you arranged any plan?" asked Stronghand.

"The first step will be to warn the young lady of our intentions, that she may prepare to accompany us; the next will be to reach the exterior of this building, and the last to pass the gates."

"The doors are all locked."

"Yes, and barred and bolted."

"There will be a chance, then, for the exhibition of a little of my handicraft," laughed Stronghand.

"I'm afraid, my dear Mark," returned Rupert, "your operations will be rather limited without tools."

Stronghand smiled in return.

"I am not quite so destitute of appliances as you seem to think," he said.

As he spoke he unbuckled a small strap which crossed his shoulder next to his skin, and with a slight tug, pulled up a small leathern pouch fastened with a flap and button at one end.

His comrades looked on inquiringly.

"In this little bag, I have everything necessary to cut the stoutest iron bar, or pick the strongest lock that was ever put together."

As he spoke he unbuttoned the pouch, and revealed an assortment of steel implements of various sizes, and several round bars of the same metal.

Rupert's eyes flashed triumphantly.

"I understand you now, old fellow," he cried; "I have only to glance at those well-tempered implements to bid farewell at once to all doubts of our being able to get out."

"They are the work of my own hands," returned Stronghand, with some little pride, "and I can depend on them."

"There is one thing has struck me," suggested Rupert, "that as we are known to be the Governor's guests, our departure might not be questioned in the least, and we might be shown out without suspicion, and with all possible courtesy."

"If so, so much the better," answered Stronghand; "it will save us a world of trouble, and the Governor the expense of new locks."

"Then suppose, as a commencement, I make my way to the young lady's chamber, and bid her prepare for her flight?" said Rupert.

"Poor little bird, she'll be ready enough, I'll be bound," remarked Stronghand.

"It is not unlikely she may be asleep. At all events, I can easily wake her."

Rupert took a step towards the door, but paused, and turning to his comrades said—

"Your hands, my friends."

Stronghand and Firebrand extended their arms, and a mutually friendly clasp was given and returned.

"Whatever may be the result of our attempt to-night, we stand or fall together."

"Ay, together!"

"And now to warn Helen Mountjoy."

Rupert approached the door, and turned the handle softly, but it refused to open. It was locked!

Rupert looked significantly at his companions, who returned his glance with equal comprehension.

"What does this mean?" he said.

"I suppose his Excellency is afraid we should walk in our sleep and fall into the death trap," returned Stronghand, with grim irony.

"I thought, as he wished us 'good-night,' there was mischief lurking in his smile," remarked Firebrand.

"Never mind," laughed Mark, "we'll prove our independence of him or his locks either."

As he spoke he dived into his pouch and brought forth a curious looking steel hook which he fitted into a bone handle.

"Now then, Senor Governor," he exclaimed.

He was about to insert the instrument into the keyhole when Rupert's voice arrested him.

"Stay, Mark, a moment!"

He paused and turned to his comrade, who was looking from the only window in the room into the court-yard beneath, "a better plan has suggested itself," said Rupert.

"What is that?" asked Stronghand.

"From what I can judge," said Rupert, "we are under the very chamber in which the young lady is confined."

"Well, my friend?"

"If so, by resting my foot upon the ledge outside, I can step on to the projecting buttress and reach the sill of the upper window. A few words will be sufficient to explain our plan, and it will be less likely to excite attention than the noise of opening the door, or the tread of footsteps in the passage."

"As you please, Rupert," answered his comrade; "but still this door and the door of the young lady's chamber must be opened before either we or she can pass out."

"True; but in the meantime she can prepare herself, and there will then be no delay, since when we once make our start we must go on—there will be no possibility of going back."

"Very well. Am I, then, to wait till you return before I commence operations?" asked Stronghand.

"Yes, I think you had better."

The window of the room in which our adventurers were located was protected by iron bars that opened on a hinge, and was secured on the opposite side by a padlock.

This, however, Mark, with a smile of derision, unfastened with one of his instruments, with no greater effort than a single turn of the wrist.

The window was then opened, and Rupert stepped out on to the ledge, steadying himself by grasping Firebrand's hand.

"I am right," he cried, as he reconnoitred his prospects. "There is the buttress, and above it the window I wish to reach."

"Be careful, captain," said Firebrand, a little apprehensively.

"Trust me," answered Rupert, as he glanced down for an instant, "this is just the kind of position to make a man particularly careful. I'm all right," he added, "I'm as sure-footed as a mule, or a cat."

He laughed as he gave utterance to this remark, and then steadying himself and measuring his distance, he sprang forward and alighted on the top of the adjacent buttress, stretching out his arms, and digging his nails into the interstices of the rugged stones to check the impetus of his leap.

So far all was well.

The spot on which he stood was in deep shadow, as was also the embrasure of the window he had just quitted, but the casement above was flooded with light from the moon, whose rays shone brightly into the chamber of Helen Mountjoy.

Rupert thought it would have been better if the luminary had been a little less bright.

He looked around him carefully on all sides, but saw no one.

The ramparts beneath seemed quite solitary and deserted.

Not even a single sentinel on his night watch appeared, nor did any monotonous tread fall on his ear.

All was silent.

Selecting a spot where the stone was broken away, he placed his foot in the cavity, and with an energetic effort sprang up, and grasped with both hands the edge of the window-ledge over his head.

Then extending his left arm he seized the iron bar that barricaded the embrasure, and pulled himself up until he knelt securely on the massive sill.

Precisely at the same moment Stronghand's supple wrist turned the steel picklock in the keyhole of the room beneath, and the door without the least noise or creaking swung open on its hinges.

He had listened to his comrade's counsel, but in this instance followed his own.

Some peculiar sound appeared to have attracted his notice, for he hastily pulled the door to and stood listening intently.

Rupert glanced into the chamber, and in a few seconds descried the young lady he sought.

She was lying on a couch, and apparently wearied with long watching, had fallen asleep there.

Rupert tapped softly at the window.

Helen, who appeared to be a light sleeper, opened her eyes and started up.

The shadow of Rupert, cast upon the floor, alarmed her, and she sprang from the couch and gazed apprehensively at the intruder, as she supposed him.

Rupert, by signs, entreated her to be silent, and to open the window.

This, after a little hesitation, she did.

"Be not alarmed," he said, in a tone at once respectful and assuring, "I am an Englishman. The same who spoke to you from the other side of the door in the earlier part of the evening, and my comrades are here disguised, and we intend to leave the fort to-night, and to deliver you from your captivity, if you be minded to accompany us."

The poor girl's eyes sparkled with joy at the prospect of deliverance, and she exclaimed—

"O yes, yes! take me from this horrible place—pray do! You spoke of my sister—is she safe?"

"Yes," replied Rupert, "I am going to take you to her."

A fervent thanksgiving burst from the young girl's lips.

"The door is locked," she said eagerly, "how can I join you?"

"It will be opened shortly," returned Rupert; "in the mean time, be prepared. Either I or one of my comrades will come for you when we are ready to start."

"O do! do!" she cried, with intense earnestness—"pray do not forget me!"

"I would rather forget myself!" returned Rupert, gallantly.

At this moment, to the great dismay of the latter, a voice at some distance shouted—

"Hallo!"

He glanced hastily around, and saw distinctly the figure of the sentinel on the ramparts, his steel breastplate and morion glistening in the moonlight.

"I must be gone! I am observed!" hastily exclaimed Rupert. "Do not show yourself at the window."

"Hallo!" again shouted the sentinel.

"What an infernal noise the fellow makes!" thought the young captain, as he prepared to descend; "if I were a little nearer I'd stop his bawling."

Rupert was in the full moonlight, and the guard could see him distinctly.

Grasping the iron bar as firmly as before, he allowed himself to drop to a perpendicular position.

As he hung suspended for a moment the sentinel deliberately raised his musket.

"Bang!" echoed the report.

But Rupert had dropped into his former shadowy position on the top of the buttress.

He was perfectly unharmed, the ball only just striking the stone window ledge his hands had just quitted, against which it flattened itself.

CHAPTER XXXIX.

THE EXECUTION.

HIS sudden disappearance caused the sentinel to think he had killed the trespasser, and to congratulate himself on his accurate aim, and, the report having alarmed the guard, there was very speedily a rattling of arms, and the sound of hurried footsteps heard.

The sentinel having made his statement, the guard hastened to the spot, according to his directions, to pick up the body, but no body was to be found.

Rupert in the meantime had regained his room, the window was closed, and the padlock refastened.

"Confound that fellow and his gun," exclaimed Rupert, as he brushed the dust from his doublet; "where is Stronghand?" he asked, in surprise, as he looked round and missed his comrade.

"I am here," cried Mark, as he hurried into the room with the utmost precipitation, hastily locking the door after him with his steel instrument.

"Quick, quick!" he cried in a low tone rapidly, "off with your clothes and lie down. The alarm is raised; the governor swears the devil is in the place, and has summoned the guard. He will come round assuredly."

Doublets and trunk hose were hastily dragged off and thrown in a heap on the floor, and our three adventurers plunged into the capacious bed and quickly pulled the coverlet over them.

"Why did you open the door, Mark?" said Rupert, reproachfully, "I warned you not."

"It was fortunate for you I did," returned Stronghand, "but it was not that that awoke the governor, but the report of the sentinel's musket. I suspect he was popping at you."

"You're right, he was. The only satisfactory part of the affair was that he didn't hit me."

"All's well that ends well," says our great dramatist, Will Shakespere, so we'll forgive the honest sentinel wasting his powder, and ——

"Sh! hark!" whispered Firebrand, suddenly, "the Don's raising the house in earnest now."

They were silent as they heard the governor shouting at the top of his voice, in the passage.

"Be quick, you drowsy laggards!" he roared. "I might be murdered in my bed, or carried off by the fiend himself, before you come to my assistance!"

A clattering of arms was heard, as the troopers, roused from their sleep, came running in twos and threes up the vaulted corridor.

Then the sergeant's voice was heard bawling them into order.

This being effected, the governor cried fiercely—

"Follow me!"

Tramp! tramp! tramp! came the soldiers.

"Halt!" shouted Don Xavier.

They stopped at the door of the chamber in which the Englishmen lay.

The key rattled in the lock, and the door opened.

Then came a flashing of lights, and the room was filled with the smoke from the links of the torch-bearers.

The Don looked in cautiously, and, seeing nothing but a heap of clothes lying in the centre of the room, entered boldly.

He looked round suspiciously.

His eyes roamed from the ground to the ceiling, and from the ceiling to the ground.

He looked up the capacious chimney, under the bed, and in the bed, where the Englishmen slumbered in a state of soundness, that, under the circumstances, was something marvellous.

"All safe there!" muttered the Don, in a thoughtful puzzled tone. "Forward! rascals!" he bawled the next moment to the link-bearers, at the door.

He passed out, the door was closed, and locked, and, in a short time, silence once more reigned in the fortress.

The events just related had, however, created such a stir and excitement in the garrison that any further attempt to leave the fortress that night was utterly impracticable.

"Poor Helen," said Rupert pityingly, "we must keep her in suspense for a few hours longer."

Our adventurers being tolerably tired with their night's work, soon fell into a slumber that was not feigned, and slept profoundly, until a loud hammering at the door aroused them from their repose.

It appeared to them that they had not slept more than a few minutes, and none of them felt disposed to shake off the blissful feeling of drowsiness in which they were steeped.

But there was a necessity that they should rise, and accordingly Rupert sprang from the bed and awoke his comrades.

"By the rood!" exclaimed Stronghand, as he raised his massive form very unwillingly from its recumbent posture, and rolled himself on to the floor, "I would fain have slept on till noon, if I had been permitted."

He yawned loudly, and Firebrand catching the infection, yawned in concert.

They had scarcely donned their garments, when the Governor looked in.

"O, you are up, senors," he said, "that is right! I would not have had you miss the execution of these English varlets on any account. Come with me, and let us take a morning draught, and a slight meal to keep the cold air from our stomachs."

The Englishmen followed the unfeeling commandant with moody brows to the chamber they had occupied on the previous evening, where the morning meal was served.

They had barely finished when the drums rolled in the court-yard, and the sergeant of the guard entered to inform the governor that the time for the execution had arrived.

Don Xavier bolted his last mouthful with a rapidity that threatened to choke him, and gulping down a goblet of wine, rose from his seat and accompanied by his guests,

followed the sergeant to the courtyard where the sentence of death was to be executed.

The morning was cold and chill, a thin mist hung suspended in the air, and wrapped the old fortress in its grey mantle.

The drums continued to peal forth their monotonous sounds, and presently a grated door opened and from it slowly emerged, guarded by a file of soldiers, the unhappy Spaniards whose position had arrived at such a critical point.

Their arms were pinioned, and their faces, naturally dark, were now livid with the foreshadowing of their approaching doom.

They looked appealingly towards the Governor, but he turned contemptuously away.

Rupert put in a word of appeal in their behalf, which Don Xavier utterly scouted.

Slowly they advanced to the fatal spot.

As they reached it the loud bell of the fort gate rang loudly.

"Who is that so early?" demanded the Governor.

"It is Don Ferdinand, your Excellency's nephew," said one of the domestics.

"Good, good!" exclaimed the Don, joyously, "this will be a treat indeed for him. Welcome, welcome," he cried, as the tall figure of Ferdinand Ribeiro, became visible through the mist.

No sooner did the three condemned men catch sight of him than they uttered a shout of joy.

"Don Ferdinand! our friend!" they cried exultingly, "we are saved! we are saved!"

Pinioned as they were, the three Spaniards rushed forward with the utmost eagerness to meet their friend, whose timely arrival had caused a sudden pause in the proceedings.

"Ferdinand!" they exclaimed with one voice, as they advanced.

The young man thus addressed, absolutely recoiled with amazement, as he gazed upon his companions, thus bound, and apparently on the verge of execution.

"What!" he cried, in a tone of bewilderment, "Lorenzo, Juan, Captain Diegos! what in Heaven's name is the meaning of this?"

"The meaning is," returned Don Xavier, who did not like the turn which affairs seemed to have taken, "that these men are impostors!"

"Impostors!" re-echoed Ferdinand, in amazement.

"Ay, impostors!" shouted his uncle. "English heretics, spies, who speak our language and have dyed their features, in order to cover their treachery and impose upon our credulity."

"It is utterly false," cried the three Spaniards, addressing themselves to Ferdinand, with great volubility, "as you yourself know. His Excellency your uncle is bewitched with some evil spirit, who has filled him with terrible delusions."

The Don glared fiercely and indignantly

THE SENTINEL'S SHOT.

at them at the bare idea that he could by any possibility be subject to anything so puerile.

But his nephew turned to him and said—

"My dear uncle, you are undoubtedly deceived. These gentlemen are my particular friends—Captain Lorenzo Ortez, Senor Juan de Vasquez, and Captain Diegos."

"It is true! it is true, your Excellency!" cried the prisoners with one voice.

"How can it be true?" roared his Excellency, his yellow parchment complexion becoming purple with rage—"how can it be true," he reiterated, "when the very gentlemen you name are standing there?"

As the Don spoke he pointed with fierce derision to Rupert, Mark, and Firebrand.

If ever our friends needed their coolness and presence of mind, they needed it now.

Circumstances had reached that critical point when their safety seemed to hang suspended in the balance of fate.

If Don Xavier took their words that they were what they represented themselves to be they might yet be safe.

If, on the contrary, the Governor believed the assertion of his nephew, and the prisoners themselves, the tables would be completely turned against them, and the muskets of the soldiers would be speedily pointed at the Englishmen's breasts.

Not that our heroes had the least intention of quietly submitting to such a fate.

In proportion to the emergency of their position so their coolness and determination increased.

They felt their blood coursing rapidly through their veins, as their position rushed distinctly before them.

What of that? They were Englishmen! They had been in peril before, and would not shrink from it now.

Besides they were fast friends—sworn to stand or fall together, and on that mutual oath they knew they could depend.

A comprehensive rapid glance from one to the other was the assurance that this was perfectly understood.

Still they had all their work before them.

They knew full well that the discovery of their identity would be to convert all within the precincts of the fortress into implacable foes.

Spain was fierce and intolerant against heretic England—as they termed her—and in none of her sons' breasts did the fierce flame of bigoted hatred burn more vindictively than in that of Don Xavier.

The three Spaniards, whose lives had been all but sacrificed, were burning with indignant rage, increased tenfold by the treatment and terror they had endured.

The Governor, whose bloodthirsty instincts had received a check, chafed at the delay, and determining fully to have some one shot, turned to our heroes.

"You hear, Senors, what is affirmed of you!" he cried in a savage, irritable tone.

"We must be very deaf not to, your Excellency," returned Rupert quietly.

"Answer me to the point!" continued the Governor, with increasing irritation, "is the affirmation true?"

"It is exactly as you choose to accept it," said Rupert, in a tone of indifference. "If you take the word of those fellows," pointing, as he spoke, to the three Spanish captains, "we are, of course, spies, heretics, impostors, and whatever else you may have the impertinence to call us. If, on the contrary, you believe our report, then are we loyal subjects and true gentlemen, worthy of the highest consideration and respect!"

There was an ironical tone in Rupert's speech, and a scornful smile on his face as he uttered these words that annoyed and puzzled the Governor greatly.

Besides, his reply was very indefinite.

There were too many ifs in it to satisfy Don Xavier.

"Tell me, once for all, have you been deceiving me all this time?" he exclaimed.

"Deceive you—a man of your Excellency's penetration?" Rupert inquired, with sarcastic surprise.

The bombastic Governor could scarcely believe it was possible. Nevertheless he was puzzled.

He was unwilling to confess himself mistaken, and yet he felt there was some great error hanging to his heels.

"I hardly know what to think!" he growled. "I am inclined to believe the devil and his imps have taken possession of the fortress!"

"I am inclined to agree with your Excellency in that particular," returned Rupert, still sarcastically. "I thought so from the first moment I entered it."

Convinced in his own mind that he and his companions must in a few moments be discovered, he cared little how he aggravated the cruel Governor before they threw off the mask.

"There must be some spell working in the air,' continued the Governor, looking up fiercely into the misty atmosphere, as though he almost expected to encounter some demoniac visage scowling down upon him.

"But, whatever it be," he continued, in a pompous, blustering manner, "one thing is certain. Here are six men, three of whom claim the names and identity of the other three. Now the point is—since they cannot possibly be the same persons—which is right and which is wrong?"

Don Xavier curled his moustachios and looked fiercely from the Englishmen to the Spaniards, and from the Spaniards to the Englishmen.

"Which is it?" he shouted.

"These gentlemen are right, uncle," replied Don Ferdinand, indicating his friends, in the midst of whom he stood; "there is not the least doubt of it. I would swear it by my honour, and this holy symbol."

As he spoke the young Spaniard drew forth a small ivory crucifix from his breast, and kissed it devoutly.

He had already severed the ropes with which his friends' arms were pinioned, and they were beginning to gain confidence.

"Yes, yes," they cried, "we are true Spaniards and men of honour, who have been grossly maligned and insulted by those demon Inglese—those accursed heretics—those ——"

They paused suddenly, and approaching the Governor, said in a low tone not unmixed with apprehension—

"They cannot be men: if they had been, could they have disarmed us and bound us hand and foot as they did?"

There was a prodigious shaking of heads in negation of this.

"No, no, no! it is impossible," they continued, "they are evil spirits of Sathanas!"

CHAPTER XL.

THREE DEMONS.

THIS suggestion made the whole body, Governor, nephew, captains, and soldiers, cross themselves devoutly, and look anxiously towards the Englishmen, who stood calmly and with apparent utter unconcern, with their eyes fixed upon the speakers.

The manner in which Rupert had played with the governor had given them time to collect their thoughts, and they were now ready for the worst and prepared to meet it.

The opinion of their supernatural power, however, had gained ground, and it seemed possible that to this impression they would owe their safety, but suddenly the governor remembered the past night.

"Spirits do not drink wine!" he thought, "spirits do not go to bed. Spirits would not stand there to answer questions as they have done! I do not believe they are spirits!" he muttered, between his teeth, "but I will know—that I will. Hark, ye, whoever ye may be," cried Don Xavier, bursting from his soliloquy, addressing the Englishmen, "it appears to me that you have deceived me—made a fool of me."

"You are one ready made," returned Rupert, coolly.

"Ha, what is that? you call me fool, do you?" cried the governor, stamping his foot with rage.

"You hear?" he exclaimed, turning to his countrymen, foaming with rage, and pointing his finger at Rupert—"he calls me fool! I will tell you what he is, he and his confederates: they are three cowardly, sneaking dogs of Inglese! spies, who came crawling into our country under false colours, who dare not show their own white faces. But I will teach you a lesson!" he shouted, addressing himself to our heroes. "You, who so nearly caused the death of my brave countrymen with your lying impostures, shall die the death they would have died! You shall be shot like dogs, and your bodies shall rot in the depths of the death-trap! Think of that and tremble."

The Don had worked himself up to a pitch of magnificent fury, and seemed in his excitement almost inclined to rush upon them and drag them with his own hands to their doom. Great, therefore, was his astonishment when the only reply the Englishmen vouchsafed to this terrible threat was a contemptuous laugh.

Before the Governor could recover himself Rupert replied—

"You bombastic cowardly combination of superstition and cruelty, let me tell you first that I and my companions scorn and defy you!—next that we are Englishmen, who love their country and their Queen as truly as they detest the arrogance, bigotry, and vindictive cruelty of Spain, who, not content with the hope of overcoming in fair fight, gloats over the prospect of torturing her prisoners. But, in the name of England, we despise your proud boasting and your arrogant threats! in the name of England we three Englishmen defy you and all within these walls! we defy your weapons, bullets, and death-traps! If we must die it will be back to back with our swords in our hands and our faces to our foes, and our last cry shall be for 'England and our Queen!' Now let him who seeks to take us come and try!"

Rupert, Mark, and Firebrand drew their weapons, and calmly waited the result of this bold speech.

The Governor either was or pretended to be so incensed that he could only reply by vehement gesticulations, the purport of which manifestly was, that the sooner the three audacious foreigners were made to bite the dust the better he would be pleased.

The three Spaniards, being unarmed, made a rush towards the musketeers, and shouted to them to lend them their swords.

These being eagerly handed to them, they, headed by Don Ferdinand, bounded forward furiously to the attack.

The Englishmen drew back close to the arched door at the entrance to the fortress, and met their advance with the utmost coolness.

Ferdinand and Captain Ortez fastened upon Rupert, whilst Juan de Vasquez and Captain Diegos engaged with Stronghand and Firebrand respectively.

It was in vain, however, that the Spaniards —who, to do them justice, were skilled in the use of the rapier—lunged with fierce impetuosity at the Englishmen.

Every thrust was parried with a calm indifference that was a little more than contempt, and which was so palpable that it roused the Spaniards to a pitch of the bitterest aggravation.

"Come out and fight, cowards!" shouted Captain Ortez, scornfully, who had tried in vain to hit his antagonist.

"Must we drag you forth?" cried Don Ferdinand, taking up his friend's tone of profound contempt.

"If you can!" returned Rupert, in a quiet, dogged manner.

"If we can! Ha, ha! We'll soon see!"

The impetuous Ferdinand made a straight lunge, and endeavoured to close with his antagonist, who had two weapons to parry with his single blade.

But he paid for his temerity, for Rupert with a sudden sweep of his rapier, dashed the blow aside, and as he advanced shortening his sword, plunged his keen blade through Don Ferdinand's throat.

The steel passed out at the back of his neck, but Rupert rapidly withdrew it, in time to receive a desperate blow from Lorenzo, which, however, he turned aside, and before the captain could recover himself, he received a sharp downward blow from Rupert that laid his face open from the temple to the jaw.

Both the Spaniards lay prostrate on the ground, wallowing in their blood.

Almost at the same moment, Stronghand disarmed his adversary, and bringing down the hilt of his sword with tremendous force on his skull, Juan de Vasquez fell in a heap like an ox beneath the stroke of the pole-axe.

Fireband's opponent, Captain Diegos, met with no better fate; his sword having broken off short at the hilt, the weapon of his adversary smote him in the breast, and passed out under his right arm, piercing his heart in its passage.

Thus in a few moments, four foes had been brought to the ground.

The Governor was aghast at this unexpected result.

He had drawn his weapon, but dared not advance to revenge the death of his friends.

But there still remained his guard of musketeers.

"Present!" he shouted.

Six muskets were instantly pointed at the breasts of our heroes.

"Fire!" cried the Governor.

A loud report followed, which was echoed by an ominous ringing laugh.

When the smoke cleared away a little, the Englishmen had disappeared.

The Governor turned pale with disappointment and terror.

"They are not men, but fiends," he muttered; "even bullets refuse to touch them."

Suddenly he remembered the door.

"They have escaped by that. They are in the fortress—we shall snare them now! Forward," he cried.

The musketeers ran forward at the word of command, but the door slammed to with a heavy bang.

"It is fast!" they cried.

It was fast.

But our heroes were inside whilst their pursuers were out.

CHAPTER XLI.
THE ENEMY WITHOUT.

RUPERT THE READY, Mark Luton, and Fireband, on hearing the command of the Governor to "present," had very wisely used the door, near which they stood, as a means of retreat, and having entered the portal, they at once closed it, and pulled to the heavy bolts as the most efficacious way of checking the enemy from following them.

They now stood in the passage, and held a brief consultation as to the best course to pursue.

Outside the door they heard the Don blustering and raving.

At one moment he was shouting for help for his wounded friends—at the next crying to the musketeers to batter in the door with their muskets.

Of the four Spaniards who had fallen in the first mêlée, Juan de Vasquez and Captain Diegos were past all surgery.

The remaining two contrived, with a strong effort, to stagger to their feet; but, being themselves totally unable to continue the attack, they quietly sank down again.

In the meantime the soldiers were hammering away with the butt-ends of their muskets at the massive door.

In the excitement of the moment it did not seem to strike the Governor that there was a postern door by which they might enter.

During this delay, however, our Englishmen held a hasty council of war in the gloomy passage, the only light to which came from narrow openings in the upper part of the walls, which served for little more than to render darkness visible.

They looked up the passage, but saw no one.

It was quite deserted, but the consternation seemed to have spread, for the alarm-bell began to sound.

It may seem strange that three men could have in a few minutes spread almost a panic in a fortress that contained more than a score of soldiers at least.

Probably the majority did not know the precise strength of the enemy, but imagined the English had landed, and were advancing to storm the gate.

Voices were heard shouting in the distance.

Still the hammering at the door continued.

"Ah!" cried Stronghand, "you may hammer, my friends, and bend your muskets double before you will burst these bolts."

"We shall have to fight for it, Mark," exclaimed Rupert, "though by St. George of England, unless the men are more worthy the name of soldiers than the Governor and his friends, I do not apprehend much danger."

"It would be to our advantage if we were a little better acquainted with the ins and outs of this hole," remarked Firebrand.

That which did not strike the Governor, who was too much concerned for his individual safety to think much of ought else, suddenly occurred to Rupert.

"There must be a postern gate," he cried, "and this entrance being effectually secured, it is of every importance that we should also fasten that."

"Yonder," said Stronghand, "is the gluttonous old Governor's supper-room."

He pointed straight up the passage as he spoke.

This reminded Rupert of the antechamber, and—by a natural train of thought—of the young English lady who was imprisoned in the adjoining chamber.

"That poor girl!" he said, in a tone almost of self-reproach, "what is to become of her?"

"She must be rescued," Stronghand remarked.

"By the Holy Rood, yes!" returned Rupert.

"For my part I am resolved not to leave this place alive, unless she goes with me."

"We can accomplish that, I think," said Firebrand.

"We must!" exclaimed Rupert, vehemently. "And now for the postern gate!"

With hasty steps our adventurers traversed the stone passage, until they came to the middle, where the treacherous death-trap masked the dark abyss beneath.

Here they paused for a moment, for at this spot the passage branched off right and left into two narrow outlets.

"One of these must lead to the postern, I should think," said Rupert.

His companions acquiesced in this opinion.

The shouts were now heard more distinctly in that direction.

"As we have only swords," suggested Stronghand, "I think one of those iron-spiked maces would not be the worst of weapons in a hand-to-hand struggle."

He sprang up, seized the handle of one that hung against the wall, and brought it down in his grasp, and with it the whole mass of weapons and helmets to which it was attached, that fell with a crash on the stone floor.

His companions armed themselves in like manner.

They now grasped each his mace.

Very formidable weapons they were, too, in the hands of those who were strong enough and bold enough to wield them, and such were our heroes.

"Now," said Rupert, "let us separate. You, Mark, take the right passage, Firebrand the left. I will go and speak a word of assurance to Helen Mountjoy, and rejoin you almost immediately."

"But should you be intercepted?" remarked Stronghand, apprehensively.

"Well, Mark, if I am I must endeavour to baffle my foes, or if brought to bay I must fight my way through them. It is not the first time I have had to do so."

"But one against so many?" returned Mark.

"I do not fear!"

"Nor I for myself, nor for you, Rupert, while we are together. Then we are like the bundle of sticks in the fable. But separate—"

"Never fear, my dear Mark," cried Rupert, "our good angels will watch over us. Besides, it is absolutely necessary that I should speak to Helen. She will have expected to see me ere this, and not having done so, and hearing this alarm, the poor little bird will kill herself fluttering her wings against her cage. No, no! Go you on, my friends, as I have directed. The laws of chivalry command us to rescue our fair countrywoman at any hazard. Go you and secure the postern gate, then we can stand a siege. I will meet you there."

The shouts and confusion rose audibly on the air without.

Stronghand and Firebrand departed by their respective passages, and Rupert went straight forward.

He entered the room where they had feasted on the previous evening.

The table was laid for a sumptuous breakfast, but there was no time to think of that at that moment.

He passed through into the antechamber, and tapped at the door.

"Is that you, sir?" inquired Helen, very eagerly.

"It is, lady," returned Rupert.

"Are you come to set me free?"

"I have sworn I would do so, and I will keep my word," he replied; "but you must wait until I come for you."

"But I am so anxious!" she exclaimed, piteously.

"Not more so, fair lady, than I am myself," Rupert answered, "but the alarm is given, and to take you into the midst of strife would be but to expose you to perils, which in the confusion we might be powerless to avert. Wait for me, and trust me, and I swear on the honour of an English gentleman I will return for you if I am alive myself."

"Enough, I believe you," replied Helen, in a tone of perfect confidence.

Rupert retraced his steps hastily, and as he advanced, the sounds of conflict reached his ears.

He took the left passage, and redoubling his speed went forward.

Turning again to the left at the end, guided by his ear and following the windings of the narrow path, he came at length upon a small open space, where the postern gate was situate, and where the contest was progressing successfully but unequally.

Stronghand and Firebrand had not succeeded in reaching this gate in time to close it against the advancing guards.

They were entering in a body, when Stronghand, clearing the way with his ponderous mace, scattered them right and left, and placed his back against the door, while Firebrand, seizing one end of a heavy chain that rivetted firmly to the door itself, hooked the other end on to a massive staple fixed in the wall at the side, and this diminished the aperture, so that a man could barely wedge himself through singly.

As to bolting it it was impossible, from the weight of the bodies pressing against it from without.

This, however, gave them time to deal with those who had already entered, and with deadly effect.

Six soldiers lay prostrate, their steel caps and their skulls within them, crushed by the formidable weapons the Englishmen wielded.

There were six still remaining, who being hemmed in like rats in a trap fought desperately, first discharging their muskets, but without effect, and then using them as clubs.

CHAPTER XLII.

THE ATTACK ON THE STAIR.

WITH an exulting cry Rupert rushed forward.

"For England and the Queen!" he shouted.

One of the dark-visaged soldiers aimed a desperate blow at him with the stock of his musket, which had it taken effect would have, in all probability, killed him on the spot.

But Rupert, lithe and active as a young panther or an Indian, skilfully evaded the blow, and brought down his mace upon the steel morion of the soldier, who fell prone to the earth with an ominous dent in the top of his casque that let daylight into his very brain.

He neither spoke nor moved again.

In the meantime the most vigorous efforts were going on, on the other side, to force open the gate, but the chain held it fast.

Of the six Spaniards who were in the inclosure at the time the gate was chained up, and the contest commenced in these close quarters, three only remained.

The odds were now become even.

In fact our heroes being only three to three, had forborne to strike, being willing to give quarter if they were asked.

Whether the Spaniards attributed this forbearance to inability on the part of the Englishmen to continue the combat, or whether urged on by a vindictive thirst for the blood of those who had so lately made nine of their comrades bite the dust, one of the three suddenly made a desperate bound towards the chain, and would have unhooked it from the staple in the wall.

His hand already grasped it when Rupert whose quick eye anticipated the treacherous movement, brought his mace down with tremendous force upon the Spaniard's knuckles, reducing the man's hand to a battered mass.

The poor wretch yelled with agony, and Firebrand terminated his miseries by a *coup de grace* from behind.

But Rupert, in thus disabling the man, had struck the staple so violently that he completely wrenched it from its hold in the wall.

The chain being thus removed the door, pressed upon as it was from without, burst open, and the living tide poured in.

Our heroes now found themselves confronted by an infuriated body of men who swore with the most terrible oaths to be revenged upon the accursed Inglese for the death of their comrades.

And thus Rupert, Stronghand, and Firebrand had all their work to begin again.

Still they did not despair, but with knitted brows and nerves that did not quiver, save with the strong energy of stern determination, prepared themselves for a second struggle.

There was one advantage in their favour.

The sudden opening of the door brought their foes in with such an unexpected impetus that they rolled one over the other.

Several fell to the ground, and those behind fell over them.

This gave Firebrand an opportunity to bolt the door.

His comrades in the meantime took every precaution to hinder those who had fallen from rising again.

Their death-dealing maces were terribly effective, as the heap of bodies, either lifeless or powerless on the ground, bore witness to.

Still they found themselves confronted by at least a dozen soldiers.

Their arms, too, were growing somewhat tired with wielding the heavy weapons they were using.

Luckily for them there was a narrow staircase behind them, which Rupert espied just as the assailants, with loud yells, made a rush towards them.

It was the work of an instant to retreat step by step, slowly, and keeping their faces all the time turned to their enemies, who came on with stealthy pace, like so many tiger cats crouching for their spring.

But now a new peril awaited our heroes.

The sentinel upon the upper turret, behind them, who had fallen asleep at his post, and only just awoke, startled by the tumult, and ignorant of the cause, and feeling that he ought to do something to atone for his negligence, discharged his musket towards the head of the stairs.

The bullet grazed the left arm of Firebrand, near the shoulder, inflicting a painful but not dangerous wound.

But it sealed the man's doom.

Firebrand rushed forward, leaving his comrades to defend the stairs, and grappling with the sentinel, hurled him headlong from the battlements of the turret into the court-yard beneath.

At the same moment the mass of men below, encouraged by Firebrand's disapearance, bounded forward with a savage yell.

But our Englishmen were not to be scared by noise.

Down fell the spiked maces, and down fell a victim at every blow.

Stronghand, during this last attack, had been wounded in the thigh by a thrust from a pike.

He had scarcely noticed it in the heat and excitement of the attack, but it bled profusely, and he was beginning to feel symptoms of faintness.

Firebrand's shoulder also grew stiff and inflamed.

Rupert seeing how matters stood, whispered to his comrades—

"We must make short work of this if we wish to triumph. Are you able to make a last effort that shall put an end to the fray?"

"Yes," they replied.

He whispered to them an instant, and then they ascended the stairs rapidly as though retreating.

The bait took.

Those that remained below rushed forward, when, as they reached the topmost stair, the Englishmen turned and fell upon them with such fury that the were completely staggered.

A panic seized the few that remained.

Rupert, dropping his ponderous mace, drew his sword, that was like a feather in comparison.

With this he cut down one and transfixed another.

One of the men at the bottom of the stairs levelled his musket at him.

Rupert drew forth one of the pistols he had appropriated from the Don's antechamber, and presented it.

The sight of the pistol disturbed the

soldier's aim, and the ball passed over Rupert's shoulder.

The effect of the discharge of the pistol was more deadly; the ball pierced the musketeer's shoulder.

Stronghand, with a last effort of strength seized two of their assailants by the throat, and hoisting them completely off their legs, hurled them crashing over the battlements, and then sank down, himself exhausted.

None of the Spaniards, however, observed this.

Those few who had the use of their legs made a hasty retreat by the arch, and dived into the narrow passages the Englishmen had previously traversed, along which they scudded like frightened hares.

Rupert pursued as quickly as possible; but in spite of his expedition, the retreating foe made such good use of their legs, in addition to their knowledge of the turnings and windings of the stone passages, that by the time Rupert gained the central passage there was not one in sight.

Not even the faintest echo of their receding footsteps sounded in the distance.

"No matter," said Rupert to himself, "there are but few remaining, and they cannot do much harm. Let them go, but let them keep out of sight. I swear I will not spare one that crosses my path in the way of hindrance or opposition!"

His blood was heated from the fierce encounter in which he had been engaged, and it would not have been well for any two Spaniards who might have encountered him at that moment.

Not that there was any immediate fear of any such attack, for the fugitive soldiers who had survived the slaughter, and who had been witnesses of Rupert's prowess at the postern gate, had concealed themselves in the snuggest corners they could find, eagerly creeping into any recess to escape the terrible demon "Inglese" as they called him.

The coast being clear, Rupert returned to the scene of slaughter.

The sight that presented itself in the narrow space in front of the postern gate, and at the foot of the stairs leading to the turret, proved how deadly had been the efforts of the Englishmen.

It was literally strewn with dead and dying.

Those who lived were completely hors de combat, from whom no apprehensions of further attack had need be entertained.

"Well my friends," he cried cheerily to his comrades, who still sat upon the steps, "how fares it with you now?"

"By my faith, Rupert!" returned Stronghand, "I must have lost blood, and plenty of it, without knowing it, for I feel marvellously weak at this moment."

"Well cheer up, my friends!" Rupert replied; "our work is done for the present, and there will be time now to look to your wounds."

"My wound is nothing, Captain," said Firebrand, with a short, dry laugh. "Save an unpleasant tingling sensation that makes my arm feel red-hot from the shoulder to the elbow joint, I feel no other inconvenience."

"That is enough for the present, my friend," returned Rupert, smiling at Firebrand's philosopical humour. But come, I think we shall be better for some refreshment. Breakfast is ready laid in the Don's room, so let us proceed thither at once."

"Where is the Don?" asked Stronghand, as leaning on Rupert's shoulder, who went up the stairs to assist him, he descended into the narrow court.

"I know not," answered Rupert—hidden, most probably, in one of his own empty wine barrels, like the bombastic coward he is.

"And his companions, those poor devils of spies who were going to be shot, and Don Ferdinand?" inquired Firebrand doubtfully.

"I imagine they have all met the reward of their merits," said Rupert; but never mind them. Let us first restore exhausted nature by eating the Don's breakfast. I believe a cup or two of good wine will go far towards putting new life into us."

"With all my heart, comrade," answered Stronghand, eagerly; "never did the prospect of a draught of wine appear so agreeable."

Stepping over the heap of dead bodies as best they could, our heroes made their way to the Don's apartment, where the morning meal still remained untouched.

There was a profusion both of food and wine.

"Come!" cried Rupert, filling three bumpers of the generous vintage, "let us drink to the happy termination of our enterprise, thus far successful."

His comrades drank, and the draught had an immediate and revivifying effect.

"And now eat, comrades," continued Rupert. "I will join you in an instant; I am only going to inform the young English lady that we shall soon be ready to start."

He passed into the antechamber and tapped at the door.

"Is it you, sir?" cried Helen, eagerly, from within.

"Yes, lady," returned Rupert, in a cheerful tone; "all is well thus far, and I am come to open your prison door."

The young girl clasped her hands with grateful delight.

"Oh! thanks, thanks!" she cried, eagerly.

"Do not be alarmed, Miss Helen, at the noise I may make, my key being a somewhat clumsy one. Be kind enough to stand from the door."

He raised the formidable mace he carried in his hand as he spoke, and with one blow dashed in one of the massive panels.

A second blow knocked out another—and a third reduced it to a complete wreck.

"Are you going to bring down the fortress on our heads, captain?" called out Stronghand from the other room, as the crash reached his ears.

"No, my friend," returned Rupert, facetiously; "I am only trying a new-fashioned key, and it creaks a little."

The wine and food had already revived Mark Luton's spirits, and Rupert rejoiced to notice the cheerful tone of his voice.

Having opened the fair captive's prison door, he courteously approached her.

"I congratulate myself at last," he said, "on being able to address you in my proper character."

Helen Mountjoy took his hand with grateful impulsiveness, and pressed it to her lips.

"My generous preserver!" she exclaimed, "how can I ever repay you for thinking of me?"

"An Englishman is always repaid, madam," returned Rupert, gallantly, "for any act of service to a lady, by the mere pleasure of performing it."

The young girl blushed at the compliment, and then asked—

"Am I to come with you now?"

"As soon as possible," answered Rupert; "breakfast is ready in the other room, and as we may need all our strength, I think if you have not yet broken your fast you will be wise to do so."

His eye fell at that moment on the chest of clothes, and an idea suggested itself.

He turned to Helen, and said—

"I am sure you are too sensible, and too much alive to the danger of our position, to be offended at what I am about to say; but in this chest are many suits of male attire; if you would be advised by me you would for the present consent to conceal your sex by adopting one of these; we know not what vicissitudes lie before us, and the step I propose, may be of great advantage to you in the future."

The young lady coloured for a moment, but she understood the necessity, and saw that Rupert was right in his suggestion.

"I will do as you advise, sir," she answered.

"And at the same time," continued Rupert, "select an additional suit for your sister; it may be as necessary for her as yourself."

"I will do so."

"I will leave you now, lady," said Rupert. "When you are ready call to me, and I will introduce you to my comrades."

He bowed respectfully to the young girl, and, raising the thick arras, passed through into the breakfast-room.

During the interval he led his companions to their bedchamber, where he bound up their wounds with strips of linen obtained by the sacrifice of one of the Don's sheets, which he tore in strips.

By the time these necessary operations were performed, Helen Mountjoy had arrayed herself in her male attire, and almost as soon as they returned to the breakfast-room she called to say she was ready.

Rupert went to her immediately.

He smiled as he gazed upon the transformation, whilst Helen blushed crimson at the novel position in which she found herself.

"You do justice to your disguise, Miss Helen," said Rupert, assuringly; "beautiful as a woman you are no less handsome as a youth. Come, comrade," he added, jocosely, "let us join our friends."

Helen gave him her hand, smiling and blushing, and together they entered the breakfast-room.

"Allow me to introduce to you our new comrade," he cried, in a jovial tone—"Captain St. Helen!"

Stronghand and Firebrand rose and cordially welcomed the blushing captain, and requested her to be seated, and join them in their morning repast.

Rupert had assumed a lightness he did not feel, in order to relieve the embarrassment a young lady would naturally feel at being thrown amongst strangers (albeit they were friends) in the costume of the opposite sex.

His comrades understood Rupert's intent, and so well did they enter into his plan that Helen found herself in a very short time no longer strange or embarrassed, but unreserved and quite at her ease in the protecting company of her countrymen.

The meal being finished, our heroes, mindful of the future, packed up as much as possible of the food and wine for after emergencies.

Helen had selected a suit for her sister Adela, and this also was added to the baggage.

"I think now," said Rupert, "the sooner we are outside the walls the better."

"I quite agree with you there, captain," said Stronghand, "and at the same time we may congratulate ourselves that there is no one to oppose our departure."

They rose to go, Firebrand undertaking to carry the provisions.

"I think," said Rupert, "we will depart by the postern."

"Yes, it is nearer the outer gate," acquiesced his comrades.

They accordingly made their way thither.

Helen shuddered as she gazed upon the scene of the late carnage.

"Oh, how terrible!" she exclaimed to Rupert.

"We had no choice, lady," he said; "it was sheer desperation. We were hemmed in by superior numbers on every side, and had we not fought like tigers, or demons, or —or Englishmen," he added, smiling, "against such odds, we should have been annihilated. We had no choice between cutting down our foes as you see them, or allowing them to cut us down—we, therefore, chose the former."

Stronghand placed his hand upon the bolt of the gate, when Rupert gently laid his hand upon his arm.

"Sh!" he ejaculated, in a low tone.

"What, captain?"

"I think I hear something!"

"Remain where you are," whispered Rupert, "we will retreat into the archway."

In an instant they were out of sight, Rupert placing himself so that the top of the wall over the door was within range of his vision.

Stronghand remained crouched close to the door, listening intently.

There was a murmuring of voices on the other side, and then a scraping of feet against the wall, as though some one was endeavouring to scale it.

"Ha, ha!" laughed Stronghand to himself, as he placed his mace against the door and drew his sword; "I'm ready for you, my adventurous friend, whoever you are. If you put even your nose beyond the inside edge of the wall, I'll have it off."

He had hardly expressed himself thus when the head of a yellow-visaged soldier, with a formidable moustache, appeared over the top.

CHAPTER XLIII.

THE MAN ON THE WALL.

THIS was one of the survivors of the mêlée, who had fled from Rupert's pursuit and concealed himself until all was quiet, and then dropped from one of the windows and rejoined his companions.

"Is all clear?" whispered a voice below.

"Yes!" answered he of the moustache, "save of the corpses of our brave troops; diavolos! what a heap!"

Stronghand with a grim smile clutched his sword firmly.

"You'll add one more to the number, my friend, if you're not careful," thought Mark.

"Hoist me a little higher," whispered the soldier to his comrade below, who was evidently assisting him to mount, "Santa Maria! you're heavy!—there!" This was accompanied by a vigorous upward jerk that almost shot the climber headlong over the wall.

It was only by clutching the top with his hands and knees, he saved himself.

Stronghand had already stretched forth his hand to grasp him by the leg, and drag him to his doom, when a sudden thought prevented him.

"We may gain intelligence from this fellow," he thought "that will be of more service perhaps than his worthless carcass."

Accordingly keeping his sword in his grasp, he allowed himself to fall forward, as though prostrate from a wound.

The soldier on the top of the wall having recovered his balance sat astride it, as he would have backed a horse.

He listened intently, and then looked down ruefully at the heap of dead below.

"Do you hear anything, Sancho?" asked a voice from the other side.

"No!" returned the other.

"Suppose you drop down, and penetrate the interior cautiously, you may perhaps discover what those infernal Inglese demons are doing," suggested the voice.

"And perhaps run into their very jaws; no thank you, I've had enough of them for one day," returned the other.

"But the Governor desires——"

"Does he? Then let the Governor come and search for himself. All I mean to do is to drop down and unbolt the gate."

He was about to descend, when Stronghand gave vent to a deep groan.

"Hullo!" ejaculated the man pausing, "what's that?"

He recovered his position and looked down.

"Who spoke?" he asked.

"I did, comrade," returned Stronghand, in Spanish, in a tone of assumed faintness.

"Ah! you are wounded?"

"Yes, to the death. You have escaped?"

"I have, bless the saints! I ran while I had the chance. I can fight with men, but not devils!" said the soldier, crossing himself.

"How many got away?"

"Only four."

"How were they able to save themselves?"

"I know not. I only know that I shut myself up in one of the chambers, and got out of sight under the bed."

"They did not find you then? Happy man!" groaned Stronghand.

"It was a miracle they did not," the man continued, "for the whole three of these demoniacs came in while I was there. What for, think you?"

"I know not."

"To tear up the Governor's sheets to bind up their wounds; I saw them do it."

Stronghand felt almost inclined to laugh.

"Where are these demons now?" he asked, in a smothered voice.

"Diavolos! it's more than I can tell; but I think they are feasting in the Governor's dining-room. What infernal impudence!"

"Dreadful!" muttered Stronghand, his broad sides shaking with stifled laughter.

"And the Governor, where is he?" he inquired.

"In the guard-room with his nephew, Don Ferdinand, and Captain Lorenzo Ortez, who are both badly wounded," returned the soldier.

"He's in an awful rage," he continued, "and commanded these Inglese to be taken dead or alive."

"Why does he not come himself then and take them?"

"He dares not leave his nephew, who has got an ugly thrust through the neck."

"Ah! he is afraid to come!"

"If he were, these devils are enough to make anybody afraid. But we shall trap them yet!" cried the man confidently.

"How so?"

"I've managed that safe enough," chuckled the soldier, giving his moustache a twist.

"Indeed! What have you done?" asked Stronghand, with an additional moan of apparently unbearable anguish.

"I'll tell you," returned the other, with evident admiration at his own skill, "I've placed a guard of a dozen arquebusiers close at hand outside the gate."

He pointed down, as he spoke, to the gate beneath him.

"Yes! Well?"

"Well, these Englishmen, when they have gorged their fill, will be sure to come out by this gate. The moment it opens, 'click, bang!' go the twelve muskets, and they will fall, ha, ha! riddled with bullets!"

"Take care! take care, my friend," said Stronghand, faintly gasping, "these—men, being—demons are bul-bullet proof! O, O!"

he groaned, "water, comrade, water," groaned the counterfeit sufferer.

"Diavolos, you must get your own water," cried the selfish soldier, in a growling tone.

"But I'm dying!"

"Can't help that!"

"But I have a treasure—a sum of money —I have saved for my wife, and—O! O!" groaned Stronghand piteously.

"Treasure! money!" exclaimed the man on the wall, whose avarice was excited by the words of his supposed dying comrade.

"Y-es."

"Where?" cried the man, eagerly bending over.

"In—in—O, my breath fails me, I cannot speak."

"Diavolos! I shall lose it," exclaimed the avaricious soldier, excitedly. "Tell me where?" he repeated.

"In-in," murmured Stronghand indistinctly as though almost at the last gasp.

The soldier, whose avarice was excited past control, and who could not endure the idea of losing his dying comrade's money, which he intended to appropriate to his own use, without further hesitation dropped down from his perch on the wall, at Stronghand's side.

"Where is the money? Where?" he exclaimed, with intense anxiety, shaking his supposed comrade remorselessly. "Santo San Nicholo, he will die without telling me. Where?" he repeated, fiercely.

The dying man raised himself on his elbow for an instant, and, without a word, grasping the unfeeling brute by the throat, flung him on to his back, and pinned him to the ground with his powerful arm.

At the same time he placed the point of his keen weapon at his throat.

"The smallest sound or cry, and you shall swallow this," he hissed in the man's ears.

The terrified Spaniard thus entirely at the mercy of his enemy, lay trembling, with his eyes almost starting out of his head, and as quiet as a mouse, hardly daring to breathe.

"Now," whispered Stronghand, "order the twelve musketeers to leave their present post, and go round to the outer gate."

As he uttered these words he gave the prostrate Spaniard's windpipe a gentle squeeze, such as a cat might give a rat.

"O, O, I'm chok——"

"Silence, you cur, or I'll choke you outright," exclaimed Stronghand, under his breath.

"Give the order, and speak up boldly, if not——"

Here he tickled the man's throat with the point of his rapier.

"I will! I will, merciful demon!" gasped the Spaniard.

"Comrades," he exclaimed after clearing his throat, "are you there?"

"Yes, have you discovered anything?"

"I have."

Here he glanced at the sword blade ruefully.

"What?"

"The three Inglese dem—I mean gentlemen."

"Are they here?"

"They are at breakfast. They will not come out by the postern, but by the front gate. I heard them say so. (Santa Maria forgive me for the lie!) Order the musketeers to go there at once."

"And you?" demanded his comrade.

"I shall remain here on the watch," returned the man, with an abject look of terror, as though he doubted much whether he would long be in a state to watch, or do anything else but keep his dead comrades company.

In a moment or two there was a slight clatter of arms, and the sound of footsteps, proclaiming that the twelve musketeers had departed.

No sooner were they out of hearing than the captive Spaniard implored with great earnestness to be released.

Stronghand, who felt the utmost contempt for the selfish cruelty the cringing fellow had shown, in his behaviour to, as he supposed, a dying comrade, hoisted him from his legs, and threw him against the wall with such force that the breath was well-nigh shaken out of him.

He rebounded, and fell upon a heap of dead, where he lay gasping, and uttering a broken mixture of exclamations and lamentations.

"Lie there," cried Stronghand, sternly, "and if you dare to move for an hour from this time, your life is forfeit."

"Now let us depart," he exclaimed. "Are you ready, captain?" he added, turning to Rupert.

"Yes."

Firebrand unfastened the bolts of the door, and looked out cautiously.

No one was in sight.

They accordingly moved forward towards the outer gate of the ramparts.

To reach this they would have to pass the guard-room, but they felt that beyond a few wounded men they would meet no opposition there.

As for the warder who kept the keys of the gate, he could easily be mastered.

Stronghand and Firebrand went first.

Rupert, encouraging Helen, who seemed inclined to be a little apprehensive, followed.

"Courage, fair lady," he said, "our worst peril, I think, is over. Ere long, I hope, you will be united once more to your sister."

This seemed to cheer Helen Mountjoy greatly, for her eyes sparkled, and she went forward with a brisker step.

But almost at the same moment they were startled by loud shouts proceeding from the spot to which they were hastening.

"It is the Governor's voice!" cried Rupert; "once let me come within reach of him, I'll stop his shouting."

At this moment the Don's shouts were answered by shouts from the musketeers, who had left the postern and assembled at the gate where the contest first commenced.

"Confusion!" muttered Rupert. "It will never do to risk a contest in this open space, and with a woman in our midst!"

"What is to be done, captain?" asked Stronghand.

"We must retreat into the fortress once more, that is if the postern gate is still open, as I think it is, and hold our own as we did before."

At this moment the alarm bell sent forth its peal, and the Governor himself appeared coming from the guard-house, and beckoning on the musketeers, who turning suddenly round the angle of the fort came in sight, and ran forward at a brisk pace.

"Be not alarmed lady," said Rupert to Helen, soothingly; "once within the gate we are safe."

They hastily retraced their steps, and the advancing guards, seeing them retreating, uttered loud "Vivas!" and increased their speed.

But the Englishmen had the advantage.

To their great joy the postern gate was still open.

They felt assured now of victory.

The Governor stood shouting and cheering on his men.

"Shoot the heretic dogs! cut them down, crush them!" he bawled.

Some of the musketeers in obedience to the command of the Don, discharged their muskets as they ran.

But the weapons of those days were not breech-loaders, nor were the men who fired them riflemen, and the Englishmen replied with a shout of derision, as the bullets flew past them very wide of the mark.

"Forward!" cried Rupert, "the gate is—" he paused suddenly as he observed, at that very instant, the gate slowly swinging to.

"Treachery by heaven!" cried Stronghand between his teeth, "this is the work of that Spanish dog, whose brains I ought to have battered out against the wall!"

"Pause not! we may yet be in time!"

They had now reached the gate, but alas! it was closed, and an ominous grating sound behind told that the bolts were being fastened.

Their pursuers, too, were rapidly gaining ground.

CHAPTER XLIV.

THE DEATH TRAP AT WORK.

WITHOUT a word Stronghand sprang up from the ground and clutched the top of the wall; and then, by a powerful effort of strength, he suddenly drew himself up and launched himself over to the other side, just as the treacherous Sancho was, with a grin of triumph on his yellow features, drawing the second bolt.

With one sweep of his brawny fist Stronghand swept the Spaniard aside, and then at once drew back the bolts.

Not a moment too soon—for, as Rupert with Helen and Firebrand rushed in, a volley was fired that hit nothing but the stone wall, and a shout of baffled rage announced the failure of their pursuers.

"Safe once more!" cried Rupert, exultingly.

"Aye, captain, safe!" echoed Stronghand, "and now to deal with the skulking hound whose handiwork had nearly cost us our lives."

He looked round, expecting to find him sprawling on the ground.

But he looked in vain.

Senor Moustache had disappeared altogether.

"I ought to have knocked his brains out at once!" cried Stronghand, "but no matter! if he comes within my reach again this day I'll atone for my omission."

With this consoling resolution, Mark Luton picked up his iron-spiked mace.

Rupert and Firebrand seized theirs.

There was evidently a consultation going on without, in low tones, almost whispers.

Our hero fancied he heard the voice of the Governor, but could not hear distinctly:

Whatever the consultation might have been, one thing was certain, no one of the outside party seemed inclined to show so much as the hair of his head over the top of the wall.

They all seemed to have a wholesome dread of encountering the three "Demonios Inglese," as they called our heroes—in close quarters.

Firebrand cautiously ascended the turret steps, and looked over.

The musketeers were ranged in a line close under the wall, and Don Xavier was speaking in a low tone to the corporal.

At the same moment a soldier was seen skulking round the angle of the fort, and approaching the musketeers as rapidly as possible, yet with caution and apparent trepidation.

"Come here!"

Stronghand hastily ascended the steps.

The skulking soldier was now nearer, and was remarkable for being very ugly and yellow, and as being the owner of an enormous pair of moustaches.

"Is not that the fellow who opened the gate?" asked Firebrand, pointing out the Spaniard to his comrade.

"Yes," returned Stronghand, biting his lip with suppressed rage, "I ought to have knocked the dog's brains out, and I will, too, before the day's over."

Sancho whispered eagerly to the Governor, who considered a moment, and then whispered to the corporal, who said in a low tone to the men—

"Forward! quick!"

The whole party moved away rapidly, the ugly Spaniard only turning to make a hideous mocking grimace towards the parties within, not, however, for a moment imagining it would be seen.

Stronghand and Firebrand descended, and rejoined Rupert, who stood assuring Helen that all would end well.

"They have moved off, captain," said Firebrand.

"To try the other gate, I suppose," returned Rupert, with a somewhat scornful smile.

Suddenly Stronghand uttered a loud exclamation.

"The other gate !" he cried; "I understand now, fool that I was not to have done so before; that treacherous villain has escaped by the front door, and left it open! look to the lady, captain; Firebrand, follow me !"

So saying, he hurried away, his comrade at his heels.

It was now Rupert felt the great responsibility he had undertaken in rescuing Helen Mountjoy from her captivity.

But his mind was made up in an instant.

"Come with me, lady !" he cried.

With hasty steps he conducted her to the antechamber.

"Wait there, dear lady, a moment," he said.

"Alone?" she inquired, tremulously.

"Yes, it is imperative ! My presence is absolutely necessary for my comrades' safety. I will not remain long."

He hurried back to the passage.

Stronghand and Firebrand had reached the portal at the other end just as the body of musketeers burst in, with their hands upon the triggers of their weapons.

It was fortunate that it had happened so simultaneously, since the door, dashed violently open, completely masked Mark and his companion from their foes, who hurried eagerly on.

Don Xavier, sword in hand, followed gallantly behind.

Suddenly the Don caught sight of Rupert, who had just emerged from the breakfast-room, and was hurrying forward at full speed to support his comrades.

Escape seemed now impossible.

"Halt !" shouted Don Xavier.

The musketeers stopped.

"Yield yourself, heretic dog !" bawled the Governor. "If not, I order the men to fire."

Rupert glanced aside.

He was at bay, and he knew his life hung on a thread.

His eye fell on the niche in the wall—suddenly he remembered its purpose.

"The Death Trap !"

It was between him and his pursuers.

He was resolved.

"Yield, hound !" reiterated the Governor.

"Never !" shouted Rupert, "for England and the Queen."

"Fire !" roared Don Xavier.

A tremendous volley echoed through the vaulted passage, but Rupert had gained the niche in the wall unharmed.

"Forward !" shouted the Governor.

Onward came the musketeers through the dense smoke—onward to destruction.

Suddenly there was a grating sound, and then a crash, as the trap, released by the pressure of Rupert's heel, fell, disclosing the yawning chasm of the death trap, into whose jaws its victims plunged with a fearful heart-rending cry.

The Governor, who was following, narrowly escaped the fate of the soldiers ; but he, warned by the terrible shriek, pulled up suddenly, and found himself, to his horror —

On the brink of the abyss !

"Santo St. Nicolo !" ejaculated the Governor, aghast as he glared in a bewildering manner down the abyss, "what a narrow escape !"

The perspiration oozed from the Don's body at every pore at the thought, and his first impulse was — his further progress being interrupted by the chasm—to turn round and retreat by the way he had come.

However, he had hardly taken a dozen steps when he ran into the arms of Firebrand.

"So, senor Governor !" remarked the artilleryman, "you're the very man I wished to meet !"

"Santa Maria !" groaned the Governor, as the strong arms of Firebrand encircled him, "I'm lost !"

"If you remember, senor," said the latter, "not long ago you introduced me to a remarkable arm chair; I am now going to give you a taste of its peculiarities."

As he spoke, he hoisted the Don off his legs, and threw him into the piece of furniture alluded to, without the least ceremony.

The concussion was tremendous—the iron springs instantly sprang forward and clasped Don Xavier, who was rendered utterly incapable.

Firebrand, engrossed in the contemplation of his prisoner, did not remark the treacherous Sancho, who, with a spiteful grin upon his yellow features, had crept forward, rapier in hand, behind him.

"You demon Inglese dog !" he muttered, "take this !"

He drew back his hand for the thrust, when Stronghand, who had been quietly watching his preparations, dropped his mace upon the rascal's head, who fell with his skull crushed dead upon the stone floor.

Rupert now called to his friends from the other side of the chasm.

"Mark ! Firebrand !"

"Here, captain," they answered.

Rupert grasped the iron ring in the wall, and the trap ascended to its proper place.

"Now, my friends !" he cried, "our work here is ended, and the sooner we are gone the better."

"We are ready, Rupert," was the eager reply.

Rupert went at once to the antechamber where he had left Helen, whom he found anxiously awaiting him.

"Now, lady," he cried, in a cheerful tone, "all the barriers that opposed us are removed, and I have come to tell you we are ready to depart."

A vivid gleam of joy flashed over the young girl's features at his words, as she rose eagerly to accompany him.

The place seemed quite deserted as they passed into the courtyard.

Our three adventurers had well sustained the character the Spaniards had given them of demons ; their enemies were destroyed, and the fortress was reduced to a state of complete submission.

"Ha, ha !" laughed Rupert, "it would not be a bad idea to keep this stronghold, and

THE STRUGGLE ON THE RAMPARTS.

hold it in the name of her Gracious Majesty Queen Elizabeth. Not that it matters much —we can teach these braggart Dons a lesson without this."

As they passed the guard-room they looked in, and saw Captain Lorenzo Ortez and Don Ferdinand lying very ruefully on a couple of rugs, their heads being supported by pillows.

"Farewell, senors," said the Englishmen, "we wish you a speedy restoration to health."

The Spaniards groaned and turned up their eyes, as though they did not reciprocate the friendly wish.

At the outer gate stood the old warder, keys in hand, looking uncommonly doubtful and suspicious as our heroes approached.

The old man, who had taken no part in the affray, had serious doubts in his own mind whether he ought to let them out.

"Where is the order for departure?" he asked.

"We have only one order, my old friend," said Rupert, "and that is our own wills, backed by power to enforce compliance."

The old man had never heard of such an order as that, and shook his head.

"You cannot pass," he said.

"Look you, friend," said Rupert, seriously, "you are an old man, and we do not wish to harm you in any way, but at the same time, if you oppose our exit, we shall be compelled to take your keys by force."

The old warder seemed to feel the force of this remark as he gazed on the stalwart forms before him, and consented to open the gates.

"I will let you out, senors," he said.

He was about to approach the gate when suddenly the tramp of footsteps on the shingle, and the murmurs of voices fell upon their ears.

Our adventurers looked at one another, and Helen noticed with apprehension there was some anxiety expressed in their glances.

At that moment the loud clanging bell of the fortress was violently agitated, and a deep voice without exclaimed in Spanish—

"Ho! warder, open the gate!"

CHAPTER XLV.
THE DEAD ALIVE.

THE voice seemed familiar to Rupert, who whispered to the warder—

"Ask his name and errand."

"Who are you?—what seek you here?" piped the old man.

The voice replied—

"Captain Pedro de Valdis and Don Alonzo D'Aquilar, with part of the crew of the wrecked Santa Maria; open the gate and conduct us to the Governor."

Rupert fairly started at these words, delivered as they were in an impressive tone by the deep voice of Captain Pedro.

It seemed to him something almost incredibly marvellous that any one from the doomed ship should be alive.

However, facts are always stubborn things, and the fact, in this instance, was too palpable to be doubted—there they were alive, and seeking admission.

It must have been them, then, he saw in the boat, and the ghastly corpse-like hue of their features must have been imparted by the lurid glare of the light they burnt.

This was Rupert's explanation to himself, and this was perfectly correct.

It was not his wish to embroil himself in another affray with these new comers.

He felt quite satisfied that he and his staunch comrades had struck blows enough that day to maintain the honour of the country to which they belonged, and the sovereign under whose flag they fought, without entering upon another engagement.

He, therefore, called the warder aside, and said—

"You can admit these men; and after they have entered we shall go; but I warn you, do not mention a syllable to them of our departure, or your life shall answer for it!"

"I will not, senor," returned the old man.

The Englishmen ranged themselves close to the wall—Helen Mountjoy standing next to Rupert.

The warder thrust the key into the lock, and turned it with a creaking sound.

The gates swung open slowly on their hinges, and completely concealed our heroes, who, from their hiding-place, watched the captain and his friend, with the sailors, pass through.

The warder pointed forward.

"Keep on straight across the courtyard, senors, till you come to the gate; you will find some one there to conduct you," he said.

They went as directed, and no sooner were they out of sight than Rupert and his comrades, with Helen Mountjoy, passed out at the portal, and stood on the sea-shore, whilst the gates closed once more behind them.

The scene looked desolate enough; the wind seemed to be rising, and the sea looked angry and discoloured.

The Spaniards in the meantime had reached the habitable portion of the fort, where they found the door open, but not a soul to receive them.

They went round to the postern-gate. There, to their horror, they found many waiting, quietly enough, in death's rigid sleep.

They entered, and traversed the gloomy passage, and at length came upon the Don, firmly fastened in the wonderful chair, and his eyes starting almost out of his head, as one of the iron springs was operating powerfully on his windpipe, and he was in a state of semi-strangulation. From this dangerous position the Governor was speedily released, and then he poured out his woes in a bitter and indignant strain, informing his listeners that three of Satan's imps, in the form of Englishmen, had held wild revel in the fortress, and bewitched everything in it.

He had hardly finished his recital when Captain Ortez, with his face bound up, and looking in his bandages like an ouran-outang with the toothache, appeared coming up the passage.

"They are gone!" ne said, in a thick, muffled voice, "those demon Inglese!"

"Gone!" cried the Governor.

"Yes! by the gate!" he exclaimed—"escaped unpunished!"

"Diavolos!" yelled the Governor, fiercely, "these fiends have massacred my troops, insulted the honour and dignity of Spain in my person, and have got off scot-free."

"My friend!" he continued vehemently, to Captain de Valdis, "I look to you and your brave sailors to follow these wretches, and avenge me!"

The brave sailors alluded to, who were half frozen and nearly famished, did not respond to the Don's animated appeal with the ardour he expected.

But Captain Pedro, having in his veins some of the blood of old Spain, and being of a chivalrous temperament to boot, seized an iron mace lying at his feet, and declared himself ready to lead the pursuit.

"Follow me, brave fellows," he cried to the shivering mariners, "the honour of Spain has been insulted! Arm yourselves with any weapons you can find, and follow me and my good cousin Alonzo; we will first punish these insolent English, and then return to taste his Excellency's hospitality.

A feeble cheer gurgled in the throats of the Spanish sailors, who forthwith seized upon whatever weapons they could find, and followed Captain Pedro and Don Alonzo.

In the meantime our heroes made the best of their way along the coast, and their progress was by no means rapid.

Stronghand, who, in his excitement, had entirely forgotten his wound, now began to feel it extremely painful, and it was with the utmost difficulty he could walk at all.

He chaffed bitterly at his slowness, and begged his comrades to hasten forward and leave him to follow as best he could.

But to this Rupert would not consent.

In the meantime, the Spanish sailors, who wished to do whatever was to be done as quickly as possible, and get back again to the fort to drink his Excellency's health, came on rapidly, headed by their captain, and his friend Don Alonzo, and a loud shout told our heroes that they were pursued.

Rupert gave vent to a muttered execration, as he turned and looked in the direction from which they were advancing.

"Those Spanish curs again," exclaimed Mark Luton and Firebrand; "will they never be satisfied?"

"Let them come an' they will," said Rupert, more calmly; "they do but provoke their fate."

The Spaniards had sighted the fugitives, and another cheer expressed their exultation.

Our heroes calmly drew their swords, and placing Helen behind them, turned their faces to the advancing enemy, with a grim smile.

They had hardly done so when another shout from a single voice caused them to look round to seaward.

To their great joy, they beheld close in shore their own snug little craft, with Peter Flight and Adela Mountjoy on board.

A simultaneous cry of exultation burst from the lips of the Englishmen, and from Helen, who recognised her sister.

"Hurrah!" shouted Peter, at the top of his voice; "there yer are—knew I should find yer! Ketch hold o' th' rope and pull her in."

This was in allusion to the boat.

They caught the end of coiled rope he flung, and hauled the boat's head up to the beach.

In a moment they were all on board but Stronghand, who remained to push the vessel off, which feat being accomplished with his brawny shoulders, he too clambered over the side and joined his friends.

By the time their pursuers reached the spot the boat was some distance off.

The Spaniards ground their teeth with spite, and shook their weapons after them defiantly, like so many infuriated savages, which our heroes returned by taking off their hats with ironical politeness, thereby considerably increasing their enemies' chagrin.

However, as one party was at sea, and the other on dry land, the anticipated retribution was necessarily postponed.

"We shall meet again, rascals!" shouted Captain de Valdis, in magnificent bass tones, and when we do——"

"BEWARE!" came distinctly wafted to his ears. across the waters.

With a scowl of contempt the doughty commander turned away and cried abruptly:

"They are not worth slaying: let us return!" and with these words they retraced their steps to the fortress.

CHAPTER XLVI.

SPRINGING A LEAK.

THE wind was increasing, and the sea as a natural consequence, growing more boisterous every moment.

The vessel seemed to feel it, for she pitched and rolled like a mad thing.

"This will not do," said Rupert.

He accordingly trimmed the sail, and with his companions, rearranged the ballast at the bottom of the boat.

After this she rode easier.

Rupert then begged his fair charges, Adela and Helen, to go below, where they would be less exposed to the keen blast and the dashing spray that broke continually over the bows.

Adela, who had warmly welcomed her young and handsome preserver back again, obeyed his injunctions implicitly, and the young ladies were soon snugly bestowed in the cabin below.

Peter then informed our hero of the cause that had induced him to leave the shelter of the cave and put to sea.

"Finding you didn't return last night, and both me and Miss Adela being awful anxious, I'd half a mind to come after you, of course with the young lady's permission."

"It's lucky you did not!" remarked Rupert.

"Well, we'd made up our minds that I ought to, but when I went to have a parting look at these three Spanish beauties that we locked up in the cave, I couldn't find 'em; they'd made a clean bolt of it somehow or other. Well, I didn't like the idear of this at all, 'cos I thought it didn't seem right. Miss Adela thought so too, so I made up my mind to stop where I was.

"Well, I makes up the fire an' spreads all the sea-weed I could scrape together for Miss Adela, and she lies down and goes to sleep, but not before she prayed that you gen'lmen might all come back safe again.

"I sat down to keep watch, but I s'pose bein' drowsy I fell asleep too. All of a sudden I starts up an' listens—an' hears voices.

"Up I jumps an' looks out, but sees nothin'. I goes quietly down th' rocky path an' peeps round the corner, an' there I sees a long boat jest landin with more than a dozen men in her.

"'Ere's a pretty go, thinks I; what's to be done now? If they comes into the cave we're done brown; but how can I prevent it? P'raps they won't see it, I thought; but p'raps can't satisfy me, because they must see it if they come this way.

"At last an idear struck me. I knowed they weer Spaniards by the jabberin' they made, and I also knowed as Spaniards in general is a werry sooperstitious race, so I resolved to go in for 'orrors."

"Horrors," laughed the Englishmen.

"Yes," returned Peter, seriously "I made up my mind to work a spill (spell he meant) a incantation, and raise a spectre at short notice as should beat all the guys yer ever saw holler.

"Well, I runs back to the cave and tells Miss Adela. Of course she wasn't particular pleased to hear about the Spaniards, but she approved of the spectre.

"In a few minutes I'd fastened a spar across a oar, an' over that hung a long piece of canvas. Then I tied up some seaweed in a piece of canvas, dumpling fashion; that was the spectre's head. On this I marked eyes, nose, and mouth, with a piece of burnt wood, and then fastened it to the top of the oar; then I delineated some skeleton ribs all down th' front o' th' ghastly objeck, and the spectre was finished.

"And did it answer your purpose?" inquired Rupert, smiling.

"I believe yer, it jest did too!" answered the enthusiastic Peter. "I'd 'ardly finished it when I heard footsteps comin' along rayther too cautious to be pleasant.

"Out I goes with the spectre in me 'and, an' plants myself at the top o' th' rocky path.

"I keeps as quiet as a mouse an' listens. Still I hears the scraping o' th' feet on the shingles. At last I peeps over, an' there, sure enough, was a Spaniard with a pair o' moustaches a yard long at least, a spyin' about with all the eyes e'd got!

"All of a sudden I observe he catches sight of the path at the top o' which I was. 'E seemed to think it might lead somewheres p'raps.

"He stood still, considerin' for a minit, an' then began to ascend.

"The moonlight jest fell beautiful on the upper part of the rocks, while all below was dark as pitch.

"On comes my gentleman pertickler care-ful, as though 'e was afraid something 'ud bite him!

"I let 'im 'ave it all 'is own way till he got about half way up, an' then I let's 'im 'ave a groan o' orful intensity.

"'E stops all of a sudden, lookin' dreadful scared like, an' begins, mumblin' someth'n about 'Maria.' For two pins e'd a turned an' bolted. 'Owever, I spose he thought it was fancy, for after a bit 'e plucked up 'is courage, an' came up a little 'igher, then I let 'im 'ave two more groans, an' 'oisted up th' spectre gradual till th' moon come right on 'is ghastly features. My eye, yer should 'a seen the man then; 'e turned all manner o' colours at once, an' rolled clean down from th' top to th' bottom as if 'e'd ben shot, roarin' out to Maria, to take care of 'him 'cos a bad character o' th' name o' Diarv'lus was after 'im. Ha, ha! that did th' business, for I saw no more of anybody.

"As the next day wore on an' you didn't come back I thought I'd embark in search of yer, an' so I did, an' I found you, an' that's th' end o' the chapter; long live th' Queen—diddledum di doodle day!"

At this moment a terrific gust of wind dashed over the surface of the ocean almost blowing the small craft out of the water, and drenching those on board with wet.

Rupert was at once at the helm, and kept the boat to her course, but he looked up and around a little anxiously.

"I understand your look, Rupert," said Stronghand, "our perils are not over yet."

"No, Mark!" answered the young mariner, thoughtfully; "we've some rough weather before us."

"I think so," returned Mark; "never did I see a more angry-looking sky."

This was no exaggeration; wherever the eye turned, nothing met its view but dark leaden-coloured clouds, that seemed in their stern gloom like so many messengers of wrath.

"Well, my friend, we must make the best of it," said Rupert, cheerfully; "perils by land and wave seem to be our lot: when it is not one it is the other."

"Perhaps, after all," remarked Firebrand, "we ought to be thankful we haven't to encounter both these at the same time."

Rupert and Stronghand smiled at their comrade's philosophy, and the latter asked—

"What course do you intend to follow now?"

"We can do little good remaining here," answered Rupert; "besides this craft of ours is scarcely fit for a long cruise, and we have on board too precious a treasure to risk its loss."

"We have, indeed," assented Stronghand, with such a deep sigh coming from his massive throat that Rupert smiled.

"Why, Mark, how you sigh! I shall begin to think a portion of the treasure is particularly valuable in your eyes. Which is the more precious, Adela or Helen?"

His herculean friend smiled, and colonred bashfully, and to hide his confusion looked to leeward.

"I have the despatch," Rupert continued,

changing his subject, "and the sooner we place it in the hands of Secretary Walsingham the better; accordingly I turn my vessel's prow towards the shores of old England."

This determination gave evident satisfaction to all, Peter especially.

"Hooray !" he shouted, "I shall see the old shop again, and dad, and the eleven little Flights, and the cat, and—"

His enthusiasm received a sudden damper from a wave that at that moment dashed over him.

At the same instant Stronghand uttered an exclamation.

"What now ?" inquired his friends.

"A vessel to leeward," he cried.

"What flag ?"

"I cannot tell with the naked eye as yet," returned Mark.

His comrades looked across the ocean, where in the distance in bold relief from the leaden clouds in the horizon, appeared the still darker hull of the ship.

"What is your opinion, Rupert ?" asked Stronghand, "is she English, French, or Spanish ?"

"If I were compelled to guess, I should say she belonged to Spain from the massive darkness of her body. No matter what she is, we have got the start, and can keep it at a safe distance."

At this moment a cry of alarm from the ladies startled them.

Before they had time to conjecture as to the cause, Adela's voice was heard—

"O, quick ! quick ! the water is pouring in here in torrents !"

"Take the helm, Mark, quick !" shouted Rupert, as he gave up his place to his comrade, and leapt down into the cavity beneath the deck.

One glance was sufficient to explain the cause.

"By heaven !" he exclaimed, "she has SPRUNG A LEAK !

The water poured in with such force and rapidity that, unless instantly checked, the vessel would in a few moments have been completely waterlogged, if not utterly swamped.

Rupert threw himself at once on his knees, and with his hand felt for the hole through which the water was rushing.

Fortunately he found it almost instantly.

It was large enough to allow his hand to pass through easily.

"Quick ! quick !" he cried, "a piece of canvas—anything—to stop this aperture."

Peter generously volunteered his head, but that was a little too thick.

Firebrand threw down a piece of canvas, but it was scarcely sufficient to remedy the accident.

The body of the boat was half full of water, and she no longer bounded through the waves as she had before, but went heavily like a dropsical invalid as she was.

The vessel in the distance, too, seemed to be making rapid progress.

Stronghand examined her through his telescope.

"Spanish, by Jupiter !" he exclaimed,

"and if she keeps up her present speed she will overtake us to a certainty."

"I don't think she sees us yet," said Rupert, as he and Firebrand prepared to bail out the water from their vessel.

As Rupert spoke a gun from the vessel boomed across the ocean.

"I don't know what to think, captain," replied Stronghand. "I'm afraid that looks as if she had seen us."

"Well the first thing to be done is to get rid of this water, of which we have many gallons too much," Rupert said.

It was a disastrous mishap, as it rendered the only retreat the vessel afforded for its fair passengers untenable.

Rupert was much chagrined, but he endeavoured to conceal his annoyance.

"I am very sorry, ladies, that you should be deprived of your shelter," he said, "but when we have bailed out the water we will endeavour to render it once more habitable."

Helen and Adela smiled sweetly, and thanked him for his care to their comfort.

"Boom !" echoed another gun.

"Confound that noisy, barking dog," cried Firebrand, irritably, "it makes me wild to hear her yelping, and have nothing with which to give her a howl in reply."

The Spaniard was evidently gaining upon them.

CHAPTER XLVII.

IN THE HANDS OF THE ENEMY.

THERE was only one chance. Night was drawing on. In the darkness they might escape their huge foe.

Rapidly the day departed, the last streaks of light showing the Spaniard evidently in full chase.

A heavy gale had blown all night.

The stopping of the leak had given way, and again the rushing waters had well-nigh overpowered the little craft.

It was with something like dismay that the first grey streaks of daylight revealed to the Englishmen the bulky galleon, like a huge leviathan, sporting in the midst of the rolling waves, not more than a mile from them.

Rupert clenched his teeth fiercely, as he contemplated what might be the result of such a dangerous proximity.

"I care not for myself," he murmured, "but for these poor girls."

The water still forced its way into the boat, in spite of all their efforts.

It was old, and the wood unsound, and would not bear much pressure, but crumbled away, as they essayed to thrust the sailcloth more firmly into the aperture.

It was as much as they could do, under these disastrous circumstances, to keep the vessel afloat, even by constant baling.

They were almost exhausted with fatigue, but their indomitable spirit, and the rage they felt at the idea of being pounced upon by their overwhelming foe, at such a disadvantage, kept them up.

The food and wine they brought from the

fort was served out, and this helped materially to sustain them.

But this could not last long.

They might by a strong effort procrastinate their fate, but not avert it.

Their unfortunate crippled vessel made now but little way, whilst the Spaniard in the pride of her strength, came gallantly on.

Presently another gun was fired from the galleon, and the shot passing high above them, went hissing into the angry waves far beyond.

But this was evidently rather to call their attention to its redoubtable presence, than from a desire to exterminate them.

Soon after they heard the voice of the Spanish captain shouting through his speaking trumpet—

"What flag?"

"English!" roared Stronghand, like an angry bull baited by dogs.

"You must come on board. You are our prisoners. If you attempt resistance or escape I shall sink you!" returned the captain.

Resistance!—escape!—both were alike impossible.

"Sink and be—"

Rupert checked the imprudent exclamation. He thought of Adela and Helen, and remained silent.

The poor girls, too, who had hoped all their perils were over, began to weep as they saw themselves on the point, of being once more in the power of their enemies.

Suddenly with a burst the stopping of the leak gave way again, and the overwhelming tide rushed in, in a volume that nothing could resist.

The hapless vessel sank almost to the water's edge, and at the same moment a boat from the galleon rapidly approached.

They had to choose between two evils—a watery grave in the Bay of Biscay, or to fall into the hands of their enemies.

It was with a feeling of bitter shame that Rupert watched the boat's approach.

"Were I alone," he said, "I would plunge into this raging sea, and struggle till my last gasp before any less potent hand should overpower me, but your lives must not be sacrificed!"

These words were addressed to Helen and Adela, but even while he was speaking there appeared to be a strong probability of such a calamity.

The waves dashed over the sinking boat, and a few moments more would inevitably seal her fate.

Suddenly a ray of hope sprang up in his heart.

"Let the worst come!" he whispered to Stronghand, " we shall at least be together on board this giant galleon."

"It don't seem to me we shall ever be there?" moaned Peter whose spirits were utterly subdued.

Nor would he, nor any of them have done so, had not the boat from the Spaniard rowed alongside at that moment and taken them in.

No sooner was this accomplished than, as though fate had interfered on their behalf till their safety had been perfectly secured, the boat they had quitted suddenly disappeared and was seen no more.

In ten minutes from that time they stood on the deck of the Admiral Galeas, one of the largest and finest ships of the Armada.

CHAPTER XLVIII.

THE SPANISH ADMIRALS.

Our heroes and their fair charges, Helen and Adela Mountjoy, together with Peter, were at once conducted to the state cabin, where they found themselves in the presence of the Duke of Medina Celi, Admiral of the Spanish fleet, and the Vice-Admiral, Hugo de Moncada.

The former was a haughty-looking but handsome man of fifty ; the latter some ten years younger, with stern, heavy brows, from beneath which his dark eyes glanced scrutinizingly at the Englishmen, and the pale beautiful girls who accompanied them.

Rupert noticed that there were sentinels posted at the door outside the cabin, in addition to those who conducted them into the interior.

He felt by no means assured as to what would be their treatment, having no confidence in the tender mercies of the bigoted Spaniards.

He sighed as he glanced at the poor girls, and though he offered up a silent prayer to heaven for their protection, he knew that as regarded himself and his companions they were prepared to meet the worst.

The Duke, after gazing at them for some moments in silence, said abruptly in imperfect English—

"Now, what account have you to give of yourselves ?"

"We are English," returned Rupert, in a firm tone, "our boat in the violent weather of last night sprang a leak ; your boat came alongside just in time to save us from destruction."

"Or rather," remarked the Duke, sternly, "to deliver you from one kind of death to consign you to another."

"If it be your custom to destroy every enemy who falls into your hands we are in your power," Rupert replied, "and know our fate. So far as I myself am concerned it causes me little uneasiness, but for these ladies, young, innocent, and beautiful, as they are, I entreat most earnestly that they may not be sacrificed !"

"Oh, no, no !" cried Adela, throwing herself on her knees before the Duke in an attitude of passionate entreaty, "you bear the stamp of nobility on your features ; you will spare not only us, but these brave men who have so nobly protected us !"

"On that point, madam, we shall decide anon," returned the Duke, coldly ; then looking towards Rupert, he said—

"Who are these women ?"

"These ladies !" returned Rupert, with indignant emphasis, " are the daughters of the worthy and princely English merchant, Master Stephen Mountjoy."

"How is it they are here?" demanded the Duke.

"They were taken prisoners on their homeward voyage from the East Indies by three of your Spanish men-of-war. Chance threw them into our company, and we were conveying them to the English shores, when the disaster overtook us that threw us once more into the hands of our foes; as a shipwrecked crew we expected at least fair treatment."

"Fair!" echoed the Admiral, with a scornful, insulting laugh. When a cageful of mice is ensnared, the cat does not inquire by what means they fell into the trap; neither do I. You are prisoners, and will be dealt with as such. In the meantime these ladies had better retire."

He beckoned a soldier and gave him some directions, which having received the man said, pointing to the door—

"Now, senoras, follow me!"

Helen and Adela glanced entreatingly towards Rupert, who hastily advanced between them and exclaimed, in an imperative voice, little suited to a prisoner—

"Stay, fellow!"

Rupert spoke in Spanish, and it caused both the Admirals and the soldier to open their eyes with surprise.

"You speak our language?" remarked the Duke.

"I do," answered Rupert, boldly, "and in your own tongue, that there may be no mistake, I demand fair and honourable treatment for these ladies. If you refuse this, be sure England will demand retribution for any insult offered to two of her fairest daughters."

"We are not responsible to England for what we choose to do," said the Duke, haughtily; "let her demand and have what retribution she pleases, and get it—if she can!"

Rupert turned from the uncourteous Spaniard with disdain, to Helen and Adela.

"Farewell, ladies," he said, in a calm sad tone, "for the present, at least; and though it grieves me deeply that we can no longer afford you help, I entreat you not to despair. Fate seems to be against us, but heaven still watches over us, and will interfere in our behalf! But should the worst come, and we should meet no more"— he dropped his voice, and added, in a low tone, to Adela— "You will think of me to the last?"

"Yes, Rupert," she replied, weeping, "to the last. Your generous devotion to my dear sister and myself has won my heart, and at this sad moment—if it will be any comfort to you to know it—the last pulsations of that heart will beat for you."

"With love?" he asked, eagerly.

"Yes, dearest, with love," she replied fondly.

A thrill of joy passed through the young captain's frame as, for the first time, he pressed his lips to those of the fair girl before him.

He then bade farewell to Helen, and they went out of the cabin with the soldier.

Peter was next disposed of very abruptly.

"Who are you, fellow?" demanded the Vice-Admiral Moncada.

"I'm Peter Flight, your Excellency!" returned the excited Peter, who thought there was a good opening for an eloquent speech; "son of——"

"I don't understand the dog. Take him away," cried the Vice.

Peter was seized by the collar and hauled out unceremoniously.

"And now," said the Duke, addressing himself once more to our heroes, "I must know more of you. Who are you?"

"We are English sailors," answered Rupert, boldly.

"What is your rank?"

"Captains."

"Umph! what is the meaning of the Spanish garb you wear?" continued the Duke, glancing at their dress.

"It requires no explanation, senor," said Rupert, coolly; "the clothes were offered us and we put them on."

"That is not sufficient," exclaimed the Duke, angrily.

"It is the only explanation you will receive from me," answered Rupert.

The Admiral glanced at him fiercely for a moment, as though he would have slain him with a glance.

Hugo de Moncada whispered to him—

"They are spies!"

"What brings you here," cried the Duke, furiously, "scouring our coasts at a time like this? You must have some motive."

"We have," replied the Englishmen with one voice.

"What is it?"

"Our duty to our Queen and country!" was the unanimous answer.

"By heaven, you shall pay dearly for your loyal devotion; it has sealed your doom," cried the incensed Duke; "that is unless your country should consider your carcasses worth ransoming," he added, with a sneer, "in which case I would accept gold in lieu of life. Know you anyone who is willing to buy you at a price?"

"Only one," returned Rupert, coolly.

"Who is that?" asked the Duke, still sneeringly.

"The most important person next to the Queen in the realm. Sir Francis Walsingham, Secretary of State!" returned Rupert, with quiet emphasis.

At this well-known name the Admirals glanced significantly at each other.

"Sir Francis Walsingham!" echoed the Duke, in a low tone to Hugo Moncada. "They are more important than I thought!"

Rupert noticed the effect produced, and a thought struck him that promised not only to avert their fate, but also to deliver the despatch, and the papers containing the plans of the engagement, into the hands of the Secretary himself.

"At what ransom do you estimate us, Admiral?" asked Rupert.

"A thousand pounds each," he replied.

"Let me write to Sir Francis," Rupert said.

"There are pens, ink, and paper," returned the Duke, pointing to a side table; "write at once."

Rupert went to the table and indited a few lines to the purpose.

"Let me see what you have written," said the Admiral.

Rupert handed him the paper.

"That will do!" he exclaimed, as he returned it, after perusing the writing, "now seal and address it."

Rupert turned away, and hastily taking the despatches and papers he had recovered from Don Xavier out of his vest, placed them with the letter he had written in a large sheet of paper, which he folded carefully.

Having done this, he secured it with string, which he sealed with wax, and stamped with the arms of Spain.

He had hardly accomplished this, when a hoarse cry was heard on deck—

"Ship ahoy!"

"Just in time," said the Duke, as he took the packet from Rupert's hand, and left the cabin hastily.

In about ten minutes he returned, followed by two others.

"I have despatched your letter, Sir Englishman," he cried, as he entered.

Rupert turned to him with a look of triumph on his features, but it quickly disappeared as he beheld to his dismay in the two new comers the persons of Captain Pedro de Valdis and Don Alonzo d'Aquilar.

There was a mutual start of recognition as they confronted each other.

CHAPTER XLIX.

RUPERT'S TREACHERY.

BUT there was a kind of superstitious terror in the glance of the Spaniards.

They recoiled as though they had been suddenly brought face to face with some evil spirit.

"Ah! demons!" they cried, in a voice of horror.

"What mean you, senors?" asked the Duke.

"Those men, your Highness, are fiends of Satan, or they could never have stood before us at this moment," they replied.

The Englishmen uttered a short, dry laugh, and the Duke looked towards Captain de Valdis for an explanation.

"That man," he continued, pointing to Rupert, "was on board the Santa Maria not more than ten minutes before she foundered. He leapt from her deck into the sea, and I with my own eyes saw him engulphed in the raging waters, yet there he stands alive and unscathed."

"I am not the first who has been rescued from the jaws of death," said Rupert impressively.

"But this is not all," continued the captain, "he and his brother fiends have carried havoc into the fortress of St. Nicholas. The ramparts and passages are strewn with dead bodies, subdued by their infernal power."

"We will test their terrible agency," returned the Duke de Medina Celi; "for myself I doubt it. What, ho, guard!" he cried.

The cabin was instantly filled with armed soldiers.

Rupert, Stronghand, and Firebrand had lost their weapons in the confusion caused by the leak in their own little vessel.

They were now on board a strange ship, surrounded by enemies, and encompassed beyond by the fierce waters.

There was, however, a look of cool determination in their eyes that proved even at that moment they had not lost their self-possession.

"Bind those men," cried the Duke.

"Never," shouted Rupert, as he snatched a weapon from the foremost soldier, and felled him to the ground.

Stronghand, with a sweeping blow from his massive fist, scattered several right and left like so many reeds.

Firebrand, too, stood with rigid limbs like a tiger crouched ready to spring.

But the Duke de Medina and Hugo de Moncada drew their weapons, and Captain de Valdis and Don Alonzo, gaining courage from their example, also drew theirs.

The soldiers presented their muskets at the Englishmen.

Further resistance would have only provoked certain destruction.

They were pinioned, and stood calmly awaiting what was to come next.

Captain de Valdis, in the meantime, repeated to the Duke the account given him by Don Xavier of the outrages committed by Rupert and his companions, until his cheek flushed with rage and shame at the recital.

"By heaven!" he cried, "demons or not demons, we will put their power to the proof! we will see whether they can resist the pressure of a hempen rope around their necks. Away with them! drag them upon deck!" he shouted "they shall swing from the yard-arm!"

The Englishmen, bound as they were, were hurried with brutal eagerness up to the deck, the Duke and his friends following.

Three ropes were quickly reeved by the admiral's order to as many blocks fastened to the yard-arms, the nooses of which at one end were placed and drawn tightly around their necks.

The other ends were grasped by brawny sailors, ready to run them up at the word of command.

The very crisis of their fate seemed to have arrived.

Still our heroes were undismayed, although it seemed hard to be dragged to death like dogs.

Rupert's blood boiled within him.

"Mark me!" he cried, addressing the Duke and his companions in their own language, "if you shed our blood in this inglorious manner, think not it will sink into the ground unrequited! So surely as we perish our lives will be demanded of you both by the voice of Heaven, and the united cry of every ENGLISHMAN! I warn you to beware of the account you will have to render!"

The Duke, eager to give the signal for their death, held up his hand.

The ropes were pulled taut, and in another

instant our heroes would have been swinging from the yard-arms, when a vivid flash of lightning blazed across the dark sky from pole to pole, followed by a peal of thunder loud enough to wake the dead, and then there swept over the surface of the ocean a hurricane so terrible that the giant vessel quivered in every plank as though panic-stricken.

The crew looked in each other's faces somewhat apprehensively, but they had little time for surmise, for the angry ocean came on rolling a vast broadside of water against the whole length of the galleon, that reeled over as though it would have succumbed to the mighty shock.

But the wave having spent its fury by deluging the decks and sweeping the crew like so many half-drowned rats against the starboard bulwarks, the vessel righted again.

Rupert, who had recovered his feet, was the first to speak.

"Look to your topmasts!" he shouted. "You are overweighted aloft! Remember the Santa Maria!"

His voice, ringing out clear and distinct above the roaring of the storm, impressed the Admiral, who gave orders to reef the topsails at once.

This being done, he advanced to the Englishmen who were still bound.

"You are good sailors," he said.

"We ought to be," returned Rupert, doggedly.

"You know the English coast well?"

"Yes."

"The navigation of the Channel is difficult and dangerous, is it not?"

"So dangerous that let those who seek to approach our shores beware the rocks that line it, whose sharp points will pierce the bulky sides of your unwieldy ships as a needle would a sheet of tissue paper. Beware, I say! Many will go there—few return!"

"Harkye, Englishmen," said the Duke de Celi, "your lives are in my hands."

"Well!" coolly ejaculated our heroes.

"I will spare them on one condition," continued the Duke.

"I make no conditions until we are released from these degrading cords," exclaimed Rupert, indignantly.

At a motion from the Duke's hand they were instantly unbound by three sailors.

"Now, Duke, I can listen to you," said Rupert, haughtily.

He detected fear in the Spaniard's concession, and felt his own superiority.

"What are the conditions on which our lives are to be granted us?" he asked.

"Simply," returned the Duke, "that you undertake to pilot a certain number of our vessels to the western coast of England, where we wish to effect a landing."

Stronghand and Firebrand were about to utter an indignant refusal.

Already their mocking scornful laugh rang in the air, when to their utter consternation and dismay they heard their comrade Rupert give his consent.

"I accept your terms," he cried; "I pledge myself to guide you to the western coast."

Mark Luton and Firebrand were fairly beside themselves with rage and shame.

"I will not live at such terms," cried the former, indignantly.

"Nor I," echoed Firebrand.

"I would not have believed had I not heard it," continued Mark, "that you, Rupert, would have bought even your life at the price of treachery! You not only disgrace yourself, you have disgraced, insulted us, branded us with the stigma of cowardice. Friends, comrades, as we have been, we are so no longer. S'death, you shall pay dearly for this!"

In a fit of uncontrollable passion, Stronghand snatched up a marlinspike, and rushed towards Rupert.

The weapon, deadly in the strong hand that wielded it, would have descended on his comrade's skull but for one circumstance.

He encountered the calm, bright glance of Rupert's eye, that never faltered or blenched before the fierce gaze of his angry comrade.

It seemed to say to him in its silent expressiveness—

"Do you believe me to be such a traitor?"

The giant paused.

"No, no! it is impossible, I cannot believe it."

The weapon dropped from his hand, and Rupert smiled upon his friend, who understood him.

He had saved their lives!

CHAPTER L.

ON THE ROCKS.

THE despatches forwarded by the dexterous manipulation of Rupert, had reached the hands of Secretary Walsingham, and given him valuable information.

This being enclosed in the same packet as the request for the ransom in Rupert's handwriting, led the astute statesman to divine that he was in some peculiar emergency.

To extricate him and his friends, therefore, from peril, Sir Francis at once consented to pay the sum demanded, on the safe delivery of Rupert, Stronghand, and Firebrand, on English ground.

The early dawn was just breaking when three Spanish galleons—the Admiral Galeas, the St. Matthew, and the Santo Fernando—might have been seen off the coast of Cornwall, between that county and the Scilly Isles, about thirty miles to the westward.

In full confidence of the Englishmen's skill, the Spanish Admirals had resigned the entire conduct of the vessels into their hands.

Rupert took the helm of the first of these; his comrade, Stronghand, that of the St. Matthew; whilst Firebrand steered the Santo Fernando.

Our heroes, inhaling once more the breeze of their native shores, felt their hearts bound within them at the enterprise they had undertaken.

Rupert had, at imminent risk of discovery,

despatched a letter by a fisherman, in cypher, to the secretary, informing him of his plans.

There was a strong ground swell, and the vessels rolled heavily as they rose and fell on the treacherous tide, from the bosom of which rose such formidable masses of hidden rocks.

But all was quiet on the decks.

The Duke de Medina Celi was counting the moments when he should anchor in sight of the English coast.

Rupert at the helm looked anxiously round for the vessels guided by his comrades, but a light mist hung over the surface of the ocean and hid them from his view.

" No matter, they know the signal and will see the light," he said to himself.

This light was the beacon from St. Agnes' Tower, erected to warn mariners from the treacherous rocks that rose like a barricade along the coasts of the Scilly Isles.

Several hundred English troops rested on their arms beneath the giant lighthouse of St. Agnes, waiting the arrival of the foe.

.   .   .   .

Gradually becoming more and more distinct, the glimmering light of the beacon pierced the mist like a small star.

Rupert, who was watching anxiously for the first glimpse of the light, could scarcely refrain from a shout of exultation.

His comrades, Stronghand and Firebrand, at the helms of their respective vessels, had seen it simultaneously, and though separate from each other, the same ejaculation had burst from their lips—

" It is time !"

" We must have all the sail the vessel will bear," said the Englishmen to their respective captains, who took their word implicitly.

The order was given to crowd all sail and executed, and a brisk breeze from the Cornish coast blew directly against the Scilly Islands.

The huge leviathans made their way with unusual celerity, whilst Rupert and his companions, their eyes fixed upon the beacon light, changed the vessels' course imperceptibly, till their bows were turned straight towards the terrible rocks.

The Duke, in his cabin, was poring over the ship's chart and exulting in the skilful pilots he had secured, meditating whether he should set them free when they had served his turn, or execute them after all.

Suddenly there came an appalling crash !

" Santa Maria !   What is that ?" gasped the Duke, as he staggered from the cabin on to the deck.

The grey light of morning was sufficient to reveal the nature of the catastrophe.

The Admiral groaned as he beheld the three giant vessels hopelessly impaled upon the rocks.

His frenzied eye glanced wildly round and encountered the triumphant gaze of Rupert, who, having performed his task, had resigned the helm, and now stood, sword in hand, awaiting the issue.

" Traitor ! Villain ! Liar ! You have betrayed, deceived me !"

The Admiral made a fierce Rupert, who at the first blow sword from his hand, and passe through his body to the hilt.

Then, ere the Duke's lifeless corpse reached the deck, arose a deafening shout, as the English soldiers swarmed over the vessel's sides.

The contest was brief but fierce ; the Spaniards hemmed in by their foes, and the sea and rocks beyond, having everything to lose, and nothing to gain, fought with the desperation of despair.

Suddenly arose the cry of—

" Fire ! Fire !"

Then from the portholes of the St. Matthew burst forth the flames, and soon the grey morning was mingled with the glare of the burning vessel.

The flames, fanned by the wind, spread rapidly, and the vessel had burnt down to the water's edge.

Then there was heard a loud explosion, and all that remained of the St. Matthew blew up in a torrent of bright sparks.

Stronghand had joined his comrade Firebrand on board the Santo Fernando, and that also was now in flames.

" Leave the vessels !" shouted Rupert.

As they were about to descend, piercing shrieks were heard both from the cabins of the Admiral Galeas and the Santo Fernando.

" It is the cry of women !" said Rupert ; and I knew not there were any on board."

Oh save me ! save me, Rupert !" shrieked an agonized voice.

" Good heavens ! 'tis Adela Mountjoy !"

" And Helen !" exclaimed Stronghand, " her sister."

In a state of intense excitement the Englishmen went below, and shortly discovered the recesses in which the young ladies were confined under lock and key.

The luckless Peter had been almost forgotten, being stowed away in the hold ; but Stronghand heard his voice, and set him at liberty.

As they were lowered into the boat, the morning mists cleared away, and the British fleet appeared in sight.

" Now, dearest, you are safe !"

" Yes, love !" she replied, " through you."

Rupert rowed his lovely charge to the nearest vessel ; before they reached it the Admiral Galeas and the Santo Fernando blew up.

Stronghand, Firebrand, and Peter soon after joined them on the deck of the Queen Elizabeth, the former seeming to have made the best of the opportunities, inasmuch as the fair Helen smiled sweetly upon her colossal admirer, and appeared to consider herself as the lawful property of her preserver.

Master Stephen Mountjoy escaped from his Spanish captors, and in due time rejoined his children in England.

He was present at their union with Rupert and his comrade Mark Luton, to whom he gave them willingly, with his blessing to boot.

[THE END.]